Hugh Miller started his
Pathologist, but his oth
flexible work pattern. H
as a stills photographer
John Grierson. He mad
teaching films, and then
marketing of professiona
books on magic and gambling. A full-time writer for many years now his novels include the bestselling AMBULANCE, TERMINAL 3, THE DISSECTOR, THE SAVIOUR and recently, novelizations of MINDER and McVICAR.

Also by Hugh Miller:

TERMINAL 3

Hugh Miller

VICTIMS

Futura
Macdonald & Co
London & Sydney

A Futura Book

First published in Great Britain in 1983
by Macdonald Futura Publishers Ltd

ISBN 0 7088 2049 2

Filmset, printed and bound in Great Britain by
Hazell Watson & Viney Ltd, Aylesbury, Bucks

Futura Publications
A Division of
Macdonald & Co (Publishers) Ltd
Maxwell House
74 Worship Street
London EC2A 2EN

The author wishes to thank Wing Commander David Nicoll for his generosity in providing much historical data and scarce research material. I am also grateful to my brother, Jim Miller, for geographical guidance. My indebtedness to the scholarship of such men as David Kahn, John Toland and Brigadier Peter Young is beyond estimation, and I would point out that historical discrepancies and flights of fancy in this novel are mine, not theirs. I thank dear Nettie for her patience, which is monumental.

To my agent, Mark Lucas, I am especially grateful. His objectivity, enthusiasm and encouragement have been invaluable.

For my mother and father

Man is preceded by forest
and followed by desert

PROLOGUE

July 20th, 1944
There were ten windows and they were all open. Even so, the heat in the room was stifling. Admiral von Puttkamer, in defiance of protocol, had unbuttoned his shirt collar and was standing close to one window, inhaling the faint breeze and ignoring General Heusinger's drone.

The Führer was the only man sitting. He had his back to the door and he nodded every few seconds as Heusinger delivered his report. The news was bad, but Hitler remained impassive, twirling his spectacles in one hand, clutching the handle of his magnifier in the other. Around him the other senior conference members leaned down across the huge map, gauging his mood and muting their reactions to the disastrous communication from the Eastern Front.

The door opened and Heusinger stopped talking. Hitler turned and smiled as Field Marshal Keitel ushered in the latecomer, Colonel Stauffenberg. The colonel was only thirty-seven, but already the war had robbed him of an eye, his right hand and forearm, and three fingers from his left hand. He limped into the room clutching a fat, brown briefcase under the stump of his right arm, and saluted the Führer awkwardly.

'Sit down, sit down,' Keitel urged him softly. 'The conference has started.' He led the colonel to a chair a few feet to Hitler's left, and asked if that would be close enough. Stauffenberg had asked to be seated as near to the Führer as possible, for the war had also made him deaf.

Standing opposite and apart from the other officers, SS Captain Stefan Gaiser watched as Stauffenberg eased his briefcase to the floor and pushed it against the heavy oak support of the map table. The man was sweating, Gaiser noted. That was hardly surprising on such a hot day, but the sun generally reddened a man's skin. Stauffenberg was deathly pale and his face shone, as if it had been sprayed with a fine mist. He had the look Gaiser had seen often, on men under interrogation, men who had something to hide.

'Poor bastard,' Captain Freital murmured, inching closer to Gaiser. 'He left more of himself on the Western Desert than he brought back.'

'He looks nervous,' Gaiser said.

Freital shrugged. 'His news is probably as rotten as the rest.' He glanced at his watch. 'With any luck, he won't have time to deliver his report. Mussolini's due to arrive at Rastenburg at three o'clock. The Führer wants to leave as soon as possible.'

Gaiser moved closer to the table, still watching Stauffenberg. There was definitely something wrong. He was looking at fear. The colonel was making the proper responses to Heusinger's resumed narrative, but the pitch was wrong. The colonel's heart was beating to a tempo different from the others' in the room, and when he glanced up for one instant Gaiser knew, for certain, that the man was close to panic.

It would have been easy to make the panic surface. Gaiser only had to move himself into Stauffenberg's line of vision and stare down at him. Wehrmacht personnel had reason to be nervous of SS officers at the best of times. A man smothered in fear, sighting the challenge in Gaiser's pale-blue eyes, would soon crumble. They always did.

The Führer asked Heusinger to pause for a moment and leaned closer to the map, locating a reference. The others leaned closer too. All eyes were on Hitler's magnifier as he moved it over the territory in question, and at that moment Colonel Stauffenberg stood up, eased himself away from the table and silently left the room. Only Gaiser saw him leave.

Captain Freital had been staring out of the window, dreaming, and he jumped slightly when Gaiser touched his arm.

'I want to slip out for a moment,' Gaiser whispered.

Freital shook his head. 'Better not. The drill is clear-cut, you know that. Guard officers remain on hand until instructed otherwise.' He winked. 'Cross your legs and do sums in your head. It won't feel so bad then.'

Gaiser moved away, walking slowly to the far end of the room, hearing Heusinger's doom-laden rumble, watching the other officers bobbing their heads obediently in time with their master. There was no point in trying, of course. To leave the Führer's presence in these circumstances was forbidden. He had to be protected by his own. There was no easy way of knowing what Stauffenberg was up to, not without raising an alarm, and that was the last thing Gaiser wanted to do. One thing was certain: Stauffenberg was not coming back to the conference, he had left the room slowly enough but in his heart he had been running.

Then Gaiser realized that the colonel had left his briefcase behind. To make certain, he walked around the end of the map table and looked under the empty chair. At first there was no sign of the case, but then Heusinger's aide reached behind the massive support column and picked up the thing, or tried to, then eased it with his foot until it was on the other side of the leg. It looked heavy. The aide moved his feet into the gap he had made and joined the others in their scrutiny of the map.

'The position at Peipus is serious,' Heusinger said, and the Führer nodded sharply. The others followed suit. At the other end of the room, Captain Freital beckoned to Gaiser. Not caring, for once, how much noise his boots made, he began striding smartly towards his brother officer. He knew that an emergency was developing.

'Unless the army group withdraws from Peipus,' Heusinger said, 'there will be a catastrophe of such proportions . . .'

Gaiser was six feet from Freital when the briefcase exploded. There was sudden, roaring darkness beyond the core of the blast and Gaiser felt himself lifted and thrown against the wall. He forced himself to his feet, coughing on the smoke and covering his head against the showering glass. Direction was meaningless, he only knew the wall was at his back. The floor had shifted and risen, timbers were splitting and falling all around him, and when he moved forward he stumbled on the twisted body of an officer who was groaning and clutching at his ears. On hands and knees Gaiser made for the gaping doorway, a bright anchor point in the smoking chaos of the room, and he clambered out into the passage beyond, spitting and coughing as the acid fumes burned in his throat.

After a few seconds he was able to stand again. His head spun and his ears were ringing, muffling the noise still coming from the conference room. Oddly, there was no one else about. Then he saw Keitel, stumbling from the doorway. He was doubled over and hanging on to the arm of the Führer, who came walking out of the wreckage like a man in a trance. His face was blackened and his uniform was hanging in tatters. Both men were covered in sharp splinters, and Hitler's right arm was bleeding.

'This way,' Gaiser said, then said it again, louder, realizing they were probably as deaf as he was. He took the Führer's injured arm and held it to his chest, guiding the way out into the air. On the grass they paused and Keitel began a coughing fit that threatened to force him to his knees.

'Quickly!' Gaiser shouted, drawing the Führer, still dazed, behind him. Keitel took several huge gulps of air and followed. In less than a minute they were across the open ground and standing outside the concrete bunker.

'What is happening?' Hitler was blinking through the soot caked around his eyes, trying to tug his arm free from Gaiser's grasp.

'An explosion, sir, a bomb.' Gaiser tightened his grasp. 'You must come inside, quickly.'

The Führer blinked at Keitel, then nodded once. 'Yes. Inside.' He looked for a moment at Gaiser, then nodded again and allowed himself to be led into the bunker.

Later, when Hitler's wounds had been bathed, his injured arm bound and the splinters painstakingly removed from his legs and chest, he asked Gaiser to remain with him. The order was curt, but the implication of trust was clear enough. Gaiser was feeling ill, there were pains in his neck and legs, but he stood by the side of the bed until Dr Morrell had checked Hitler's heart carefully and administered an injection of Brom-Nervacit.

'You will feel calmer now,' Morrell said.

But Hitler was growing increasingly excited. He kept turning his head from side to side on the pillows, addressing anyone who came within reach. 'Now I have them! Now we can act!'

'You must try to rest.'

'Rest is for the dead!' Hitler was beginning to laugh, and when one of his secretaries came into the room he took her hand and squeezed it. 'You see, my girl? Everything has worked out well for me again. It's proof, still more proof!'

When Bormann appeared he was greeted with the same hysteria. Cautious as ever, he took the Führer's hand between both of his and agreed, quietly, that the escape had been miraculous.

'I am unharmed! Ask Dr Morrell. My pulse is *normal*!'

Bormann nodded his belief, then looked sternly at Gaiser. 'Why are you here?'

Hitler looked up at the young officer, dirty and dishevelled, still at attention by the bedside. 'He helped me, he brought me out of that inferno with Keitel.' Bormann stepped back, still frowning, as Hitler disengaged his hand and laid it on Gaiser's arm. 'He is one of the very few, I tell you . . .'

Gaiser felt the fingers tighten on his wrist. The pain screamed in his head and his legs hurt so badly he could barely remain upright. But the Führer's eyes were on him, the old man was smiling at him, touching him. It was the greatest moment of Stefan Gaiser's life.

BOOK ONE

1922

Charlotte Malcolm, the only daughter of Sir George and Lady Malcolm of Handcross in Surrey, met Leonhard Gaiser in the autumn of 1908. They were guests at one of the regular weekend parties given by Angus Brodie, a London-based historian of private means and mammoth ego. The gatherings usually comprised his friends, admirers and correspondents, and he often said that their real purpose was to promote an interchange of ideas and interests among people who were fundamentally alike. Objective outsiders, however, described the house parties as elitist gossip festivals, with a collection of guests carefully chosen to suit Brodie's incurable activities as a matchmaker.

There was no need for Brodie to throw Charlotte and Leonhard together. Almost from the start, when they were introduced in the opulent, lawned garden of the Kensington house, the two young people found themselves drawn to each other.

Leonhard was classically handsome, tall and slim with careful Teutonic bearing and a clarity in his eyes that was both bold and sensitive. A single, thin duelling scar – produced, he assured Charlotte modestly, with only a sharpened cane – ran from one high cheekbone to the corner of his mouth, underlining rather than marring the symmetry of his features. As he talked to his companion in his clipped, precise English, he would frequently push back the soft blond hair from his forehead. He might have stepped down from one of Charlotte's dreams.

Charlotte was overwhelmed. Like Leonhard, she was visiting Brodie's house for the first time, and although she had felt timid misgivings about the grandeur of the company she would be joining, she had never expected anything like this. The young man was quite simply stunning. For once, character matched appearance and bearing. She felt her heart pound.

By Sunday morning they were inseparable, and they already knew a good deal about each other. Brodie assisted the growing union by keeping out of the way and making sure everyone else did. Charlotte and Leonhard were left alone in the library while the others played croquet or drowsed in the summer house. After they had been talking and sipping lemon tea for a few minutes, Leonhard suddenly put his cup aside and leaned forward in his chair, his expression serious.

'Charlotte Malcolm,' he said, 'I think I have fallen in love with you.'

Her first reaction was to cry. In the twenty-four hours since they had first met a fierce tension had been building inside her. As the pleasures she experienced in his company had mounted, as she had found reality measuring up to her romantic ideals, the anticipation of an end had begun to weigh ever more painfully on her. He would, she had been sure, walk out of her life as coolly as he had entered it. Now he had taken away that fear, but she still felt that the whole thing was just a dream.

Leonhard was frowning. 'Have I upset you?'

'Oh, no. No.' She blushed and looked at him through her tears.

'But I startled you.' He smiled and reached out to touch her hand. 'I do assure you,' he said, 'that what I have told you is quite true.'

She had never been bold. She was a daughter of privilege who had been raised in a quiet house and had taken the quiet into herself. She was studious and otherworldly, immersing herself in books. Her forays into society had been few and unrewarding. Until now.

Leonhard rose and put his arm around her, gently drawing her close until her composure returned. He kissed her forehead, and when he spoke again his mouth was close to her ear, brushing the long dark hair. 'Tell me, do you have any feelings for me?'

Charlotte did not trust herself to say anything. Gently, after wondering again at how Providence could have stored up so much for her and then delivered it all at once, she nodded.

The courtship proceeded by long letters and brief visits over the following eight months. The letters were never passionate; instead, they corresponded about their interests, the books they had read, the tales of myth and legend in which they were both immersed. Passion was reserved for the times they were together.

They were married in London in September of 1909. The wedding was a major social event, but the honeymoon was the beginning of an agonizing withdrawal that took Charlotte eight years to complete.

She began hating her husband two days after their marriage. The honeymoon hotel at Interlaken was cold and austere, and that had not helped. The wedding night was terrible for both of them. Before, Charlotte had thought she was conditioned to accept the consummation, she had even believed she was eager for it. But a sense of duty on her part and an awareness of his rights on Leonhard's had inverted everything. He was forceful where she needed to be coaxed, and he became demanding at the moment when she was least able to give in. He bruised her and strove like an animal to penetrate her, and when he failed she could not comfort him or conjure up any warmth. He accused her of humiliating him, of denying him his rights as a husband, and when Charlotte began to cry hysterically, Leonhard told her that tears could not move him.

On the second night he struck her, a stinging blow on the temple that left Charlotte dazed and bewildered. While she lay under him in shocked silence he threw up her knees and forced himself into her. Charlotte remained silent even though the pain was excruciating. She made not one sound as he bit her shoulder and grunted against her ear, and when he had finished and lay beside her, stroking her breast and telling her that truly he did love her, she felt her silence become part of her. The sense of loss was too acute even for tears.

By the time Stefan was ten, he understood that his mother and father moved in separate orbits, even though an appearance of unity was strictly maintained. Their home in the country outside Dorfen was large and bright, a place built for noise and boisterous laughter. When Leonhard entertained his friends there was certainly a lot of laughter and plenty of noise, but Charlotte always withdrew at those times, and even on the few occasions when she was present for the sake of appearances she formed no part of the gaiety.

The boy was sturdy and intelligent, and in looks he strongly resembled his father. His endless energy tended to suggest that he was his father's boy to the core, but in fact Stefan had inherited his mother's introspective nature. He had learned that it was easy to please his father, but a great pleasure to make his mother happy.

Leonhard adored his son. When Stefan was old enough to walk without an adult's help, he was taken along on afternoon fishing trips and visits to neighbouring estates. At fairs he was encouraged to ride on donkeys and compete in running events. He learned to ski before he was eight. He was educated at home by a private tutor from the age of four, and his learning was carefully supervised by his father. The heroic myths were fed to the boy relentlessly: he learned the ideal of *Blut und Boden*, blood and soil, and he was made to understand that he carried an inheritance of dignity and honour, an inheritance he must support and pass on in his turn.

Stefan also learned his family's history, in the minutest detail. His ancestors had been Prussian soldiers and landowners for three hundred years. They had also been scholars, preserving the literature of their territory and adding to it, forever compiling records and maps and bulky histories. The boy's lineage was littered with heroes – in his own lifetime his uncle had died in combat at

Ypres. His father, not quite forty, had been invalided out of the army after taking a bullet in his chest at Compiègne. As the boy absorbed the facts and figures he was simultaneously shown the honours – medals, scrolls, framed obituaries and letters. He was reminded, constantly, that his inheritance was not only a privilege, it was a responsibility.

Only in the evenings did Stefan spend time with his mother. Those were the warm periods that he looked forward to, the times when he had to be no more than a boy, playing checkers or helping to make lemonade or just sitting on the floor, listening, as that quiet woman read to him about Sherlock Holmes, Barnaby Rudge and King Arthur. During the day, although his mother was still there, she became a figure in the background of domestic continuity, against which his father operated as prime mover.

A few days after his thirteenth birthday Stefan asked his mother about England. He had grown up speaking German and English with equal fluency, but he knew practically nothing about her country. The previous year he had met his grandmother, Lady Malcolm, and he had promised he would go to England and visit her. But his mother tended to avoid the subject after that. All she ever said was that they would go to England later, when there was more time.

Now, she seemed prepared to say more. They were sitting at opposite ends of the scrubbed wood table in the huge kitchen. The late sun was on the boy's back, warming him, and it glinted on the brass his mother had suddenly stopped rubbing. She gazed at him for a few moments, puckering her mouth; then she smiled, though her eyes remained serious.

'It's all very difficult, Stefan. But I'll try to explain.' She put down her work and folded her arms. 'The war has separated us from England. Your father fought for his country, and relatives of mine fought on the opposite side. Things have grown a little easier in the past few years, but there are still some hard feelings.' She looked down at the table, as if she was remembering something. 'Your grandmother longs to see you, and I know you would love England, especially at this time of year . . .'

'Then why don't we go?'

'We can't. Not yet.'

Stefan peered at her eyes, recognizing the sadness in them. 'Is it because of Father?'

'I suppose so.' She looked away.

'But I want to go. I want to see all the places you've read to me about. I need to see them, Mother.'

'Need to?'

He could not explain why he put it like that, but he was sure he had said the right thing. And he felt like insisting. 'Please, ask Father, make him say yes.'

'We'll see.' Charlotte picked up her duster again.

Stefan watched her for a minute, memorising the way she sat in the orange-gold light, turning the bright metal in her hands. His mother radiated a marvellous peace, a sense of comfort. It was the only English thing he knew, his mother's serenity.

He began to hope very hard that she would be able to talk his father around. He had begun to understand why he felt so strongly. In England, he was sure, his mother could show him something *real* that echoed the stories she told. Already, Stefan knew that his father's tales and legends had no more life or warmth than his medals and the other relics that surrounded them.

That evening, long after Stefan had gone to bed, Charlotte sat by the fire in the kitchen and worked at strengthening her resolve. Self-pity, she knew, would have helped, but all her compassion and concern had long ago centred on her son.

Charlotte was ill. Five years before, the family physician had told her that the recurring bouts of weariness and blurred vision she suffered were the result of a temporary nerve lesion, a passing disorder of the spinal cord. But the ailment persisted and took on a pattern. For an hour and sometimes longer each day, usually in the afternoon, Charlotte went about her household duties with the feeling that she was walking on soft cotton, and her sense of touch at those times was as hazy and inaccurate as her vision. A specialist, visited secretly a few days after Stefan was nine, formed an initial diagnosis of slow, spreading sclerosis of the dorsal columns in the spinal cord. At a second consultation two weeks later, the diagnosis was confirmed.

'You are young,' the doctor told Charlotte, 'and the disease is moving forward very, very slowly.' That was all the reassurance he could offer. Within herself, Charlotte knew that however gradually her illness grew, it nevertheless signalled a predictable end: the process of dying had begun in her.

Every night, it seemed, Charlotte dreamed of England. She would be there with her son, walking in quiet shaded woods, watching with Stefan as wild deer made their timid approach and fed off the leaves of young trees. It was always summer in her dreams, and always there was the comforting solitude of open places and the lush gentility of sun-warmed nature. Charlotte was pining, and as the boy grew older urgency spiced her longing.

But Leonhard stood between Charlotte and her hopes. She was afraid of him and even in her imagination she was no match for his ranting and his threats. At last, alone in the firelight, Charlotte acknowledged her need for determination and found a way, finally, to stand up to her husband. All she need do, in the predictable barrage of rancour, was remember that she was dying – by infinitely small stages, but dying nevertheless – and that the future she wanted for her son would be just as doomed if she delayed taking a stand much longer.

She rose and drew her hands nervously across her apron.

She found her husband in the gun room. Without preliminary, and with too much nervous haste, she told him she wanted to take the boy with her to visit his grandmother.

Leonhard was perched on top of an oak stepladder, oiling the stock of a shotgun. He blinked at his wife as if she had said something crazy, then he went back to his oiling, shaking his head as he did so.

'But he has a right to go there, and he wants to.'

'I don't wish to discuss it.'

Charlotte had no skill in argument, certainly not against Leonhard. When he invited no discussion, it was worse. Nevertheless, she stood her ground.

'I may just take him, whatever you say.'

Now he smiled at her as he put the gun back on its rack. 'Don't be stupid, my dear.'

'You're so full of spite!'

He came down the ladder and stood looking at her, narrowing his eyes. 'You can talk to me about spite? For thirteen years you've wielded spite like an axe.'

Charlotte shook her head violently. 'I won't be drawn into that argument again, Leonhard. We are discussing our son. He wants to visit England. He's half English, you've no moral right to keep him from going there.'

Leonhard turned away from her and began running his fingers along the shiny barrels of the pistols that were racked along the top of the ammunition cabinet. Because of the injury to his lung, he had to avoid any excitement that increased his rate of breathing. He was calming himself now.

'He doesn't belong to you,' Charlotte said.

He turned to face her. His jaw was trembling. 'Your shallowness appals me. You can see nothing but trivialities and surfaces. Stefan is a German, he has been raised in the traditions of his country and already he thinks and acts as a German. In England my son is an alien, an enemy. I will not have him going there.'

'The war is over!'

'It is never over.'

Charlotte moved a few steps closer to the door and set

her hands on the back of a chair for support. 'Very well,' she said quietly, 'you have issued your ultimatum. Now I shall issue mine.' What she was about to say had been in her mind for months, and she had often wondered where she would find the strength to bring it out into the open. 'I believe that the boy is being stifled by you. Your approach to his education has been one-sided and you've deliberately channelled his curiosity and energy to shape him into a Junker.'

'You mentioned an ultimatum,' Leonhard said.

'Stefan is still a child and before it's too late I want him to have free will. I want him to make up his own mind about loyalties and persuasions.' She inhaled shakily before going on. 'My Uncle Thomas has made a proposition. When Stefan is seventeen he can apply for entrance to Cambridge University, and I want him to take that opportunity.'

'Never!'

'Then I will leave you.'

Leonhard was still, wide-eyed as if the room had turned dark. 'You would resort to that?'

'Yes, I would.'

Disgrace had never touched the Gaisers, not in three hundred years of honourable history. They were Catholics, rooted in a tradition to which marriage and the solid structure of the home were fundamental. Leonhard put his hands over his face for a moment, struggling again to settle his breathing. 'Charlotte, you are talking like a mad woman.'

'I'm trying to enforce sanity,' she replied. 'I mean what I say. I will leave you for good if you block Stefan's progress.'

He brought his hands away from his eyes. Disbelief was still etching furrows on his forehead and cheeks. 'What depth of hatred brought you to this?'

Her courage was running out. She went to the door and opened it slightly. 'It wasn't hatred, Leonhard. But it might have been, if you had had your way.'

August, 1944

Three weeks after the explosion at Rastenburg, Reichsführer-SS Heinrich Himmler was in possession of a list of over two hundred people who, according to his aides, were directly implicated in the assassination attempt. The ringleaders were already dead, but a memo from the Chancellery in Berlin maintained that there was evidence of massive complicity in the crime, and that special anti-uprising squads were being formed to eradicate the subversion for good.

On 10th August, Captain Stefan Gaiser was temporarily transferred from executive duty on the Führer's staff to lead an interrogation team based at a former post office less than a mile from the Chancellery.

At first Hitler had been reluctant to permit the appointment, but Secretary Bormann was persuasive.

'Captain Gaiser has wide experience of this work,' he told the Führer. 'I know how much you value his presence, but we must also remember that the subversive scourge must be wiped out, completely. Gaiser is talented in uncovering criminals. He trained under Heydrich and he has commendations from Reichsführer Himmler himself. We must put the best men we have into this purge.' Naturally, Bormann omitted to mention that he personally disliked Gaiser, and that it would be a relief to have him out of the way for a time. He was not likely to confess, either, that he was deeply jealous of the young officer. That was something Bormann would never admit, even to himself.

The two rooms assigned for use by the interrogators were dark and bare, each fitted with a low overhead lamp, a table and one chair. In the corner of each a booth had been constructed where a clerk could make shorthand notes of the proceedings, without offering visible distraction to those being questioned.

At nine o'clock on the morning of the 10th Stefan Gaiser gathered his team around him in the disused kitchen of the building and outlined the procedure.

'The list we have is divided into two: Certainties and Probables. I will work on the Probables. You four will work in pairs, alternately, questioning the Certainties.' One of the earliest directives from Heydrich had ordered that an interrogator should always be fresh and never, ever, look tired. Stefan had the talent and experience to ensure he would manage on his own, and he had fewer people to question. 'What you have to obtain from each prisoner is a list of all living relatives and friends. Do you understand that?'

His four subordinates were experienced at interrogation, too, but their credentials were mediocre. The eldest, Leutnant Prager, had spent a year with the Schutzpolizei and a further year with Kripo, the State Criminal Police. The other three, Ullmann, Dreesen and Brandt, held the rank of leutnant and worked on personnel clearance at the R.S.H.S., the main office of Reich Security. Only one of them, Ullmann, looked like a thug. He was tall and fat. The skin beneath his eyes hung in slack pouches and his nose was hooked and lopsided from three separate fractures. As he listened to Stefan his mouth hung open, the lower lip puffy and scarred. He had been a street fighter for the National Socialists in the early days and only his subsequent record of lunatic courage with Einsatzgruppen squads had ensured him a good, safe post now that he was officially an invalid. Ullmann had an artificial leg, and he was proud of the limp it gave him. By comparison, Dreesen and Brandt looked like glorified clerks, which they were.

'Why do we ask them for that kind of information?' Ullmann wanted to know.

'You don't have to know why,' Stefan told him sharply. 'Simply get a list from each, and be sure it's complete.'

Leutnant Prager was nodding. 'We promise them a favour if they talk, do we?'

Stefan shrugged. 'Do that, or anything else you know will persuade them.' It hardly mattered if the lists were not complete. Under questioning, each individual on the forthcoming lists would be asked for a similar catalogue of relatives and friends. In time, every living associate and relative of the men behind the bomb plot would be located and executed. That was the way Reichsführer Himmler wanted it.

Dreesen had a question. 'Captain, these Certainties as you call them, have they any idea that they have been condemned?'

'They know they've been found guilty. There is solid proof against every one of them. They can't be sure if co-operation with us will help them. If my advice is worth anything to you, I'd suggest you make your questioning appear to be a simple matter of documentation. They are all in the dark, so I think they may respond best to firm, straightforward interrogation.'

'What will happen to them afterwards?' Brandt asked.

'They will be shot.'

After some further, minor questions, Stefan outlined the rest of the procedure. He explained that a full record of each interview would be copied down by a clerk and passed on in typed form to the Reichsführer's office. 'The names of the particular interviewing officers will appear on each report, so be careful. Future assignments and promotion prospects could depend on how you conduct yourselves. It's not often Reichsführer Himmler reads such reports himself, but this time I think he will.' He could see them tensing already. Himmler's name was like a magic wand. 'Right. The Scharführer in charge of the prisoners has all the necessary documentation. If any of you need to talk to me, I'll be in Room One. Don't barge in on your own, however. Tell the Scharführer.'

Klaus Metzler had been waiting outside Room One for

only a few minutes, but already his nerves were ragged. Several times he walked to the small mirror set in the wall at the end of the passage and straightened his cap, flicked invisible dust from the SS runes on his lapel and patted his black tie. He was immaculate, as he always was, but he went on fussing with his uniform until Stefan Gaiser appeared.

'Klaus! What brings you here?' Stefan took his hand and shook it warmly. 'I thought you were still stationed at Natzweiler.'

'I am,' Colonel Metzler told him. 'I'm back here on the anti-putsch business. I gather that's what you're doing.'

Stefan nodded. 'Are you on interrogations too?'

'No,' Klaus said, and his eyes wavered for a moment. 'Not the interrogations.'

'Oh. I see.' Stefan felt like an idiot. They had known each other for years. After eighteen months at adjoining desks in the Headquarters of SD, they had been posted together to Poland, and it was there that Klaus Metzler had demonstrated the special ability that gained him his quick promotion. By a fluke and some inspired guessing, he had uncovered a small Werhmacht black-market ring, selling food and fuel to the inhabitants of Warsaw. He was as dispassionate about the discovery as he was about anything else that could be laid out on paper: there was an irregularity, a breach of regulations, and Klaus prepared his evidence and submitted it to his superiors. Within eight hours four officers and three non-commissioned officers had been found guilty and executed. Two weeks later Klaus was assigned to a special Guard brigade in Berlin, and a month after that he was elevated to the rank of major. Somewhere between then and the winter of the following year, the major's talent for unemotional procedure was translated into action. Stefan saw his name and his new rank, Standartenführer, in despatches from Russia. Klaus had been one of the few officers chosen for leadership of the Einsatzgruppen, and he had distinguished himself: within a space of six months, the three thousand men of the murder squads had slaughtered almost half a million people. It had been stupid of Stefan to think his old colleague was in Berlin to carry out interrogations.

'I only expect to be here for a few days,' Klaus said. He was staring at the toes of his shiny boots.

'Then it's back to Natzweiler,' Stefan said chattily, taking in the nervousness.

'Yes. I, ah, wanted to discuss something with you urgently, Stefan. If you could find the time.'

Stefan smiled at him. 'You outrank me, Klaus. My time is yours.' He gestured to the door of the interrogation room and they went inside. The pale light bulb in the enamel shade cast a circle of light over the solitary chair in the centre of the floor. The table was in the shadows at the far end, and it was there for the interrogating officer to lay his papers on, and to sit on if he wished. Ideally the person being questioned always sat at a lower level than his interrogator.

'Sorry it's so gloomy.' Stefan put his folder on the table and offered Klaus the chair.

'No, I'll stand.' Since the door had closed behind them, the colonel appeared more nervous than ever. He walked around the edge of the pool of light for a few seconds, head down and hands clasped behind his back. Then he stopped and peered across at Stefan. 'What I have to say is difficult.'

'We've known each other for a long time,' Stefan said.

'That's true.' Klaus drew a pale hand across his forehead, pushing back his cap and revealing the deep furrows in the skin. He would be no more than forty-five, but he looked older than fifty. In the early days, he had always seemed younger than his age. 'It's your list of suspects I've come about. I saw it this morning and I couldn't believe my eyes.'

'What's wrong with it?'

'Among those Probables is a man I once knew very well.'

'Oh?' Stefan made an effort to sound casual. 'Which one?'

'Helmut Rascher.'

Stefan opened his file and located the name. 'I see he's a doctor.'

'That's right. A Luftwaffe staff surgeon.'

Stefan read some more of the details on the closely typed sheet. 'His complicity in the assassination attempt is only faintly in doubt, I'm afraid.' He looked up. 'I don't think I can do anything for him.'

'That's not what I came to ask.'

Stefan knew what Klaus wanted, but he kept up the mask of puzzled innocence. 'What, then?'

Klaus finally took the chair and sat with his feet tucked under the edge. The shadow from the lamp obscured his face. 'Stefan, until two years ago Rascher and I were friends, drinking companions. He was on the research team at Dachau when I was a liaison deputy there. We got along very well together, we had similar tastes, identical views on some things. I haven't seen him since my transfer to Natzweiler, but two years is nothing, is it?'

'I don't follow,' Stefan lied.

'Damnation, I'm an associate! And associates, friends, even distant cousins are being rounded up by the Gestapo in wagon loads!'

'You're also a senior officer of the SS, Klaus. That has to count for something.'

'What? Are you serious? Did you hear what went on at the trial in the Kammergericht two days ago?'

Stefan had heard, and he had personally sent out the Führer's instructions to the judge, Roland Friesler. 'Proceed with harshness,' Hitler had ordered, 'and with lightning speed.'

'It was hellish,' Klaus said. 'Grotesque. They dragged Field Marshal von Fitzleben into the courtroom without his false teeth and dressed up in tramp's clothes. That maniac Friesler did nothing but scream abuse at him. And the other seven defendants were treated no better.

They were all found guilty without proper evidence being presented. That's the tone of this witch-hunt, Stefan. Fanatical ruthlessness, mindless butchery. Himmler's list of two hundred has quadrupled in two days.' Klaus stabbed a finger against his chest. 'I'll be on the list if they find out I knew Rascher.'

Stefan examined his watch impassively. 'I think you're panicking unduly,' he said quietly. Klaus would have panicked even more if he had seen what had happened to the eight condemned men from the Kammergericht trial. Stefan had seen it, faithfully recorded on film and shown to the Führer the same day. In a small room at the Plötenzee prison they were stripped to the waist and each had a piano-wire noose placed around his neck. They were then hung from meat hooks in the ceiling. One man took twelve minutes to die. Hitler timed it.

'You have to help me,' Klaus moaned. He was on his feet again, hands clenched at his sides.

'But how? My job here is to force confessions from the Probables, and then to obtain a list of relatives and friends. Every word said by myself and the prisoners will be written down by a Gestapo clerk. There's no room for flexibility in the rules, Klaus. If Dr Rascher mentions your name . . .'

'Don't let him!'

Stefan sighed. 'How do I do that?'

'God Almighty, you're an expert in interrogation! You can do it! Talk to Rascher before he comes in here, warn him . . .'

'Impossible.'

'Stefan, there must be something . . .'

'No.' Stefan shook his head firmly. 'There's nothing. You're familiar enough with this kind of thing. How many pleas for help do you have to turn away in a week? The system is rigid, too rigid to allow me to help you. Besides, it's not only the doctor you have to worry about. What about all the other people who know about your friendship?'

'Hardly anybody did. We always drank in my quarters or his. And always late at night, after work.'

'Even so, someone will know about it. I can only advise you, Klaus. If you feel you are in danger, make a run for it. God knows there's enough chaos to lose yourself in, these days.'

Klaus changed then. His eyes hardened and he cocked his head, looking at Stefan with something like hatred. He was no longer pleading. 'Very well,' he said calmly, 'I have honoured my promise to myself.'

'What are you talking about?'

'I came here determined to plead with you as a brother officer. I felt I could rely on a former colleague to offer as much help as he could. Without pressure.'

Stefan looked at his watch again. 'I'm sorry, Klaus, I must get started. If you've something further to say, please say it quickly.'

'I will.' His hands were on his hips now, he was growing more confident by the second. 'As a last resort, I'm determined to lean on you, hard. It doesn't come easily to me, this kind of thing. I am a man of honour, I've done nothing to shame my oath.'

'Klaus, what the hell are you talking about?'

'I have certain information about you that would have you sitting in that chair, under interrogation, within the week.'

'Rubbish.'

Klaus shook his head slowly. 'No, not rubbish. Fact. I have a long memory, Stefan, and it's wide-ranging. Three years ago you were in charge of security around the Führer's headquarters train at Mönichkirchen, remember? You did well, and a year later you were part of the travelling furniture, you were on security and executive duty at Obersalzberg, Rastenburg, Vinnitsa. You were one of the outer circle.'

'I'm flattered that you've taken such an interest in my progress, Klaus. Now will you get to the point?'

Klaus smiled. 'Oh, I've watched you, I've watched a lot

of my old colleagues. It's been a yardstick for my own progress, you might say. You, Stefan, were one of the golden boys. You rose fast in the Führer's esteem. And all that time, you were betraying him.'

The colour rose in Stefan's cheeks. 'Klaus, I'm warning you . . .'

'No, I'm warning you. You'd better do something about Dr Rascher out there, or your neck will be in as much jeopardy as mine.' He began pacing back and forth before the table on which Stefan was leaning, watching the light glint on the burnished leather of his boots. 'I know about you and the little SS girl. And I know some of the things you do . . .'

Stefan pushed himself away from the table. 'I don't know what you're talking about.'

Klaus swung on him. 'Yes you do! And it would take only one breath of it from me to set a full-scale investigation going. You know what would happen.'

Stefan lowered his head. 'She is all I have.'

The colonel smiled. 'So you will do as I ask?'

'No.' Abruptly Stefan took three steps backwards and drew the Luger from his holster, levelling it at Klaus' chest.

'Stefan – what . . .' Klaus began to move forward and the bullet hit him in the throat. He flew back and landed on his face beside the table. Before he had even stopped falling Stefan was beside him, yanking open Klaus' holster, pulling out the pistol and firing a bullet high into the wall by the corner. He wiped the smoking gun on his armpit and wrapped Klaus' lifeless fingers around it, then ran to the door with his own gun still in his hand. The door opened before he reached it and Leutnant Brandt rushed in.

'What happened?' He stared at the crumpled body by the table, then at Stefan. 'Who's that?'

One of the clerks came in and Stefan grabbed him by the arm. 'Get on to Gestapo headquarters! Right away! We need someone down here.'

'Who is that?' Brandt asked again as the clerk ran off along the passage.

'Standartenführer Metzler,' Stefan told him. 'Deceased.'

The Gestapo major took the story down neatly, with all the detail appropriate to a security-grade report. When everything was on paper he offered Stefan a cigarette, apologized for the length of the procedure, and then asked if Stefan would mind repeating his account.

'Again,' the major said, 'it is a matter of procedure, as you know.'

Stefan gave the officer an understanding smile. 'I told Colonel Metzler that I would not compromise my loyalty to the Reich.'

The major cleared his throat. 'Forgive me interrupting again, but I must ask you, Captain – are you absolutely sure the colonel didn't mention the name of his friend on your interrogation list?'

'I'm positive. When I had refused a second time to help the colonel, he spun on me in a rage and drew his pistol. I brought up my foot and kicked his hand aside just as he fired, and by the time he had aimed again my own gun was out and I shot him.'

The major asked a few more questions about where Stefan had been standing when the shots were fired, how long the colonel had been in the room before the shooting and approximately how long it had taken to raise the alarm. 'Details, details,' the major crooned, closing his notebook finally and thanking Stefan for his co-operation.

'Attention to detail has played a large part in the growth of the Reich,' Stefan said.

'Oh, of course, I know that, Captain. And I know the value of being meticulous.' Rather sheepishly, he put on his cap and left, pausing at the door to thank Stefan again.

The interrogations started at 11:30. The first man brought before Stefan was an analytical chemist who worked on quality control at an explosives factory on the outskirts of Berlin. He was called Lindt, he was thirty-five years old, and before the war he had controlled a laboratory with over forty assistants, engaged on research into synthetic fuels. He looked frightened, and the sight of the tall young officer did nothing for his composure. When Stefan offered his introductory smile, the man just stared back at him with wide, sunken eyes.

'Do you know why you are here, Joachim Lindt?'

The man shook his head.

'You are suspected of having dealings with a certain army officer, a man who sought your advice on the construction of time-bombs. Surely you know that?'

'I know nothing.'

Stefan stepped close, letting his toe strike one spindly leg of the chair. 'Come now, that will do you no good. We know you submitted designs for miniature explosive devices to the patent office before the war. We also know you are skilled in devising detonators which operate through the action of acid on a copper wire. Such a device was used in the abortive attempt to murder the Führer.'

'I had nothing to do with it!' There was no defiance in the man's voice. He merely sounded scared, like a guilty child denying something because that was all he could do.

'Do you deny that you were visited by a Wehrmacht officer several months ago? Do you deny he called at your place of work and spoke with you?'

'I have to see so many people . . .'

'But this one was special. He was implicated in the bomb plot. He has confessed his guilt.' It was not true, the officer in question had disappeared, as had many others.

Sweat began to break out on the man's face, the same kind Stefan had seen on Stauffenberg. 'If he says I was involved he's lying! I only drew a diagram for him . . .'

'Ah! You're remembering. You drew a diagram. And you gave him something.'

Lindt nodded eagerly, seeing his confession as a road

out of his nightmare. 'Some wire. He needed the wire for the detonator. And the correct dilution of acid.'

'And you knew what he was going to do with what you gave him?'

'Of course not!'

Stefan walked to the table and looked down at his list. He had eight more men to interrogate. This one was guilty of nothing. He was a minor expert in time-bomb mechanisms and he had been used, that was all. Stefan would recommend that he be released. That would count for nothing, perhaps. The Reichsführer's definitions of guilt and complicity were widening every day. He turned back to face the prisoner, ready to speed the interrogation to its end, when the door burst open and Dreesen rushed in.

'I told you not to come in here!'

'I'm sorry, I forgot.' Dreesen was breathless. He had been running. 'Can I speak to you, please?'

'Is it urgent?'

'In a way.'

Stefan called to one of the soldiers by the main door to come and stand by the prisoner, then he went out into the passage with Dreesen.

'What's so important, then?'

'It's really weird. I was standing in the room with the other prisoners when it happened.'

'Get to the point, Dreesen!'

The lieutenant caught his breath. 'The Luftwaffe doctor, Rascher I think his name is, he was sitting there picking at his ear, then he pulled out this thing like a blob of wax and stuck it in his mouth. I actually saw him do it, as calm as you like. Then his eyes rolled back and he fell off the chair. He's dead.'

Later, as the Gestapo rolled into action again, Stefan sat on the table in his interrogation room and wrote his own explanation of why the day's work had been so seriously delayed. On all sides people were screaming for speed, but even Himmler would accept delays if they were properly documented.

On balance the day had been a good one. Poor shivering Lindt, the chemist, probably knew less about time-bombs than Stefan. One time-bomb had been defused right there in that room; Metzler had been the detonator.

He checked his watch and decided to have lunch. On the way out he saw the Gestapo major again.

'At least it's one less for you to tackle,' he said to Stefan.

'That's true,' Stefan replied. 'But there's always another one to fill the gap.'

On the street he paused, sucking in the fresh air. Always one more, he thought. How many more?

The campaign map, spread carelessly on the desk in the study at the Berghof, presented a picture of desperate emergency that only Hitler himself refused to accept. Even Bormann, striving to mirror his chief's grim confidence, began to admit at least some of the defeat. On the sullen morning of 24th August he stood by the Führer's desk and stared bleakly at the map, his foot tapping softly as Stefan Gaiser reported the priority order of the day's business.

'Dr Goebbels' emergency policy is to be implemented from today,' Stefan said, reading from the list on top of the stack of papers he was holding. 'The Führer's signature will be necessary.'

'A formality,' Bormann muttered, still looking at the map. 'Put the document with the others on my desk. The Führer has already approved the plan.' He sighed. 'All music halls, theatres, music schools and cabarets will be shut down within the week. Orchestras will be disbanded, the publication of fiction will cease and all but two illustrated papers will stop publication. Actors, dancers, musicians and journalists will be put into uniform or into munitions factories.' He looked up and eyed Stefan coldly. 'Barrels are being scraped vigorously.'

Stefan nodded and ran his finger further down the list. 'There's the matter of the directive to all Wehrmacht units. I only have a note here. You suggested that the point be raised with the Führer today.'

'Yes, I've already drafted the statement. Disintegration within the ranks and among the officers is to be curbed with a sharp warning. Deserters' families will be arrested. What else?'

'The Führer is to be asked to send a follow-up directive to Reichsführer Himmler concerning the dismantling of the internment camps.'

'You don't really have to mince your words, Gaiser. Not with me. They are extermination camps, and we should feel no shame about their existence.' Bormann stepped away from the desk and stared thoughtfully through the window. 'We have to be so careful of misguided good intentions. It would certainly appear wise to remove the camps in the present situation, and I know there is some high-level panic because of the Russian advance. But we have to balance our thinking. Eichmann reports that his task is near its end. Like myself he believes in strict continuity – a job started should always be seen through to the finish. That is the basis of progress.'

'I agree,' Stefan said. 'But the camps are a severe embarrassment. I'm sure that is why so much pressure is being put on the Führer to speed the demolition.' He consulted his papers. 'The original order to Reichsführer Himmler was issued ten days ago, and so far nothing has been done.'

Bormann returned to the desk. 'An order to dismantle all of the camps except Auschwitz will be issued by Himmler before the end of the year. Meanwhile, I'll issue a few comforting memoranda to the worriers. There's no need to burden the Führer with the matter any further. Strike it from the agenda.'

Stefan did as he was told, then proceeded to read out

the remaining business for the day. Bormann nodded his assent to each item and when the list was exhausted he beckoned for Stefan to come and stand beside him.

'Look at it carefully,' he said, waving his hand over the map. 'Where, in your opinion, does the hope shine through?'

'It's hardly for me to—'

'Nevertheless. Look at it. Tell me candidly if you can see *one* opportunity for us.'

This was not like Bormann. He rarely missed a chance to show his dislike for Stefan, and all the time they had been obliged to work together the Führer's watchdog had kept up a stiff, formal barrier between them. But since the week before, when Hitler had recalled Stefan to his personal staff, Secretary Bormann had given off traces of a weary abdication: the defeat that Stefan saw hollowing the eyes and voices of so many officers lately was beginning to seep through, even to him.

'It's rather depressing,' Stefan said.

'You see nothing hopeful?'

Hitler demanded optimism of everyone around him, and would fly into a rage if he thought that any of his staff were less convinced of victory than he was. Stefan glanced at Bormann for a second, scanning the puffy, tight-mouthed features. All he could see was straightforward curiosity, and perhaps a little anxiety.

'Military strategy isn't my strong point, sir. I can only see the facts here. They don't seem to hold any message, apart from the obvious one. The Red Army offensives have been devastating. The Wehrmacht has been defeated or surrounded all the way from the Baltic to the Ukraine. To the north we have at least fifty divisions completely surrounded, and in the south the Romanian oilfields are falling to the Russians.'

'They're closing on Warsaw, too. The Führer has issued orders to have President von Hindenburg's coffin removed from the tomb at Tannenberg. It's only a matter of hours,

I think, before we lose Paris. It's a mess, Gaiser. We are falling on every front.'

'You believe there is no hope at all?' Stefan risked the question.

'Why do you think I asked you in the first place?' Bormann spread his hand flat on the centre of the map, shaking his head. 'I've looked at the picture, so have you, so have dozens of people better qualified to interpret it. We all see the same thing. Yet the Führer *knows* there is a chance for us. If only he would say what it is he understands from this chaos.'

The surge of feeling subsided suddenly and Bormann stood erect. 'You understand my concern, don't you?' His voice was controlled again, the taut monotone he used when he addressed subordinates. 'Our leader has a gift for strategy and I am aware that he has a plan to rescue our honour and convert defeat into triumph. But he says nothing. I only see glimpses of his certainty when he nods his head over this map and looks up with that light in his eyes. The generals have to be reassured. All they need is a promise. Every day I pray that the Führer will say something to them . . .' Emotion was edging into his voice again and he stopped talking.

Stefan began to understand a little more about Bormann's loyalty, and his loneliness. 'Perhaps,' he said, 'it is part of the Führer's plan to remain silent until his generals are at the limits of their endurance. Men in that condition respond magnificently to any hope they're offered.'

'Perhaps.'

Later that day Stefan was called to the study again, this time by Hitler, who sat propped in a leather chair while his physician, Dr Morrell, applied an auroscope to his right ear.

'Come in, Gaiser, come in.' The old man was smiling, beckoning with his left hand for Stefan to stand by the table opposite the chair, where he could be seen clearly. Hitler's right hand, Stefan noticed, was jammed firmly against his knee, but the tremor was still visible. 'The good doctor is checking to see how many more of my seams have cracked in the last twenty-four hours.'

Stefan stood by while Morrell completed his examination. The Führer's health had deteriorated sharply since the bomb attempt at Rastenburg. His heart had gone into a slow decline, making him listless and irritable, and he was plagued by persistent earache and partial deafness. There were recurring pains in the head and attacks of dizziness, making it necessary for Hitler to walk with his feet spread apart to keep his balance. A recent cold had caused inflammation of the sinuses and an almost total loss of appetite. The Führer was fifty-five years old, but that afternoon he looked twenty years older.

Morrell finally stood back and gave his patient a wry smile. 'The advice is the same as before,' he said. 'Rest and more rest.'

'No more medicine?' Hitler asked.

'No new medicine, Führer. The regimen should remain the same, at least for the time being.'

Before taking his leave, Morrell administered an injection of Tonophosphan, a phosphorous preparation that helped to promote a sensation of physical comfort, although it did nothing to reduce the levels of the Führer's ailments.

'Well then, Gaiser,' the old man mumbled as Morrell closed the door, 'you are looking well.' He rubbed his arm over the spot where the needle had entered. 'I can almost remember when I felt as sturdy as you look.'

'The health of the spirit is the important thing,' Stefan replied. He had read *Mein Kampf* several times, carefully.

Hitler nodded approvingly. 'But it can burn out the body, I think. My mission has consumed me. My body is a collection of pains and weaknesses, held together by determination.' He motioned for Stefan to sit in the upright chair beside his own. 'I don't make a habit of meeting my staff in shirtsleeves, as you are aware, but the matter on hand is urgent.' He waited for Stefan to sit down before he went on. 'I believe you are a man I can trust.' His voice was hoarse and quiet, and Stefan had to lean forward in his chair to hear properly. 'I have watched you during the past few years and I find that you embody some virtues of correctness and dedication peculiarly suited to your work. I do not say this to flatter you, Gaiser.'

Stefan knew that. The Führer was simply putting him on his honour. 'I am grateful for your trust, sir.'

'I want you to go to Munich.' He pointed to a sealed envelope on the desk. 'The address and other details are there. You will locate a lady called Margarete Slezak – there is a picture of her in the envelope. If she has moved to another address, or even to another town or city, I still want you to find her, and accompany her back here to the Obersalzberg, as my guest.'

Stefan promised he would do everything in his power to find the woman, and rose to leave.

'She is to be treated with the utmost courtesy,' Hitler warned him. 'I am sure a man of your charm and bearing will have no difficulty in putting Fräulein Slezak at her ease. And one other thing. You will make no mention to anyone, not even to Secretary Bormann . . .'

'I understand, Führer.'

'Good. Leave at once, then.'

In his quarters, after packing and changing into a fresh uniform, Stefan opened the envelope and looked at the woman's picture. She would have been about thirty when it was taken, and she was stunningly beautiful. Her blonde hair was worn high on her head and soft ringlets framed her round, even-featured face. Her eyes were most striking of all, large and bright and a match for the Führer's in the intensity of their stare.

Stefan knew her. She was forty-three now, still single, still living in Munich. Her beauty had not so much faded as mellowed: she still commanded the attention of men, and she never lacked escorts. Her address was different from the one written on the slip of paper and Stefan was glad of that. He could stay longer in Munich on the pretence of looking for Margarete Slezak, then go directly to her apartment when his other business was finished.

As he waited for his transport to arrive he made no effort to speculate on the Führer's reasons for wanting to see the woman. To Stefan's certain knowledge they had not met for over ten years. In many ways Hitler was a romantic, but it was likely he was so sentimental, especially at that time and in his low state of health, that he would want a simple reunion with an old lover. In the absence of anything firm to go on, Stefan declined to guess any further. It was a habit his SS training had given him, and he valued it.

He was in Munich by late evening. As a special aide of the Führer he was given a fine suite in the second best hotel in the city. There he dined alone, and drank half a bottle of scarce *tafelwein*. Just before ten he went down to the foyer and made a call from the public telephone booth. After a moment a man answered, his voice muffled.

'I'm here,' Stefan said in English.

'In Munich?' The other man's voice was clear now, a richly accented American.

'That's right. Meet me.'

'Sure. One hour.' There was a brief, cackling laugh. 'You sonofabitch. I thought you were miles away.'

'Naturally.' Stefan dropped the receiver and stepped out into the foyer.

There was time for a drink, he decided. Time to drop the tension and just float, if only for half an hour. Then he could start to worry again.

1927–1930

In his will, Sir George Malcolm had made extensive provisions for his daughter. There was a summer cottage at Pevensey Bay in Sussex, a ten-room house with two acres near the family seat at Handcross and an annuity of £2,000. Two years before his death in 1919, he had been keenly aware that his only child was desperately unhappy in her marriage, and the will stipulated that the properties be kept in good order for Charlotte until such time as she returned to England.

She came back in the summer of 1927. She was thirty-nine and had managed to keep her grace and good looks intact, although some relatives quietly observed that she brooded a great deal, and her hand shook slightly when she held a tea cup.

Stefan came with her. He was now fifteen and a full inch taller than Charlotte. The resemblance between the boy and his father had become more noticeable now that Stefan had reached puberty, and it was his appearance, coupled with his slightly accented English, which made it difficult for the aunts and uncles to show him much warmth. He was the son of a Prussian officer who had fought against England, and he looked and sounded the part. None of the Malcolms, apart from his grandmother, could feel any kinship with him. Everyone was content to let the boy and his mother lead their withdrawn existence on the small estate called Deanfield.

Only Charlotte's mother, Lady Malcolm knew the full story behind her daughter's separation from her husband. Charlotte had given her the details not long after she came back, because explanations were in order, and Lady Malcolm could be relied upon to be discreet when retailing the facts to other members of the family.

'Leonhard's illness turned him into a violent drunkard,'

Charlotte told her mother. 'The lesion in his lung deteriorated so badly by 1923 that he couldn't go fishing or hunting any more. He had to rest until noon every day, and in the afternoons he still had to be careful. Even walking became a difficulty. I believed he would go back to his writing, but he didn't. The impulse had died, I think; so had the vision. He became very bitter.'

She went on to say how vicious he had become, too. He stopped bothering with threats. He acted directly on urge, and several times after arguing with Charlotte he tried to hit her with his walking stick. Once, the blow landed. Charlotte suffered a cracked bone at her elbow, but she was luckier than a maid who had her knuckles smashed when Leonhard caught her dusting, against his orders, in his sacred gun room. Only Stefan had escaped the belligerence, the abuse and the maudlin, drink-soaked bouts of self-pity. He had been Leonhard's last hope.

'I had intended to wait until the boy was older,' Charlotte said. 'He already knew he would be trying for Cambridge when he was nineteen, but I felt he would need more maturity to understand why I would be leaving Dorfen, too. I waited as long as I could.'

'And how will Leonhard fare?' Lady Malcolm asked.

'He's in the care of nurses at a clinic in Munich. He went berserk when he knew we were leaving. It took three of our estate workers to hold him when he came raging after me into the kitchen. He struggled so hard he ruptured some vessels in the damaged lung. I don't think he will survive long.'

'And you have no qualms about leaving him, now that he's so ill?'

'Mother . . .'

Lady Malcolm understood. 'And what about Stefan? How will the uprooting affect him?'

'I believe his destiny lies with us.'

The first year at Deanfield was a period of rapid change and growth for Stefan. During quiet mornings and evenings when his mother sat in the cosy drawing room and sewed, Stefan would stay near her, methodically absorbing his English grammar, mathematics and history. The intensity of his education at Dorfen had already brought him close to university entrance standard, and two afternoons a week he was visited at Deanfield by a tutor from London, Eric Brown, who carefully set down the guidelines to ease his way into Cambridge.

On Tuesday, Wednesday and Friday afternoons, Stefan went out on his own, encouraged by his mother, to see places and get acquainted with people. At fifteen he could easily be mistaken for someone much older, and he had inherited his father's ability to impose himself upon situations. Within two months he had made tentative friendships in two neighbouring villages, and when he found there was a lot of prejudice against Germans, he began passing himself off as a Swiss. By late autumn Stefan knew the taste of English draught beer and the pleasure of riding in gymkhanas. He learned to play cricket, shoot clay pigeons and master the rudiments of shove-ha'penny. When people learned gradually that he was the grandson of Sir George Malcolm, a few discreet invitations to parties and dances were dropped through the letter-box at Deanfield.

'You must accept as many as you can,' his mother told him. When Stefan occasionally said he was concerned for her, the way she stayed home so much and rarely saw anyone but himself and the servants, Charlotte assured him she was fine. She was happier than she had been for years, she insisted. 'Go to your parties and your dances, Stefan. Absorb the gentleness of people.'

Towards Christmas of 1927 Eric Brown suggested that Stefan spend a weekend as his guest in London. 'It will be a break for you,' Brown said to Charlotte, who never really found the boy a burden. 'And it'll be a big adventure for Stefan. I'll entertain him royally.'

Charlotte hesitated only momentarily before agreeing. Eric Brown was about thirty-five, perhaps a shade flamboyant for a tutor, but intelligent and intensely good-natured. On reflection, Charlotte could think of nobody better suited to introduce Stefan to the Capital.

Eric lived in an apartment near the house where Stefan's parents had first met. The place was spacious and well-furnished, with some Augustus John charcoal sketches in silver frames on the walls and art nouveau bric-a-brac on the glass-topped tables.

'Not a typical scholar's garret,' Eric confessed when Stefan first arrived. 'I have private means. One day I'll learn to stop apologizing to myself for not being a stereotype.'

Stefan was enchanted by the place. Beyond the showy sitting room there was a small, square room with a desk, a swivel chair, a reading lamp and hundreds of books covering all four walls. 'All tastes catered for,' Eric said. 'History, science, poetry, literature in three languages, some bound American comic magazines and an encyclopedia or two. Feel free to browse.'

The guest bedroom was splendid. The bed itself was a slender-framed, chrome four-poster with fine lace curtains and a white damask counterpane. It sat regally against the centre of the wall opposite the door, on a woollen carpet so spotlessly white that Stefan was tempted to remove his shoes before going in. There was a bathroom *en suite*, and opposite it, a dressing room fitted with Victorian mahogany trouser press, matching tallboy and wheeled full-length mirror.

When Stefan had completed his inspection Eric asked him if the quarters suited him.

'They're magnificent! I imagined you lived in a room the size of a shoe box with a leaky fanlight and no heating.'

Eric laughed. 'On the money I earn, that's exactly how I'd be fixed. But as I said, there's a private income. My father makes tin boxes and my mother dotes on me.'

Stefan had never thought of Eric Brown being anybody's son. He had a smooth, adult confidence and the slightly worn face of a man who was self-contained and happy. People like that never had the air of attachment. Even a wife would have been a surprise.

Eric had made arrangements for a theatre visit that first evening, and when they were both changed and ready to go out, he suggested a dry sherry. After a minute, it became clear that Eric had planned this as a time to explain about himself.

'In my father's opinion, I am a wastrel. I never advertise that I have a doctorate in philosophy, Stefan, but I have, and I cost my old man a few quid getting it. He had pictures in his head, of course. He saw me as a distinguished scholar, a teacher in some lofty capacity, probably winding up as chancellor of some university. After receiving my doctorate, I began to worry my people by lolling about the house all day, and only going out to get drunk or to stuff myself in some restaurant. Eventually the old man tackled me about it. And I explained. I'm privy to the thinking of Plato, Livy, Socrates and the rest: I'm a disciple of Nietzsche, Lenin, Kierkegaard – in short, I'm full of contradictions and I love them all. And what I am inside, I also am outside. I drift from one magnetic activity to another. Work – one clearly defined job – would suffocate me. I really am the wastrel my father calls me.'

'Am I your only pupil?' Stefan asked.

'You are, indeed. I have other jobs. I lecture once a week on comparative religion. I read proofs for a publisher. I'm writing a biography of Pascal to which I add maybe a hundred words a month. Then there's my translation of Ovid, and my postage stamps. I buy them up at seedy markets all over London, then sell them through small advertisements in collectors' magazines.'

'You're extraodinary,' Stefan said.

'And you are brilliant, young Stefan. With enough ambition you'll do anything you want. But you also have the mark of the anchored man. You might rise very high in your chosen field, but you'll miss the variety of life because your dedication will blinker you.'

'So I'm here to be taught a lesson?'

'Certainly. I want you to learn to dilute the intensity in yourself. I want you to enjoy. You have the kind of drive that eventually squeezes out the capacity for laughter.'

That night they laughed a great deal. They had front row seats at the Pavilion and saw Cochran's revue, *One Dam' Thing After Another.* Artistes Stefan had read about in newspapers and magazines paraded only a few feet from where he sat – Jessie Matthews, Sonnie Hale, Greta Fayne, Max Wall and Douglas Byng. The music was loud and tuneful, the comedy fast and well-timed. Afterwards, as if he were trying to trap the mood, Eric hailed a taxi and told the driver to take them to an address in Tite Street, Chelsea.

'What happens now?' Stefan asked as the cab trundled down Sloane Street.

'More variety,' Eric said.

In the sitting room, dining room, stairway and kitchen of a large terraced house, about a hundred people were standing, sitting, leaning and lying in overflowing groups that sounded, collectively, like dozens of shifting, buzzing cells that exploded randomly with laughter. Stefan had never been to so large or casual a gathering. Eric led him by the sleeve past girls in shimmering dresses and skullcap hairdos, men with wide trousers and cigarette holders, over kneeling couples playing pontoon on the carpet and through a group trying to sing *Ain't She Sweet.*

'Ah!' A fat man, completely bald and wearing a blue silk dinner jacket and a wide cummerbund, came waddling at them from the door leading on to the garden. 'Eric, the light at the end of my tunnel!' He wrapped arms like bolts of cloth around Eric and squeezed him, then turned his attention to Stefan. 'And is this your young friend from the country?'

Eric made the introductions. The man was Dorian Goode, owner of the house and host for the evening.

When Stefan responded to training and bowed stiffly as he shook Dorian's hand, the fat man gave a wheezing gale of laughter.

'What's wrong?' Stefan asked.

'Nothing, dear boy,' Dorian apologized as soon as his breath came back. 'It's a long time since anyone showed me that kind of respect.' He patted Stefan's shoulder. 'Do let me get you a drink.'

Stefan looked enquiringly at Eric.

'Champagne,' Eric said.

Stefan had never tasted the stuff before and he drank warily.

'Just take it steadily,' Eric whispered. 'Enjoy, but don't wallow.'

For almost ten minutes their host conducted a monologue about his recurring boredom, the cost of living in style, and the problems of being overweight.

'Women took me seriously when I was thin. It's so ironical. In those days I'd neither the funds nor the energy to take advantage of their interest. Now I'm a bit of a joke, yet I've the strength of a bull and enough money to make any woman happy. Ridiculous.'

Eric suggested that Dorian put himself on a strict diet.

The big man shook his head, making the rolls of fat on his neck shift like wedges of pink fondant. 'On principle, I could never subject myself to any kind of discipline. Perhaps I pay a high price for my self-indulgence, but I'd rather do that than turn myself into a soured Spartan.'

Years later, Stefan would learn that Dorian Goode was one of the most disciplined people he had ever met, but at that moment he could feel nothing more than distaste for his decadence.

A little later, when Dorian had moved on to another group, Stefan asked Eric what the man did for a living.

'He's a professional diarist,' Eric said, with a trace of mockery. 'Under two different names, neither of them his own, he produces little gossip columns for American society magazines. That's why he has these parties. He can bring the scandals into his own sitting room and pick up all the dirt he needs without straining himself.'

'I don't think I like him much.'

With his second glass of champagne clutched in his hand, Stefan accompanied Eric from group to group, listening to what was said and only speaking when he had to. After a while it was obvious that most people thought he was older, and a couple of times he forced himself to grin at innuendoes he did not really understand. Moving across the hallway towards the dining room, he paused for a moment and saw himself in a mirror several feet away; he did not stand out from the others as much as he had imagined, and in the dim amber light he did look much older. That comforted him, and his confidence began to grow.

In the dining room he was introduced to a tall, square-faced man called Harold Fisher. He was about sixty and he moved with the cautious pace of a man whose body had become fragile. Harold was a theatrical impresario, Eric explained, and then reeled off a list of famous actors and actresses who had been associated with the Fisher empire. But Stefan was only half listening. He felt himself blushing, not unpleasantly, under the candid stare of a petite, beautiful girl standing beside Fisher. It was hard to tell her age. There was dark make-up around her eyes and her mouth was a glossy scarlet, a vivid contrast to her pale skin and short, jet black curls. Stefan had never seen a girl look so quietly confident, and he guessed at once that the confidence came from intelligence, not arrogance.

'Never mind my history,' Fisher grumbled amiably, cutting off Eric's flow. 'Tell us about friend Stefan. What's his line of business?'

'I'm still a student,' Stefan said. He had already agreed with Eric that it was the best thing to tell people.

'And a brilliant one,' Eric said, patting Stefan's shoulder.

Fisher turned suddenly, realizing the girl was beside

him, and he ushered her gently forward, his eyes twinkling with a fatherly pride. 'This is my little Emma.' He squeezed her arm and she smiled faintly, glancing momentarily at Eric before returning her stare to Stefan. 'You've met this rascal Brown already, my dear. This other gentleman is called Stefan.'

'How do you do.' Stefan shook her hand.

'Stefan what?' Emma asked.

'Gaiser.'

'Oh. You're a German.' She said it in a flat, unemotional way, betraying no special reaction to his nationality. 'How long have you been over here?'

'Not very long,' Stefan said, 'but I am staying in England now. My mother is English.'

'He's my guest for the weekend,' Eric said. 'I'm showing him a slice of life in the wicked city.'

Fisher chuckled. 'I hope he knows what he's letting himself in for.' He raised a warning finger. 'Hang around with this rogue too long, and you'll wind up seeing a slice of life in Wandsworth prison.'

They all laughed. Then Emma said, 'I'm sure Stefan couldn't be corrupted that easily.' Her eyes were still firmly on him.

'Why does everybody think I'm a villain?' Eric asked. 'Just because I don't do a regular job, I drink a lot, sing in the street occasionally and chase duchesses – does that make me bad company?' Stefan knew he was trying to reduce the tension.

'You have a face for the gallows,' Harold Fisher said, and rumbled with laughter.

Eric and Fisher began reminiscing. Stefan smiled and laughed with them dutifully. Emma's gaze remained fixed, and she did not smile.

Eventually Eric drew Stefan away, and as they helped themselves to drinks from the sideboard Eric let out a whistle. 'That Emma. She's bad news.'

'I thought she looked rather nice.'

'They said the same about Lucretia Borgia. Listen,

Stefan, I've a certain responsibility to keep you out of trouble. Let's just stick with the superficial crowd until it's time to go home.'

They circulated and chatted until the early hours, and Stefan learned a lot. He discovered, for one thing, that Eric Brown was not usually so civilized and restrained when he attended parties. It was clear from the way people greeted him and nudged him in the ribs and whispered and sniggered in his ear. Stefan realized that his tutor was making a special effort, and he appreciated that. Another thing he observed – and stored up for examination – was that a lot of the guests were very lonely people, and almost all of them had one thing in common: deep anxiety to capture time and hold on to it.

As they were getting ready to leave, Eric stepped aside to say goodbye to some friends, and Stefan felt a hand on his elbow. He turned and saw Emma.

'It's been nice meeting you,' she said. 'It's a pity your stay has to be so brief.' Then she handed him a small ivory card. 'If you can manage it at all, give me a ring on Sunday morning. Make it early. I think there are some aspects of London life Eric will miss out of your visit, and that would be a terrible shame.'

When she walked away he looked at the card. It had her name embossed in gold type. There was nothing else on it. In a mild panic he twisted the card and turned it over. Then he saw the exchange and number pencilled on the back.

It was almost four when they got back to Eric's apartment. As soon as Stefan had eased off his shoes he felt the tiredness sweep over him.

Eric was wandering about the sitting room, dropping his tie, jacket, cigarettes and wallet on random tables and yawning. 'I'm exhausted.' He paused with one shoe in his hand and looked at Stefan. 'I'll let you sleep late tomorrow. We've nothing on the programme until eleven o'clock. I thought you'd enjoy a visit to the National Gallery.'

'Fine,' Stefan said, and started moving towards his room.

'Did you enjoy yourself?'

Stefan nodded. 'It was marvellous, Eric. I'm grateful to you.'

'It was fun for me too. I enjoy playing the benefactor occasionally.'

'Eric, that girl . . .'

'Emma Fisher?' Eric scratched his head. 'I don't want to labour the point, but you're a minor, Stefan. Men twice your age have run into trouble with her.'

More and more Stefan was becoming irritated at the way his age formed a barrier between him and his instincts. 'Is she really as bad as you make out?'

'I don't want to discuss her.' Eric sat down and started removing his other shoe.

'I got the impression she was quite pleasant.' Stefan had already decided two things: he would take up the girl's invitation, and he would say nothing about it to Eric.

'You got the wrong impression. Take your tutor's word for it. Put your affection where it belongs – with Archimedes, Dickens and Gibbon.'

'How old is she?'

Eric sighed. 'Twenty-two, as far as I know.'

Stefan shrugged, striving to be casual. 'I thought her father was quite nice, too.'

Eric started laughing.

'What's so funny?'

'Your innocence. Harold Fisher isn't Emma's father. He's her husband.'

Saturday was as exhausting and as entertaining as the day before. The visit to the National Gallery was followed by lunch at Ye Olde Ham Bone, an artists' club in the West End. Afterwards, Eric suggested a round of the traditional tourist sights – Trafalgar Square, Buckingham Palace, St Paul's and the Tower. At the Prospect of

Whitby they had beer on the terrace and watched the small trade vessels chugging back and forward through the slimy water around the docks. In the evening they went to the theatre again, the Old Vic this time, and watched a performance of *Twelfth Night.* Instead of a party, Eric took Stefan to a night-club, a dingy, smoke-filled cellar called Anna's, where they drank cheap sparkling wine and watched two very thin girls tap dance on a glass floor. Around midnight Stefan complained he was tired, and Eric immediately suggested they go home.

'You must look your best for tomorrow,' he said. Stefan had told him he was going to visit a friend of his mother's.

The call to Emma Fisher was made from a telephone box in Knightsbridge. It was a freezing morning and Stefan wondered if he was being stupid: any girl with sense would still be tucked up in bed. But she answered on the second ring and sounded anything but sleepy.

'Stefan! So you decided to take up my offer.'

'If you don't mind venturing out in this weather.'

'But I love the cold! It sharpens the awareness, don't you think?'

'I suppose so. Where were you planning on going?'

'You'll find out later,' she said. 'Have you got a pencil?'

He fumbled in his jacket and wrote down the address she gave him on the back of an envelope.

'Find a taxi, if there are any about. It should only take you about five minutes. I'll be waiting with hot coffee.'

Outside the call box Stefan stood and looked along the deserted pavement. The steam from his lips and nostrils curled in front of his eyes, adding to the morning's unnatural, dreamy stillness. For one insecure moment he was missing his mother and the friendly warmth of Deanfield. Then he shook himself, turned up his coat collar and began striding towards a cab rank. His father had once told him that a man was never alone or lost, when he had his determination, and Stefan was holding on to that thought. Even so, he was still a little nervous.

He was actually keeping an appointment with a beautiful, married woman.

The address was a white-painted mews house at the fashionable end of the Bayswater Road. Emma had the door open before Stefan had finished paying the driver.

'You look frozen!' she said, and pushed him ahead of her into the tidy little sitting room. 'Take off your coat and warm yourself at the fire. I'll get the coffee.'

She vanished to the kitchen and Stefan stood with his back to the fire, gazing round the room and admiring the quality and quiet good taste of the furnishings. He had expected something more flamboyant, more theatrical, but the place had the look of a country home, rather like his mother's at Pevensey Bay. There were two large oil paintings on opposite walls, a Turner seascape and a portrait of Emma, looking as ominously straight-faced as she had when he first saw her at Dorian Goode's party.

Stefan could hear the cups chinking in the kitchen. Swiftly, he took three strides to the sitting-room door and had a look at the hall stand. All the coats were Emma's. There was no trace of anything belonging to a man, not even an umbrella. He went back to the fire and stood waiting, hands clasped behind his back.

'Here we are.' Emma came in with a tray and set it on the low table in front of the leather chesterfield. She was wearing a dark blue cashmere dress that made her complexion much rosier than Stefan had remembered. It dawned on him that this was the first time he had seen her in daylight, and she seemed even more striking now. She turned and smiled at him.

They sat together on the couch and Emma put her visitor at ease by doing all the talking. She explained that the house was her own weekend place, her retreat. Harold – she never once referred to him as her husband – respected her need for time on her own, and she never saw him between noon on Saturday and Monday morning.

'The weekly programme of receptions, parties, openings, dinners – it's all great fun, but there's no room for peace. Harold thrives on the hubbub, I'm the one who falls to pieces.'

Looking at her, Stefan could hardly believe it. Nor could he see her as Eric's scarlet woman.

'Usually I spend Saturday evening here, alone, reading, playing the gramophone, just relaxing. On Sundays I like to go out and visit the places Harold would never take me.' She smiled. 'He's really quite a snob.'

They had a second cup of coffee, laced with rum this time, because Emma said they would need something to fend off the cold. She told Stefan a little more about herself – she had been in the theatre at seventeen, and would have been yet if things had not changed so dramatically, and she admitted that her one big ambition was to become something very special in her own right – and then she began asking him questions about himself.

Stefan gave her the revised history that he had concocted and rehearsed since his arrival in London. He was the son of a German landowner (he said his father was dead, and he knew it would soon be true, anyway) and he had come to settle in England with his mother immediately after his father died. He had inherited an interest in history, and hoped to pursue his leaning at Cambridge. He gave his age as nineteen and he could see that Emma accepted that without hesitation. He added that he had always been in love with the image of England, and found that the country lived up to his dreams. The last part was not quite true, but it was a convenient way of avoiding argument.

'That's very curious,' Emma said.

'What is?'

'You being such a dedicated Englishman inside, and yet you're so German looking.'

'You think so?' He knew he looked like his father, but it had never occurred to him that there was anything in his appearance that signalled his race.

'I'd say you were the perfect Aryan.' She sounded amused. 'It's not simply the precise way you move or your

European manners. You're made differently from Englishmen. That special squareness of the shoulders. The terribly fair hair – and your eyes are so blue . . .' She began to laugh. 'I'm embarrassing you. I'm sorry.' She touched his hand lightly. 'Just be glad you're the way you are. There's something deliciously sneaky about being one thing on the outside and another inside. And besides, I think German males are lovely.'

Before Stefan's blush could take hold she was on her feet and putting her cup and saucer on the tray. 'Time we were moving,' she said.

'Where are we going?'

'Down among the real Londoners.'

Within half an hour they were at Petticoat Lane. Starting at the Bishopsgate end, Emma led the way through the packed crowds and kept up a running commentary on the place as she elbowed her way from stall to stall.

Stefan had never seen such a variety of traders in one place. Men and women bundled in overcoats and scarves roared their prices and rattled their wares and did everything but manhandle the shoppers into buying the goods. On one twenty-yard stretch of road there were stalls selling blankets, crockery, fruit, toys, hot chestnuts, ironware, clothing, seafood and clocks. The din and the bright lights and the sense of being carried along by the crowd made Stefan light-headed. Emma reached behind her and grasped his hand, and then suddenly they were on a wider stretch of road and walking side by side, still holding hands.

'I adore this place,' Emma said, and she leaned her head on Stefan's shoulder. 'The people are so alive. You know they're not playing at living.'

At a corner they stopped and watched an auction of turkeys. Emma looked on entranced as the butcher hoisted the carcases and bellowed his offers, but Stefan wanted to move on. Christmas was never quite the pleasure for him that it was for other people.

At a stall selling cheap jewellery and trinkets Emma bought a little silver-plated watch fob and gave it to Stefan. 'A keepsake,' she said, and kissed him on the cheek. He promptly bought a brooch in the shape of a heart and pressed the tissue-wrapped gift into her hand. After only a short hesitation, he returned the kiss.

They had lunch in a large, bare-floored shop that traded exclusively in the traditional meat pie, mashed potatoes and peas in thick green liquor, served on large oval plates and eaten from marble-topped tables. Emma was like a delighted schoolchild, filling her mouth and trying to talk through the obstruction.

Later, when they were back on the street, she asked if Eric was expecting Stefan at any special time.

'No, not at all.'

'That's good,' Emma said, and she looked at him again with that still, thoughtful expression.

His feelings were confused. Any experiences with girls in the past had been childish, tentative, uncertain. Now he was on the brink of something different. In the taxi on the way back to the house, Stefan watched her profile and wondered at the complexity of a real, grown woman, the very first woman with whom he had been friendly. Though saying and doing very little, she hinted at vast expanses of understanding and experience. He was fascinated by her, and rather frightened.

The warmth of the sitting room was extraordinary. Stefan had forgotten how cold it was outside; when he held his hands in front of the fire the knuckles were blue.

'Let's have a drink,' Emma said, warming her own hands for a moment, then slipping off her coat. 'Something really strong, to drive out the chill.'

She went away to the kitchen and came back with a bottle and glasses.

They sat down on the couch again and drank. Stefan found the liqueur so rich, it practically evaporated on his tongue, and the fumes from the rim of the glass were as delicious as the liquid itself. He finished one glass and

Emma refilled it, giving him almost twice as much as before.

The room was becoming very warm, too warm. It was growing dark outside and Emma had closed the curtains. Stefan felt the room shrink. Sweat began to break out on his forehead.

'Take off your jacket,' Emma said. 'There's no need to stand on ceremony. I'm boiling, too.'

Halfway out of his jacket, Stefan froze, mesmerized, as Emma unbuttoned her dress and slid it down her body. She glanced at him, tilting her head to one side and smiling as she stepped free of the garment. 'Am I shocking you?'

'No. Not at all.' He had never been so uncomfortable in his life. The enticement she presented was cancelled, agonizingly, by his lack of confidence. This was the territory he had hoped for, but it was totally alien.

Emma kicked off her shoes and sat next to him in her cream satin slip. She took some of her brandy, savouring it with closed eyes and a soft moan, then opened her eyes and fixed him with her stare. 'You look better without a jacket,' she said. 'Less formal.' She reached out a hand and stroked his arm through the shirt sleeve. 'Stefan, do you like me?'

'Yes. Of course I do.' He was trembling, and he knew she could feel it.

'Have you had many girls?'

He shook his head and looked down into his glass. A moment later he felt her breath on his cheek, then her mouth, warm against his ear.

'I get terribly lonely,' she whispered. Stefan glanced aside from the glass and saw her knees curled beside him on the couch, smooth and shiny in the grey silk stockings. He was petrified.

'It gets unbearable, Stefan. Today has been marvellous. Just being with someone. Someone so lovely.' She put her hand on his stomach and he almost dropped the glass. Emma moved back and he turned to look at her. She was different, her eyes were dilated as if she might cry, but she was smiling. 'You're so shy! It's beautiful!'

From the burning in his cheeks he could tell how he looked, and that made him feel worse.

Emma put down her glass and threw her arms around him. She moaned and kissed him on the mouth, softly, longingly. Stefan sat as still as a rock, terrified of moving. He had dreamt of being with girls this way, and in his dreams he had been so competent, so much in command.

Emma unwound herself and stood up, holding out her hand. He looked at her with something like pleading in his eyes, then took her hand and followed her out of the room and up the narrow stairs.

The bedroom was small and opulent. The walls were covered in a dark floral fabric, and when Emma threw back the quilt Stefan was suprised to see that the sheets were black silk. He had never seen such a thing. The drink had hit him harder than he realized and when he moved now the floor seemed to shift.

'Sit down, my darling.' She put him on the edge of the bed and undressed in front of him. Stefan watched, agitated now and edging away from his terror. She took off everything but the stockings, which were supported by red garters, and when he averted his head slightly Emma told him to look at her. She was standing three feet away, her hands at her sides, her legs apart. She was so beautiful Stefan wanted to cry.

'Does the handsome German find me attractive?' she said.

She took a step towards him and Stefan had to close his eyes. The image burned behind his eyelids, her soft rounded belly, her thighs taut in the stockings, the compelling dark tuft between her legs. She put her hands on his shoulders and he moved towards her.

'There, baby, there . . .'

Emma undressed him and when he was naked she made him lie on the dark sheets while she looked at him.

Finally Stefan had to tell her. 'Emma, I've never done anything.'

She was kneeling beside him, and he saw the wonder spreading on her face. 'Never?'

He shook his head.

'Oh, you *darling!*' She rolled on top of him, pushing her breasts hard against his chest and panting in his ear, letting her fingers play up and down his sides and trapping his thighs within her own. 'God, you're perfect!'

And at last Stefan was able to respond. He rolled on his side and took Emma with him, holding her close with one arm while his free hand explored her breasts, her thighs. After a few moments the terror came back. He had no clear idea how to go further.

Finally Emma took control again. She made him lie very still on his back, and with her hand and her mouth she brought him to such a peak of excitement that Stefan thought he would go mad. Then she straddled him and put him inside her, and in less than a minute it was over.

Much later, when Stefan could lie beside her and feel almost indifferent about their nakedness, he started to voice his growing curiosity about Emma. To begin with, he wanted to know if her husband knew she was unfaithful.

'Our marriage doesn't work that way,' she said. 'Faithful means loyal. Harold would never betray me and I would never betray him. Right at the beginning we knew there would be this one area where total sharing wouldn't work. I didn't care, neither did he.'

'And you're both happy?'

'Very.'

They talked for another hour, and then they made love again. This time it was more savage, a boisterous enjoyment of each other's bodies, and afterwards Stefan felt clean, invigorated.

When it was time for him to leave Emma saw him to the door. She was wrapped in a thick woollen robe that made her look childish and vulnerable, and when Stefan looked at her he did not want to go.

'You have my number,' Emma said. 'Call me again when you're in London. But not too soon, Stefan.'

He understood. He kissed her, thanked her for a perfect day, and left.

Only one thing marred the rest of the weekend. No amount of gaiety could conceal Eric's uneasiness on Stefan's return. Clearly he had lost the last marks of innocence.

Leonhard Gaiser died in March, 1929. He succumbed to lobar pneumonia after surviving four major haemorrhages, and although he never left the hospital during the last two years of his life, he remained lucid to the end.

In his revised will he left everything – his land, house, possessions and money – to Stefan. A sealed letter addressed to the boy was brought to Deanfield by the German lawyer handling the estate. After the necessary documents had been signed and the box of title deeds and shares and bank books had been handed over, Stefan went to his bedroom and read the ten pages of sentimental rambling and of the smouldering hatred that had kept his father alive long past the expectation of his doctors.

Leonhard blamed all his troubles on Charlotte. She had rejected his love from the earliest days of their marriage, he wrote, and she had spent the remaining years taking away everything that afforded him warmth. The most evil act of all had been when she took the boy to England and kept him from seeing his father, or answering his letters. Broken and ill, Leonhard had sustained himself on memories of Stefan's childhood, and on the certainty that he had planted seeds in his son that would flower in spite of Charlotte.

As Stefan read the intense, close-written lines he began to feel remorse, despite Leonhard's cruelty to his mother. Not all of his father's anger could be shrugged off as delusion. Stefan had no doubt that his emotional life had been painfully bleak, and the man *had* been capable of charm and kindness. He pitied his father the burden of grief he had carried to his grave.

On the final page, Leonhard returned to the strict, patriarchal tone of his earlier dealings with Stefan. He warned his son to be on his guard against influences that would weaken the spirit or obscure the vision. The words were impressed into the paper in a strong, clear hand:

> You are a Gaiser and the name carries honour. There is no power in any man to undo the past, even when he is under pressure to try. Rejoice in a heritage of strength, proclaim your birthright and reject corruption. Blood and Soil are your watchwords, my son, you are a German. In my dying I will hold that pride close to me, and I will pray to the last breath that you fulfil your duty and my hopes.

Stefan was rich. At a time when Germany was suffering a financial crisis, his father's capital had remained safe in overseas investments and bullion deposits. There were three hundred acres of prime farm land, orchards, several sawmills fed from a private forest, a large dairy, tenanted cottages and revenue from two flour mills powered by a waterfall on the edge of the estate. In hard currency Stefan inherited the equivalent of £400,000, plus a regular share and rental income of £3000 a year. The house where he had been born was under the management of stewards, and an estate supervisor saw to the collection of rents as well as overseeing the fifteen domestic and contract employees. Stefan was not over-impressed with his sudden affluence. Wealth meant freedom, but he had always felt free and he had no extravagant tastes or ambitions. He transferred half of his fortune to his mother, since the will carried no proviso forbidding such a thing. When the minor flurry of paperwork and property transfer had been attended to, he went back to his life as it had been, promising himself that some day he would visit Dorfen and look at the estate again.

He had seen Emma Fisher three times in sixteen

months. Their friendship deepened, and as a result of that and some other outside help Stefan's maturity catapulted forward. While other seventeen-year-old youths were tiptoeing into society, the handsome Anglo-German from Deanfield was establishing himself as a talented amateur sportsman in his county, and in places as far-flung as Yorkshire, Northumberland and Somerset he was gaining a name as an elegant party-goer and discreet seducer among the daughters of the gentry.

Eric Brown had helped considerably. He was convinced that Stefan had learned enough to enter Cambridge with his hands tied behind his back and Eric saw it as his duty to push his pupil around the circuits until his social graces were on a par with his intellect. Charlotte took quiet pleasure in what was happening – or at least in what she was allowed to see. Stefan was turning into the kind of man her father had been. He had an easy charm, he could be witty, he bore himself with instinctive dignity and he could prevail in a situation without even raising his voice.

Charlotte would have been less content if she could have seen even a little way beneath the surface. Her son engaged in sport because he suffered from fierce physical tension. His wit covered a temper that was shortened by his taste for whisky. He prevailed in situations as often by quiet threat as by strategy, and Stefan's choice of female partners would have given his mother sleepless nights.

Deeper still, Stefan was becoming a political animal. World events registered with him and conclusions were formed by a process that seemed automatic. He foresaw the Wall Street Crash a full two months ahead of time, and at one London party he made himself memorable by asserting that Trotsky, who had been officially expelled from the USSR, would go to Turkey, which he did. Publicly he could discuss the restoration of the Greek Senate and the repercussions of the Catholic Party winning the Belgian elections, while privately he studied the movements of the Brownshirts in Germany, and marvelled in silence over the treachery and cunning of Adolf Hitler.

In the early spring of 1930 two things happened which made vast changes in Stefan's view of life. The first was Eric Brown's suicide, and the second was the scandal that followed.

Eric killed himself by drinking a bottle of lysol in the small, book-filled study of his apartment. He was found sitting in his chair by the woman who cleaned the place, and within an hour word reached Stefan at Deanfield.

At first, Stefan could not believe it. It was not possible that Eric was no longer in the world. He walked round and round the small estate, racking his brain to find one reason why a man so full of life and so capable of enjoying it should end it deliberately. The news crushed him. He sat on a shaded bench and cried for the first time since childhood.

He went to London that evening. He called Emma and he could tell she was glad to hear his voice. It was Saturday and she was alone at the mews house. She asked Stefan to come round as soon as he could.

They sat in the curtained sitting room and stared at each other for a while, both drawn with shock, sipping Scotch and trying to find words to encompass their grief.

'Can you thing of a reason?' Stefan finally asked.

'Blackmail, perhaps,' Emma said quietly.

He was shocked. 'What grounds could anybody have for blackmail?'

She stared at him hard for a moment, then switched her gaze to the table in front of her. When she spoke again she sounded evasive. 'It happens, doesn't it? People can be vicious, Stefan.'

'Emma, what does that mean, exactly? Vicious about what, in Eric's case?'

She sighed. 'You don't know, do you? You, of all people. I thought you never mentioned it because you were being loyal to your friend . . .'

He was on his feet, agitatedly fumbling with his glass. 'Tell me, Emma!'

'Eric was a homosexual.'

He froze, gaping at her. 'I don't believe it!'

'He was, all the same.'

Stefan sank down on his chair. Fragments of memory came flashing back and he scanned them, hunting for clues. There was nothing, nothing at all. Eric Brown had been his friend and his guide.

'How did you know?' he asked finally. 'I never guessed, not once.'

'Gossip travels, especially if you spend all your time in the heartland. Eric was discreet, and he was more than a little bit ashamed. A man like him could cover up a lot, Stefan, but he couldn't really protect himself. It only takes some bastard with determination . . .'

'But why would he kill himself?'

'I think it's understandable enough. Have you any idea what the police do to that kind of man? And if a homosexual goes to prison, the other prisoners put him through hell.'

Stefan was shaking his head. 'Poor Eric,' he whispered, and felt the pain grow wider and deeper.

It was past midnight when they went to bed. Emma slept with her body curled against Stefan's back, while he remained awake, watching the soft stirring shadows on the wall, remembering. The enormity of the loss made Stefan's heart jolt as he recalled the laughter, the wisdom, the hours spent at Deanfield and the weekends in London, Yorkshire, Norfolk. Eric Brown had been his only friend.

In the morning Emma noticed a difference. Stefan was brisk and preoccupied over breakfast, and when she asked how he felt he told her he was better, now that he was taking some of Eric's advice.

'What advice is that?'

'He told me never to leave scores unsettled.'

'Stefan, you're not going to start playing the vengeful friend, are you? You've no idea what you're taking on.'

'Just leave it to me,' he said sharply, then he smiled to her, seeing the hurt on her face. 'I'm simply going to do what's right. And don't fret, I'm not quite so vulnerable as you think.'

Later he telephoned his mother and told her he would be staying over in London for a few more days. Next, Stefan called Thomas Malcolm and asked if he could see him that afternoon.

At two o'clock he left Emma's place, and twenty minutes later he checked into Brown's Hotel in Dover Street. After bathing and changing his clothes he took a taxi to his uncle's home in Clarges Place, at the centre of Mayfair. A maid opened the tall black door and told him to go straight to the study, where he was expected.

Uncle Thomas was sitting behind his vast Victorian desk with several buff folders open in front of him. He was in his sixties, with very white hair and a moustache so neatly trimmed it looked as if it had been sculpted. He was as tall as Stefan and when he stood up to greet his nephew he grinned in the same fond way he always had, as though he still saw a little boy in front of him.

'It's grand to see you, Stefan.' He pumped Stefan's hand. 'How have you been, then? Still working hard for Cambridge?'

'Yes, still working,' Stefan assured him. 'There's been a setback, though.'

'Oh, dear.' The tone of voice had not altered over the years, either. Thomas Malcolm was still overdoing the concern. 'Nothing *too* serious, I trust?'

'My tutor has killed himself.'

The shock on Uncle Thomas' face was instant. He had personally appointed Eric Brown three years before.

'I suspect he was being blackmailed, or threatened.'

'And what makes you think that?'

'I found out yesterday he was a homosexual.'

The very mention of the word appeared to remind Uncle Thomas he was not addressing a child. His face hardened. 'I clearly made a big mistake.'

'No, you didn't. Eric Brown was a good tutor, the best. He was imaginative, practical, encouraging – and he was my friend.'

'Yes. Well.' The old man was examining his fingernails. 'You always seemed to get along well. It's all very sad.'

'I've come to ask your help, Uncle.'

'In what respect?'

Stefan's voice was steady. 'I want to find out who caused Eric's death.'

'Stefan, that's wild talk . . .'

'I've thought about it, Uncle. My closest friend is dead. Somebody killed him. I mean to know who.'

Uncle Thomas squared his shoulders. 'You're still a boy, and you're full of boyish ideals. I'm telling you now to forget the whole matter. Your friend is gone, so the proper thing to do is mourn him and cherish his memory. Beyond that there is nothing you should want to do.'

In that moment Stefan changed before his uncle's eyes. He rose and glared down with determination and hard-eyed assurance. 'If you won't help me, I'll find out the hard way. But I *will* find out.'

'Stefan . . .'

'My mind is made up.'

Thomas Malcolm sighed. 'I don't have access to the kind of information you want.'

'You can open just about any door you want, Uncle. I've been aware of that for a long time. I read the papers.'

The old man was quiet for a minute while Stefan continued to stand in front of the desk, waiting.

'Listen to me,' Uncle Thomas finally said. 'I can't deny that I admire your motive, so far as I understand it. And I must say you strike me as a young man capable of handling himself sensibly. If I help you, it must be on the understanding that you remain sensible throughout. If Eric Brown was being blackmailed and you can prove it, then the proper processes of justice must be observed. Do you understand?'

'Yes, of course.'

'And you must also consider your mother's feelings. Conduct yourself with discretion.' He looked at his watch. 'Come back here this evening about nine.'

It took Stefan four days to find the man he was looking for. He spent most of Monday morning reading the police notes his uncle had provided, and the picture of Eric that emerged was a sordid, shadowed profile of a man with two lives, who had obviously lived in continual fear of discovery. In a file box at Eric's apartment the detectives had found letters, diaries and photographs, and from the summary of their contents Stefan compiled a list of associates that he knew the police would never interview, since three of them had royal connections.

That same morning the newspapers carried copy on the suicide story. Eric was depicted as a degenerate waster with an unspeakable private life, a worthless profligate with unnatural tendencies who had been destroyed by his own style of living. The material rated front-page coverage because of Eric's social contacts, and one paper had a photograph of a dozen well-known theatrical people, with Eric smiling in the middle. That afternoon Stefan rang Eric's father, whom he had never met, and told him that his son had been a good and honest man, the opposite of the picture the newspapers chose to present. Mr Brown was grateful for the call, and he thanked Stefan warmly.

On Monday evening a youth who was known to his friends as Primo had a call from a strikingly handsome stranger who wanted to know when he had last seen Eric Brown. Primo was a gossip, but only with people he trusted. He told his visitor that he had a bad memory, and besides, his movements were his own affair. To Primo's amazement and pain the stranger stepped forward and slapped him hard on the face, then repeated the question. Swallowing back his hysteria, Primo insisted that he couldn't remember when he had seen Eric last, and he added a piping threat to call the police. He received another blow and in tears he finally said that

Eric had been in the Maddox Club on Thursday, and he had been with a girl called Susie Drew, whose name and address were on Stefan's list.

Susie was tougher than Primo, and her hostility towards Stefan was instantaneous. Even when Stefan told her that he had been a close friend of Eric's, she refused to talk.

'Anybody can claim to be a friend,' she said, a sneer on her small painted face. 'Eric knew a lot of people; I think he paid for knowing too many.'

'I think that, too,' Stefan said.

'What you think doesn't concern me.'

'You were with Eric on Thursday. He died on Friday night. There must be something you can tell me.'

'There's nothing. Get out of here.'

Stefan put his hands on her shoulders and pushed her back against the wall. Susie would have kneed him in the groin on sheer instinct, but something stopped her, something in the intensity of his eyes.

'Eric was in trouble and by Thursday it must have been showing.' Stefan spoke softly, his face close to the girl's. 'Tell me what you know about that.' His fingers tightened.

'You're hurting me, you bastard!'

'Talk, and the pain will go away.'

'He was on edge all evening,' she mumbled. 'He was drunk, had been all day as far as I could gather. It had something to do with Fisher.'

'Fisher?' A pulse throbbed suddenly in Stefan's brain.

'Harold Fisher. Eric said he wouldn't leave him alone.'

'Tell me what you know about Fisher,' Stefan breathed.

'He's a shit. A high-living predator with a vicious streak when it comes to other people's misery. He's hurt a lot of men and women, some of them very big.' Susie lowered her head and sighed.

Stefan released her and turned to leave. Susie followed him to the door, rubbing her shoulders.

'Keep my name out of whatever you're up to,' she said shakily.

'I will,' Stefan said, and closed the door without looking back.

The jolt was enormous. On his way across town in the taxi Stefan kept turning his earlier picture of Harold over in his mind. Fisher had been so static, so much in the background, a willing cuckold, benign, a harmless absentee whose existence never hampered his, Stefan's, visits to Emma's bed. It was hard to re-cast him as a villain. Getting out of the cab on Charing Cross Road, Stefan decided to call Emma.

He told her what Susie had said, and listened for any trace of falseness in the response.

'I can't believe that,' she said, and it sounded convincing. 'Harold barely knows – knew Eric. Why would he have anything to do with what happened?'

'He's hurt people in the past. Or so I'm assured.'

'Businessmen are always hurting other people.'

'Yes, I know.' Stefan saw the reflection of his mouth in the small mirror above the coin box. It was taut, he had never been aware before that it could look that way. 'Emma, I think I called you to apologize, in a way . . .'

'You mustn't do anything,' Emma cut in. Her voice was sharp.

'I have to find out. You know that.'

'But don't *do* anything, Stefan. I don't want Harold hurt!'

'Emma, I'll ring you later.' Stefan put down the receiver.

Fisher was not at his office, and his secretary said she had no idea where he could be reached. A library copy of *Who's Who* listed two clubs under the impresario's entry, and Stefan found him at the second. Fisher came into the guests' bar with the same stiff-legged gait as before, his hands held awkwardly away from his sides. He frowned questioningly as Stefan approached.

'I understand you wish to see me. I don't believe we've had the pleasure . . .'

'We've met,' Stefan assured him. 'My name's Gaiser. My friend Eric Brown introduced us.'

'Really? I meet so many people, you must forgive me.' Fisher took the handkerchief from his breast pocket and dabbed his mouth with it. 'I was on the point of leaving, Mr, ah, Gaiser. I hope your business with me will be brief.'

'I doubt it. Perhaps I could talk with you later, somewhere a little more private.'

There was no mistaking the wariness in Fisher's eyes. 'I'm a busy sort of chap, y'know.' He looked at the big mahogany-cased clock above the door. 'If you'd care to ring my office, perhaps my secretary could arrange a mutually suitable time . . .'

'It's rather more urgent than that,' Stefan said.

'Indeed.' Fisher had straightened, and now his eyes were firmly on Stefan's. 'Perhaps if you gave me a clue, Mr Gaiser? Just what do you want to talk to me about?'

'Eric Brown. I assume you've heard he's dead?'

'I did hear something, yes.'

'Well that's what I want to talk about. Eric's death, or, more specifically, your part in it.'

A muted anger discoloured Fisher's cheeks, and he glanced towards the hall porter, who was looking directly at the pair of them. 'I've no idea what you're talking about, young man, but if you think you can march in here and . . .'

'Let's go where it'll be less embarrassing for you,' Stefan said calmly.

For a beat Fisher stood where he was, then he turned sharply and went to the cloakroom. When he came back, wearing his overcoat and carrying a black velour hat, Stefan noticed that the fragile manner had disappeared.

'I'm leaving now,' he told Stefan. 'Kindly don't trouble me further. The consequences could be uncomfortable for you. Do I make myself plain?'

'I'll come with you,' Stefan said, and walked smartly to the door, holding it open.

Fisher glared at him, buckling the brim of his hat as his fingers clenched. After another glance at the porter, who was now looking discreetly the other way, he strode past Stefan and out on to the pavement.

'Shall we take a taxi?' Stefan asked, and waved his arm at a passing cab. The driver pulled in and Stefan stood back to let Fisher get in first. As he ducked his head past the driver's window he gave an address in Mayfair. The drive took less than ten minutes, and neither spoke.

The terraced house was in the same late-Victorian style as Thomas Malcolm's. Fisher rapped the brass knocker and a manservant in a dark suit and striped waistcoat opened the door. Fisher marched in ahead of Stefan and halted halfway across the hall.

'In there, if you please,' he said, and pointed to a half-open door. 'I'm afraid I can only give you a few minutes.' The chill in his voice matched the new vigour of his movements.

The room was an over-furnished salon, muffled with Persian carpet and hung with a variety of pretentious canvases whose value, Stefan suspected, was as high as their vulgarity was great. He stood and gazed at a picture of pre-Raphaelite sheep grazing on post-Impressionist grass, letting Fisher grow impatient behind him. Finally he turned, and saw that Fisher had taken up an aggressive stance, feet apart and hands clamped on his hips.

'Right, Gaiser. Say your piece, then go.'

Stefan nodded and folded his arms. 'Just before Eric Brown died,' he said, 'he was worried about the way you were leaning on him.'

Fisher sneered. It was startling to see, the instant cancelling of the refined, withdrawn expression. 'Is that so? And what are you, Mr Gaiser – apart from being an interfering foreigner? Are you one of Brown's ilk? You don't look like a pansy.'

'What were you doing to Eric?' Stefan moved closer, and although Fisher stayed where he was his eyes wavered.

'I know you *were* up to something, I can see it written all over you.'

'I was setting something right, and Brown was part of it. I've nothing to reproach myself for.'

Stefan shook his head slowly, staring at the revised Fisher, the hard-eyed, spite-ridden reality behind the smooth social façade. 'I think he killed himself because of you.'

'Think what you like! Brown committed suicide because he hadn't the guts to live openly with what he was!'

'And you, of course, had threatened to tell people what he was.'

'It's none of your damned business!'

'You're going to tell me what you did.'

Fisher blinked at the gaunt enigma in front of him and struggled to maintain his bluster. 'Setting yourself up in judgment on me, are you?'

'Yes, I am,' Stefan took a step closer and this time Fisher moved back.

'Brown was involved in some mucky affair with the son of a friend of mine. I broke it up, that's all.'

'And then you went on leaning on Eric.'

'To make sure he was properly warned off, yes.'

Stefan lowered his head. 'You kept threatening to expose him, didn't you?'

'He was warned that his family would find out.'

'But why? You're in the theatre, homosexuals are hardly anything new or repulsive to you. Why did you get so vicious with Eric?' With a shock, Stefan realized he was suddenly looking right into Fisher, reading the totality of the narrowed, hate-filled eyes, the unsteady mouth, the concentrated loathing that centred directly on *him*, on his very existence. 'You filthy bastard!'

'Now look here . . .'

Stefan's right hand closed on Fisher's throat, a firmer and more muscular throat than he might have expected, and choked off the sound. 'It wasn't Eric, it was *me*! You took out your jealousy on a good man who never hurt a soul in his life!'

Fisher gurgled and Stefan tightened the clamp, jerking his arm straight and standing clear of the flailing arms. In an instant he saw everything: the urbane impresario, mindful of appearances, feigning indifference to moral codes and seething with bitterness and inadequacy. In the same instant Stefan learnt something else about himself: he was capable of killing.

Fisher's foot came up suddenly and rammed into Stefan's groin. Riding the pain, Stefan kicked the older man twice, once on each shin, and put him on his knees. 'You're filth, do you hear that? Filth!' Stefan released the grip on Fisher's neck and stood back. In a flurry of legs and arms Fisher was on his feet and rushing at the desk. He lifted a thin ornamental knife and spun on Stefan, whining like a demented animal.

Stefan was not conscious of what he did then. A clear mechanism of defence took control and he caught the knife on its downward sweep, deflecting the drive inward on Fisher. The glittering edge sliced through the man's left cheek, taking away a disc of flesh and releasing a bright flow of blood.

'Aah! God, no! No!' Fisher dropped on all fours, blood dribbling on the backs of his hands. He began to moan and shake his head from side to side.

Stefan watched for a moment, calming himself with the pain and the fright, then he left.

That evening Stefan called Emma again. She was withdrawn but not cold, and she accepted what he told her.

'I was wrong,' she said.

Then they said goodbye.

Later Stefan sat on the bed in his hotel with a bottle of brandy beside him and a warm glass in his hand, remembering some things, realizing others for the first time.

He rose and looked at himself in the mirror. Hardly anything boyish remained. Stefan looked the way he felt, a man with the rehearsals of childhood behind him. Cold anxiety touched him then, and he wondered about the future.

During the next few days the changes were rapid. Thomas Malcolm sent for Stefan and put the facts clearly. Fisher was raising hell. He had influence that went very high and depressingly wide, and he had begun to apply pressure along social channels that could damage Stefan far more than simple police action.

Like a weary, reluctant judge passing sentence, Malcolm told Stefan that his chances of entrance to Cambridge had been neatly blocked, probably for good. On top of that there was now a growing scandal, with Eric's death at its centre, and Fisher on the perimeter stage-managing the gossip, the press stories, the social amputations. Thomas Malcolm's concern was divided evenly between Stefan and his mother.

He went on to explain that Charlotte had to be caused as little pain as possible. The one way to ensure that was for Stefan to remove himself from the scene completely.

It was finally agreed that Stefan should return to Dorfen for an unspecified period. He could supervise his estate and simultaneously deprive the gutter press of copy.

On the last day of March, 1930, Stefan said goodbye to his mother and took ship at Southampton. The weather was clear and his mood, for all the uncertainty, was bright. He looked forward to a short stay at Dorfen and a chance to revise the plans for his future. He had no way of knowing, on that sunny morning, that he would never see England again.

August, 1944

Ralph Farrell was at the rendezvous point before eleven o'clock. He took a seat in the corner of the small restaurant, where an artificial potted palm screened him from the door. He ordered a bowl of onion soup, some bread and a glass of milk, then leafed through a copy of *Signal* magazine while the waiter filled his order.

Farrell was wearing the grey service tunic, breeches and riding boots of a Wehrmacht colonel. In the breast pocket beneath the silver eagle emblem he carried papers to show that he was Horst Luckmann, serving with the 77th Artillery Corps. At other times and in other places he was an SS Standartenführer, a Luftwaffe major and a lowly Wehrmacht Schütze. Sometimes he wore plain clothes and carried the documents of a Gestapo investigator.

There were several other officers in the restaurant, and Farrell was pleased about that, for he did not attract special attention. He was just another tired soldier snatching an hour away from duty. His brown hair was clipped close to the scalp, like everyone else's, and he sat with his cap on his lap and his holster unbuttoned. Even his face was right. Dark grey eyes, puffy from fatigue, and a white crescent scar on the bridge of his nose, a souvenir from a Bronx street fight twenty years before, looking like a shrapnel wound.

Stefan Gaiser arrived just after eleven and the two men greeted each other in German. Farrell's order arrived at the same time and Stefan sat opposite, watching his companion eat and glancing round occasionally to see the effect he was having. As usual, his uniform was making other diners nervous.

'I distinctly heard three guys shit themselves when you walked through that door,' Farrell murmured through a mouthful of bread.

'It's my aura,' Stefan said.

'It's your fuckin' decor. You look like the blue-eyed Angel of Death.' Farrell slurped his way to the bottom of the soup bowl and mopped up the dregs with the last wad of bread. 'Nice,' he breathed, then sank the entire glass of milk in one go.

'Careful,' Stefan said, 'some of it's going in your mouth.'

Farrell dabbed his lips with his napkin and sat back in the chair. He grinned behind his screen of palm fronds and folded his arms. 'You're looking good. What brings you to the big city?'

'I'm on an errand for our leader.'

'Let me guess. He wants you to get him an air ticket to Buenos Aires.'

Stefan asked the waiter for coffee, and waited until it arrived before explaining about the Führer's wish to entertain Margarete Slezak at the Obersalzberg. 'Maybe it's an attack of nostalgia. She's an old flame.'

'He told you that?'

'No. But I did some research on her, years ago. Magda Goebbels introduced the couple in 1931, just after Geli Raubal committed suicide.'

'What's the griff?' Farrell asked.

'Not much,' Stefan said. 'They had a discreet relationship for a while, then Fraulein Slezak disappeared for a couple of years, or she seemed to. She's still in Munich, though. I've seen her.'

'You're some snoop,' Farrell said admiringly. 'While we're on this useless information, is there any truth in the stories you hear about the Führer's leadless pencil? One guy even suggested that Europe caught it in the neck as a direct result of Hitler having a limp dick.'

'I wouldn't know.'

'You surprise me.' Farrell looked at his watch. 'It's late. I don't want to sit here too long, getting my face printed on somebody's memory. Do you have anything for me, aside from gossip?'

Stefan nodded and put a cigarette packet on the table. 'It's all in there.'

'Can you give me a preview?' Casually Farrell opened the packet and took out a cigarette. The coded information was on a tissue at the bottom of the packet.

Stefan gave him a light and said, 'I've detailed the locations of two Intelligence agencies in Berlin. I was lucky to get them. One's in Charlottenburg and the other's at Tiergarten. They've got very quiet frontage, but the people inside are working like ants.'

'Anything else?'

'The names and descriptions of two men. One is American, the other one's a German. Colepaugh and Gimpel. They'll have new names on their papers by now, but I don't know what they are. What I do know is they're going to America, soon. They were briefed at a very high level; von Ribbentrop's in on it personally.'

'So what are they? Saboteurs?'

Stefan shook his head. 'It's an Intelligence operation. If I get any more, I'll be in touch.'

Farrell pocketed the cigarettes. 'That's something I wanted to mention. If we don't get a runner soon, the straight line between you and me is going to get visible. The SD bloodhounds are hotting up around here. Have you found anybody yet? What about the girl you talked about?'

'Soon,' Stefan promised him. 'Just be patient.'

'Right. I'll push along then.' Farrell stood up and put on his cap. The waiter scuttled across with the bill and Farrell handed it to Stefan. 'Charge it to the Führer,' he murmured.

Five minutes after Farrell had gone, Stefan settled the bills and walked to the door. Before going outside, he paused and looked slowly around the room. Soldiers and civilians were avoiding his eyes. One Wehrmacht officer gave him a feeble smile. Stefan stared at the man until he looked away.

He drove back to the hotel in the staff car he had requisitioned from the Gestapo pool. Outside the entrance he sat with his hand on the ignition key, trying to make up his mind. Finding a go-between was probably more urgent than Farrell thought. In the past month two OSS agents had been picked up by the police, and it had been their geometrical pattern of operations that had let them down. Soon, he had told Farrell, and soon it would have to be.

Stefan switched on the engine again and began heading the car through the darkened streets towards the north of the city. He had planned to wait until tomorrow before going to see Gretl, but if he went now, the painful part might be over by morning.

Farrell took a long walk when he left the restaurant. Keeping a steady strolling pace he passed block after block of tall, silent buildings, holding the zigzag clear in his head, homing on the Prinzregentenplatz.

Farrell had made five similar journeys in the past six months, always at night, though not always in Munich. Just as he could steer himself through the streets and alleys of this city without visible markers, he could move from district to district in Berlin, from Steglitz to Wilmersdorf, Köpenick to Lichtenberg, Tempelhof to Kreuzberg. He reckoned that whatever a homing pigeon had, he had it too. If he ever needed to make a run for it across Germany, he could do it without taking one wrong turning.

He remembered facts with the same instinctive precision. Tonight he was carrying the details of one particular story at the front of his mind, using the cool statistics to hone his determination.

In March, 1942, the Germans erected the concentration camp Treblinka B, near Warsaw. By the autumn, it was ready for full-scale business. Two railway transports were dealt with every day. After unloading at the siding, all the prisoners were gathered in one place, then the men were separated from the women and children. The people were told that they would stay in the camp for a short time, and after the necessary bathing and disinfection, they would be sent farther east to work.

The victims were all Jews. They had to remove their clothing and shoes, and then they were herded into several large chambers. The old and the weak were hurried along with blows from rifle butts, whips and boots. A lot of them fell: the ones behind fell over them. Small children were simply thrown into the chambers. When they were filled to capacity, the chambers were hermetically sealed, and steam was forced in under high pressure. The people died in great pain. Jewish menial workers removed the bodies and buried them in mass graves.

Among the deputy administrators at Treblinka B, Albert Kropp was notable for his energy. He worked long hours, and even when the camp was running at full stretch, he would scream for higher productivity. 'We are in the business of making dead Jews,' he jokingly told the other soldiers. Kropp's brutality was as formidable as his enthusiasm for the job. Endless stories about him had filtered through, but one in particular had remained with Farrell. An elderly Jew from Poznan had argued with guards since his arrival at Treblinka. He wanted to know what was to happen to his few remaining valuables, and he demanded to know where his wife had been taken. Kropp had stood by for several minutes, watching the old man and listening to him, then he ordered two guards to lead the prisoner to a shed some distance from the extermination chambers. There, in the presence of the guards, Kropp confronted the shivering, naked old man and screamed abuse for almost five minutes. And then he took an axe to him.

Early in 1944 Albert Kropp was invalided out of the camp service. He had fallen from the doorway of one of the railway freight wagons used to transport prisoners, and the injury he sustained to his spine had left him lame and unable to stand for long periods. He now worked as a records clerk for the SS in Munich. At the end of July he had moved to a new flat, and the address was as clear in Farrell's head as the other details: Apartment 5, 22 Prinzregentenplatz.

Farrell knew the kind of image he presented to people and he had the full act ready when he began to climb the stairs of the apartment block. He was tall and broad, straight in the back and stiff-necked, with a square jaw that could menace by moving forward an inch. He had studied real German officers and discovered that a lot of them strengthened their presence by narrowing the eyes all the time and barely moving their lips when they spoke. Tough New York kids did the same thing but not so well, not so carefully. Farrell had the technique perfected.

He stopped on the third landing and took out his pen torch. The numeral 5 on the door in front of him was new. It was made of a shiny alloy like brass, just like the small plate underneath with the deep-etched name, A. KROPP. Farrell knocked twice and waited, then knocked again. After a minute there were sounds behind the door.

The man who opened the door was in dim silhouette, and he would have been as tall as Farrell if he had not needed to lean on a stick.

'What is it? Do you know what time it is?'

'Almost midnight,' Farrell said in German, 'and I apologize for disturbing you. But it's important. May I come in?'

'If you must.'

They walked along a short dark passage and into a living room. Kropp had been reading. There were books open on the table under the single shaded light, and other books were piled on an armchair by the fire.

'So you're a studious man, Herr Kropp.'

'I am not a civilian,' Kropp snapped. In the room light his sharp features had the shadowed scowl Farrell had seen before on wounded, embittered men. 'On active duty I attained the rank of SS Hauptsturmführer. I still hold the rank, even if I can no longer serve as a soldier.'

'Oh.' Farrell dropped the stiff face that had got him through the door and smiled at the other man. 'I had no idea you'd been a real soldier.'

'What do you wish to see me about, Colonel?'

Farrell gave no sign of having heard the question. 'What have you been studying, Kropp? Advanced butchery?'

The fact that he was trapped in his own flat, with a possible assailant, came home to Albert Kropp in sharp stages. The hostility was glowing through Farrell's smile, his voice suddenly had a harsh edge and there was aggression in the way he kicked one chair aside to examine the books piled on another.

'I am drafting new forms for my department,' Kropp said huskily. 'There is a need to save paper . . .'

'How many forms does it take to get somebody wiped out?'

Kropp backed away, gripping tightly on his stick. 'I demand to know why you are here!'

Again, Farrell ignored him. He was leafing through books, letting them drop on the floor. When Kropp turned and hobbled towards the passage Farrell kept his back to him and snarled, 'Don't try it!'

'You have no right . . .'

'Right?' Farrell spun round, still holding one of the books. 'You're talking about rights? Listen, Kropp, you don't have an idea what rights mean, and you're not eligible for any. I've done some research on you, and you come out looking like Jekyll and Hyde. You were quite a scholar, once. History, languages.' Then, in grating English, Farrell said, 'You soaked up all that and you still managed to come out an ace slaughter man.'

The change of language and inflection startled Kropp so badly he dropped his stick. He clutched his checked dressing gown about him with one hand and grabbed the edge of the table with the other. 'Who *are* you?' Dismay, outrage and fear danced across his face.

'I'm somebody who pukes when I see garbage.' Farrell grabbed the lapels of the dressing gown and bent Kropp back across the table.

'Please!' Kropp screeched. 'My spine!' He was shuddering with pain.

Farrell was unmoved. He pressed down harder and listened to Kropp's voice diminish to a hiss in his throat. 'I had to get a look at you first. I had to see you, motherfucker.' He jabbed his knee up into Kropp's groin and stood back. The man fell on the floor, curled forward in agony, his pain far beyond vocal relief.

Farrell strode into the hallway and pushed open the bedroom door. He put on the light and opened the wardrobe. The Nazi adherence to pattern was amazing. Just where he expected to find it, in a box under some folded sheets, there was an ornamental bayonet in its fancy, scrolled sheath. Farrell yanked it free and went back to the living room.

Kropp lived through almost all of the following three minutes. When Farrell had finished his arm ached and he threw the bloodied weapon across the room. Without pausing or paying any more attention to the mutilated corpse, he went to the kitchen and wiped the blood from his boots with a towel. He washed his hands, examined his uniform to make sure there were no marks on it, then left the flat as quietly as he had entered, making sure the door catch dropped behind him.

On his way back across the city he whistled softly to himself – a German tune – and slowly began to consider the details of another story he had picked up from OSS Intelligence files. An officer called Hauffe, on operations with a Death's Head Division, had distinguished himself by single-handedly killing forty people, the staff of a Belgian hospital where Royal Air Force evaders had been hidden. His two revolvers, according to reports, were almost red hot by the time he had finished. Hauffe was being transferred to SD duties in Munich within the month. Farrell whistled as he strolled on, letting the edge develop again. He had almost forgotten Albert Kropp.

1930–1934

Some remnants of Leonhard Gaiser's influence remained at the old house, triggering memories and imposing a sense of responsibility. The place was in excellent condition, and if some of the more rigorous domestic routines had been relaxed, there was still enough old-style discipline in the staff timetables to ensure order. To his surprise, Stefan found himself enjoying the place much more than he had as a child.

With his father gone the house and estate gave a greater feeling of space and friendliness, and with the revised outlook of a man Stefan began to understand the way property could reinforce a person's confidence. During the first two months he wrote to his mother every week, telling her how the business of management came easily to him, passing on stories about the employees on the estate, and explaining that, as a bone-deep Englishman, he could enjoy the pleasures of a visitor and the easy acceptance of a native German.

Charlotte replied occasionally, but the tone of her letters showed that she was disappointed. Stefan should have been in England, every second line carried the reproach, and if Charlotte properly understood the need for his exile, she preferred not to face the facts.

Stefan had decided some time before that his mother was withdrawing from the world by stages that he could never arrest, even if he were back at Deanfield living with her.

During that summer, serious endeavour and free-wheeling leisure consumed his time, and by late autumn he began to realize that his situation was as good as it was ever likely to be.

He offset the emptiness at the centre of his life by developing his interest in politics. Each morning, after spending an hour with the estate manager, he would take a pot of black coffee from the kitchen and go to his father's old study, where he would read the daily papers from Europe and England until early afternoon. He began keeping large, indexed notebooks and crammed them with events and statistics. Civil disobedience had started in India. The new Italian naval programme was getting underway with some speed. The London talks on Egypt and the Sudan had broken down, and there was a Kurdish uprising on the Persian-Turkish border. Stefan took down unconnected events and stored them, waiting for connections to form, and through all his researches and careful predictions he kept one clear eye on a development that fascinated him. The provincial assembly elections in Germany were becoming a star chart for revolution.

Then came the Reichstag elections in September, and Stefan felt his certainty harden: the Nazis, as people had started calling them, became the second strongest party in the German Reichstag, and Adolf Hitler was the name on everyone's lips.

In October Stefan wrote to Malcolm, telling him about life in general and explaining his fascination with the growth of the Nazi movement:

> 'The tactics of Hitler's campaign for supremacy are crude by any standard, but on such a large scale that they are overwhelming. He uses pageantry to pull the people up off their knees and convince them they have strength, and he calls back the old gods and myths to remind the Germans they are the children of tradition. Cheap sentimental tricks and brutal displays of strength are being employed to mesmerise the public, while Hitler applies his genius for political manipulation in the background. Something quite terrible is happening here, and although I find it distressing I am also gripped by it. I want to stay as long as I can, certainly for as long as it is safe.'

Since late summer, Stefan's leisure time had been spent mainly in Munich, where he enjoyed the crowds and indulged the urge to mingle with men and women more sophisticated than the people at Dorfen. At least once a week he made the twenty-mile journey, occasionally staying for several days at a time.

Girls, it seemed, were everywhere, and they were a lot more friendly and approachable than the women he had met at parties and dances in England. During the first six months Stefan entrenched himself with a dozen different people, making friends of them, reliable company graded neatly to suit any mood. In October, on an evening when Stefan felt quite content to sit alone in a hotel bar and listen to the overlapping conversations, he was suddenly confronted by Sara Alterman.

'I'm sorry to trouble you,' she said, 'but I believe you're sitting on my scarf.'

Stefan looked round. The girl was small and dark-eyed with a glinting, self-possessed stare that held a friendly challenge.

'My scarf,' she repeated, and smiled.

Stefan got up and pushed back the chair. 'It's a little crumpled, I'm afraid.' He handed the girl the scarf and noticed how small her hands were, and how smooth.

'My fault. I shouldn't have left it there.' She pointed to a table nearby where three young people were sitting, two men and a girl. 'We were standing at the bar for a while, and when we came back you had taken this table.'

'I apologize for everything,' Stefan said. 'Let me buy you a drink. Or perhaps your young man would object?'

'I'm not with anybody in particular.' She was still smiling, and she lingered the way people did when they had no pressing need to be away. 'We all met this evening.'

'Ah.' Stefan took her elbow gently and began moving with her to the other table. 'Let me buy you all a drink, then.'

The introductions were easy and good-natured. The

young men looked relieved at the arrival of another male, and after a couple of minutes Stefan realized why. There was a third girl, who had been in the cloakroom. Stefan had evened the numbers nicely.

The men, Felix and Gerd, were older than Stefan, but their behaviour belied it. Felix was plump and serious-faced, even when he laughed. He worked as a government clerk, he told Stefan, and soon he hoped his friend Gerd would be able to give up his job in a printing works and take up a post for which Felix had recommended him.

'The only trouble is,' Felix said, 'Gerd's too soft with people. He'd be processing applications for state housing, and he'd probably fall for every sob story he heard.'

Stefan could believe that Gerd was a kind and gullible man. He was slight, with a thatch of dark curly hair and big, gentle eyes. He kept sneaking glances at one of the girls, Ilse, and blushing when she said anything to him.

Pairing went as smoothly as the introductions. Gerd had found a suitably dominant and talkative partner in lanky Ilse, and the heavy, smouldery-eyed blonde called Marie kept her gaze firmly on Felix. Stefan was pleased that there was no need to compete for Sara's attentions: if it had been necessary he would have done so, however. The girl fascinated him.

For half-an-hour the talk centred on status and ambition. Felix and Gerd both wanted the security of pensioned employment at administrative level. Ilse was a student nurse, and wanted to be a matron – or marry a doctor. Marie, who had a well-developed talent for innuendo even though she was still in her teens, informed the company that she had plans involving a lot of fun, for at least ten years, and then a secure marriage to someone who wouldn't keep too sharp an eye on her.

'I'll never get married,' Sara said.

'You'll have to turn down a lot of proposals,' Stefan said. Seated, she looked tinier than ever, and had a disturbing fragility.

'I'll stay buried among the books and just pop out occasionally to have the odd lover or two.'

'Books?' Stefan's fascination was growing.

'I work in my father's bookshop.'

Stefan was on the point of quizzing her when Felix cut in.

'And what is it you do, Stefan?'

'I don't do anything, really,' he said candidly. 'I manage my estate, study politics . . .' He saw it in an instant, the same reaction taking the five of them. Easy friendliness withdrew and left uneasy respect behind.

'Your estate? You have an *estate*?' Sara did not sound disbelieving, but there was no mistaking her surprise.

'My family place,' Stefan explained, and wished he had said something else, some revision of the truth that would have slotted neatly into the circumstances. Felix was stunned. Gerd, Ilse and Marie were all shifting uncomfortably. Sara was beginning to look amused.

'Tell us about your place,' Felix said.

Stefan told them. The full explanation appeared to ease everyone a little, but the undertow of shock remained. What was a landowner of the Prussian officer class doing *here*, sitting at a table making friends with members of the struggling middle class? Without being asked the question openly, Stefan answered it.

'I come to Munich regularly, to get away from the stuffy atmosphere of duty. I like being here, it puts some colour and excitement into my life. If I stayed out at Dorfen all the time, I'd turn into an old man in five years.'

'You've got a double life, then,' Sara said. She was delighted.

Stefan nodded. 'At home I'm the responsible man of property. I cope with the mechanics of serious privilege and carefully guard my privacy.'

'What about us?' Sara said. 'Would we be excluded?' The others looked at her as if she had just handed out an embarrassing insult.

'No. But only on one condition.'

'And what's that?'
'I wouldn't want any of you to accuse me of trying to buy your friendship.'
The ice was broken. While Sara was firing a salvo of questions at Stefan, Felix went to the bar and bought another round of drinks. They talked and laughed until the bar closed.
'Why don't we all meet up again next week?' Felix suggested. Everybody looked at Stefan before speaking.
'Excellent,' he said, and they were all agreed. A time and place was arranged. They started to disperse.
'May I walk you home?' Stefan asked Sara.
'It's a long walk.'
'I'm sorry. Let me take you in a taxi, then.'
Sara shook her head and smiled. 'I'd prefer the walk, if it's all the same to you.'
On the way across the lamplit city, they talked. Sara told him about her work in the bookshop, and was coaxed into naming a few of her favourite authors. She liked many of the popular writers, and one or two of the more serious ones, such as Max Kretzer and Hermann Sudermann. Stefan nodded and smiled as she talked.
'One I *don't* like,' Sara said, 'is Paul Ernst.' She looked up at Stefan. 'What do you think of him?'
Stefan's opinion of the prolific poet, novelist, playwright and critic had been formed long ago, so he did not hesitate. 'An intellectual crowd-pleaser,' he said. 'A fake.'
Sara nodded, pleased. The breeze had blown her short hair down across her forehead, making her look younger than before. 'The Nazis are fond of him, of course.'
It was easy to spot the challenge, and Stefan could forgive Sara for making it. 'That's because Ernst has a cheap, cult-building message,' Stefan said, and watched the small pucker vanish from Sara's eyes.
Before the trip was over Stefan knew she was twenty and quite uncertain about the future, she had a vague feeling she might like to travel, but so much depended on her father. He had been in business in Munich for thirty-

five years and he was set in his ways. Since the death of Sara's mother the old man stayed indoors most of the time, and relied on his daughter to be his assistant, housekeeper and occasional companion.

Outside the small bookshop with its square-paned windows, tucked away at the end of a short street near the Scheidplatz, Stefan squeezed Sara's hand.

'It's been a nice evening,' he said. 'I like you a lot, Sara Alterman.'

The following day, instead of going back to Dorfen as he had intended, Stefan returned to the bookshop at noon. He stood by the window for a few minutes, pretending to read the titles of the volumes stacked on the display stands. The only person he could see inside was a man, elderly-looking with a crisp fawn jacket and pince-nez, sitting behind a counter with a large lectern at one end. Finally Stefan went in, ducking through the low doorway.

The old man looked up from his book and nodded. Stefan nodded back, then turned to the nearest shelf and started reading the spines with his head tilted on one side.

'If there is anything special . . .'

Stefan turned and shook his head. 'Browsing,' he said. Sara's father had the same directness in his eyes, the same serenity. 'Perhaps,' Stefan added, 'if you have anything printed in English, you could show me where it is.'

The man smiled. 'Not much, I'm afraid. The demand is small.' He pointed to a shelf near the counter. 'There is Shakespeare, some Dickens and a volume of poetry. The other English works I have are rather specialized and probably of no interest to you.'

'Such as?'

The man hoisted a small bundle of cloth-bound books from under the counter and held one up. Stefan went forward and read the title.

'Hebrew writings,' the man explained, 'all by Hillel Zeitlin. Have you heard of him?'

Stefan nodded. 'One of the leading exponents of

Hasidic thought.' The look of respect on the man's face produced an urge to show off, but Stefan resisted it. 'I'd like to look at them, if you don't mind.' He was still perusing the first volume when the door behind the old man opened and Sara came in, carrying a steaming mug of coffee. She almost dropped it when she saw Stefan.

She switched her attention to her father, who was frowning cautiously, and said, 'This is Stefan Gaiser, the young man I told you about.'

'It's good to meet you, Herr Alterman,' Stefan said, and he began to feel awkward as the man's frown deepened.

'I thought you were going back to Dorfen today,' Sara said. She put the coffee down beside her father and folded her arms.

Stefan felt obliged to explain himself. Then he noticed that Sara's father was smiling.

'To think,' Herr Alterman said softly, 'they say the Jews are devious.'

They laughed. Then the old man turned to his daughter. 'If I gauge this young man's motive correctly, he's come here to claim some of your time. Why don't you go out for an hour? Maybe he'll buy you a decent lunch.'

It was a beginning, as clear as any Stefan had felt. The confident relationship of father and daughter underlined the welcome they offered, the happy acceptance.

Sara led the way to a small restaurant two streets away. 'They have Sauerbraten like you never tasted it,' she assured Stefan on the way. 'I'm mad about Sauerbraten.'

It transpired that she was also mad about red cabbage, olives and pickled cucumber. Sara ate rapidly, suspending conversation for the duration of the meal, and when she paused it was only to roll her eyes in silent pleasure. Stefan ate very little. He was preoccupied with watching the girl and absorbing the patterns of movement, the contradictions of a hearty appetite being served by the daintiest etiquette.

'Marvellous,' Sara declared finally, easing her empty plate aside.

'And so are you.' Stefan had not meant to sound too soulful, but the way he spoke made Sara frown.

'You're taking me too seriously,' she said, smiling. 'You don't know a thing about me, Stefan.' Her smile faded.

'Are there barriers for you?' he said quietly.

She looked at him pityingly. 'You know there are. *I* believe that people are just people, I believe in freedom, mingling, all the good things about being human and alive. But an awful lot of people don't share my views. It gets very hard, sometimes, holding on to the conviction that I'm no different from anyone else.'

'You've had trouble?'

'Enough,' Sara said. She sipped her coffee, then pointed to the adjacent table. 'Sometimes my father takes me out for a meal in the evenings. Last time, about a month ago, four people at that table got up and marched out as soon as we sat down. And across the road at Dorff's, the greengrocers, they won't serve me any more. It's always been there, the resentment and the hatred, but it's up on the surface now. You noticed my father's stock of Hebrew books is under the counter? He had to move them off the shelves; people defaced them.'

When they were outside again, he touched her arm gently. 'Can I see you again this evening?'

'I'd like that,' Sara said frankly. 'But listen. Can we still go on meeting the others, like we agreed?'

'Of course.'

They parted outside the bookstore. When Stefan returned to his hotel he dug out a wad of National Socialist pamphlets he had been handed on the street the previous day, and settled down to read them. His distaste, he now found, was different from before. From thinking of victims in a general sense, he had shifted to thinking of just two. Stefan was left with a gnawing anxiety, and he had no grounds for suppressing it, no reason to hope things would get better.

By December a pleasant routine had been established. The three girls and three men gathered almost every week and went dancing and drinking together. Their individual lives outside the times together were never discussed.

Stefan and Sara became lovers in November. By December Stefan knew he loved her, and that it was a unique kind of love, where the principal ingredient was friendship.

A week before Christmas the happy association of the six young people ended. In the aftermath, Stefan was left doubting his ability to read beyond façades.

The break happened in the plushest suite of the Augsburg, a large hotel on Sendlingerstrasse that Stefan always used when he visited Munich. It was Gerd's birthday, and Stefan had laid on a special celebration. There was food, drink and loud music from a gramophone, and after two hours they were all pleasantly drunk.

Gerd felt he should make a speech. As he got up on a velvet footstool and steadied himself with a hand on the wall, boozy emotion began to distort his face. After a moment he managed to contain himself and started to address his attentive audience, who were all sitting on the floor.

'I want to thank our friend Stefan for giving me a wonderful birthday, and for giving all of us a great night. I don't think anyone's been so kind to me in my life.' He had often complained, jokingly, about being the only orphan in the group. At that moment Stefan could see the jokes had covered a real feeling of deprivation. 'It's my hope that I'll be able to return the compliment one day – with the help of my friends, of course.'

The girls cheered and clapped, and Felix nodded up at his friend, smiling. In the past few weeks Felix had grown quieter, and Sara told Stefan she thought it might be his work putting a strain on him. At the birthday party Felix had been drinking red wine only, and that always made him quieter than ever. He went on nodding and smiling as Ilse attempted to get Gerd down off the stool, where he was swaying precariously.

'Wait,' Gerd shouted, 'I haven't finished! As a mark of my profound gratitude, I will allow my Ilse to give our host a kiss. A big one!'

More cheering, and as Ilse crossed to Stefan and bent down to put a stagey kiss on his mouth, everyone applauded, including Stefan.

Gerd fell off the stool then and everyone grabbed him. They took him by legs and arms and dumped him on the couch.

'Take his trousers off!' Maria yelled amid the laughter.

Glazed panic spread across Gerd's face. He tried to struggle up off the couch and that only made the others more determined. Ilse and Maria held his legs and shoulders while Sara started unfastening his braces.

'No! Please!' Gerd yelped, then as Sara undid the top button of his trousers he cried, 'A bargain! I'll make a bargain!' He sat up, panting and grinning. 'Garment for garment, Sara. What do you say?'

'It's all up to you,' Maria yelled at Sara. 'What do you say?'

Sara said nothing. Instead, she winked at Stefan and began to undo the buttons of her cardigan. The other girls screamed their delight.

'Stop it, you whoring Jew bitch!'

Everybody froze, staring across at Felix. His face was livid. He was glaring at Sara as if he wanted to hit her.

'Steady,' Stefan said, and walked across to Felix. 'What's wrong with you? Too much wine?'

'There's nothing wrong with me,' Felix hissed. He lowered his eyes. The others on the couch tried to smile at each other and recapture the evaporating mood of the party.

'Maybe you should apologize to Sara,' Stefan said.

'No.' Felix looked up again, and his jaw was set. 'I'll apologize to you, however. I should have guarded my tongue.'

'It was Sara you insulted.'

'They can't be insulted.'

Stefan turned away sharply and approached the others. He took some folded bills from his pocket and handed them to Gerd. 'Take the girls down to the bar. Get drinks, find a good table and sit down and enjoy yourselves. I'll join you later.'

He waited until they had gone before he faced Felix again. 'Right. Now you can explain yourself.'

'There's nothing to explain. You have my apology already.'

Stefan crossed to the fireplace and leaned an elbow on the mantelpiece. 'Felix, I've got a notion. I fancy I'm going to give you a pair of black eyes if you don't stop playing the sulky schoolboy. Out with it. Why did you say that to Sara? It was only a game.'

Felix folded his arms and tried to look cynical, which was difficult with his features. 'You didn't know she's a Jew?'

'It had crossed my mind. What about it?'

'For God's sake, Stefan. You're not stupid.'

'Correct. But I think you may be. Where have your ideas been coming from lately?'

With nothing less than grim pride, Felix reached into his pocket and took out his NSDAP card. Then he flipped over his lapel and let Stefan see the enamel badge with a swastika at the centre.

'You're a clown,' Stefan told him flatly. 'How long has this been going on?'

'Long enough for me to see things straight.'

'Well, I'm surprised you still managed to go around with us, Felix. I mean, with an actual Jewess in our midst!'

Felix put away his card and fumbled out a cigarette, which he lit quickly and puffed hard a few times, putting up a protective screen of smoke between them. 'As long as a month ago I'd decided to talk to you about Sara. My mind was made up but I kept quiet for some reason.' His face softened a little. 'Stefan, I've got respect for you,

you come from a fine family and you've given me your friendship. It was difficult to approach you . . .'

'You're out of your mind,' Stefan told him. 'Don't your natural human instincts tell you anything about the girl? Was she such a corruptive spectre in the days before they filled your head with that anti-semitic junk? Sara's been your friend for as long as she's been mine.'

'I was deluded.'

'Felix, I could kick your arse right around this room.'

'I know what I know,' Felix said stubbornly. 'They're trained from the time they're children to trespass, gain trust, and then betray. You can say and do what you like about it, Stefan, but my eyes have been opened. I've stayed silent long enough. Her behaviour here tonight supports everything I've learned.'

Stefan's anger had collided with the softening effect of the drink, and he began to feel sick. Suddenly the disease was off the neat pages of the journals at Dorfen and spreading through living minds, moving them to action.

He went to the bathroom and splashed cold water on his face. When he came back, Felix was gone.

Later he joined the others in the bar. They were sitting in glum silence with half-full glasses in front of them. Stefan had nothing comforting to say. He tried to apologize for Felix and everyone pretended to accept it and believe it had been the drink talking. 'An aberration,' Gerd mumbled. 'It didn't mean a thing.' But the uneasiness grew until Stefan said he was tired, and excused himself.

Sara came into the suite when he was getting ready for bed. There was no need for her to say anything. Stefan took her to bed and made gentle love to her, and when it was over Sara wept, the first time he had ever known it to happen, and she told him she was frightened. The snubs and insults were increasing, she said, and as her tears wet Stefan's shoulder she told him other things: two youths had yelled obscenities at her the day before, and one of them had thrown a stone, and when Sara got back to the bookshop she found her father sitting pale and ill-looking, clutching a letter.

'Everybody's withdrawn their credit,' Sara whispered. In the dark, Stefan could imagine the hurt on her face and he drew her closer.

'You should leave Munich,' Stefan said.

'It's our home . . .'

'Even so.'

Sara moaned softly, then said, 'Why is it all happening?'

He lay still, hugging her, feeling the waves of compassion wash over him, but he could give her no answer.

On Christmas Eve, Stefan arrived in Munich early. He brought with him a miniature banquet in three large boxes, and five bottles of wine from his father's cellar. The Altermans celebrated Christmas because Sara's father liked to acknowledge any festival where people were nice to each other. At midday Stefan turned up at the bookshop and handed over the food and drink to Sara, who had cleared the kitchen and was ready, aproned and beaming, to start cooking.

'There's more to come,' Stefan said as he helped to unpack the boxes.

'More?' Sara looked around her at the poultry, vegetables, fruit and confections. 'There are three of us, Stefan. *Three*. With what we have here, we could feed eight and leave plenty for the cat.'

'Just wait and see.' He finished unpacking and looked at his watch. 'I'll be back in two hours. Lots to do yet.' He kissed Sara on the nose and left, waving his farewell to Herr Alterman, who was busy with a customer.

Back at the hotel a lawyer was waiting. He had brought a document which, when Stefan had signed it, would empower the bank to place substantial credit facilities at the disposal of Sara's father. The matter had been discussed at length, and Herr Alterman had finally agreed, but only on the understanding that the money be treated as a loan. The major resistance had come from the bank itself, but Stefan had prevailed, with a clear threat to transfer his business elsewhere, tradition or no tradition.

When the papers were signed, Stefan called at a jeweller's and collected his Christmas present to Sara. It was a brooch with sapphires and tiny diamonds, worked in gold and silver in the shape of a flying dove. Stefan chose the box carefully, black leather with a scarlet velvet lining, and then had the jeweller wrap it in tinselled paper.

At half-past one, instead of taking a cab, Stefan began to walk through the busy streets to Alterman's bookshop. The spirit of Christmas had begun to glitter on the edge of his awareness. Before a week was out the knives would be drawn again, hate would poison the atmosphere. But for the time being, there was a gentleness, a sense of well-being in the air. Stefan was enjoying it.

At two o'clock Sara Alterman stood back from the array of bubbling pots on the stove and smoothed her apron. It pleased her to see what she had set in motion, an efficient and well co-ordinated beginning to festivity. She had learned to cook early in her life, and by the time she was twelve she could master the complexities of timing better than her own mother: when Sara cooked a meal, everything was ready at the same time, nothing had to be held or hurried. Today, she was making a special effort, and Stefan would be as proud of her as her father already was.

She turned at a loud, crashing noise from the direction of the shop. Before she had taken one worried step she heard her father shouting. When she wrenched open the door she saw first the gaping hole in the front window, then her father, shielding his eyes with his arms. Something came flying through the broken door and struck Herr Alterman. Instantly flames shot everywhere, issuing in jets from the blazing canister that had knocked the old man down.

'Father!' Sara rushed to where he was lying, and screamed when she saw he was on fire. She grabbed an overcoat from the peg on the wall and threw it on him.

All around books and shelves were burning, and fingers of flame were crawling on a dozen parts of the floor. Sara tried to lift her father and was suddenly seized with pain. Her dress had brushed the blazing waste basket and now it was on fire, the flames tearing at her legs and arms. Sara grasped at the material, ripping it from her skin. She was still screaming at her hands to fight back the pain and get free from the blazing garment when the black canister exploded.

Outside, two streets away from the shop, Stefan heard the rumble and stopped. People around him stopped too, looking in every direction. It was a sound that fitted nothing in everyday experience. When he saw men running towards the street that led to the bookshop, Stefan's heart jolted. He began to walk again, faster, and by the time he reached the corner he too was running.

He could see the flames and the smoke for an entire, agonizing minute before he reached the spot. People had already gone into the shop with coats over their heads and handkerchiefs at their mouths. Stefan ploughed after them, coughing on the thick smoke and blinking against the heat. The shop was formless now, walls and shelves and floor unrecognizable. The smoke had choked out most of the fire and discoloured everything: black books lay tumbled on grey shelves, picture frames enclosed prints barely visible through the stained glass, and the counter was a charred and smoking altar.

'Out! Get out!' A uniformed man was shoving Stefan and coughing in his face. He was a policeman, grimed like everything around him. 'There's nothing you can do here. Out!'

'Sara!' Stefan shouted the name as if it would convey his special right to know what had happened.

'I told you!' The policeman took Stefan's arm and marched him out on to the street. 'Stay there!'

When Stefan ran into the shop again, he was lifted bodily by two other policemen. They were in no mood to be gentle or considerate. They were angry men, victims of circumstance, who had been on their way to enjoy a pre-Christmas drink in the back room of a bar near the bookshop. Caught there, yards from the fire, they had to act, their uniforms demanded it. They bundled Stefan back on to the street and one of them twisted his arm sharply, warning what would happen if he interfered again.

Minutes after, while Stefan's brain seethed against the unbearable, a cordon was put around the place. The last traces of fire had been put out, and when he finally managed to get a policeman to talk to him, he learned that the two people from the shop had been taken away through the back entrance. The policeman knew nothing about their condition.

Ten hours later, standing in a cold, sterile waiting room in the city's largest general hospital, with his fingers wrapped tightly around the small package in his pocket, Stefan was given the facts. They were delivered by a young doctor with the faraway eyes of a man who had learned to distance himself from distress.

'The father is dead, I'm afraid. He suffocated on the smoke. The girl was badly burned, but the explosion lifted her clear of the worst area of the fire, so she was able to breathe.'

Stefan's lips had difficulty forming words. 'How bad? How bad are her injuries?'

'They are very bad, sir.' No emotion coloured the words. 'The damage is more than physical, however. The girl was able to breathe, as I said, but the level of oxygen in her blood was greatly reduced for several minutes.' The doctor paused.

'I don't understand. You said more than physical.'

'There is mental damage. How extensive, I can't yet say. The brain was starved of oxygen, you see.'

Starved. The word was like a club. Starved, deprived, victimized. An ache swelled into a sharp pain that attacked Stefan's chest and eyes at once, a grief pain that left him as a moan and rose again as tears. The doctor led him to a chair. Later, when he was driven back to his hotel, the pain was still there, in every part of him.

He never saw Sara again, but he saw to it that she was cared for. Scarred and with no traceable personality she was sent to a private home for the disabled in Zurich. For months Stefan fretted over his odd cowardice: nothing could compel him to go near the girl, yet she was constantly in his thoughts. In the end, when the sense of loss had grown smaller than his hate, he decided he was not a coward at all. He was a man who knew, by instinct, when to stop punishing himself.

For two years Stefan immersed himself in his work. He saw no friends. When his mother wrote he sent back the same cheery, chatty notes he always did, without ever revealing that he had grown completely separate from her, without revealing the hollowness he felt inside, or his despair about what was happening all around him.

Late in 1934, Thomas Malcolm arrived at Dorfen. Stefan was delighted to see him.

'You haven't changed a bit,' he said.

'You have,' Malcolm replied. 'I knew your father when he was just a little older than you are now. It's like meeting him all over again.'

The first day was taken up with their pleasure at seeing each other again, and after a tour of the estate and a lavish dinner Malcolm retired to his quarters.

The following day, sitting in the noon sunlight of the spacious day room, the old man explained to Stefan why he was there.

'This visit was no whim. I've no time for things like that. Stefan, I'm here in my official capacity. I've come to talk to you about a job.'

Stefan was wary. There was something he didn't recognize in Malcolm's tone. 'I'm always prepared to listen,' he said.

'Perhaps,' said Thomas Malcolm, 'I had better explain.'

Stefan was not sure whether to show surprise or

amusement at what Malcolm told him. The elaborate diplomatic front. The social and professional persona that he had developed over long years in the service of British Intelligence. The prestigious history of his own particular branch of his country's defence network.

When the old man focused more firmly on the situation facing Germany, Stefan became more attentive. A brooding anger replaced his curiosity when Malcolm began to talk about Himmler and Reinhard Heydrich.

'He's practically running the show already,' Malcolm said, 'and he's making his mark. He has files on just about every member of the party who amounts to anything. He drives his staff like pack animals and he pushes himself just as hard. Two years ago Heydrich was well down the ranks, but when he got going he was promoted to SS Major inside six months, and a year later he was a colonel. He's set up a leadership school at Bad Toelz in Upper Bavaria, and it's only a matter of time before he'll be a general. He'll be a bloody hard counter-espionage man.'

There was more. MI6 had information that Himmler was seeking control of the police. If that ever happened, an ordinary Intelligence agent working inside Germany would stand less chance of survival than a rabbit on a ferret farm.

'Which is why,' he continued, 'we are planning a new department. It'll be called Special Operations Executive.'

'What kind of special operations?'

'We foresee an outfit to handle the training of resistance groups, carry out sabotage, gather classified information. The personnel will be special, of course, and they'll be the best-trained men in the world. There'll be a section for each country if invasion should occur, and each section will train and maintain its own group of agents.'

Stefan asked when it would all begin.

'As soon as you agree to work with us.'

'I wondered when you'd come to that. It's out of the question.'

Thomas Malcolm did not answer immediately. Instead,

he looked at his watch. Then he smiled quietly as he heard the sound of footsteps in the passage.

The maid came in and announced there was a gentleman waiting in the hall. 'He's from England,' she said.

'Ah.' Malcolm stood up, pocketing his watch. 'Stefan, forgive me. I took the liberty of inviting a colleague. He has just arrived from Munich.'

Stefan shrugged. 'He's welcome, of course. Did you ask him along to help soften me up?'

'Not entirely. May I ask him to come in right away? I think you know him, incidentally.'

Stefan nodded to the maid. A few moments later a fat man walked in, wrapped in a huge black overcoat. He smiled broadly at Stefan and held out his hand. 'How nice to see you again, Mr Gaiser,' said Dorian Goode.

Stefan was thunderstruck.

Dorian unbuttoned his coat and sat down, wheezing softly. 'You've had time to talk, have you?'

'Some,' Uncle Thomas said. 'But Stefan is reluctant.'

'Naturally he is. Only an idiot would be enthusiastic.' Dorian spread his knees, allowing his belly more room. He looked at Stefan. 'There are many reasons,' he said, 'for your joining us. But there is one in particular.' He leaned across to Stefan, withdrawing a battered photograph from an inside pocket. It was a photograph of Sara Alterman.

BOOK TWO

1935–1944

Parliamentary responsibility for Stefan's appointment was maintained through the Minister of Economic Warfare, who agreed on a four-month training period before Stefan would officially become an agent of the SOE. In January, 1935, a young Englishman called Albert Murray came to stay at Dorfen. He was a thin, bespectacled graduate of Oxford, energetic and good-humoured, with a smile that flashed on and off like a lamp. Over dinner he delivered his credentials in a faraway manner, as if he could hardly believe any of it himself.

'I wanted to teach, originally. History. But politics crept in and corrupted my good intentions. The year I graduated, I was approached by MI5 with the offer of a job. I couldn't imagine myself being of any use to them, but they were persuasive. Some of my hot-headed articles about fascism attracted their attentions, I think.'

'That's roughly what happened to me,' Stefan told him. 'Like you, I'm not sure I can do what's wanted.'

'You'll surprise yourself,' Albert said. 'By the end of April, you'll be ready. Just see if you aren't.'

The weeks passed quickly. Stefan found the mass of new knowledge daunting at first, but Albert steered him through the phases of learning calmly, adapting his approach to special aptitudes he discovered in Stefan, or particular blind spots. They spent a month on codes, and after Stefan had learned to use the double transformation type, he was taught to understand the systems in use with the Germans. After that, he was instructed in the details of German military Intelligence.

He had next to learn all about the SD, and when he had done so his attention was directed to the personalities, the men who controlled and developed the complex Intelligence arm of the SS. At that point, he began to understand that SOE would like him to penetrate the SS itself.

In March, during one of the long, cold walks Albert insisted they take every day, Stefan asked when the practical work would start. For two days they had done nothing but revision. Suddenly there was a sharp pain in his shoulder and he realized he was falling. He hit the ground and rolled to the foot of the slope. When he pushed himself up, Albert was holding a stiffened finger under his nose, a symbolic pistol.

'It just started,' Albert said. 'You've done your homework. Now we have to hone your physical alertness, and make you so bloody vicious you'll frighten yourself.'

By April Stefan was ready for his final briefing.

'There's a Special Branch file on you,' Albert told him. 'It tells clearly how you left England because your sympathies were here, in the Fatherland. There's detailed information on your pro-Nazi leanings and all sorts of other stuff about the kind of upstanding fascist swine you are.' He laughed. 'You're listed as undesirable, to be taken in for questioning if you ever return to Britain. There's another file in the Foreign Office, with much the same story in it. We can't take chances, and if the Nazis ever decide to check up on you they'll know where to do their checking. You have a small criminal record too, for good measure.'

'What did I do?'

'You painted a yellow star of David on a kosher butcher's shop in Islington.'

'Good God. Is there anything else?'

Albert nodded. 'Some newspaper clippings – letters here and there you wrote to the press about the rebirth of the German nation, and how Mr Hitler's visionary ideals would benefit the British way of life. Dorian Goode wrote the letters. I think he did credit to your style.'

'You're certainly thorough,' Stefan said.

'It's the only way to be. And now we've blackened you,

you're ready to go forth and fulfil your destiny as an instrument of Hitler's will.'

When Albert left Dorfen, he insisted that he travel to the station alone. His presence in the country had been unobtrusive, and he wanted it to stay like that. In the large hallway he shook Stefan's hand and said he hoped they would meet up in London one day.

On the last day of April another Englishman arrived. He stayed only for a few hours, and in that time he gave Stefan his briefing. He was simply to ingratiate himself with the Nazis, and use his stature as a landowning son of a Junker to advance himself. At all times he must behave in a manner befittingly arrogant and ambitious – that kind of behaviour tended to take people to the top. As a sleeper agent Stefan would not be expected to pass on regular reports, and the time when he became active was largely up to himself. He was given some small tissue pads and one suicide tablet – not cyanide as he had expected, but a concentrated barbiturate. It seemed a pitifully small kit, but it made sense. On a long-term assignment an agent's cover had to be the tightest possible, so there was no use carrying hardware that could be incriminating.

'Eventually,' the man from London said, 'someone will be in touch with you. It may be in months, or years, but sooner or later you'll be given a contact. There will never be more than one.' The matter of salary had never been raised before, but the man discreetly mentioned that an account had been opened in London, and monthly amounts would accumulate to Stefan's credit.

Stefan's letter to NSDAP headquarters in Berlin produced a reply four days later, from Dr Roland Pleiger in Munich. Pleiger, who was a lawyer by profession, was organizational head of the Allgemeine SS in Munich, a general branch of the SS which counted doctors, teachers, lawyers and other professions in its membership. The Allgemeine SS had no specific function, except to remain on call, but Stefan was already aware that many of the members were doing specialized work in various phases of SS activity. Pleiger's letter was brief but cordial: he suggested that Stefan call on him at his home that weekend.

From the moment he walked into the Pleiger drawing room, Stefan could tell that his visit was not to be treated casually. Frau Pleiger had laid on a small, handsome buffet, and when the children were introduced to Stefan their tidiness and general good manners hinted strongly at rehearsal.

Pleiger himself behaved with the stiff servility of a good butler. He was tall and thin, with sparse black hair and a rather sour face that somehow suited his wing collar and heavy black suit.

'We were delighted to hear from you,' he told Stefan as he poured him a glass of sherry. 'Young men of your family and bearing are always assured of a place in the Party.' He motioned Stefan to a chair and sat down himself, carefully hitching up the knees of his trousers. 'In your letter you expressed a desire to be active with us – may I ask you to explain the extent of the involvement you seek?'

'Certainly,' Stefan said, finding it easy to play the hereditary superior in such an atmosphere of awed respect. 'For some time I've been watching the movement grow, and all along I have felt myself in tune with Adolf Hitler's aims and his hopes for our country. But it is one thing to sympathize, to applaud, and quite another to *help*. It occurred to me that my unoccupied time would be better spent in the service of the Party. As to the extent of involvement, I would gladly devote myself entirely to the National Socialist cause.'

Pleiger was beaming. 'That is laudable, Herr Gaiser. But tell me, what would you do about your domestic commitments?'

'I have none. I am unmarried, and my estate managers are more than capable of looking after my affairs.'

'Yes, of course. I took the liberty of acquainting myself

with your background in the Social Register.' Pleiger cleared his throat. 'I, ah, understand you have spent a number of years in England?'

'Yes,' Stefan said. 'My mother is English, and I stayed in England with her for a time, but my boyhood was spent here, and as time passed I found that my instincts were rooted in the Fatherland. It is where I belong.'

'Splendid.' Pleiger was nodding, as if Stefan had just successfully allayed a major doubt – and he guessed he probably had. 'Herr Gaiser, would you describe yourself as an intellectual?'

'Only insofar as I use my intellect to achieve certain ends,' Stefan said smoothly. 'But my intellect remains my servant, and it is not so wayward that it can dominate me.' The Nazis saw intellectuals as obstacles to their progress, just as they were suspicious of landowners and aristocrats who showed signs of stubborn independence. 'It is my will which predominates,' Stefan added.

Pleiger rearranged his legs, setting his feet squarely side by side, signalling an important announcement. 'This little meeting is significant for a number of reasons,' he said. 'I was asked to see you and to evaluate your potential as an administrator. As you may know, the work of the SS is broadly based and there is room for men of character and foresight at the upper end of the structure. I must say, Herr Gaiser, that you strike me as an ideal person to train for service with us.'

'I'm gratified,' Stefan said.

'I will report back to Berlin,' Pleiger went on, 'and I have no doubt you will hear from someone quite soon.' He stood up and extended his hand stiffly. 'I do not believe I am being premature in welcoming you to the movement.'

A week later, Stefan was summoned to Berlin, and at the offices of the Sicherheitsdienst he was seen by an officer called Presse, who was rather less respectful than Pleiger. Presse was slightly older than Stefan, with short red hair and eyelashes so pale they were almost invisible.

Even though he sat throughout the interview, he gave the impression he was strutting.

'Your credentials have been thoroughly investigated,' he told Stefan. 'Our standards are the highest, of course. We check the political reputation of your parents, and we examine your ancestry as far back as 1750. A record of hereditary health is compiled, and the Race Commission is asked to issue a certificate.'

'I don't believe I've heard of the Race Commission,' Stefan said.

'It is made up of SS leaders, anthropologists and doctors. In your case their findings are unequivocal. You are of good Nordic blood, and in every respect you appear to fulfil the Aryan ideal.' Presse began tapping the desk with his pencil. 'We now have to find out, Herr Gaiser, if your character matches your pedigree. Such power and authority as you possess seems, if I may say so, to have been entirely inherited.'

'Inherited, and sustained,' Stefan said, with just enough edge.

'And do you see yourself as a man with the talent for leadership?'

'There is a natural order that owes nothing to opinion,' Stefan replied. 'How I see myself is a matter I discuss with no one. The natural order is what matters, and I'd be happy to discuss that.'

Presse had narrowed his eyes, making his dislike more obvious. 'What natural order are you referring to?'

'The strong,' Stefan said, 'must dominate the weak. It is inevitable. Blood confers authority, and the power to maintain authority.'

'But does the power you mention extend to the harsher tasks of authority – could you command the respect of soldiers, Herr Gaiser?'

'If I say yes it makes no difference, you'd have to put me to the test.'

Presse moved uneasily to other topics. He asked Stefan about his political outlook and his understanding of

Hitler's plans for Germany. Stefan replied at copious length, paraphrasing *Mein Kampf* and the witless hysteria of Goebbels' propaganda sheets. When Presse quizzed him on his views of individual freedom, Stefan said that freedom had to be earned: some people, he added, should never be free, since restriction was their only hope of survival, and it kept them from harming others.

'You are half English,' Presse said finally, and he managed to make it sound like an accusation.

'Not at all,' Stefan replied sharply.

'But Herr Gaiser . . .' Presse held up the notes he had been scanning, as if they were damning evidence.

'My mother is English, which means that one half of my parentage is English. As your genetical analysts are doubtless aware, my father's bloodline holds dominance in me; I am his image, as much in character as appearance. No part of me is English at all.'

Presse shifted in his chair. 'Your mother must have influenced your views to a certain extent. And you lived in England for several years. How does a man remain thoroughly German in outlook with a history like that?'

'The same way a Negro remains black after a lifetime in a cold climate. My father instilled his character and opinions in me when I was a child. Living in England did nothing to alter that. I imagine you know something of my activities in England, anyway. They speak for themselves.'

It was clear that Presse knew nothing about the planted files, the police record or the forged press clippings, but he made an attempt at an understanding nod. 'Would you be able to remain in Berlin for a few days, Herr Gaiser?'

Stefan said he would. 'And that's part of my trouble,' he added. 'I have a great deal of time to waste.' He gave Presse the address of his hotel before he left.

At their next meeting, four days later, Presse was businesslike and even respectful. He told Stefan that he had been accepted for full-time duty with the SS, as that was where his capabilities could best be exploited. Stefan filled in the appropriate forms and was passed along to a senior recruitment officer called Schaub. He was fat and fatherly, with cropped grey hair and a small waxed moustache that he stroked as he addressed the new recruit.

'Certain formalities of candidacy are being waived in your case,' he said: 'Normally, you would spend a year working for your sports diploma, and two more years doing regular army service. After that you would be thoroughly instructed in ideology.' Schaub smiled. 'Your background makes most of that unnecessary. You will be assigned to a training camp for one month, and on completion of the course you will return to Berlin and take the oath. Following that, I believe the Head of SD, which is the main security office of the Party, has plans for you.' Among other details, Schaub mentioned that Stefan would be expected to pay for his own uniform, and during training he would receive no pay at all.

With his documentation arranged and a single bag packed, Stefan travelled the following day to Bad-Toelz in Upper Bavaria. The camp there was small, with eight buildings built around a drill square, and a sports field at the rear. This was the leadership school Uncle Thomas had mentioned when he first tried to recruit Stefan for the SOE. On the afternoon Stefan arrived, seven other recruits came to Bad-Toelz, and they were all billeted in a cement-block dormitory near the sports field. In a group of potential leaders, Stefan discovered, the struggle for leadership was fierce. Inside two days he had established a form of dominance within the group, using an amalgam of arrogance, cunning and occasional brutality.

His prime opponent in the unit was Karl Roesen, a twenty-six-year-old Berliner with a degree in architecture. He was as tall as Stefan and as powerfully built, with unwavering dark brown eyes and a mean, thin mouth. Roesen was a born state functionary, the kind of man who could be aimed in a straight line and relied upon to stick to it. He did not appear to be hampered by imagination or a sense of humour, and his keen desire to prevail over the others was apparent from the start.

The first head-to-head confrontation came when Stefan dropped his bag on the bed nearest the door. Roesen, standing at the far end of the dormitory and scowling at the paintwork, turned and snapped his fingers. Stefan ignored him and hung his overcoat in the steel locker. The fingers snapped again.

Stefan turned. 'Have you lost your dog?' he asked softly.

'My case is at the foot of that bed,' Roesen snapped.

'Then move it. This is my bed.'

Roesen came striding down the room, his coat flapping. The others were watching him. He picked up Stefan's bag and dropped it on the floor from shoulder height. Stefan went to the door, opened it wide, then returned to the foot of the bed. One sharp kick sent Roesen's bag flying on to the path outside.

'Bastard!' Roesen growled, squaring up to Stefan.

'I'd pick it up, if I were you,' Stefan said, ignoring him and replacing his own case on the bed. 'You don't want to start collecting black marks on your first day.'

It was safe to rely on Roesen's respect for the camp authorities. A winner would never run the slightest risk of soiling his record, especially on grounds of tidiness or discipline. By the time he had collected his case and flung it on the bed next to Stefan's, Roesen was clamp-jawed and scarlet.

The Commandant, Brigadeführer Eftger, addressed the new recruits on the first evening. Sternly, he reminded them that they were an élite, men handpicked for special duty, and as such they would be expected to apply themselves to the month of training with unusual energy and determination. They would remain together as a unit throughout the programme, and they would not mingle with the two other groups at the camp.

'Training will be rigorous and there will be no time for relaxation, gentlemen. You will leave this place with a fuller awareness of yourselves and of your mission. Make the most of the few free hours you have this evening. They will be the last for a long time.'

At supper, Stefan had an opportunity to study the people he would be living with for the next four weeks. They resembled nothing so much as schoolboys, gawkily zealous, rivalling each other in their attempts to be the stiff-necked, bull-headed oafs by which the state placed so much store. In a matter of hours they had paired, like with like, but overall the differences were slight. Stefan and Karl Roesen stood out by virtue of their mutual hostility, and just before lights-out Roesen made his second play for dominance.

'I vote we work to make this unit the most outstanding of the year,' Roesen declared, standing by his bed in his black dressing gown. It was a challenge, and the others responded eagerly. Stefan remained silent. A call to vote was a call to follow a lead.

'And you, Gaiser?' Roesen was staring at him and so were the others, suddenly hostile-eyed, united.

'I vote,' Stefan said, 'that you leave me out of your infantile dramas.' He glanced aside at one of the others who was trying to look dangerously menacing. 'If you don't point your scowl somewhere else, Loritz, I'll take your face for a walk along the latrine wall.'

Loritz lowered his eyes, but Roesen stepped closer to Stefan, who was sitting on the edge of his bed. 'You're only one man, Gaiser. We can make your life hell.'

Stefan rose to his feet, facing Roesen squarely. Then his right fist shot out and he punched Roesen under the heart. The big man gulped and tried to inhale, and when he did the pain pulled him to his knees. While he knelt huddled and gasping, Stefan bent close to his ear, but spoke loudly enough for all to hear.

'You can ambush me in my sleep, catch me in the showers, or just gang up on me right now. I couldn't stop any of that, but I'll tell you what I'll do if you ever try it. I'll wait, maybe for a year. Then one day I'll put all your names in a box, and I'll draw one name out. That man I'll kill.'

They all withdrew to their beds, and the lights went out while Roesen was still squatting on the floor, hugging his chest.

As the course proceeded through the second and third weeks, the overall plan became clear. Leadership, in SS terms, meant the ability to bend wills and nurture blind obedience in others. A leader, therefore, had to be a hard man, and he had to be well-informed on the roots and branches of Nazi ideology. Productive cruelty was a priceless instrument, and the recruits at Bad-Toelz learned that the hard way, as they were subjected to ever tougher drills and more punishing daily programmes of learning and inter-unit competition. They were all changing, their responses were tightening and self-pity dwindled as the prime objective became simply to get through each day and win a few hours' rest.

On top of all Stefan had already learned about Nazism and the growing structure of the Third Reich, he was obliged to absorb the naive idealism of Heinrich Himmler, among others, and he found there was a great similarity between the Reichsführer's philosophy and his own father's. Apart from Leonhard Gaiser's superior intellect, the two men could have been spawned by the same Teutonic earth mother, with heads full of Nordic mythology, runes and Aryan genealogy. In Himmler's case there was one important difference, and it could be detected in his style of writing and his recorded pronouncements: he was obsessed with total power.

As Stefan neared the end of his course he began to work for prominence in the eyes of the camp administration. He presented himself as a deeply respectful student of Reichsführer Himmler, both in his final written and oral examinations. He praised Himmler's racial and political theories and lauded his vision.

On the morning of the final day at Bad-Toelz he was summoned to the commandant's office. Brigadeführer

Eftger was expansive, beaming genially at Stefan and offering him a chair.

'This will be a hectic day. I wanted to speak to you before the flurry begins.' He offered Stefan a cigarette, which he repectfully declined. 'You have done very well, Gaiser, in fact I may say that your performance here has been exemplary. All of your instructors agree with me that your talents should take you far in the SS.'

'Thank you, sir.'

'There is a point I shall make later, when I address your training unit, but I want to make it to you privately, first, and with more emphasis.' Eftger puffed thoughtfully on his cigarette for a moment. 'The bias in this course is principally towards the elements of leadership – you will have noticed that military skills have played little part in your training. That is because it has been decided you are not to be a soldier, but rather a political functionary. The day will come when there is an armed SS, but they will be men very different from yourself. You will have problems then, and some of them exist already. When you take up whatever task the administration assigns you, there will be resistance from the military men.'

'I understand,' Stefan said. 'I am grateful that you've warned me, sir.'

Eftger sighed. 'I hope you take more notice than some I've told. Men have gone out of this camp shining with promise, and within months they've been removed from duty, or demoted, simply because they did not keep an eye on the small acts of sabotage perpetrated by the soldiers in their midst. When you are gifted with single-minded purpose, Gaiser, you can be terribly vulnerable. Watch them, and don't give them a chance.'

Later, when the Brigadeführer had congratulated Stefan again and pointed out that the Reichsführer himself would know how well he had acquitted himself, Stefan left the office with a stiff, determined expression that covered an urge to smile. Eftger's last murmured words of advice had carried the sentiment that was already etched in his heart: 'Be ruthless, Gaiser. Make them frightened of you.'

A week after he had left the camp at Bad-Toelz, Stefan was called to SD headquarters in Berlin, and there he took the SS oath.

Dressed in his uniform – custom-made by his father's old tailor in Munich – Stefan was then taken by car to a large records building in the Charlottenburg district. The place had recently been leased to the SS as a registry of workers, the driver told him, and as he was led along aisles flanked by shoulder-high glass partitions, behind which male and female clerks worked at massive ledgers and card indexes, Stefan began to comprehend the scale of the Nazis' obsession with paperwork.

He had no idea why he had been brought there. The guard who had accompanied him from the front door took Stefan to the first floor and asked him to wait by a heavy oak door, which was guarded by an armed sentry who stood motionless and stared straight ahead.

Stefan waited for ten minutes, then the big door opened wide and an aide dressed in a uniform similar to his own beckoned him inside. Stefan found himself in a high-ceilinged office, richly carpeted and furnished with oak and dark leather. A man was standing by the window with his back to Stefan, studying some papers.

'Take a seat,' the aide whispered, and Stefan sat down by the scroll-fronted desk. The man at the window turned, smiling as he looked up from his papers, and Stefan felt himself stiffening in the chair. It was Himmler.

'Gaiser?' The Reichsführer came forward, extending a bony hand and grasping Stefan's. 'I'm glad to meet you. They said such marvellous things about you at Bad-Toelz, I thought the least I could do was see you for a few minutes.'

'It's most generous of you, sir,' Stefan said. 'I hadn't looked forward to such a pleasure.'

Himmler sat down behind the desk and his eyes

glittered behind steel-rimmed spectacles. In the flesh he was very different from his photographs. Although his chin receded, it did so at a stubborn angle; his mouth was firm and positive, and there was imposing breadth in his forehead. It was as if his burning determination had reinforced his appearance, making the most of an unpromising collection of features.

'You appear to be the kind of man we need most,' the Reichsführer said. 'You are aware of your Germanic heritage, and you accurately comprehend the Führer's grand design for our future.'

Since it appeared to be good form to talk like a promotional pamphlet, Stefan replied, 'I am anxious to serve to the utmost of my ability, sir.'

'I've no doubt of that.' Himmler folded his hands and looked down at the desk for a moment. 'You have been granted the rank of Untersturmführer, and it carries heavy responsibilities. At all times, you must epitomize our highest ideals – our race, Gaiser, is the finest in the world, and the world will know it.' To Stefan's surprise, Himmler then said, 'You will be familiar with the Order of the Crown, of course. It symbolizes power, and a certain grandeur of the spirit befitting our movement.' He smiled, showing short, irregular teeth. 'Are you surprised I mentioned the Order?'

'I'm not surprised you know of it,' Stefan said, 'but you're one of the few men I have heard mention it, sir.'

'The work of Leonhard Gaiser is something I have cherished for a long time,' Himmler said. 'His books have been on my bedside table often. It was gratifying to learn that his only son wishes to work for our cause.'

'You are a credit to your father,' the Reichsführer continued warmly. Then he stood up and stepped away from the desk. 'I will watch your career with interest.'

Realizing he was being dismissed, Stefan rose and the aide appeared at his side again.

'You will be appointed to the administration of the

SD,' Himmler said, picking up his papers again. 'I'm sure you'll find the work challenging.'

'I'm sure I will, sir. Thank you again for seeing me.'

Stefan was brought down from his cloud the following day, when he reported for duty at the SD headquarters. He was shown to an office resembling an ornate sitting room, and asked to wait there. The curtains were of scarlet satin, matching the shade of the carpet, and the walls were covered with embossed, gilded paper. By the desk in the corner there was a flag, the gold, red and black standard of Hitler's bodyguard, mounted on a silver pole bedded in an oak plinth. Where Stefan sat, beside a low circular table, there was a heavy metal ashtray with intaglio swastikas around its rim, and lying by it there was a solitary Nazi armband, bearing the SS identification of single black lines above and below the swastika. The room had an overbearing atmosphere, an authoritarian threat that was emphasised by the padded silence. As the minutes passed, Stefan realized he was becoming nervous.

At ten o'clock precisely the door opened and a lean, broad-hipped man strode in. Stefan recognized him at once, although he had never set eyes on him before. He was Reinhard Heydrich, the thirty-one-year-old head of the SD.

'Herr Obergruppenführer!' Stefan snapped to attention and shot out his arm in the Nazi salute.

Heydrich nodded and waved the salute aside. 'Sit down again, Gaiser,' he said casually, and walked to the desk in the corner. He unlocked one of the drawers and took out a folder, then brought it to the table. 'We have an hour,' he said, then sat down and began frowning at the papers.

The man's appearance was a match for his reputation. He was fair-haired, with an abnormally high forehead and small, restless eyes. His nose was long and aristocratic, and as he studied the file on his knees his wide mouth tightened and slackened by turns. Without the uniform, Stefan guessed, he would have looked just as impressive;

with it, he bore the kind of authority that people would refer to as a presence.

'Right.' Heydrich slapped the folder down on the table and looked straight at Stefan. 'I think we should show all our cards. Before you went to Bad-Toelz, I had already decided there was a place for you here. I still think there is, but one or two things disturb me.' He flipped open the folder and rifled down to the fourth page. Stefan saw his own handwriting. ' "The understanding of blood",' Heydrich read, ' "and the ideology arising from that understanding, creates an élite, from which can emanate the master race so long foretold by our legends and history".' He closed the file and looked up at Stefan. 'Recognize it?'

'It's my essay, sir. I wrote it for the final examinations at Bad-Toelz.'

'And do you believe all that stuff about blood and Aryan dominance and the German master race?'

'Well, I may have put it rather floridly . . .'

'Gaiser, even the Führer doesn't believe it, and frankly I don't see how you can. We investigated you, and we came up with a picture of an activist, a man whose instincts have developed through experience, not fairy tales.' Heydrich put up a long, slender hand. 'Don't defend yourself until I've finished. I can quite see that you were being smart, telling your instructors what they wanted to hear. If that's the case, it does you credit – but if it's not, if you *are* one of those Siegfried-worshipping fanatics, I want to know right now.'

Stefan paused. He could feel the sweat prickle beneath his shirt. 'I was being smart,' he admitted. 'My father was an authority on Nordic legend, and he lectured me regularly on the principle of blood and soil. It was easy to call it all back and write it down.'

Heydrich smiled, and his eyes showed some admiration. 'It did the trick,' he said. 'I'm glad to know you're our man, after all. But bear this in mind, from the very start – in your dealings with me, I want scrupulous honesty.

Save the tricks for the people you need to delude. Understood?'

'Yes, sir.'

'Good. Now we can get down to business.'

Stefan learned a great deal over the next forty-five minutes. Apart from the syrupy ideology in the essay, Heydrich said, the extremely high leadership rating from the training camp had confirmed initial expectation. Stefan was described by Brigadeführer Eftger as forceful, energetic, intelligent and naturally dominant. He was also the closest thing to an aristocrat that Himmler would allow near the SD. That special feature, added to the others, had decided Heydrich. He wanted Stefan on his personal staff.

'I don't care a damn about the Aryan life-force. But I do care about good breeding.'

Heydrich went on to outline the power structure he controlled. Apart from the numerous offices of the SD – which existed, he said, to protect the state from its enemies – he had control of the Sicherheitspolizei, which was composed of the Reich Kriminalpolizei, known as Kripo for short, and the Geheime Staatspolizei, otherwise known as the Gestapo. His powers were almost as wide-ranging as Himmler's, although the Reichsführer was still technically Heydrich's direct superior.

'I have a straight line of communication with the Führer,' he told Stefan. 'And that is valuable. You will have a similarly direct contact with me, and I'm sure you'll find it indispensable.'

As he talked, Heydrich displayed a certain absence of respect for Himmler. He said nothing openly derogatory, but he managed to make it plain that he put up with the Reichsführer only because, for the time being at least, he had to. It was just as clear that he saw no danger in speaking so candidly to Stefan, and it was easy enough to see the reason; on his own admission, Heydrich had so much information on everyone in the Nazi movement that he was practically invulnerable.

By stages they reached the point where Stefan's duties with the SD were discussed.

'We have to make distinctions when we talk of threats to the Reich,' Heydrich said. 'The ordinary police forces deal with individual cases, isolated instances of sabotage or sedition. The SD keeps an eye open for ideological dangers, the growth of factions and movements hostile to the administration. I'm keen to strengthen my interrogation branch, Gaiser, and I think that may be where you would do especially well. At present I'm maintaining pressure on the Communists and the Social Democrats. Do you fancy you could interrogate an underground Communist, Gaiser?'

'I'm prepared to learn,' Stefan said.

'Good. You'll have your first lesson this afternoon. Until then, I suggest you familiarise yourself with the code of procedure for SD officers, and here—' he picked up the SS arm band and handed it to Stefan, '—wear this all the time, because in conjunction with this—' Heydrich lifted the white braid triangle with the black letters SD that had been under the arm band, '—it'll put the fear of hell into people before you open your mouth.'

As the morning wore on and Stefan sat alone with the procedure manual, he began to understand better why Heydrich was giving him such special treatment. The walls of the small office he had been given stopped short of the ceiling, and Stefan could hear the activity in other offices around him. The SD, it appeared, was populated by as many thugs and ruffians as other wings of the SS. Clerical officers, secretaries, even senior investigation officers muttered, shouted and bawled at each other in language that was as rough as their accents. Now and then a softer voice would surface, and Stefan distinctly heard a woman who spoke the way they did in the nicer districts of Munich, but in the main it was a bear pit. Heydrich was of the officer class, and there must have been times when he pined for someone around the place who could communicate in something more than the basic two hundred-word vocabulary that was assailing Stefan as he tried to absorb the information in front of him.

After lunch in the building's small canteen, where a dozen or so officers introduced themselves one after another with overdone heartiness, Stefan was approached in his office by another member of Heydrich's personal staff. He was an Obersturmführer called Hubert Feder, a pale, expressionless man in his thirties with greying hair and spectacles like Himmler's. He uttered a brief, halting speech of welcome, and explained that Stefan would be working with him that afternoon.

'You'll have to do no more than watch and listen,' he said. 'Interrogation isn't exactly an art, and everybody adopts his own style, but there are certain general rules worth observing.'

They travelled in the elevator to the basement of the building, and when they stepped out Stefan felt the depressing chill of the place at once. It was large, low-ceilinged and dark, and at the end opposite the elevator there was a long row of barred cells. To the left, four doors lay open along the grey stone wall, each emitting a glimmer of light.

'The interrogation rooms,' Feder said. 'Deliberately uninviting, of course.'

They went into the first room. It had dark green walls, a single ceiling lamp, one chair under the lamp and a table against one wall. It was a layout that would become familiar to Stefan, a working environment designed to induce fear in a suspect and diminish his hope.

'For optimum stage dressing,' Feder said, 'it would be best if you sit yourself on a corner of the table and look as if you're studying the case notes.' He handed Stefan a clip board with a blank sheet of paper attached to it.

Stefan eased himself down on to the edge of the table and watched as Feder took up a spread-legged stance in front of the chair. He appeared to be thinking, perhaps mentally rehearsing; after a few moments he moved to the door and touched a white button on the frame. Stefan heard a cell door being opened and slammed shut, and as Feder took up his stance again, a uniformed guard came in, leading the prisoner by the arm.

'Sit,' Feder said quietly.

The prisoner was in his twenties. His hair was ruffled and there was a dark purple bruise on his left cheek. Stefan noticed he wore no shoes, and the belt had been removed from his baggy trousers, making it necessary for him to clutch them around himself. He looked very frightened, and he sat down the instant Feder ordered him to.

'Benjamin Conrath. Occupation: bricklayer. Married, with two children.' Feder read the facts off his sheet of paper, then looked at the prisoner. 'Correct?'

'Yes.'

'Yes, *sir*.'

'Yes, sir, that's correct.'

Feder stepped back a few paces, like someone taking in an exhibit in its entirety. 'And you are a Communist.'

'No! I've told them that already, I'm not a Communist, and I don't know anything about Communism!' Conrath's voice was hoarse, and Stefan guessed he had made plenty of denials before he had been brought before Obersturmführer Feder. There were dark lines below his eyes, as if he had gone without sleep for too long.

'Have you been told the consequences of lying to us, Conrath?'

'I've been told nothing. All they've done is accuse me.'

'Well, listen carefully.' Feder moved in close again, so that Conrath had to strain his neck to look up at him. 'If we establish that you are a Communist, or have Communist associations, and that you have worked against the interests of the Reich, then you will be sent to Dachau. Do you know about Dachau?'

Conrath shook his head.

'It is a place for enemies of the Reich. It is a hard place to survive in, Conrath, terribly hard even for a man with your constitution. Just think how hard it might be for a woman and two small children.'

Stefan felt his stomach heave. Conrath's evident misery had been heavy enough before Feder mentioned his family. Now there was stark concern on his face. Stefan had a flashing thought about guilt, his own guilt by association, just by being there and allowing this to go on.

'My family aren't involved . . .'

'But you are?'

Conrath began to cry. His head slumped on his chest as the sobs hissed between his clamped teeth.

'You are, aren't you?'

'It's nothing . . .'

'Tell me, anyway,' Feder said, and his voice had gone soft again, hinting at mercy.

'I passed on some leaflets for a friend, that's all.' Conrath wiped his eyes on his shirt sleeve. 'It was just an errand, a favour.'

Feder nodded understandingly. 'Your friend, who is he?'

'Otto Kreisch.'

'And why did Kreisch not deliver the leaflets himself?'

'It wasn't a delivery, exactly.'

'What, then?'

Conrath spoke so quietly Stefan could barely hear him. 'I gave the leaflets out to people I know, people I drink with.'

'Because you are a Communist and you wished to spread the gospel of Marxism.'

'No,' Conrath groaned. 'Otto Kreisch isn't a Communist, either. His leaflets are about workers' rights. He has theories, he talked to me about them – he's a schoolteacher, you see, he teaches my own daughter. He's a kindly man, he's not a threat to anybody.'

'Tell me,' Feder said, 'do the theories of Herr Kreisch run contrary to state policy?'

'They vary. He suggests alternatives. His concern is for human beings.'

Feder was nodding. 'Human beings like yourself, articulate bricklayers. Jewish bricklayers. Kreisch is a Jew also, I presume?'

'Yes. It's no crime.'

'But the international Jewish conspiracy is, Conrath.' Feder had become cold again, businesslike. 'I want you to tell me the names of your associates, and I want a list of people you know to be associates of Kreisch.'

It was over in another ten minutes. Conrath reeled off names and Feder wrote them down. When he appeared to hesitate, just once, Feder reminded him that he was endangering not only himself, but his dependents. The warning produced a small surge of names and approximate addresses, and when Conrath had finished Feder urged him to be sure there were no more, and he read off the names already mentioned, in case there were omissions.

'That's all,' Conrath said wearily.

'Very well.' Feder nodded at the guard, who had remained by the door, and he came forward and hoisted Conrath out of the chair.

'Can I go home now?'

Feder stiffened. 'Home? Why should we return you to your home?'

'But I've told you all I know!' Conrath howled.

'On your own admission you're a dissident, an enemy of the Reich, and you associate with other dissidents. We don't set dissidents loose on the streets, Conrath.'

'What'll happen to me?' Conrath was standing at an angle, gripped at the armpit by the guard, his head sunk forward with an expression of sheerest anguish.

'You will be transported to Dachau, in due course.'

'Oh no, please, my family . . .'

'They will no doubt join you in the concentration camp, Herr Conrath,' Feder grunted, and turned his back. The guard dragged Conrath away.

'That was an easy one,' Feder said as he dropped the list of names on the table with his other notes. 'The only thing to be learned there, I think, is that it's always best to leave the major threat until the actual interrogation, when the prisoner has already been under prolonged stress.'

'How long has he been in custody?' Stefan asked.

'Three days. He was picked up in a beer hall following information that he'd been seen handing papers to people.'

'And he wasn't asked any questions until now?'

'That's right. As he said, all they did was accuse him. It works very well – it's standard.'

Stefan had no wish to show any concern for the prisoner, but he had to know what would happen to him. 'He'll really be taken to Dachau?'

'Yes, and there he'll undergo much more intensive questioning. Some facts can bury themselves in a man's mind. They have methods at Dachau for bringing them to the surface.' Feder sucked his teeth thoughtfully. 'I don't know much about the place, really, and I don't think I want to know.' He picked up his notes and looked at them. 'Ah. The next one should present some challenge.' He went to the door and pressed the button, then moved to the wall opposite the door and leaned there, his hands in his pockets.

The guard brought in a woman of about forty. She was barefoot, as Conrath had been, and her face had been bruised too, on the chin and along the line of the left jaw. She was wearing a baggy dress of loose-woven grey canvas material, and from the way it hung on her Stefan knew it was all she wore.

When the guard pushed the woman down on to the chair the beauty of her face was apparent for a moment as she tilted back her head, shaking her long brown hair from her eyes. Stefan was reminded of his mother; the dignity was imposed by the eyes and the fine symmetry of the facial bones.

'So *you're* the troublemaker,' Feder said languidly as he pushed himself away from the wall. 'I'd expected someone much tougher-looking. Female agitators usually have a little hair on the upper lip, and the odd tattoo.' He glanced at the paper in his hand. 'Irma Rode. Occupation: painter. Single. Have I described you correctly?'

'Name, occupation and status are as stated,' the woman said, and Stefan was instantly impressed with the strength of her voice. 'But you are wrong to call me a trouble-maker. I've done no more than defend my rights.'

'Traitors have no rights, Irma.'

'I am not a traitor! And I am not a person who can be talked to in this fashion by the likes of you.'

'Oh?' Feder raised his eyebrows theatrically, looking first at Stefan, then at the prisoner. 'You're someone special, are you? I must apologize, no one warned me. I was misled into believing you were a painter of daubs, who lives like a pauper in an attic in the Ramersdorf district of Munich. What has been missed out, or wrongly reported?'

Irma Rode began to say something, then apparently changed her mind.

'If that much is wrong,' Feder went on, 'then the rest might be wrong too. If so, we owe you an apology. As I understand it, you made derogatory remarks in public about the RSHA, and the SS. You also took the trouble to paint a swastika with four snakes' heads on it. And I'm advised there is strong evidence that you have several times written letters of complaint to the intellectual press in France and England, talking of your hardship under the – what did you call it? – the mounting oppression of jack-booted hooligans in positions of power. Now have we got all that wrong?'

'I am an artist,' Irma Rode said quietly and firmly, staring back at Feder. 'I have an artist's integrity and an artist's right to free expression. You have no right to imprison me and ill-treat me for my opinions.'

'I see. So in your view, a child with a loaded gun, firing

it off at random, is merely expressing himself and should not be discouraged. Is that what you believe, Irma?'

'You know perfectly well it isn't!'

Feder's voice hardened then and he leaned close to the prisoner, almost shouting in her face. 'But you think it is your right to malign the Party, to spread lies and misinformation, and to work at the subversion of government programmes without hindrance! The word artist is a label to cover every level of decadence, immorality, criminal sloth and treason, Irma Rode! I am the one who should feel offended at having to talk to *you*!' He turned away abruptly, walked to the table and snatched up the file of notes. 'You can be indicted on at least five charges, and every one of them is serious.'

'I don't recognize the authority of you or of your charges!' the woman said defiantly.

'You have no choice. The law is not something you choose, or do not choose, to obey.' Feder's manner became brisk as he began to pace in front of the prisoner, staring at the notes as he did so. 'We know you have proposed the formation of an artists' resistance group. We also know you have sympathisers. I want to have the names of these people, and I want them quickly.'

'You can go to hell!'

'If you do not start giving me names within ten seconds, your acquaintance with hell will start a great deal sooner than mine.' Feder looked at his watch, then at the woman.

'I'm telling you nothing.'

'Eight seconds.'

Stefan felt the sweat on his palms. There was nothing counterfeit about Feder's calm or his certainty. He knew the woman would talk, it was apparent in his easy movements, the casual assurance in his glance. Irma Rode sat tensed in the chair, her mouth clamped shut, her beautiful eyes no less defiant than before.

'Three,' Feder said, looking steadily at his watch. 'Two. One.' He dropped his arm and looked at the prisoner. 'Well? Are you ready to tell me?'

'You've had my answer.'

Feder nodded at the guard, who turned and left the room. While he was gone Feder turned his back to Irma Rode and pretended to scan his notes again. Stefan saw the woman's determination begin to waver, and the impulse to defend her was so powerful he had to look away.

When the guard came back there was another soldier with him, and they carried a chair between them. It was made of dark, heavy wood and there were two stout arm supports with straps attached to them. They set down the chair beside the one Irma Rode sat in, and at a slow-nodding signal from Feder both men lifted the prisoner and pushed her down on the new chair. For the space of four heartbeats that Stefan felt in his throat, the woman's defiance held, then she began screaming as the soldiers strapped down her arms.

When the guards stood away from the chair Feder moved close, addressing the prisoner in a reasonable, conversational tone. 'The drawing of one fingernail is unbelievably painful,' he said, 'and you have ten.'

Irma Rode was crying and talking, producing an angry, frightened babble that distorted her face and gave her the authentic appearance, to Stefan, of a sensitive animal being taunted by children. He remembered his haste, once, to kill a rabbit he had seen caught in a bear trap. The spreading peace on the creature's face as the bullet struck home had done something to relieve his distress, but he had never forgotten the message of misery and agony delivered by the small, writhing body. He was holding his breath now, willing the woman to talk and save herself, when Feder spoke again.

'Are you sure you want to put yourself to all that pain?'

'I have my rights!' the woman screamed.

One of the guards stepped close to the chair and bent over the prisoner. Stefan glued his eyes to the clipboard and set his teeth hard as the first screech hit his ears. The aggrieved noise was like a siren, telling Stefan what he had never quite suspected, that the nightmare he had foreseen was underway, and probably had been for a long time. He sat motionless in spite of every urge to move, to *help*, and prayed for Irma Rode to lose consciousness.

She was very strong. After the first small atrocity, when the guards and Feder stood watching closely, the woman summoned a new defiance. Perhaps because she had discovered she could hold her integrity against terrible pain, she raised her head and showed Feder her tight-shut lips.

Impassively, Feder motioned for the guard to repeat what he had done, and in less than five seconds Irma Rode's will buckled under the onslaught of a new pain that drowned the other with its force.

'I'll tell you,' she said, when she was able to speak.

'That is very sensible of you. Guard, bring a glass of water.' Feder turned to take a fresh sheet of notepaper from the table, and Stefan saw nothing melodramatic in his face. He had the placid expression of a man getting on with his job.

Three weeks later, Heydrich watched from an observation cell as Stefan interrogated a prisoner himself. Stefan did not know Heydrich was there, which was just as well. The knowledge would perhaps have overloaded his shock and confusion when he saw who the prisoner was.

Recognition did not come immediately. The man was tousled and sat with his head lowered, his chin pressed on his chest. His alleged crime was sabotage: two SS vehicles had been set alight outside a school where teachers were undergoing routine questioning. On the evidence of the civil police the prisoner was certainly guilty and a conviction through the civil court would have been certain. But the crime had political overtones, so the man had been brought to SD headquarters to have his background sifted and his future decided. Stefan read the notes swiftly, then told the prisoner to look up. There was a jarring moment of rejection, something bordering on fright, and Stefan swallowed sharply, struggling to show nothing.

'Your name,' he snapped, not needing to know.

The large, gentle eyes blinked at Stefan. There was recognition, but it was suffused with terror. 'Eber,' he croaked, 'Gerd Eber.'

Stefan glared at his clipboard. Had they stumbled on something? Did they know? His reason said no, it was impossible, if they knew about the old days with Gerd then they knew about the same old days with Sara. Pain shot along Stefan's arm and he realized he was gripping the sharp edge of the clip too tightly.

'Sit up, Eber. I want you to sit up when I address you.' With his eyes Stefan tried to convey his own confusion, but Gerd's fear was obliterating the signal. He was as scared of Stefan as he was of any other Nazi officer. His face was older, it had probably grown that way in the past twelve hours since he had been arrested. Pain and fright had made chaos of his features.

'I would like some water,' Gerd said.

'In due course.' Indecision was not natural to Stefan, but he found himself on a cliff edge, frightened to jump. Whatever he did, however lenient he tried to be, Gerd would be finished. It was clearly right, sensible, *imperative* that the interrogation go ahead like any other, but the prospect of such callousness gave Stefan pause. To lose everything, he had only to acknowledge his friend. To maintain progress, he needed only to stifle every decent impulse. Stefan's eyes bored into Gerd's, imploring forgiveness.

The guard by the door shuffled his feet. Taking that show of impatience as his springboard Stefan spun and threw his clipboard at the table, making a crash that brought the guard to attention and made Gerd jump up in his chair.

'Your thirst should be the least of your worries, Eber!' The harshness of his voice was painful to his own ears but Stefan rode forward on the surge of pretence, deadening his mind with the well-rehearsed cant. 'What kind of lunatic zeal drives saboteurs of your calibre?'

Something in Gerd rallied and he put back his head, moistening his lips before he spoke. 'I have a regard for human dignity, as perhaps you once had . . .'

The personal reference triggered Stefan's caution and he snatched up the clipboard from the edge of the table and waved it menacingly. 'Dignity? You? You have your delusion, nothing else.' Stefan glanced at the notes, wondering behind his agitation how someone like Gerd could have been driven to open acts of defiance. 'A clerk, living off the earnings of a whore, talks about his dignity – his humanity? It's laughable, Eber.'

'I have a brain!' Gerd's eyes were defiant, and the glint of hatred there was a pain that cut right into Stefan. 'I can tell when people are being reduced to robots . . .'

'You have a vacuum, ready to be filled with the easy-to-soak-up pap handed out by the Communists!'

'I have *choice*,' Gerd whined, 'and I won't give it up!'

'Choice!' Stefan growled, no longer able to look at Gerd, wanting the ghastly charade to be over. 'You exercise choice the way an animal would. There's law and order, but you chose to disrupt it. There is decency, but you *chose* to set up house with a prostitute.'

'Erika is not a prostitute!' The anguish beat like a club on Stefan's brain. *He was doing this to a friend!*

'She has three convictions. All for street soliciting.'

'That was a long time ago!'

Stefan waved the clipboard again, making an elaborate show of dismissing the matter. *What the hell was Gerd doing in Berlin anyway? What kind of macabre coincidence was this?* The notes showed that Gerd had been transferred from Munich three months before, to work on the programme of civil deployment, listing the citizens available for war work should the need arise. A straightforward fact. Again, Stefan wondered if someone had known about the old days. Again, he rejected the notion.

He straightened and shook an imperious finger at Gerd. 'I know what I know, Herr Eber, and you imagine what you imagine. That gulf isn't worth spanning. So let's stick to what we know to be a fact. You destroyed two valuable vehicles belonging to the SS, and you did that as a demonstration of your solidarity with the Communists. Before you leave this room, you'll tell me who your associates are, and what future acts of delinquency are in your squalid cooking pot.'

'I have no associates,' Gerd said.

'Don't be ridiculous. You're a mob type, Eber. Only in a lump can you feel anything like potent. Your talk gives you away. Group thinking, collective banality.'

Hours of sleeplessness, punishment and uncertainty had eroded whatever reserves of real courage Gerd possessed. The breaking point was near; Stefan recognized it and wanted to hasten the moment.

'I don't deny I set fire to those cars,' Gerd said. 'But I did it alone, it was my own idea.'

Again Stefan tried to use his eyes, he tried to beg Gerd to give in, to avoid any more suffering. But Gerd saw only the Nazi, the tormentor.

Stefan shook his head. 'A man will always confess a smaller crime to distract attention from a larger one. You're one of a mob, Eber. Tell me who the others are.'

'I told you, there's only me.' Gerd was looking at his knees, moving his feet in agitated circles.

Stefan leaned closer and put a hand on the drooping shoulder. 'You know we can force the information from you?'

'I'm ready for that,' Gerd said shakily.

The creation of physical fear, Stefan had discovered, was easiest when the threat was unseen, unspecific. If the likelihood of harm lay elsewhere, results could be spectacular. Stefan walked to the table and pressed a black button set into a wooden box. It was connected to nothing.

After a minute, during which Stefan stayed by the table, staring at the notes, Gerd said, 'What are you doing?'

'Studying your pathetic history,' Stefan said, without looking up.

'That thing, that button . . .' Gerd's voice had the unsteady, exhausted sound of a man who had run too far and for too long.

'It's a signal,' Stefan said levelly. 'Your beloved Erika is now being questioned. What you don't wish to tell us, she probably will.' The lie was like an obstruction clogging Stefan's throat. One glance and he could see the pain flash across Gerd's face, widening his eyes, pushing him to a new limit of terror.

'You inhuman bastard!'

Erika, for all Stefan knew, was probably at home. There was no record of her arrest, as yet. If she had any sense she would be hiding somewhere. 'Any expedient is justifiable, Herr Eber, when it comes to protecting the order of the state. If you have any concern for this woman, you'll talk to me now, and quickly.'

For an endless second the space between them was electric, a cord of pure tension as Gerd tried to hold out and Stefan tried just as hard to will him to give in.

'All right,' Gerd said at last. 'I'll tell you.'

Stefan pressed the button twice, then walked back to the centre of the floor. Beyond all reason he hated himself in that moment. He wanted to close his hand on Gerd's shoulder and tell him it was all right, he would be safe. There was no such hope, and instead Stefan raised his pen over the clipboard, waiting.

Later, when Gerd had issued his list of names and outlined a few projected acts of sabotage, he was led back to his cell. He did not look back at Stefan, and when he was gone Stefan let loose a shuddering sigh that hovered on the edge of a groan, a sound of misery.

To have known that Gerd was in SS custody would have been pain enough: to have been the instrument of Gerd's torment was a fact so obscene that in the aftermath Stefan felt a wave of nausea, and the bile rose in his throat before he could swallow it back.

In the evening, before he could get drunk enough to blunt the sharper barbs, the memories came edging in, the agonizing pictures and echoes of times that could not be brought back, times that were now only a punishment to recall. Stefan wept for his friend, and for everything of himself that he had lost and renounced. That night Stefan dreamt they were all together again, Sara, Gerd and the others, sitting around a table laughing, with Stefan laughing loudest of all, while their little raft of carefree friendship floated slowly into the jaws of change – brutal, merciless change.

One morning in early September Stefan heard a voice through the office partition that made him stop what he was doing and listen, trying to remember. It was a woman's voice, melodic and soft among all the harsher sounds around it, and when he heard it one more time Stefan did remember. On his very first day with the SD, that had been the gentle female sound that had made the rest seem so coarse, as it did now.

Stefan got out of his chair and snatched up a folder, then marched with it out of the office. He saw her at once, standing by the desk of the departmental audit clerk. She was small and beautiful, and in the instant she glanced at him Stefan smiled and nodded, as if they knew each other. The audit clerk had gone off to the other side of the room and Stefan went straight to the vacated desk and put down his folder.

'Good morning,' he said. 'Are you being attended to?'

The girl looked surprised. She was in civilian clothes,

which could only mean, in that place, that she was a detainee or a minor employee. In either case, it was hardly appropriate that an officer of the SD would want to offer assistance.

'I thought perhaps I could help you,' Stefan added. He hoped the warmth of his approach would take some of the chill out of his appearance.

'I'm waiting for the clerk,' the girl said. It was an educated voice, calm, with no need for arrogance or submissiveness. 'I have to take some papers back to the office.'

'And what office is that?'

'Ordnungspolizei. I'm an administrative clerk there.'

Stefan's mind raced to the nearest opportunity. 'If you're going back there right away, I can give you a lift.' His work entailed occasional visits to the civil police headquarters to collect lists of suspects under street surveillance.

The girl quietly agreed to accept the offer. Ten minutes later she was sitting in the staff car beside Stefan, her fat wallet of papers clutched on her lap.

It was raining. Large drops were drumming on the hood and streaking down the windscreen. On the short dash to where the car was parked, the girl's hair had been soaked and flattened against her head. The change in her appearance was surprising to Stefan: from round-faced, wholesome elegance she had been transformed to a starker version of herself. She revealed the beauty that had lain under the applied embellishments of hairstyle and composure. She looked uncomfortable, and Stefan apologized to her.

'I should have brought an umbrella,' he said.

'I'll be fine,' she assured him, staring at the windscreen.

The engine was turning, but Stefan delayed putting it into gear. 'What's your name?'

'Bauer.'

Stefan smiled at her profile. 'Is there a first name?'

'Gretl.'

'And I'm Stefan.'

When she turned her head to look at him, it was clear that the discomfort was only partly to do with the soaking she had received. SS officers, and officers of the SD in particular, were discouraged from making social contact with civilians, and the civilians were as much aware of the fact as anybody.

Stefan eased the engine into bottom gear and pulled out into the slow traffic. 'I'm sorry if I've embarrassed you,' he said, and before Gretl had time to pretend she did not understand, he added, 'I tend to forget I'm not permitted to be human when I've got the uniform on.'

When Gretl looked out through the fan-shaped segment where the wiper made the street visible again, she was smiling.

At Ordnungspolizei headquarters Stefan accompanied Gretl to the second floor and explained to her department controller that he had given her a lift because the weather was so bad. The controller, with great diffidence, thanked Stefan, and voiced the hope that it had not been too much trouble.

'Not at all. I was coming over here anyway.' Stefan glanced across to Gretl's desk, where she was already seated and sorting through the papers she had brought. He waited until she looked up, then he nodded to her and smiled before taking his leave.

He allowed two days to pass before getting in touch with her again. The personnel files, as expected, were eloquent on the matter of her background. She was twenty years old, a graduate in administrative studies from the Berlin College for Women, and her father was a respected lecturer in politics and military science. She lived alone in a small apartment near Lutzow Strasse, and her social life appeared to be restricted to weekly theatre visits and occasional dinner engagements with her father. It was a practice with the SS to make a careful study of the social backgrounds of all personnel, whether they worked directly for the department or for its satellites. A grading system was adopted with these studies, and Gretl had been awarded a 'B' rating, which practically qualified her for sainthood. It occurred to Stefan, the second time he read Gretl's file, that she had to be a very keen Nazi, or simply a nice, level-headed girl with more than her share of discretion. The file said she was politically and ideologically stable. Stefan hoped she was the kind of person who just went along with the rules in the interests of a quiet life.

By singling out the precise quarter of police administration Gretl was concerned with – recruitment analysis for the northern sector of the city – he was able to have his call put through to her desk without having to ask for her by name.

'This is Untersturmführer Gaiser, SD headquarters,' he said stiffly, as soon as he heard Gretl's voice. 'I require some information.'

'I will help in any way I can,' Gretl assured him coolly.

'How many men under the age of thirty-five have been assigned to street duty in your sector during the past month?'

There was only a moment's pause, then Gretl said, 'We have eighteen men in uniform, Herr Untersturmführer, and twelve in trainee posts with existing surveillance units.'

'I see. And men over thirty-five? How many of them in the same period?'

There was no pause this time. 'No men over thirty-five have been freshly recruited or assigned this year,' Gretl said.

'One more question.'

'Yes?'

'How many forms do I have to fill in before you can have dinner with me?'

The silence was formidable.

'You haven't fainted, have you?'

Gretl cleared her throat softly. 'Do I know you?'

'You've met me.' Stefan put on a stricken voice to add, 'Don't tell me you've forgotten so soon?'

'Of course not.' She was speaking very quietly now. 'This call is irregular, you must know that . . .'

'The only irregularity is that you haven't answered my question about dinner. I thought tomorrow evening, if you're free. The *Königshof*. Please say yes. It'll cut down the number of irregular calls.'

'But really, I don't even know you properly . . .'

'Matters like that,' Stefan said, 'are generally best attended to over dinner.'

Gretl sighed. 'Very well.'

'Good. I'll pick you up at nine.'

'You know where I live?'

Stefan grinned. 'Naturally. The boys in the SD always do their homework. I'll see you tomorrow, Gretl.'

The call had broken more ice than Stefan expected. Over dinner the following evening Gretl chatted easily, and she displayed a lot of curiosity about her escort.

'I always believed the SS were aloof as a matter of policy,' she said. 'I don't know of one other girl who's been out with one of them.'

'We're not *all* out of the same mould.'

'Just the same, I'm still finding it hard to believe.' She sat with her hands on the table before her, the fingers curled softly around her brandy glass. The dress she was wearing, peach-coloured silk that touched only the outer curves of her shoulders and dipped in a graceful curve across her breast, gave Gretl the appearance of quality that matched her confident interrogation. 'Out of uniform, you look more like an aristocrat than an official of the state. What did you do before?'

'I was a scholar, of sorts.' Stefan was staring at her, as he had done for most of the evening. It was dawning on him just how difficult it might be, getting close to someone without ever being able to tell her the truth about himself. 'I needed to be more active, so I joined the SS.'

'I wasn't aware you could just join. It's an élite body, after all.'

'That's what we tell people.'

She smiled at him and sipped her brandy. 'You're being evasive, which means I'm probably being too inquisitive. I apologize.'

'No need for that. If I'm handing out vague answers it's because I'm impatient to ask a few questions of my own. Will you tell me something truthfully?'

'Of course.'

'Have you truly been enjoying this evening?'

She nodded. 'I'd go so far as to say it's one of the most enjoyable evenings I've had.'

They sat together in the warm restaurant for another hour, sipping coffee and brandy. Gretl told Stefan some more about herself and Stefan pretended to do the same.

After he had taken Gretl home, he drove to his own apartment and sat outside in the car, listening to the cooling sounds of the engine and prodding the small pain at the centre of his happiness. The need for honesty had never been so strong in him, he would never be able to express himself fully as long as there was deception. But the reasons for deception had never been more obvious or insistent.

Stefan spent a long time in the car, rationalizing, but in the end he still felt the same. He was engineering, he knew, a special kind of loneliness.

They saw each other eight times in six weeks, and on the ninth occasion Gretl accepted Stefan's invitation to dine at his apartment.

'I had no idea you could cook,' she told him and spread her hands in wonder at the display of dishes on the hotplates in his kitchen.

'I can't. If you want to compliment the chef later, you'll have to walk two blocks.' Stefan lifted the lid from a small saucepan. 'Recognize the aroma?'

Gretl put her face close and sniffed. 'Traudl! You went to the trouble of getting Traudl to make all this?'

'It was hardly any trouble. The real trouble would have been me trying to open a couple of cans.' He kissed her on the cheek. 'I hope you enjoy it.'

The darkened little sitting room seemed to huddle around them as they ate. Stefan had bought two bottles of French wine and when they were almost finished with the second one Gretl announced that she was no longer sober.

When the meal was over, there was coffee, a liqueur, and the dim cosiness of the sitting room. Gretl sat down on the narrow couch, holding her glass in both hands, and Stefan sat down beside her.

'It was a lovely evening, as usual,' Gretl said.

'As usual,' Stefan whispered, and put his arm around her shoulder, drawing her close. 'Do you realize it's the first time we've really been alone together, apart from in the car, or standing outside your apartment?'

Gretl nodded. 'It's nice.' There was a tremor in her shoulder, like the restlessness of a young animal nervous of its surroundings.

'We must do it more, Gretl.' Stefan brushed his face against her hair, tightened his fingers momentarily on her shoulder. 'When other people are around, they dilute our atmosphere.'

'Very poetic,' she said.

'It sounded rather chemical to me.'

When she laughed, a little too heartily, he turned her towards him and took the glass from her. They had kissed like that only once before, three days earlier, and the memory of it was a perfect overlay as Stefan closed his lips on hers. He drew away after long seconds and looked at her.

'Stefan . . .'

'You're not afraid?'

'No.' She moved her head on to his shoulder, and with her mouth by his ear she said, 'I can't help being nervous.'

'I know.'

They kissed again, and while Stefan held her mouth

close to his he began to caress her, and when finally there was enough trust in the gentle sagging of her body he raised Gretl up and put her face against his shoulder as he led her into the bedroom.

Their lovemaking was smooth and unhurried, and long before the soft throes of his climax Stefan knew he was in bed with a woman of experience, a gloriously warm, competent lover whose nervousness was reserved for thresholds.

Later he asked her.

'I first made love when I was fifteen,' she said. 'You couldn't call it an affair, it was too furtive, there was only the sex. The man was almost four times my age.' She paused. 'Shocked?'

'A little,' Stefan admitted.

'It wasn't a matter for shock. He was very kind and gentle, I was shy, trusting. He was one of my father's friends, a doctor. It made him very unhappy, even though he wanted me so badly. He used to cry.'

'How long did it last?'

'Until I was sixteen. On my birthday I decided it had to stop. I told him so and he accepted it. I think he was relieved one of us could make the decision.'

'And since then?'

'One man,' she sighed. 'It began happily, but he was young and jealous, I couldn't move without him wanting to know where I'd been, who I'd seen. It finished a year ago.' Gretl inhaled deeply, and her breast pressed softly against Stefan's palm. 'Until I met you, I was pretty sure I couldn't stand the strain of a relationship with anyone, any more.'

With unconcealed feeling, Stefan kissed her cheek, her forehead, and moved closer to her. The bleakness touched him again, the periodic awareness of his charade. He had stolen the love of a complete woman and she loved someone who was only half real.

'Now tell me about you,' Gretl said.

'Me.' He rolled on to his back and folded his arms.

'There isn't much to tell.' Nothing of the truth, certainly, he thought. Stefan Gaiser was inaccessible, only the fake was available for inspection. Somewhere there was a decision to be made, there was *always* a decision that could stop the growth of something unpleasant. He waited for it to present itself for consideration, while his mouth delivered the smoothly edited facts. 'An affair with a married woman when I was still in my teens. Another affair later, with a bad ending. It's a history much the same as yours, in outline.'

'And your career absorbed the rest of your time and your energies, is that it?'

'I suppose so.'

'What about your family?'

'They're dead.' He began to tell her about Dorfen, the parts he could tell her, leaving out the violence of his father and inventing a death for his mother. Then the decision came to him suddenly, in mid-sentence. Stefan saw it and accepted it without faltering on a word. In time, he vowed, he would tell Gretl everything, he would set his mind on a future when that would be possible. In the meantime he could only go on with the sham, and hope she would forgive him for it when the time came.

'Are you a person who believes in fate?' Gretl asked him.

'I'm not sure.'

'I believe in it,' she whispered. 'I had an eerie feeling, the very first time you took me to dinner. It was as if I'd been waiting, and I'd known who I was waiting for.'

He laughed softly. 'All the lovable people in the world are romantics.'

'Then you must be one, too. I love you so very much.' She rolled close to him and put her head on his chest. 'Do you want to love me for a long time, Stefan?'

He nodded, but remained silent. There *would* be a time, he swore again, and when it came he would still want this woman with him.

At Christmas Heydrich sent out his customary SD progress report to Hitler and Himmler. A paragraph in the staff organization section was set aside for Untersturmführer Gaiser.

> Within only a few months this young officer has set standards for interrogation and related procedures, and he continues to exceed previous targets in relation to the number of his interrogations and positive case conclusions. In addition to his routine work he has assisted energetically in the groundwork planning for the SD expansion programme. Untersturmführer Gaiser observes only the highest standards, bringing a quality to his duties which is an inspiration to other officers.

Stefan spent the holiday period with Gretl. They stayed locked in her apartment for two days, and only emerged when Gretl felt bound by duty to go and see her father. When Stefan returned to his own apartment, there was a telegram of congratulation from Reichsführer Himmler.

In January 1936 Stefan moved into a new, larger apartment in the south west of Berlin at Reifträgerweg, only a few minutes' walk from Heydrich's large detached house. Although his rank remained unaltered, his privileges expanded, and he now had a staff car, a maid whose salary was paid by the Government, and free access to Heydrich's social circle.

Six months of concentrated work for the SD had seasoned Stefan's outlook; what had begun as lockjawed disgust had turned into a routine with an upward spiral, a day-to-day programme of furthering himself without doing too much damage to innocent people along the way.

He had learned how to quieten his conscience, and he had gained the knowledge from Heydrich himself. The great goal in the SD was completed paperwork; closed cases and concluded investigations formed a bulwark that had to be thickened and made taller as a prime objective.

Heydrich had explained it to Stefan when they attended a birthday party for Reichsführer Himmler in October.

'We're all judged on our record,' Heydrich said. 'And records are what give you and me the power to judge others. The more detailed the records, the better. The state of Germany's security can be gauged at any moment by simply checking the files at headquarters. A man's reliability can be gauged from a check of the files on his family and associates, and so on. Without our records, we're impotent.'

That was the key to Heydrich's indifference to the suffering that went on daily. Everything, everybody, ended up as paper. The tortures, the deprivations of people's lives were merely transient matters on the road to tidy reports and completed dossiers. Stefan could not accommodate such barren objectivity in his heart, but he could adopt it as an expedient. There was a trick to avoiding concern for people, and it lay in pretending that only the paperwork was real.

By stages Stefan had become Number Two Interrogation Officer. He could have been Number One, if Heydrich had not liked Feder so much and kept him in his position out of long-standing respect. The small brass nameplate had been taken off the cubicle Stefan first occupied at headquarters, and it had been replaced with a much larger plate, on the door of a larger office. There was a personal secretary now, a squat sexless brunette who showed Stefan the kind of respect usually reserved for people at Heydrich's level. Life had altered dramatically. Stefan Gaiser was a respected officer of the SS, a man with a clearly-mapped future in the hierarchy of the Third Reich. He was also a man hated by more people than he might have guessed, people to whom his name represented as much brutality as that of Heydrich.

In the summer of 1936 Heydrich appointed Stefan to the post of Controller in the SD records and statistical unit, at that time situated in Berlin. Stefan's brief was clear-cut: he had to enforce discipline, and maintain a constant watch for security risks among the three hundred personnel.

Stefan took to the job as if it were an act of atonement. From his office on the top floor of the building – a room not unlike Heydrich's own at SD headquarters – he operated a reign of terror that worsened his public reputation and simultaneously revived his faith in his mission. His victims now were all loyal Nazis, and he bullied them without mercy. Modelling his style on Heydrich's, he appointed no confidantes and kept fellow officers at a distance. Through a team of secretaries he stepped up the work load on every member of the staff: records had to be filed in duplicate, and the sub-divisions in the index were multiplied, so that one reference point in any given record could have as many as five sub-references, which in turn could be further adorned with offshoots. After two months there was a congratulatory memo from Reichsführer Himmler, and by late summer extra staff were drafted in to cope with the masses of microscopic detail that were now appended to official dossiers and statistical analyses. Stefan worked like a demon, maintaining standards to a hair's breadth of his own specifications, punishing defaulters harshly and never issuing praise. In August, he was informed that he would shortly have his first formal introduction to the Führer.

The audience, to Stefan's surprise, was private. The usual form was for promising young officers to be introduced at official gatherings such as banquets or receptions. On those occasions Hitler would be given a brief summary of the officers' achievements, and there would be a handshake, a word or two of praise from the Führer, and nothing more. But on the warm afternoon Stefan was ushered into the large private office on the first floor of the Chancellor's residence, there were only three other people present. Bormann sat behind a desk by the side window and an aide sorted through maps and papers at a long table along the opposite wall. Hitler was at his desk near the centre of the floor, and as Stefan entered he stood up and extended his hand.

'So you are our new broom,' he said, and he squeezed Stefan's hand warmly. 'Reichsführer Himmler and Obergruppenführer Heydrich have been lavish in their praise for you.'

Stefan murmured something about being flattered. There was no chair for him to sit on, so after shaking the Führer's hand he stood back stiffly and hoped he looked less awkward than he felt. Bormann, he observed, was staring. He always seemed to be staring.

'We are pleased with your revisionist policy at SD records, Gaiser,' Hitler said. 'I have also examined your previous record in interrogation work. You appear to fit a mould which the principles of our movement imposes, and you fit it extremely well. Tell me, what shape does your present ambition take?'

'Still that of the mould, Führer. I am keen to exert myself to the fullest in the service of the Reich's best interests.'

Hitler nodded. In the golden light of the large room he looked well, and his blue eyes were brightly attentive. 'But specific ambition, tell me about that.'

After a moment of thought, Stefan said, 'I would like to gain a total understanding in internal security work, Führer. The SD is large and growing larger. I know I have administrative flair, but I think I would administer best from a position of complete knowledge.'

Again Hitler nodded, while Bormann went on staring. 'So you feel that the security of the Reich is your mission. Good. Splendid. I think I can promise that you will gain all the experience and understanding you are seeking. All the Reich will ever ask of you is that you maintain your present high standards of service.' Hitler stood up and shook Stefan's hand again. 'It has been a pleasure to meet you, Gaiser.'

The interview had lasted less than two minutes, but as he left the building Stefan knew he had broken an important barrier. Hitler's time was precious, and even ambassadors rarely spent more than a few minutes with him. Wheels were turning, Stefan assured himself. The ground was shifting.

One week after the audience with Hitler, Heydrich appointed a deputy to Stefan's department. The man was a former divisional head at SD headquarters, and was charged with the task of learning the administrative ropes at the records and statistical department. He was to be Stefan's successor, and it took three months of punishing tuition to get him ready: the man had been the brunt of so much bullying himself that he could hardly wait to take control of the whip. Stefan had fashioned a duplicate, one without foresight or much ingenuity, who could take up where he had left off. The new Controller would go through the motions of control in an environment Stefan had shaped, as Heydrich put it, to work like a high-efficiency treadmill.

From December 1936 to June 1937, the pace of Stefan's life accelerated and his store of experience became so crammed and varied that he scarcely noticed the time passing.

'Regard the next six or seven months as a period of advanced training,' Heydrich told him. 'And if you find the time, try to spot a few of your future enemies.'

For a month Stefan worked in the counter-espionage decoding station in Munich, where he learned that spies in London, Paris and Washington regularly sent in reports that were in the main superfluous. He was glad to be away from the role of administrator, however, and he spent the time in Munich catching up on his reading and visiting the theatres. That period of comparative relaxation proved to be a mistake, for in early January he was transferred to a special security squad investigating the activities of civilian police in Berlin, and there again he was expected to leave a deep SS imprint behind him.

The sudden change of gear affected Stefan's health. He was an interrogator again, harrying police officers suspected of low sympathy towards the political administration. Stefan was leaning on men who were themselves trained leaners, and the work was exhausting. There were sleepless nights, days when he could only assert his special qualities by resorting to barbarous threats, weekends taken up with drug-induced rest and occasional fits of despair. When Stefan's term of duty with the squad was over, he had lost ten pounds in weight and gained more enemies than he could count. He determined, after that, never to let up again, for the torture of renewed effort was more than the strain of sustained drive.

For several weeks he joined an élite bodyguard unit, and realized quickly that he was being tested under fire. His duties included the setting up of security arrangements in advance of tours and visits by Himmler, Göering and Goebbels, and active guard work at four receptions attended by Hitler. As usual, Stefan worked at being a loner, even within tightly-formed groups, and again he made enemies, SS enemies who had resented him in advance.

The first time Stefan killed a man, he simultaneously put himself beyond the reach of all his latest opponents, and ensured that a number of the older ones would give him a wide berth in future.

A rally of the Hitler Youth was being staged in Nuremberg. Thousands of humourless children stood in square formations, facing the granite dais with its fluttering standards. Beyond the young fanatics there were an estimated twenty thousand more people, the enthralled populace come to gaze at and be hypnotized by another display of superhuman unity and might. Effectively, the Hitler Youth formed a safety barrier between the uncoordinated crowd and the Führer's dais, but even so the security precautions were massive. A side guard of eighty uniformed SS men stood to attention with cocked guns in their holsters: the holster flaps had been modified with brass clips soldered to the flap edges, so that they appeared to be closed but were in fact open, and pistols could be drawn in a second. A further one hundred plainclothes Gestapo men were in the crowd with revolvers at the ready in their coat pockets, and on either side of the dais there were ten SS officers, facing the daunting rectangles of well-scrubbed boys and ready to shoot anything that moved the wrong way.

Stefan, positioned at the end of the row on the left of the dais, had sighted his target a full five minutes before the Führer's arrival. Others would have noticed the man too, if they had not been so confident in the safety of their numbers, or so moved to emotion by the relayed music. The uniform was wrong, for a start: the man was dressed as a Wehrmacht Feldwebel, and he had attached himself to the edge of a group of similarly uniformed spectators, but he was wearing his marksmanship lanyard between the third and fourth tunic buttons, instead of the second and third. Even at a distance of ten yards his nervousness was obvious. He looked around too much, and he did not stand like a soldier. He also looked down at the ground when another soldier turned his way, and not once did he match the mob responses around him as standards went up and tunes hit their crescendos.

When the first flank of Hitler's party began to file on to the dais, Stefan lost all remaining doubt. He had seen the hundred faces of deception, seen them and seen through them, and the man he was watching had now abandoned his own weak front for the worst giveaway of all, a stern, immobile expression that his features could not support.

At that range and angle, Stefan decided, the man could not shoot with any accuracy – and the short time at his disposal made the likelihood even more remote. If he was a Communist, or a member of some other fanatical group, he would be prepared to risk his life, so there was every chance he *would* fire a shot, however wild. He might even try to rush the dais. Stefan went on watching for another minute, and as the crowd grew agitated at the imminent arrival of the Führer, he saw the man take his first short step forward, and on the second step his hand went deep into his tunic pocket. The hand was halfway out again when Stefan took his decision. He strode out of rank and heard the officers beside him gasp. He looked straight at the impostor in the ill-fitting uniform, willing the man to see him, to turn and run and have at least some chance. But instead the man pulled out his Stechkin automatic and levelled it. Stefan's Luger came up first and two bullets hit the man in the chest, knocking him back into the group of soldiers. For a moment there was chaos, during which Stefan stood still, a focus of order, an answer to the sudden mystery.

The advantage of any win, large or small, is that it opens a momentary gap for further success. The lesson of the follow-through, as demonstrated by Heydrich, had not been lost on Stefan. His report later that day, neatly typed while the dead man was being identified as an old-style Anarchist, not only underlined his own alertness, but implied saddening lack of that quality in his fellow security officers. The reverberations of that report echoed on for weeks, and as some officers were demoted and others disciplined, all of them assigned Stefan Gaiser to their unspoken lists of men to be avoided.

The coming of war did much to consolidate Stefan's position. The Nazi machine looked outward now, the pre-war obsession with nest-cleaning diminished. As Poland was invaded and Danzig annexed, as Pomerania and Silesia were overrun and the Russians began their assault from the east, Heydrich started behaving like a naughty child whose parents were away. He created the RSHA, absorbing a dozen semi-independent security units into the Reich Security Main Office. He built internment units in Poland, and under Himmler's admiring gaze he began implementing the biggest act of racial suppression in history.

As an energetic and trusted associate, Stefan Gaiser was promoted to SS Hauptsturmführer, Captain, and he was granted a free hand in forming his own internal security unit.

'You're a specialist,' Heydrich told him, 'and you know your ground well enough to be left alone. Keep up the pressure, Stefan. We have a reputation to maintain.'

By 1940, when Norway and Denmark were being invaded and Churchill had formed his National Government in Britain, Stefan was running a security agency in Berlin which bore the official title of Reich Security Special Investigations Branch: elsewhere, among people with reason to hate or fear the administration, the square building on the Reichenhallerstrasse was known as the Black House. On 14th June, the day the Germans entered Paris, a Wehrmacht Oberstleutnant called Klausmann arrived at the Black House and asked to see Captain Gaiser on urgent business. He waited for an hour, and when he was finally shown into the Director's office he found Stefan seated behind an enormous desk, drumming his fingers and frowning at a sheet of yellow paper in front of him.

The seniority of Klausmann's rank did not matter in that place. Stefan was SS, and he controlled his own investigation division, which gave him the right to remain seated even when a Wehrmacht General walked in. He waved Klausmann to a chair and told him to state his business.

'I've come to return this to you,' Klausmann said. He handed Stefan a small silver-plated watch fob.

Astonished, Stefan turned the trinket over in his fingers, recognizing the fine scratches on its surface, remembering the feel of its chased edges. Emma Fisher had bought it for him on his one and only visit to Petticoat Lane. He squinted across at Klausmann, questioning the man with his eyes.

'I had to bring something you would recognize.'

'You're not making yourself clear, Oberstleutnant.' Stefan closed his fist around the fob, the way he had held it often in the first days of his relationship with Emma.

He was giving Klausmann a look of irritated puzzlement and scanning his face for a sign of deception.

'I admire your caution,' Klausmann said, smiling. 'You left that trinket at your mother's house in England.'

Stefan went on staring.

'Your mother is in reasonably good health, although she has not been properly well for years.'

'One minute to explain this babble, Klausmann, then I get the guard in here.' There was nothing Stefan could detect, not a flicker. The man appeared to be genuine, but appearances meant nothing.

Klausmann sighed, gazing at the ceiling for a moment. 'My name really is Klausmann, and I'm in the Wehrmacht. Like you, I am a servant of Whitehall.'

Stefan reached for the intercom button.

'One thing,' Klausmann said hastily, 'one small thing that may convince you. Six months ago I met a man in Zurich. His name is Albert Murray. He spoke of you affectionately. Apparently he once gave you a very sore shoulder.'

Stefan jabbed the intercom. When the guard opened the door a look of alarm spread across Klausmann's face, and that was enough for Stefan.

'Guard, see that we are not disturbed, for any reason.'

The guard left and Stefan sat back in his chair. 'You took long enough to get in touch,' he said.

Klausmann took a few seconds to compose himself. 'I think you were warned it might take a long time,' he said finally.

'Have you any idea what I've been through? Do you even have a notion of what I've done in the interests of making myself a good Nazi?'

'Yes, well, the job is demanding, isn't it? None of us ever believed it would be a picnic . . .'

'But *this*,' Stefan jabbed his finger on the desk, 'this job, Klausmann! No sane man outside Germany would believe what it entails. And all the time the feeling, the conviction sometimes that I was in it for keeps, abandoned . . .'

'I can guess,' Klausmann said. 'But the risks, you understand. The whole operation is so fragile. A year ago there was a move to reassure you that you hadn't been forgotten, but the man concerned lost his cover and had to go back to desk duty in London.'

'One man?' Stefan resisted the urge to raise his voice. 'Surely there was somebody else? All I needed was to know the Department still existed. There's nothing in Reich Intelligence reports to suggest it does, or ever did.'

Klausmann nodded. 'Precisely. The very best secrecy is maintained by taking the fewest risks. You were appointed an agent of SOE.' His voice went very low at the mention of the name, even though the walls and door were as thick as any in Berlin. 'But officially, SOE was not formed, and had no real function, until this year. There were drawbacks, objections, administrative hazards, the usual trip-wires of bureaucracy . . .'

'I couldn't care less,' Stefan hissed. 'I was dumped here, right in the middle of this cesspit, and *left*.'

'I understand how you feel,' Klausmann said. 'But the waiting is over. You become active as of now.'

Stefan sighed. 'So what happens?'

'Well, you were recruited as somebody rather special, and that's how you'll stay. You've done a lot better than anyone suspected you would, so no untoward risks will be taken with your cover.' Klausmann smiled placatingly. 'You will have low-line contact.'

'Meaning?' Stefan said acidly. 'I've been out of touch for a while, remember.'

Klausmann folded his hands, looking more like a schoolteacher than a soldier. 'SOE has several sections. And there will be more as time passes. You will have contact with none of them. Instead, it's been arranged that you make your communications through an American agent, operating on behalf of the US Central Office of Information.'

'When?'

'You'll be told. The agent himself will make contact, and from then on he will be the only line you'll have.'

Stefan slapped the top of the desk. 'Can't you give me an idea? Will it be a week, a month?'

'Perhaps longer.' The slight apology in Klausmann's voice only irritated Stefan further. 'For the present, you must rest assured that you are an important component of British Intelligence inside Germany. Great value is being placed on you.'

'I'm gratified. And meanwhile I'll go on persecuting men and women who commit the crime of democracy, and a lot of others more innocent than that.' Stefan leaned across the desk, tapping the yellow sheet of paper as he did so. 'Have you any idea what this is, Klausmann? It's an execution order. One sweep of the pen and I'm a murderer. I've been avoiding these for a long time, but I can't any longer. And next, I know, they'll expect me to start laying the hammer on the Jews, whole families and communities of them. What in Christ are they playing at in England? They know what's going on, why can't they let me pass along what I know? I could have stopped a lot happening these past two years, if only I'd had a line out of here . . .'

'They cherish you,' Klausmann said simply. 'Risk has to be minimal. When the time comes, you'll be in a position to pass on as much as you can. On orders emanating from the office of the Prime Minister himself, you are to be used only when the optimum levels of safety can be implemented. No other agents of SOE will know you even exist. You are precious, console yourself with that.'

Stefan waited another two years. During that time he was occasionally relieved to learn that other agents were operating near him, although he never knew who they were. Reich security reports listed breaches of top-level communiqués, interceptions of radio messages and frequent acts of sabotage that could only have been perpetrated by British spies. Americans, notably since the bombing of Pearl Harbor in 1941, had started to operate inside Germany, Poland and France. The security forces were being harassed, but the war went on, and the covert business of genocide went forward by leaps and bounds. By January 1942, Stefan was still at the Black House, with occasional breaks to join the Führer's entourage. Silently he prayed for someone to call on him, to prove that he really was on active service.

In March, when he was rejoicing that the RAF had bombed Lübeck, Stefan's small pleasure turned to the coldest despair he had ever experienced: he accompanied Reichsführer Himmler to the sprawling complex of buildings and wired compounds at Oswiecim, the place the Germans called Auschwitz.

Although he saw nothing of the horrors he would learn about later, the gas chambers, the ovens, the sheds full of spectacles, teeth and human hair, Stefan nevertheless knew he was in the midst of something too atrocious for one mind to comprehend. The place had a smell of death, and as Himmler prattled on about the need for efficiency in deploying Jewish labour, and the equal need for a firm administrative policy to handle the growing numbers of deportees, Stefan looked through windows and into compounds and saw misery etched on the faces of men, women, and children too young to cope with sustained cruelty and deprivation. The visit was intended by Himmler to be an informative event for promising young men under his command: Stefan found it so informative that on the same evening he swore he would give it three more months, and if no one made contact in that time, he would remove himself to England, whatever the consequences.

By the end of April, he had revised his plan. He would still wait until June, and if he was still in operational limbo he would *still* quit, but on the way back to England he would do more damage to the Germans than a formation of tanks. The idea of revenge sustained him through weeks of continuing so-called security work against German citizens and Poles, and Stefan's dreams became filled with schemes for sabotage, mass disruption and selective, retributive killing.

In May, something happened which eased the pressure on Stefan's mind and brought back his capacity for patience and hope.

Heydrich was appointed head of the Einsatzgruppen, the extermination squads that slaughtered Jews in their tens of thousands in the occupied eastern territories. The impetus of that authority carried Heydrich forward suddenly faster, making him more remote, even from Stefan. Keeping his own counsel and manipulating every advantage, he soon engineered for himself the appointment of Reich Protector of Bohemia-Moravia. Within weeks of taking the post, Heydrich had earned himself an alternative title among the Czech people. He was called the Butcher of Prague.

On the afternoon of 27th May, careless as usual of his personal safety, Heydrich left his castle in Prague to drive to the airport. At a sharp bend in the road two Free Czech agents, flown in from London, appeared a few feet from the car. One had a Sten gun, which refused to fire when he pulled the trigger. His companion had a pistol and a grenade, and after a moment of frozen panic he threw the grenade at the side of the car. It exploded but Heydrich appeared to be unhurt. He leapt from the partial wreckage, firing his pistol as his attackers ran off, and then suddenly he collapsed. A week later, despite the efforts of several eminent surgeons, Heydrich died of the gangrene that had been caused by a small wound in his back.

There was something magical for Stefan in Heydrich's assassination. The puppet master had gone, it *was* possible for the people to overthrow something so ultimately vile and seemingly invulnerable in its black omnipotence. Even on the 6th June, when Himmler ordered a reprisal for the death of his deputy and let his senior murder squad destroy every man, woman and child in the Czech village of Lidice, Stefan could sustain his hope. One charmed life had been cancelled; therefore so could the others.

Then in late July Stefan was visited at his home by a man in a heavy overcoat, horn-rimmed glasses and a wide-brimmed hat. He showed both the maid and the armed adjutant in the hall his documentation, which said he was Johann Kasche, a regional overseer with the Gestapo Political Investigations Department: his identity card bore the stamp of the ultimate authority, Himmler's full police title spread in capitals across the open wings of the eagle – REICHSFÜHRER SS UND CHEF DER DEUTSCHEN POLIZEI IM REICHSMINISTERIUM DES INNERN. The adjutant, daunted into near silence, led the man to the upstairs room where Stefan worked during the evenings.

When the identification had been flashed again and Stefan decided it would be as well to stand for his visitor, the adjutant left the room, taking with him the warning that they were not to be disturbed.

'What precisely can I do for you?' Stefan asked.

The visitor removed his hat and threw it on a chair, then took off his glasses and put them in his coat pocket. 'You could give me a drink,' he said in English, 'if you've got anything better than the Kraut piss I've been swallowing for the past couple of months.'

Stefan blinked at him. In his best clipped German, he said, 'I beg your pardon?'

The visitor grinned and started unbuttoning his overcoat. 'Your Uncle Thomas sends his apologies for the time you've had to wait.'

Stefan went on staring, his mouth tightly shut.

'Jesus, you're careful, aren't you?' The man scratched his stubbly hair for a moment. Then he said, 'Dorian Goode is still as fat as ever. How's that?'

It was the fierce candour of the man's eyes that made Stefan relax suddenly. It was always hard to tell the truth when it was merely heard: seeing it as well as hearing it, Stefan felt a sharp pang that was like a homecoming. 'Sit down,' he said in English. 'I've got a bottle of Johnnie Walker somewhere.'

They both had a drink before another word was said. Watching the man swallow his Scotch, Stefan recalled that he had been holding an image of someone thin and furtive. The visitor was built like a prize-fighter, and he looked every inch the extrovert.

'My name's Farrell,' he said as soon as the first glass was drained. 'Ralph Farrell. In OSS stage-talk, I'm Janus.'

Reich security and counterintelligence had compiled a small file on OSS. It had been officially formed only recently, under the direction of a General Donovan, known in military circles as Wild Bill. The function of the Office of Strategic Services was vague, to the Nazis at least, but it appeared to have supplanted the Central Office of Information, which had been a national security organization. In Berlin circles it was believed that OSS was probably an outfit geared to assist resistance movements.

'Can I take it you're my contact, at long last?' Stefan asked.

Farrell nodded. 'Your one and only line out.'

'It was a bit risky, coming here . . .'

'Naw.' Farrell waved his glass and Stefan refilled it. 'I bet my papers look as real as yours. And who'd recognize me afterwards, anyway?'

Stefan shrugged. 'You're probably right. I haven't had any practice at real spying. All my time so far has been taken up being a Nazi.'

'You did a good job,' Farrell said. 'The big worry in London was that you'd get assassinated before you could go operational.'

'It could happen yet. I've made myself unpopular.'

'And well-informed, I hope.' Farrell savoured the drink, rolling it on his tongue.

'Oh yes, I know a lot. And I've known a lot that would

have been useful before. So much of my time here has been a waste.'

'You'll have a chance to make up for that. As much as you can get, I'll take off your hands and pass along. When there's a need for anything specific, I'll always let you know.' Farrell took a folded slip of paper from his pocket and handed it to Stefan. 'That's a list of places in Munich where I can meet you without any trouble. We can work to a rota.'

'Munich? Wouldn't it have been easier to work here in Berlin?'

'Easier, yes. Safer, no.'

'Whatever you say. I'll be glad enough to work against the system for a change.'

Farrell was shaking his head gently, smiling. 'It's hard to believe you aren't one of them. Just for a second when I came in, I got the feeling I'd made a mistake.'

'No mistake,' Stefan reassured him. 'Talking of credibility, have you had any trouble passing yourself off as a German?'

'None. I've been speaking the language since I was a kid. All our neighbours were German immigrants, and my mother spoke it as fluently as English. The rest's easy. I just exaggerate everything I do.'

'But your cover – isn't it kind of difficult, with you not having the background I have? I mean, they can trace me all the way back, and on paper it looks fine.'

'I've got no single identity,' Farrell said. 'I turn up as somebody different every two or three days. I've got three safe addresses, so I get to relax occasionally. Also, I'm in touch with other OSS operatives, and we can help each other when there's any danger of the cover getting blown. Another big help is Nazi bureaucracy.'

'How do you mean?'

Farrell smiled. 'Their paperwork's so clotted and complicated, nobody really knows nowadays just who orders who else to do anything. If you're OK for identification, then you're just about fireproof. I get the feeling I could go around with a Field Marshal's ID and get away with it.'

They talked for a few more minutes, then Farrell left. Before he went, Stefan gave him a summary of troop movements in and around Stalingrad. He had picked up the information by memorizing a report he had read upside-down on a desk at the Chancellory.

In bed that night, letting his thoughts drift alternately between Gretl and his new, cleaner image of himself, Stefan began to feel the hardening of his resolve, a sensation that had been delayed, it seemed, for ages.

'*I'm at work*,' he whispered. Now it was no longer theory, no longer a dying expectation. Farrell gave him confidence, too; he looked and sounded competent, he had the marks of a winner. All the foul yesterdays, the deepening seven-year rut of involvement, looked more like a route-map for success now.

On the edge of sleep he saw his mother, perhaps the first clear thought of her for years, and then he saw Eric and Sara. Symbols, Stefan decided, beloved reminders of what peace and freedom meant for him. It made him feel warm when he saw himself as a crusader, fighting for the right of people to be who they were.

He smiled against the pillow, realizing there was more of his mother's sentimentality in him than he had thought. There were worse ways to be, and he believed he was acquainted with most of them.

Between August 1942 and the summer of 1944, Ralph Farrell received enough information from Stefan to fill a small history of the period. In frequently exhaustive detail, Stefan passed on advance warnings of such events as Rommel's offensive at Alam Halfa, the all-out assault on Stalingrad, and the renewed air attacks on London. He even supplied drawings of the V-2 rocket, and provided site details of the rocket-building installations at Peenemünde. The figures for penal transportations were reported just as faithfully, together with all the information Stefan could get on military deployment, weapons manufacture inside the Reich, actual army strengths and a welter of facts about the concentration camp system, including names of prominent detainees, camp superintendents, throughput of prisoners and the estimated weekly rate of executions. Stefan worked like a beaver, and as his stature within the SS continued to increase, so did the quality and quantity of his messages.

July 1944

An impromptu meeting of the Three Wise Men – Douglas Cheever, Rollo Nesmith and Thomas Malcolm – had convened when Cheever and Nesmith, out to a meagre dinner at the Savoy, had bumped into Malcolm in the bar. Although the men worked as a team, they rarely had the opportunity to get together without the stifling attendance of other Whitehall people, principally those on the staff of the Ministry for Economic Warfare.

'Not an opportunity to be missed, this,' Nesmith said. 'Why don't we find ourselves a table somewhere and have a natter?'

The team was unique, even by wartime standards. Between them they controlled the movements of over one hundred agents known, in Intelligence circles, as Prebendaries. The name had been decided upon by Rollo Nesmith, whose customary melancholia thrust most of his ideas in the direction of the Church. A Prebendary was a spy possessing talents that set him apart from ordinary agents: Nesmith had responsibility for a team of safe-crackers, Douglas Cheever controlled a swarm of multi-gifted assassins, and it was Thomas Malcolm's job to oversee the élite among the sleepers inside Reich administration. Although all three worked specifically for Special Operations Executive, their Prebendary exercise was generally accepted as being something apart.

Thomas Malcolm ordered brandies and was surprised when the waiter did no more than nod and walk off.

'Things must be looking up,' Cheever murmured. He was the youngest, a man of forty with thinning hair and permanently tired eyes. 'Last time I asked for a brandy in a restaurant bar they laughed.'

'It's Malcolm's style,' Nesmith said. 'He can seduce obedience out of anything that moves.' Nesmith's jowls waggled for a moment, indicating that he was being humorous. Of the three, he was the only one actually sure of a knighthood and that gave him an edge of authority, although in terms of power they were all strictly equal. Patting his large stomach thoughtfully, Nesmith added, 'Next thing you know, he'll be wangling us caviar.'

Cheever made a face. 'Not with the brandy, I hope.' His eyes went a shade sadder. 'I can't remember when I last tasted a good, dry white wine.'

'Ahem.' Nesmith patted the table softly. 'Since we've managed to foregather without the shrikes and buzzards for once, I think we might have a policy chinwag.' He blinked at Cheever. 'What's this I hear about Churchill poking his nose into the Dutch thing?'

'What's the Dutch thing?' Thomas Malcolm asked.

'Freiwilligen-Legion Niederlande,' Cheever said, displaying his grasp of German pronunciation. 'The Dutch SS, in other words.'

'So?' Thomas Malcolm looked from one man to the other. 'I know who they are. But what's this about Churchill?'

'The gang in question,' Nesmith said, 'was officially disbanded in May last year, at Grafenwöhr in Germany. They were badly shot up, and the Dutch resistance assassinated their leader, Lieutenant-General Seyffardt. We were happy to write them off the books, but it appears they're massing again, or trying to.'

Cheever was nodding, and he took up the story as soon as Nesmith paused. 'Some of my chaps were on to the people behind the new volunteer group. They reported back and I was on the brink of giving the order to make erasures when Winnie put the block on it.'

Thomas Malcolm was surprised. 'That's not like him at all. It's not really his style to interfere in our affairs so pointedly, for that matter.'

Rollo Nesmith tasted his brandy and made his best effort at a smile. 'I've heard a theory. He's got a little espionage unit of his own going in the Netherlands. If it's true, we might be in for some shocks. Loss of control, for one. It's always been agreed that we be left alone, but nobody ever made it a law. My informant reckons that our leader, in his wisdom, believes the existing service isn't up to scratch.'

Thomas Malcolm was suddenly and uncomfortably aware that Nesmith and Cheever were staring at him.

'It could be,' Nesmith said slowly, without taking his eyes off Malcolm, 'that Churchill's loss of face in certain quarters is forcing him to look for a few new areas where he can shine. There's no denying that recent rumblings have attracted his attention to our patch.'

Swirling his brandy, Thomas Malcolm said, 'I presume you're referring to the disappointing show put up by our man inside the Nazi circus.'

Nesmith nodded. 'That, among other things. There's no point denying it, your nephew hasn't exactly lived up to expectations.' The reference to kinship was accompanied by a swift, sidelong glance at Cheever, who was trying to look suitably embarrassed. 'It's got to a point,' Nesmith went on, 'where we might well be asked to report on the matter, to no less a predator than the head of the Political Warfare Executive. Once we admit a defect to that estimable gentleman, we might as well forget any ideas we had about independence.'

'I have the feeling,' Thomas Malcolm said sharply, 'that I'm being blamed.'

'Not at all,' Nesmith assured him. 'The Gaiser chap was not your choice alone; he impressed other people. And he's not the only agent, God knows, who's disappointed us.'

Cheever cleared his throat. 'Nobody expected quite so much of the others,' he pointed out. 'The stuff Gaiser's been sending in could be picked up, for the most part, from the intercept radio outfits. And when something *does* look good, it's usually all wrong.'

Thomas Malcolm had decided he did not want his brandy. Staring at the table cloth, he said, 'I admit, I don't understand it. He's a good chap, I'd stake everything on that. The poor quality of material he's been sending us is as big a mystery to me as it is to you.'

'Now, now,' Nesmith said soothingly, 'I'm sure it'll all work out fine. Gaiser could be under all sorts of suspicion and pressure, for all we know . . .'

'You wouldn't think it, looking at the press pictures.' Cheever was making no attempt to hide the acid now. 'I wouldn't be surprised to hear he's been made deputy Führer, next.'

Before Thomas Malcolm could say anything, Nesmith put up a hand. 'End of topic, gentlemen. Let's sup our brandy and rake over a few of our other worries.'

The matter was left there, but it burned in Thomas Malcolm's mind for the rest of the evening. His personal hopes for Stefan, amounting to a paternal pride, had been sliding fast, in spite of every emotional argument he could raise. The information was useless most of the time, as Cheever had implied so heavily. It was feeble, inaccurate, often downright misleading. And it could start a landslide for the Three Wise Men.

On his way home that night, driving through a sluggish rain across London's dark streets, Thomas decided that it was best, for his morale and his professional efficiency, to put the whole matter from his mind. It would no doubt be raised again, soon enough, on some classified memo or other. Until that time he would replace his small despair with a stubborn, unthinking hope. At any minute there might be a reversal; Stefan would pass along a piece of monumental intelligence, and all doubts, rumours and misgivings, would be cancelled. Much better to hold on to that attitude, Thomas told himself, than face the depressing facts.

August, 1944

Going to live in Munich had been something Gretl Bauer had dreaded, but the reality had proved pleasant. Her transfer from the administrative offices of Ordnungspolizei, the civilian police, to the records and statistical unit of Sicherheitspolizei, the security police, had meant her leaving Berlin, the city where she had grown up. None of the expected wrenches had taken place. The people in Munich were the same as those in Berlin, Gretl's work became more varied and interesting, and she saw just as much of Stefan as she had before. In addition, she now had a larger and more comfortable apartment.

Because Gretl worked daily with the raw materials of official secrecy and could accept the keeping of secrets as a part of living, she had no difficulty in believing that her relationship with Stefan should be a fact known only to themselves. He had explained it all to her carefully and Gretl found no flaws in Stefan's argument. She had not looked for any. He was an officer of the SS engaged on work that put him close to the Führer, and such men were expected to keep themselves apart from civilian society, except on official occasions. Gretl Bauer was an ordinary government employee. No one would object to a girl like her going out with soldiers, but SS officers, particularly those who moved in the circle of power around Hitler, were beyond her reach.

When Stefan arrived that night Gretl looked radiant. He had seen it happen often – the smallest of pleasures would light up her face, a reaction that sophistication and experience had never diminished. She hugged Stefan and buried her face against his shoulder, but when she looked up at him her wide blue eyes were brimming with tears.

'If I'd known I was going to upset you, I wouldn't have come,' Stefan said.

'Silly.' She touched his arm and wiped her eyes. 'Your timing's perfect. I was feeling sorry for myself tonight.'

Stefan ruffled her short hair, dark gold in the lamplight. 'Come and sit down. Tell me your troubles.' He kissed her cheek and led her to the small settee by the fireplace.

'It's my father again,' Gretl said. 'He's had a visit from the PK men. This time they're accusing him of spreading Communist ideology.'

'Your father's big enough to weather it.' Stefan had never met Konrad Bauer, but he was familiar with the man's record. He was an old-school liberal, a minor diplomat who had pre-war ties with Goering. His job for the past two years had been to indoctrinate members of the hastily formed SS Legions in Denmark, Holland and elsewhere. Once or twice in the course of his duties he had been criticized for passing on a diluted brand of Nazism. The objections, Stefan knew, were purely technical. No one doubted Bauer's loyalty.

'He doesn't keep up with the revisions,' Gretl sighed. 'Half the time he's preaching from the early manifestos and policy booklets. He gets so worried when Propaganda Kompanien go on at him. I wish they'd let him retire.'

'Maybe they will,' Stefan said. 'I'll see if anything can be arranged.'

Gretl moved closer to him. He could feel the tension draining out of her.

It was going to be hard to bring up what was foremost in his mind. The mood was soft already. Gretl was at her most feminine, at her most vulnerable, bathed and fragrant, wrapped in her dark pink robe. The room was warm, the silence like a balm. Stefan closed his eyes for a minute. Then Gretl provided him with an opening.

'We're losing this war, aren't we?'

Stefan turned to her.

'I'm aware of it all the time. All the hysteria, the desperation. And the way the security clamps are coming down. The anxious little memos flying about. Everything.

Germany's losing. I think we all know it at the department, but nobody says anything.'

'Nobody would dare.'

'Tell me Stefan, truthfully. Is there any chance?'

'There might be.' He was suddenly aware of the enormity of what he had to tell her. She knew already that he was less than a hundred percent loyal to the cause, that much had emerged when Stefan knew for certain that she hated more about the Nazi administration than she liked. And when he knew that she would keep things to herself. But it didn't make it any easier.

'Stefan, what's wrong?'

He hesitated. 'My love, everything is wrong. There just is not enough time . . .'

Kissing her hair, he sank into silence once more. She must not suffer. Whatever happened, she, alone amongst them all, must not be allowed to suffer.

They sat there, silent, still.

In the bedroom he marvelled at the beauty of her, bending naked by a chair and placing her robe over the back. Gretl Bauer had the distinction, unique in Stefan's experience, of being flawlessly attractive from every angle. His habit as he undressed was to catalogue, setting her down feature by feature in his mind, savouring his mingled lust and tenderness.The whisper of her short hair against the skin of her neck. Her shoulder blades, so small and fine they barely cast a shadow on the smoothness of her back, and above each firm, childish buttock, the near-impudence of a dimple. The smooth, tapering thighs, the fine down. He was staring at her when she turned, facing him with the easy-limbed candour that had grown from the first shy nights at his apartment.

'Are you going to stay like that forever?' she asked him.

Stefan realized he was frozen with his shirt half off. Smiling, he finished undressing and threw himself under the covers.

'I'm cold,' she whispered against his chest.

'Then I'll warm you.'

He put his hand on her back and slowly Gretl straightened, pressing herself close to him.

'You'll tell me I'm being a romantic again,' she said, 'but I keep wishing it could be like this all the time. This comfortable, I mean. This secure.'

Stefan was losing himself in the fresh scent of her skin, running his fingers over her back and shoulders. The need to make love increased slowly, gently impeded by the soft sensations of touching, tasting. Gretl's mouth had the familiarity he ached for when he was in his cot in Berlin, and her soft probing kisses gave him a sense of unity that was overwhelming. To be loved with such sensitivity came as close as ever to taking away his pain.

A whimper, barely audible, escaped Gretl's lips, and a new pleasure was on Stefan, a carnal revelling triggered by her hand curling around his penis. The innocence, the *cleanness* of Gretl made it all the more exciting to know she felt the need for this. Stiffening within her touch Stefan moved her on to her back and began licking her breasts, teasing the nipples with his tongue while his hand traced small circles on her parting thighs.

Paradise, he thought, and knew he meant it, would mean it always. The dark language of the flesh was not awkward to them, they had a fluency that had needed no learning.

As Gretl arched her stomach against Stefan's face there was a sudden break. Soft mental images hardened abruptly into unwelcome clarity. He saw Farrell and felt the alien chill of their traffic with each other: there was also the bleak awareness of the mission that had brought him to Gretl's apartment. Stefan clenched his eyes shut and strove to evade the perverse, deadening intrusion of duty.

'What's wrong?' Gretl reached for him, fear and worry in her eyes.

'Nothing,' he said, and realized he had been motionless above her on stiffened arms.

'Darling. Please.' Her arms were on his sides, trying to draw him down.

'Sorry, my love, sorry.' The warmth of her against him was salvation. With renewed urgency he kissed her eyes, cheeks and neck, with unusual haste he poised himself between her legs and allowed Gretl to guide him into her. Stefan rolled on his side, maintaining the steady rhythm, almost covering himself with her. Without willing it, he was hurrying, as if he might be deprived of his climax, and Gretl was adjusting to his pace, panting against his cheek, thrusting with her small, strong hips. With stiff-fingered hands Stefan traced and gripped the backs of her thighs, her buttocks. He heard his own snarl as his mouth closed on her neck and clamped there in a rough kiss as his back stiffened and release came. As he lay beside her, he realized that his face was wet with Gretl's tears.

For almost an hour he soothed her, holding her in his arms, crooning gentle solace when she said she had been frightened. Over and over he apologized and told her there was nothing wrong, nothing changed in the way he felt about her. Finally she slept.

The job had never entered the bedroom before, the clammy tendrils of duty had always stopped short at the door. Stefan argued with himself that it had happened only because he had lost the courage to ask for her help. A deeper voice told him he was some rarefied kind of bastard even to consider asking Gretl at all.

He sat up and folded his arms, watching her sleep. In that condition of mind, with his fondness for her brimming, he could never ask Gretl to take any risk, however slight. Daylight, of course, would make a difference, daylight and a few more hours of increasing urgency. But for the moment Stefan rejected that practical wisdom. The biggest truth before him was that he had used her as a shield and a diversion, as a whore. The priority was to gain her forgiveness for that.

The Obersalzberg, Hitler's fortified mountain near Berchtesgaden in South Bavaria, was ringed by two fences. The outer fence was nine miles long, the inner one almost two miles. Under the directions of Martin Bormann, forests, farms and small estates had been eradicated until an area of two-and-a-half square miles lay within the enclosure. Whole networks of payed roads had been made, there was a vast garage building, a barracks and even a hotel for the Führer's visitors. Thirty million marks had been spent on the access road to the Berghof, Hitler's house on top of the mountain, which had to be reached finally by an elevator blasted into the rock.

When Margarete Slezak stepped out on to the verandah she swayed and Stefan had to take her arm.

'I'm sorry,' she said. 'It was so dark in the elevator. The sudden brightness made me dizzy.'

'The altitude too, probably.' Stefan led her towards the main door. 'We're almost six-and-a-half thousand feet above the valley. I think you should rest for a few minutes before seeing the Führer.' Stefan had managed to contact Hitler that morning on his private telephone, and his orders were to take the guest directly to her quarters.

There were three uniformed guards by the door, who all smiled and nodded to Stefan. He led the way into the large hall and pointed to the stairway, where a maid was waiting with folded hands.

'If you will go with the girl, she will attend to you.'

Margarete Slezak thanked him and walked away. Stefan watched until she was halfway up the stairs. She had the controlled bearing of an aristocrat, and she was still very beautiful. When Stefan had called at her apartment early that morning she had received him calmly, and showed neither particular pleasure nor resistance when he passed on the Führer's invitation. They had travelled within two hours of that meeting, and throughout the journey the woman had expressed no curiosity about the visit. Whatever her business with Hitler, Fräulein Slezak had embarked on it with admirable self-assurance.

One of the girl stenographers came out of her room and waved to Stefan. He crossed to her and she informed him, in a half-whisper, that the Führer wanted to see him in the tea house. Stefan was amused. Bormann was obviously being kept out of the picture and the old man was passing on his orders through the clerical staff. Bormann would still know something was going on, of course, and he would be annoyed. It was very satisfying.

The walk to the tea house was long and narrow. It was patrolled by guards and Hitler's own two police dogs. Both animals knew Stefan and one trotted at his side for most of the twenty-minute walk, lifting its head and occasionally licking his hand. That was another aggravation to Bormann. He made elaborate displays of fussing and playing with the animals when the Führer was around, but they always ignored him, or they growled.

The tea house was built on Hitler's favourite vantage point, overlooking the Berchtesgaden valley. It was a round, single-roomed building, twenty-five feet in diameter, with small windows let into the wall at regular intervals. The helmeted guard by the door nodded sharply as Stefan approached. He tapped the door, and there was a muffled response from within. The guard nodded again and stood aside to let Stefan enter.

Hitler was in his easy chair by the round table. There was a tray beside him set with a teapot, crockery and some biscuits. He motioned for Stefan to sit down, then he leaned forward with obvious difficulty and began lifting the teapot.

'Let me do it, Führer.' Stefan poured fresh tea in the old man's cup and half-filled one for himself. From the corner of his eye he could see the tremor in Hitler's shoulder, and when he looked up and replaced the teapot, he saw that the deep-lined face was trembling, too. The lips were dark brown, as if something noxious had dried on them.

'Is the lady installed with us?'

'Yes, sir,' Stefan said, and eased down into a chair. 'She appeared to enjoy the journey here.'

'Good. You had no trouble finding her?'

'A little. She had moved a few times.'

Hitler nodded, rubbing the back of his right hand. His face was the colour of tallow, and his cheeks had sagged further since Stefan last saw him. It was clear he had suffered one of the frequent attacks Dr Morrell called palsies. They drained the Führer and left him listless for hours. The long walk to the tea house must have added its share of fatigue.

'Tell me,' Hitler said, 'is she still as handsome as her photograph?'

'A most attractive lady, Führer.'

Hitler seemed relieved. He pushed himself forward, leaning closer to Stefan. 'I'm grateful for your diligence, Gaiser. And I want you to remain diligent until Fräulein Slezak leaves. Speak to no one about her and answer no questions, from anybody. When the lady is ready to leave, I want you to return to Munich with her and conduct her safely home.'

'Of course, sir. How long will she be staying?'

'For as long as she wishes. I've suspended the normal afternoon routine for the duration of her stay. I will use the living room at the house, and Secretary Bormann has been instructed to leave me undisturbed. Try to see that nobody persuades him otherwise.' Hitler smiled. 'I am not expressing a lack of confidence in Secretary Bormann. I simply think his zealous approach to work can defeat his discretion, occasionally.'

'I understand, Führer.'

They talked for a few minutes more, and then Hitler said he wanted to rest. Stefan left him and returned to the house. In his quarters on the upper floor he sat by his desk and smoked a cigarette. He had not anticipated another visit to Munich so soon. In the records office downstairs there were at least five documents he had planned to copy during the coming week. With the uncertainty surrounding the length of Fräulein Slezak's stay, he would have to work overtime. OSS and OSE were always hungry for information. The files Stefan had in mind were too complex to copy quickly, so he would have to think of something else.

Then he remembered the camp file. The Allied Intelligence agencies were compiling a black book of Nazi war crimes with a view to a prosecution case after the war. Through Farrell, Stefan had been encouraged to compile a piecemeal dossier on the concentration camps in Germany and Poland. The material had less urgency than the other intelligence he gathered, but it was wanted nevertheless. In a few hours Stefan could have numerous detailed notes down in code, and however soon he had to go back to Munich, he would not go empty handed.

It took less than an hour of searching in the classified files to locate the latest information on three camps – Wolzec, Westerborg and Mauthausen. As usual, the aides and adjutants who came and went through the tall, narrow room ignored what Stefan was doing. The Führer often instructed him to compile statistical analyses of anything from the number of casualties on the Eastern Front to the weekly consumption of coal by German industry. Even Bormann had stopped asking him what he was doing.

He made pencil notes in a modified Pitman shorthand on the margins of pages covered with inked notes on other matters. The coded details were deliberately faint and quite invisible to anyone who did not know they were there. When Stefan had used up the margins of fifteen quarto sheets, he went back to the first row of files and took a quick look inside one that had puzzled him. Inside were three hand-drawn maps and five slips of paper covered with typed notes. The contents and the loose arrangement did not tally with any of the other files, and on a swift impulse Stefan decided to borrow the entire folder.

Back in his quarters he transferred the shorthand to eight pages of a miniature notebook he carried in the side of his boot. Then he carefully erased the original notes.

The mystery file remained a mystery for nearly an hour. The notes were sparse, in a hand that Stefan eventually recognized as General Jodl's, and the style had the clipped, disjointed manner of the General's speech. The maps were sketchy approximations of territory in Belgium and Northern France, with certain areas lined heavily in red. The Bastogne—Brussels—Antwerp line was heaviest of all. Stefan decided to copy the maps as precisely as he could, tracing them on to thin paper and duplicating the colours. As the accompanying notes seemed to follow no order, he made one long transcript and set it before him. After two readings a vague sense emerged.

On the third reading, using the maps in conjunction with the notes, Stefan began to get excited.

What he was reading was a first draft for a battle campaign, a huge offensive aimed at the destruction of Allied forces and supply bases in the West. The word 'potential' cropped up frequently, as did 'possible' and 'probable'. This was what Hitler was fond of calling a Likelihood Study; dozens of such files appeared every month, but they were never so hurried or disorganized as this one. There was no date on the notes, but they had to be recent or Stefan would have seen them before. And for all their vagueness one certainty showed through: the chosen line of initial attack would be in the Ardennes, where General Troy Middleton's US 8th Corps was formed along a seventy-five mile front, from Monschau south to Echternach.

Stefan looked up from the notes and stared at the blank wall, wondering. He could transmit everything to Farrell, and hope that Allied Intelligence would make a clearer picture of it. Or he could wait, watching and listening, until something solid emerged.

After a few minutes consideration, he decided to wait. It would serve no good end to alert the Allies to something that might not happen, and it could be damaging to trigger a campaign of defence on the strength of plans that could change, as often happened, overnight. If the notes and maps were a seed, Stefan would hang fire until he was sure the Führer intended planting it.

He put the file aside and hid the copy in the spine of his bound volume of *Signal.* Folding the sheets of camp data ready for passing along to Farrell, he paused, caught again by a thought of Gretl. It was the gentlest of pictures, something he could hold vividly for minutes on end. Once, in a rush of sentiment, he had told Gretl that thinking about her that way was like stepping near a warm fire on a cold day.

Then he shook himself and got back to what he was doing. 'Priorities,' he murmured. 'Progress.'

Dinner had not been a success. Margarete Slezak spoke barely a word, and Hitler, clumsily trying to use knives and forks with hands that were almost useless, had quickly lapsed into a sullen, nervous silence that matched his guest's. He shouldn't have tried to resurrect the past.

Crossing the hall afterwards, Margarete passed Bormann, who was standing in a doorway glaring at her. She acknowledged him with a curt nod and kept on walking. Bormann stayed where he was until she had gone upstairs, they he crossed to the salon and knocked on the door. There was no reply, so he opened the door and stepped halfway inside.

'Führer . . .'

Hitler was sitting on the couch, a small figure among the furnishings and adornments. He looked at Bormann as if he barely recognized him.

'Führer, I know you didn't wish to be disturbed . . .'

'Then why do you disturb me?'

'For one thing, I was concerned. I just saw that woman Slezak leave here.'

'That is no business of yours, Bormann. Was there something else?'

Bormann closed the door and approached the Führer. 'You look ill, sir. Shouldn't you be retiring? I'll call Linge and tell him to prepare your bedroom.'

'I'll call Linge myself when I'm ready to. I've asked you, is there something else?'

'Field Marshal Keitel, Führer. He urgently requests to see you. Tomorrow, if it's possible.'

'Ask me again tomorrow and I'll tell you.' Hitler rubbed his eyes wearily. 'I have plans to make, I will want to see a number of people. I will do it when the time is absolutely right.' He appeared to remember something. 'Has there been any communication from General Jodl?'

'Not yet, sir.'

'Get in touch with him. Tell him I'm growing impatient. He'll understand.'

'Very good, Führer.'

'Now leave me. I wish to be alone for a time.'

Outside, Bormann saw Stefan Gaiser coming out of the records room.

'Gaiser, a word with you.'

They went into one of the empty stenographers' rooms and Bormann closed the door. Stefan stood by the desk, watching the twitchy annoyance on the other man's face.

'I've just seen Margarete Slezak,' Bormann said. It sounded like an accusation. 'Do you know why she was brought here?'

'No, sir. I was simply ordered to bring her.'

'Yes, yes.' Bormann drummed his fingers on the side of his trouser leg. 'Your loyalty to the Führer does you credit, but understand, there are times when he doesn't know what is in his own best interests. At present he needs to be shielded from influences that could damage him. Now if you have even a clue as to why that woman is here, I want you to tell me.'

'I swear, I have no idea,' Stefan said.

'He looks terrible. Ill. Despondent.' Bormann had his faraway look again. 'If I gauge it correctly, he's on the verge of deciding about Ardennes. He needs to be in strong spirits for something like that. It's crucial.'

Stefan was suddenly alert, recalling something he should have remembered before, when he was scanning the mysterious maps and notes. On the day after the explosion at Rastenburg, while he had been in the medical centre being treated for his shock and bruises, Hitler had apparently issued an official directive demanding a renewed and fanatical determination from all men fit for service. Later, four men had been taken into an inner chamber of the field bunker to discuss the war situation. One of the men had been Chief of Staff Guderian, and later Stefan picked up the story by simply listening to a conversation between Guderian and one of the others present at the conference, General Jodl. Hitler had been told of a respite in the East, as the Russian summer offensive exhausted itself. There was, however, pressure in Belgium and Luxembourg. Hitler had behaved excitedly, telling everyone he had made a momentous decision. The nature of the decision had remained a mystery to Stefan, and he had been inclined to ignore what he heard anyway: in the murmured opinion of Guderian, the Führer had still been suffering from the effects of his ordeal. Since then Stefan had heard nothing, and he had decided that Guderian was right and that the scheme, like so many others, had been allowed to evaporate.

Now, he pretended some familiarity with the facts. 'A campaign of those proportions would certainly need stamina and clear thinking.'

'We must all remember to stay quiet about this, Gaiser. The Führer rightly distrusts a great number of people, and in my opinion there are more he doesn't suspect yet.'

He turned to open the door again, then paused. 'Have you any notion when Fräulein Slezak is leaving?'

'None at all.'

'The sooner, the better,' Bormann mumbled. 'She should not be here at all. The Führer grows sentimental when he's ill or tired.' He opened the door. 'Perhaps, if you're not too busy, you could send a signal for me, to General Jodl. Say simply that the Führer is impatient.' He narrowed his eyes. 'If my judgement's correct, Jodl will be the architect of the battle plans. That's what he's best at.'

On his way to the radio room Stefan reflected on how vulnerable Secretary Bormann could be when his vanity came anywhere near the surface. He could never resist boasting about his astuteness. If his pride persisted, he could soon be indispensable to the Allied war effort.

Later that night, after spending two hours alone in the salon, Hitler went to his bedroom and allowed his valet, Heinz Linge, to undress him and put him in bed. When Linge had gone, Hitler pressed the small button by his bedside and lay back to wait for Eva Braun.

She answered the summons in less than three minutes. Even so, she had taken time to brush her hair, and when Hitler saw her he smiled warmly.

'You're a very refreshing sight,' he said, and patted the side of the quilt. 'Sit here, my love.'

Eva had trouble restraining her tears. She sat by him and stroked his cheek, trying to think of something to say, hoping her recent distress did not show.

'It has been a bad day, Eva. I need to be comforted.'

The following day Margarete Slezak returned to Munich and Stefan went with her. In the late afternoon, after taking Fräulein Slezak to her apartment, he booked in at the hotel he had used before, and at five o'clock he called Farrell. They arranged to meet, and in accordance with the rota of contact points they had devised, Stefan made a mental note to get to the *Taschenlampe*, a soldiers' nightclub in the east of the city, before eleven o'clock.

At six he went to Gretl's apartment. As usual her surprise and pleasure warmed him, and Stefan made every effort to appear normal. He had been in the apartment for only ten minutes, however, when Gretl confronted him.

'Now.' She put her hands flat on her grey skirt. 'You must tell me.'

He sighed. 'Last time . . .'

'Last time you started, I think, then you decided against it and I didn't object. But now I want you to get it off your chest.'

Stefan stood up and walked to the fireplace. He had rehearsed the moment, but a starting point was hard to find.

Gretl fixed him with wide eyes. 'Stefan. I thought I *knew* you.'

He drummed his fingers on the mantel then faced her squarely. 'There are things you must know and believe, Gretl. The first is that you're the servant of a criminal regime. The biggest there's ever been. Those mountains of honourable propaganda and the libraries of high-sounding laws are the window-dressing for a bunch of gangsters. Blood-lusting gangsters. You've heard about the concentration camps?'

'A little. People don't really talk about the camps. There are whispers, sometimes.'

'They're terrifying places, Gretl. And there are a lot of them. Do you know what they're for?'

Gretl shrugged. 'Containment, I suppose. That's one of the words they use.'

'They exist,' Stefan said, 'for the suppression, torture and murder of human beings. Men, women and children, possibly in their millions . . .'

'That can't be true.' Gretl said it flatly, with the tone of someone who simply knew better.

'It's true, I'm in a position to know it is. In four years

the camps have mushroomed, with no publicity. They built nine of them between 1940 and 1942. I'm sure the local people were assisted to believe the compounds were for ordinary criminals and political offenders. You may not know the names now, Gretl, but you will some day. Auschwitz, Neuengamme, Guson, Natzweiler, Gross-Rosen, Niederhagen . . .'

'Stefan, they can't be murdering people. It's unthinkable. I've seen some of the men who administer the camp transports – they're human beings themselves, they're not the kind of animals you're talking about. I mean, the thought of *millions* of people being killed – it just sounds impossible.'

'Once you accept murder as an expedient, the scale hardly matters. And when genocide's the game, half measures get you nowhere.'

'That's horrible.' Gretl was staring at the fire. 'I see plenty of documents. Deportation orders, internee lists, things like that. They don't suggest anything so barbaric. Just the opposite, in fact. It's all so orderly, civilized.'

'Paperwork makes everything palatable,' Stefan said. 'I used to live in a nice paper-padded cell myself.'

'But there must be some good men in positions of power. What about the generals? Surely they don't support the kind of things you're suggesting?'

'A lot of them don't. But it doesn't matter. Terror's the big weapon these days. Military strategy doesn't come into it.' Stefan was becoming agitated. He unbuttoned his tunic and loosened his collar. 'The generals who haven't been slaughtered for their complicity in the bomb plot have to struggle against habitual megalomania and SS obstruction. Hitler was never an army man, he just doesn't get on with them. The SS hold the reins, Gretl, and words like decency and honour aren't in their vocabulary. While the generals are out losing their battles, Himmler's thugs are waging their own war against the Jews and any other subhumans they can lay hands on.'

Gretl looked up at him. 'Are you part of that?'

Stefan watched the tightening of her mouth. 'I have been,' he said.

'Has it ever seemed right to you?'

'Of course not.'

'I'm confused,' There was no accusation on her face, only the small worry Stefan had seen before, and ignored.

'Gretl, I climbed because I'm efficient. It had nothing to do with enthusiasm. That's as much of an explanation as I can give you, for the moment.'

Gretl held out her arms to him and Stefan sat down again, drawing her close, stroking her hair. 'Why have you told me all this? It hasn't helped me to understand anything.' She kissed his cheek. 'I see your picture in magazines, standing near the Führer. I've seen you riding in the car behind his in Berlin. I try not to be puzzled, really I do, but when you do so well in the regime, and yet condemn it . . .'

'I'm not on their side,' Stefan said. 'Believe that, along with the rest.'

'Is there more?'

'One more fact for you to absorb, then a confession.'

Gretl put a hand over her eyes briefly. 'I don't really think I want to hear any more . . .'

'Please, you must listen.' Stefan touched her shoulder the way he always did when he wanted to impress his sincerity on her. 'I've seen the progress figures from Auschwitz for July. They were exterminating twelve thousand Jews a day. This month the numbers could be higher.'

Gretl's head turned. 'Twelve thousand . . .'

'Every day, by every means possible.'

Gretl tried to resist the weight of what he was saying. 'Stefan, are you telling me you're thinking of *opposing* them?'

'I already do.'

'Tell me what you mean,' she said quietly.

He told her. The words were chosen with care, so that Gretl knew no more than she had to. Stefan said he worked against his masters at every opportunity, and he passed information to an American spy every time he visited Munich. He watched her absorb that, and saw her turn pale.

'My God,' she said, 'I wish you hadn't told me.'

'I had to,' Stefan said.

'But why? How can I ever have peace of mind knowing that?'

'I told you because it was time you knew. I'm still the Stefan Gaiser you've known all along. It's who I am that matters, isn't it? What I am should make no difference.' He thought how fatuous it sounded.

'But you just can't do that, Stefan.' Gretl's voice was uneven. 'I *worry* about you, about your safety, sometimes at work I get paralysed just thinking what might happen to you in Berlin. How do you expect me to cope now? And why did you say it's time I knew?'

'Because I need help.'

'Help? From me?'

'There's no one else I can rely on.' Slowly, in a voice laden with gentleness, he explained the need for a go-between. The line had to be more flexible, he emphasized, less visible.

'But I'd be terrified!' Gretl gasped. 'I could never do anything like that!'

'There would be no danger, my love. No more than the everyday danger of walking those streets out there.' He drew her close for a moment. 'You would simply carry small pieces of paper from one place to another.'

'No, Stefan.' She said it firmly, pulling back to look squarely at him. 'I'm not sure I even agree with what you're doing . . .'

'Think of the other things I've told you.'

'Even so.'

'I'm not a bad man, Gretl. I'm truly on the side of the angels. Do you still love me?'

'Of course . . .'

'Then trust me, and help me. I want us to have a decent future after this war's over.'

'You sound like a propaganda magazine.'

'Believe me, I wouldn't have raised any of this if there had been an alternative. Without your help, I *will* be in great danger, and so will all I'm working for.'

She was close to tears. 'Part of me wants to help, Stefan, but it's so frightening . . .'

Stefan cupped his hands around her face. 'I would never expose you to any risk, my darling. Just remember, you can *trust* me, as much as anyone in the world.'

As usual, Farrell was at the rendezvous first, dressed as a Wehrmacht colonel again and sitting in the darkest corner of the dingy little room.

'Hang on,' he hissed when Stefan started to say something. Farrell was holding a glass of wine motionless under his chin and staring at the thin, elfin face of the girl singer who was trilling a sentimental ballad about old Berlin. Stefan sighed and waited.

When the song was over and the scattering of clients applauded dutifully, Farrell said, 'There's something about that kind of woman I really take to.'

Stefan glanced at her. She had the figure of a child and her movements were angular and exaggerated. 'Maybe she brings out the protective part of your nature. She looks like an elegant waif.'

Farrell shrugged. 'She puts a little whine across my heart, whatever it is about her. Mind you, it's so long since I had any tail, even the old whores down at the Rummelplatz get my nuts in a knot lately.' He sighed and drank the remainder of his stale wine. 'What I'd really like to screw is one of those BDM Group Leaders.'

'The League of German Girls is sacred,' Stefan said, ironically.

'I'll bet. Reserved for top brass, as after-dinner treats.'

'They wouldn't dare try it. Hitler gets very touchy about people defiling the flower of German womanhood.

Besides, they're mostly in factories now. They don't look the same in overalls.'

'I suppose not. But who eats candy with the wrapper on?' He eyed Stefan slyly. 'How do you make out for women, anyway?'

'I'm saving myself for marriage.'

'Horseshit.'

Stefan had placed the cigarette packet on the table. 'There's additional material on the camps in there. I can get some of the more urgent stuff within a week or two.'

Farrell nodded, helping himself to a cigarette. 'Do you know anything about the SS units posted to Dobrush, a couple of years back?'

'Dobrush?'

'It's in Russia, in the Gomel region. Two units of the SS used the population as a walking shield when they carried out their battle formation attacks.'

'I hadn't heard about that. Who needs to know?'

'How should I know?' Farrell blew smoke into the air above him and watched it spread. 'I get little queries like that all the time. You would, too, if you used a radio.'

'I wouldn't want to do you out of a job.' Stefan's look hardened.

To change the subject, he told Farrell that he had arranged a go-between. He described Gretl Bauer and outlined her qualifications for the work without saying a word about his close involvement.

'Recruiting her wasn't easy, Ralph. She's nervous, but she fits our need very tidily. Treat her carefully. I've arranged to see her regularly after she makes the drops to you, so if there's any two-way trade needed, she'll be able to pass on anything you want me to know. Just don't make it too heavy. I don't want her getting scared.'

'Sounds great,' Farrell said. 'How exactly did you hook her?'

'That doesn't matter. She'll do the job.'

'She's fully briefed?'

'Yes. It's all here.' Stefan tapped the cigarette packet.

'She knows the times when you'll be by the phone, and she has the rota and transfer procedures. I've varied things here and there – I don't think you should do too much lingering together.'

Farrell nodded approvingly. 'Looks like we're getting streamlined at long last.' He raised his glass. 'Here's to improved communication.'

'And fruitful results,' Stefan added, sipping the wine and trying to ignore the bite of the tannin. 'I've a feeling there's hot news coming your way soon.'

'Like what?'

'A major offensive. In the Ardennes.'

'The Ardennes,' Farrell said, and shook his head. 'Now I know that bastard's crazy.'

'I don't think he can be underestimated, not even now.'

'It's his funeral. What does he want to do? Break through to the Channel coast?'

'I imagine so,' Stefan said. 'He's been encouraged lately by the stories about bickering among the Allies. They're divided, so they're vulnerable.'

'Sure. And what's going to unite them better than an offensive in the west? Jesus, they do agree on some things. Like the need to get this fight right into the heart of Germany. Where's the punch-power going to come from, anyway? I haven't seen any Intelligence reports that talk about big resources of fighting men. Just the opposite. The Wehrmacht's on its ass.'

'I don't know any of the facts yet,' Stefan said. 'But when I do, I'll pass the information along.'

'Do that. I can always use a laugh.'

The girl had propped herself on the stool under the weak spotlight again. As she began her song, accompanied by an old man picking uncertainly at the keys of a battered upright piano, Farrell put the cigarette packet in his pocket and murmured, 'I'd really love to prong her.'

Farrell showed no signs of wanting to leave, even when the girl had finished her song and returned to the room behind the chenille curtain. Perhaps, Stefan thought, the general darkness of the club made him feel safer than usual; there were certainly fewer lights than before.

'I'm going back to the hotel,' Stefan said finally. 'I have to get back up the mountain tomorrow.'

'Finished here, are you?'

'Yes, the visitor only stayed for one night. She's home again.'

'Did you find out why Uncle Adolf wanted to see her?'

'I haven't a clue.'

'He's fucking senile, going back over the high spots in his past.' Farrell took Stefan's hand and shook it warmly. 'Keep out of trouble, kid. Your country needs you.'

Near midnight the singer came back to do her final number. There were about twenty men in the club, most of them sitting in groups at tables, talking and drinking. A few went on talking when the girl began singing, others became silent and attentive. Alone at his corner table, Farrell was the most attentive customer in the place.

She was sensational, in his estimation. The stuff of dreams and memory, a tiny doll of a girl with the drive of a demon locked up in her narrow, fragile body. The clue was in her eyes, big brown orbs that were half-lidded most of the time, but when she opened them wide the sparks were there, the glittering power. Her voice echoed it.

He had known them all his life, girls like her. They stood out in any crowd, even in groups where the other women had bigger breasts, firmer bodies and faces that were prettier. When Farrell was fourteen he had tried to seduce a girl like that and wound up being seduced by her. She had scared him with her self-assurance, her lively eyes and emotionless face, her skill. Since that time he had met a lot of others and it had always amazed him the way they operated to the same set of rules and procedures, as if they belonged to a network and were planted across America and Europe to bedevil him at secretly arranged intervals. If there was one feature that stood out, it was their capacity to startle him, even though he always thought he knew what was going to happen. To Ralph

Farrell that was magic, for he was not an easy man to shock.

The song ended and Farrell was on his feet, still clapping his hands politely, crossing the floor to intercept the girl before she vanished behind the curtain.

'Fräulein . . .' He closed on her just as she drew the curtain aside.

The girl turned and looked up at him, the small face bland and confident.

'I enjoyed your performance very much.'

'Thank you.' She moved forward an inch and he detained her with a hand softly on her arm.

'Perhaps you would join me for a drink?'

'I am sorry.' She smiled faintly and tried to move on.

'Please,' Farrell said, and he knew the intensity of his gaze was telling her they were a match, two of a special kind.

'I have an appointment,' the girl said. She ducked under the curtain and Farrell caught it, pushing it wide. As he stepped into the small room the man waiting for the girl moved into view.

'And what is your business in here, Colonel?'

Farrell stopped and watched the girl go forward to take the brandy glass her boyfriend was holding out to her. He was a fat, pug-faced man, dressed in the uniform of an SS Oberführer. He was scowling at Farrell, waiting for an answer.

'I'm sorry,' Farrell said, and took a step backwards. 'I am obviously trespassing.'

'And I am asking you why.'

The girl was standing with her back to the far wall now, drinking from the glass, staring at Farrell.

'I wanted the lady to join me for a drink.'

'And she declined. Twice. So you followed her into these private quarters.'

'I apologize,' Farrell said. 'I'll go.'

'Wait.' The officer came over and stood close, staring hard at Farrell. 'Show me your papers.'

Farrell unbuttoned his pocket and handed over the forged documents.

The Oberführer studied them for almost a minute, and all the time the girl went on staring. 'Horst Luckmann,' the man murmured. 'Seventy-Seventh Artillery Corps.' He passed back the papers, having made it clear that he was memorizing the name and the unit. 'I would advise you to leave now, Colonel. And try to remember that a certain measure of decorum is expected of officers.'

Farrell nodded and saluted the Oberführer, then he turned and pushed his way back through the curtain. Behind him, he heard the girl giggle softly.

People were leaving the place in groups and Farrell mingled with them, passing out on to the street and pausing at the edge of the pavement. He looked right and left, like a man trying to decide what to do next. His car was across the road, and somewhere near it there would be an SS staff vehicle. He spotted it after a few seconds, parked ten yards to the left of his.

He crossed the road and climbed into his car. Channels of decision, however precise, always left him with two answers to a problem. This occasion was no different. The fat man had worn the ominous black sleeve triangle of the SD, so he was probably big in the Gestapo, which meant he was thorough. He would follow up on that confrontation, he would make a stink. The SS were as noted for their dislike of the Wehrmacht as they were for thoroughness, so there would be some vindictive glee behind whatever action the Oberführer took – and he would go up in the air when it was discovered that he had made a blunder, that he had let an impostor slip through his hands. Farrell remembered the way the man had stared, memorizing his face. He had stared at the identification photograph just as hard. He was SS, he would never forget, and life was close to impossible for a spy with the Gestapo hot on his tail.

The answers were straightforward, but the choice was difficult.

Farrell started the engine and began to drive the car slowly round the block. Answer Number One was to pull up pegs and change the base of operations. Farrell could move to Berlin, where there was already a cover address and a network link as secure as the set-up in Munich. That way he would be out from under the Oberführer's searchlight, which probably covered less than the entire city of Munich, now that manpower and resources were stretched. Berlin was a messy place to be, but Munich would soon be no better, and the shift could be carried out easily, without further risk.

Answer Number Two was more dramatic. It was also dangerous, but there was speed and tidiness in its favour. And Answer Number Two sang in his blood.

On his second circuit of the block he saw the Oberführer unlocking his car. The girl was standing beside him, wrapped in a fur coat. Farrell drove slowly past and kept the car at a crawl until the SS vehicle came up behind him and overtook. He saw the girl in profile as they went past and felt a tight lurch in his stomach.

Her name was Lucie. She was twenty years old and ambitious. When the war was over she planned to attach herself to a man with enough wealth and influence to make her a famous popular entertainer. Lucie knew she had talent, all she needed was opportunity.

Already she was good at manipulating men. In her small apartment near the Odeonsplatz she had furniture, clothes, food and money, all provided by male friends: not one of them had ever felt he was getting less than good value.

Gerhard Rieder, the man who had come home with her that evening, was particularly generous. He had given her jewellery, perfume and clothes, and he had made arrangements for her to live rent-free in her apartment. In return Lucie had only to make herself available whenever Gerhard wanted her, and on those occasions he did not ask for much – he never made love to her, and he never stayed the night. The most he asked was that occasionally he might sit in a chair with his arms folded, and watch while Lucie made love to herself.

Tonight he was tired. Lucie made him coffee and sympathized as he talked about the pressure of his work, the long hours and shortage of men that resulted in officers slaving like sergeants. Gerhard was telling her how he had just worked almost non-stop for three days, when they heard a sound in the hallway. Lucie thought it was her cat, but she went to look anyway.

She came back white-faced, with the big Wehrmacht colonel pushing her ahead of him.

Gerhard Rieder was on his feet at once, gaping at the taut-faced intruder. 'What are you doing here?'

'Visiting, Oberführer.' Farrell held up the short jemmy that had torn off the lock. In the same action he pushed Lucie aside.

Rieder's tunic was unbuttoned and when he reached for his gun he fumbled. Farrell took three steps forward and slapped the side of the fat, enraged face. Rieder stumbled but he was strong, and he swung a wide punch that hit Farrell on the point of the chin. Farrell grunted and brought up the thin edge of the jemmy, ramming it into his opponent's armpit.

'Stop it!' Lucie screamed. She was flattened against the wall, terrified.

'Any minute,' Farrell said. Rieder had dropped to one knee with the impact and pain and Farrell's knee caught him squarely in the throat. When he fell back on the carpet one boot struck him in the groin, the other on the mouth. He was barely conscious when Farrell dropped astride him and began hammering his face with the jemmy.

Lucie was silent by the time he was finished. She was on her knees, trembling violently, supporting herself with one hand on a table leg. Farrell stood up, letting the jemmy drop on Rieder's motionless chest, and he picked the girl off the floor by her waist, setting her against the wall again.

'Please . . .' Her big eyes were turned up to him, pleading harder than her shaking voice could.

'You sing like a bird,' Farrell whispered, and he placed a hand over her mouth. For a moment she tried to struggle, then stopped. Farrell's eyes were almost sad as he spread his hand wider, enclosing her nose. Only the frightened stare remained to give her identity. She struggled to breathe and he felt soft, warm air against his palm. 'Don't try,' Farrell said, and his voice carried the concern he might show for a child. 'Just let it happen.' He tightened the clamp and turned his head aside. When he looked back at her the eyes were almost closed, and they were sightless.

He carried the body through to the other room and placed it carefully on the bed. Farrell did not look at the face, he knew there would be an ugly white patch where his hand had been. In the living room he took the papers, money and gun from Rieder's body, pocketed them, and left. As he walked the short distance to the place where his car was parked, he did not whistle or hum, and he took no care to walk with the briskness he usually affected. Farrell was preoccupied and a little depressed. It sometimes happened that way, when a tidy victory carried too many elements of loss.

On the afternoon of 3rd September 1944, the deputy head of the Political Warfare Executive in London received an informal memo in his Top Secret docket. It came from his counterpart on the parent body, SOE.

> 'Regrettably, I have to report that our fears concerning agent Gaiser have been confirmed. It is now clear that for two years he has fed us a series of communiqués that have been useless, misleading, and in the matter of the flying bomb sites at Pas

de Calais, downright mischievous. On reflection we no longer think it fanciful to assume that Gaiser is firmly entrenched with the other side – either through a change of heart or an earlier, concealed belief in Nazism. I know you will agree it is best to act on any doubt where an agent is concerned, and in this case there can be few doubts at all. An operative of 'F' section will be briefed immediately to cancel our black sheep at the earliest opportunity.'

At his home that evening, Thomas Malcolm sat in the firelight with a dry sherry in his hand, and mentally rehearsed the story he would tell Stefan's mother.

Thomas had tried to use persuasion in Whitehall, but it was useless. When an agent in the field went bad, there was no question of clemency. When the operative happened to be one so potentially valuable as Stefan Gaiser, the records showed no precedent for even the slightest flexibility. Thomas sighed at the fire, wondering, remembering.

When it was faced squarely, he decided, nobody had ever known enough about the boy. They all knew what they had been allowed to know, and what they had assumed.

'His father's image,' Thomas said to the fire. He had never forgotten the strutting Bavarian, the man who had taken all the delicate colour and the youth from his niece. Painfully, Thomas scanned the emerging logic. Sons were inclined to emulate fathers, not mothers. Stefan could be considered as a special example of that fact: he had a quiescent mother and a dominant, ranting father in his background. The father had indoctrinated the boy from earliest childhood, Charlotte had said as much. And Stefan was clever, perhaps more clever than they had suspected. It was not hard to imagine that he had been moving towards an acceptance of Nazism when Thomas and Dorian Goode had gone to see him at Dorfen.

The career of Thomas Malcolm would be badly damaged, of course. Nothing less than resignation would do, he fancied. But it hardly mattered. What hurt Thomas most was that he had made a hideous error that would bring down a lot of the power he had laboured to achieve for his department. Nothing would be the same. It was sad to fail, but it was agony to bring about the failure of other people who merited the shiniest of success.

The sherry tasted like vinegar. 'There's no telling,' Thomas murmured, setting the glass aside, 'no telling at all.'

Nobody had any doubt that the communiqués were intentionally misleading; even Thomas had stopped trying to believe otherwise. A number of men had died because of those messages, and no one could excuse the painstaking deception that had been acted upon, again and again, until it was clear the information from Berlin was a snare, not a searchlight.

Thomas had decided he would tell Stefan's mother that the boy had died as a result of enemy action. Thomas would never keep her in the dark, he would not let her go on believing that Stefan was alive. Enemy action, that was definitely the kindest way to phrase it. There would be no need to explain just who, in the end, had been Stefan's real enemy.

November, 1944
Hitler had moved his headquarters to the bunker that had been specially built for him in the garden of the Chancellery in Berlin. Conditions there lacked the organization and freedom of movement possible at the Berghof, and for an entire week Stefan laboured with Secretary Bormann to establish a system where the masses of documents and file boxes could be stored without causing obstruction to the working order laid down by the Führer.

The bunker consisted of two connected groups of rooms, set out on two levels underground. The upper group of twelve rooms ran on either side of a central passage, where meals were usually eaten. At one end of the passage there was a spiral staircase that led down to Hitler's quarters, eighteen small rooms flanking a passage similar to the one above. The passage was divided in two sections, and the one furthest from the stairs was used as a conference room. It was scarcely seventeen feet square with bare, grey-painted walls. The only furniture was a wooden bench along one wall, a large map table, a desk and a chair.

The rooms were no larger than railway compartments. Six on the lower level were reserved for Hitler and Eva Braun, and five others housed bathrooms, the power generator, and telephone exchanges. The remaining living rooms were set aside for use in an emergency by administrators such as Goebbels and Himmler.

There were three entrances to the bunker. One led from the butler's pantry in the Chancellory, another from the Foreign Office garden, while the third, designed primarily as an emergency exit, travelled between the lower section of the bunker and a heavily camouflaged door in the Chancellory garden.

Stefan's quarters, amounting to no more than a cell near the staircase in the upper section, were flanked by those of Hitler's vegetarian cook and one of his typists. Despite the crowding, and the constant presence of guards, orderlies and clerks in the passages and record rooms, Stefan found it easier to operate in the bunker than at the Berghof.

On 21st November, there was a breakthrough, a stroke of luck that Stefan could hardly believe.

A slip of paper, bearing the shorthand notes of the Führer's closest secretary, Traudl Junge, had fallen face-down on the floor beside the combination-locked operations file in Bormann's office. Stefan spotted it when he was putting the daily sheaf of unsigned requisitions on Bormann's desk, and he picked it up, a second before Bormann walked in. There was no time to pocket the paper, so Stefan just held on to it.

'What is it now, Gaiser?' Bormann was constantly on edge lately.

'The requisitions,' Stefan told him, and he waved the piece of paper as if it was another of the endless memos that dictated his daily movements. 'Too many as usual, but most of them are from sources I can't ignore.'

Bormann threw himself into his chair and slapped the sheaf absently. 'I'll weed through them later. Much later.'

Stefan left the office, slipping the paper into his pocket. In the lavatory, he propped himself against the door and examined the squiggles under the dim lamp. What he was holding, he suddenly realized, was a directive to General Jodl and Field Marshal Model.

> Operation Christrose shall hereafter be called Operation Watch on the Rhine. Different names for the offensive will be used at every level of command, and these names will be changed every two weeks. No trust shall be placed in telephone or teletype, and all communications on the offensive shall be made via courier officers of the SS. To ensure secrecy further, a network of subterfuges will be put into operation in due course. Radio operators will trans-

> mit orders to fictitious headquarters, false coded signals will be sent to genuine headquarters, and genuine signals will be radioed to headquarters hundreds of miles from their advertised locations. False rumours, for the ears of foreign agents, will be distributed among the clientele of beer halls and restaurants.

The directive was headed *Operation Christrose: Communication Five.* Stefan read it over again, wondering how much had been finalized. For days there had been frantic activity on the lower section of the bunker, and the resulting paperwork had been travelling in tray loads into Bormann's office. It was no wonder one piece had gone astray.

That night, Stefan started to move. An order was in force, banning all but selected personnel from the lower level. It was an emergency order of a type issued only when important conferences were in progress, and Stefan knew it would eventually be lifted: now, he was convinced he could not wait.

There was no danger of being seen as he moved the short distance from his own room to the top of the stairs. The double guard was at the other end of the passage and they always faced the concealed entrance doors. When he had descended the spiral steps he pushed himself into the corner by the door to the Number One telephone exchange; it was never manned at night, and when Stefan was sure the guards were on the far side of the corridor partition, he slipped into the telephone room and eased the door shut.

There was one tiny working light, just bright enough to show him the obstructions between himself and the door to Number Two exchange. Stefan pushed that door open a crack and saw the operator with her elbows on the console, the earphones buried in her curly hair. She had her back to him, but Stefan waited until the switchboard became active. The bright yellow lamp came on to the operator's left. It signalled a call from the secondary bunker, where Secretary Bormann lived apart from the others. As soon as the girl leaned over and flipped the switch, Stefan walked into the room, closing one door behind him and opening another, right beside the switchboard console. Inside three seconds he was in the generator room with its permanent odour of warm oil and the dull, blanketed hum of the motor. He stood motionless in the green light, catching his breath, then moved forward, holding the plan of the lower level in his head.

There were several unoccupied rooms ahead, all interconnected, and on the Führer's orders none of the doors was ever locked. Guards could roam that area in a random patrol, and for the present they represented the only hazard. It was well after midnight, and Stefan had seen the shift rotas: if he was any judge, the four guards would be resting in the conference section of the corridor, opposite the door of Hitler's suite. They had already been on duty for thirteen hours.

Within five minutes he was sure he had reached the key door. In the Führer's personal cluster of rooms security was provided by reinforced walls and the occupants of the rooms themselves. His living and sleeping chamber was surrounded on three sides by smaller rooms occupied at various times by Goebbels, General Keitel, or Reichsführer Himmler. The recent spate of visitors had been kept relatively secret, but Stefan knew that none of those men had been near the bunker lately, so the guests' overnight rooms would be empty, and locked. Only one room afforded access to Hitler's chamber, and Stefan was ninety-percent sure it was occupied that night. He opened the door softly and held his breath.

There was a rustling of sheets, but after a ten minute wait, Stefan was satisfied that Eva Braun was asleep. He slipped into the room, closing the door behind him. He stood silently, looking towards the bed.

Eva moved again, but then lay there, breathing softly, her hair tousled against the pillow. She looked exhausted.

Satisfied, Stefan moved towards the Führer's chamber and listened at the door.

A few minutes passed before he entered, relieved to find it in complete darkness. Beyond a wooden screen the old man's light snoring provided a stable point from which Stefan could take his bearings. He had been inside the chamber only twice before, but he had a good memory of the layout. The canvas bag with the heavy, brass-locked flap, was kept in a slotted cabinet near the desk. It was the receptacle for all the documents relating to the day's programme, and in defiance of Bormann's fussy insistence that it should be locked away, Hitler always kept it by him. On hands and knees, Stefan groped his way across the floor and finally located the bag.

Dragging it into Eva's room was not easy. The thing was packed with maps and folders and it made an alarming scraping sound when it was moved. Eventually Stefan managed to swing his load through the narrow doorway, and as he did, the Führer stopped snoring.

For five breathless seconds Stefan remained midway between the rooms, his ears aching with the effort to hear. There was a soft movement behind the the screen, a cough, then the snoring started again. Only when he was inside Eva's room with the door closed did he breathe again.

He sat on the floor, concealed by Eva's wardrobe, and sorted through the contents of the bag with a small torch. On the first search he found nothing significant. Unbelieving and on the border edge of panic, he looked again, and found a folder narrower than the others. On the front was one word: *Christrose.*

There were ten pages of typed notes, with marginal additions in Hitler's shaky script. He leafed quickly through it, memorizing as much as possible, from the startling battle plans to the map references and tree-shaped lines of command.

When he was sure he had the essence of the data in his

head, he put the folder back in the bag and returned it to the Führer's chamber.

The return journey was uneventful. The telephonist was drowsing, and there were still no guards near the stairs. It was only when Stefan was opening his own door that he was challenged.

'Who is that?'

Stefan pushed himself away from the doorway, ruffling his hair before the young guard could see him clearly.

'May I ask what you are doing in the corridor, sir?'

Stefan made moistening noises with his tongue on his palate. 'Lavatory,' he mumbled, and pointed at the door opposite. Then he noticed that the soldier was staring pointedly at his uniform. 'I fell asleep at my desk,' he yawned. 'I'll be useless in the morning.'

The guard nodded curtly and moved off again to the far end of the passage. Stefan opened the toilet door and went inside, feeling his nerve begin to falter. He sat down for a minute and thought over what he had just done, and it frightened him. He hoped, fervently, that he would never let himself take that kind of risk again.

By late the following evening, he had the message coded for Farrell. Although he had edited it as much as he could, it still took up a lot of tissue paper. He read it through twice, carefully, before he folded it and put it inside the wrapper of a bar of Wehrmacht-issue chocolate.

> *Operation Christrose* – also to be known as *Operation Watch on the Rhine*: Working from two premises, surprise and bad flying weather, three armies with a combined strength of 12 Panzer and 18 infantry divisions will attempt to break down 30 American and British divisions on a wide front, crossing the Meuse on the second day of the offensive and reaching Antwerp on the seventh day. A wedge would thus be driven between American and British forces, with results that are intended to be as damaging psychologically as they are physically.

This is clearly a last ditch offensive and everything is being thrown into the effort. The 5th Panzer Army will be given 400 new Panther Mk IV tanks, each considered to be equivalent to 4 Shermans, and new Panzer brigades will be formed to launch against Patton's southern flank. The 7th German Army has been reinforced with divisions of the Volksgrenadiers and Paratroopers trained as infantry. Four crack SS tank divisions will be used to spearhead the attack in the Ardennes: the Leibstandarte, Das Reich, Hitler Jugend and Hohenstauffen. The average age of these men, who are all noted for their fanatical bravery, is 18 years.

In outline, the plan calls for the 3 armies to attack simultaneously along an 80 mile sector held by only 5 American divisions. Unless the Ardennes is reinforced, such a plan is bound to succeed.

There will be added pressure from the revitalized Luftwaffe when the weather clears, and on the ground special units led by Standartenführer Otto Skorzeny are already primed to cause havoc. They will wear British and American uniforms and travel in captured Allied tanks and other vehicles. They will go in ahead of the attack to the first major obstacle, the river Meuse, and they will attempt to seize one or more bridges. An equally important part of their work will be to create confusion by issuing false orders, breaking communications, and undermining morale with stories of German successes. Skorzeny's operation has been given the code name *Greif*.

The proposed date for the commencement of the Ardennes offensive is 16th December. It is imperative that the foregoing details and the following maps and deployment summaries be passed on to the British and American Commands as quickly as possible.

At the weekend Stefan managed a trip to Munich on SS

courier duty. He could only stay a few hours in the city and he telephoned Gretl before she left work and arranged to meet her near her office.

They talked while Stefan drove the staff car slowly around the streets. Gretl was nervous and unhappy. Her courage at the prospect of contacting Farrell was waning.

'But there isn't room in the plan for anything to go wrong,' Stefan tried to reassure her. 'You go to the café and you wait. The man will talk to you, and he'll identify himself as Janus. Leave the transfer details to him. As long as the bar of chocolate's on the table, he'll pocket it without causing the slightest suspicion. Then you go home. Simple.'

'I'm scared.'

Stefan looked at her briefly, taking in the vulnerable softness of her face under the high, turned-up collar of her coat. He wanted to hold her, to draw her close and protect her. He rejected the sentimental impulse, reminding himself that Gretl was being exposed to a little danger to protect *him*.

'Just remember why you're doing it,' he said. 'If it's any help, I can tell you that the information you're carrying is crucial. You'll be helping to end the war quickly.'

'You don't need to lie to me,' Gretl said coldly.

'I'm not.' They had reached the outskirts and Stefan took a sharp turn, heading back in the direction of the city centre. 'You know the way things are falling apart. It should all be finished, sharply. If that information doesn't get to the right people, the war might drag on for a long time yet, and thousands of good, innocent people will die as a result. Passing on a bar of chocolate isn't such a big thing when you view it in that light, Gretl.'

'I suppose not.' She touched his hand on the steering wheel. 'But I'm still frightened.'

Stefan let her out of the car on a quiet street a few minutes later. He was as reluctant at the parting as Gretl was, and he gave her a lingering kiss before she stepped out on to the pavement. He could see, as he started to move off again, that she was on the verge of tears.

He drove around for several minutes more, delaying the time when he had to return the car to the Gestapo pool. It was a relief to be away from the crammed, frenetic warren of the bunker, to be on his own for a time and take stock.

The past two months had been frustrating and harrowing in turn, a period that Stefan felt had aged him more than any other. The frustrations had all attended his work, his real work, and Farrell's gluttony for information had been left unsatisfied for weeks. Stefan had known there was something big on the move, but the Führer's precautions had kept him right on the outside. Until now.

December, 1944

It was a feature of Gretl's nature that she would never trouble other people – especially close people – with her own worries. In the case of Stefan she believed he was already carrying too much stress for one man, so when she began to have doubts about the Allies' reaction to the information about Ardennes, she mentioned nothing, and even tried to seem brighter than she felt.

In the course of her work Gretl had access, most of it accidental, to reports that detailed Allied manoeuvring in the West. There were voluminous files issuing from Intelligence units along the River Meuse, and it was these that Gretl began to watch. Stefan had impressed on her the importance of the information she had passed along to Farrell: after each drop he would go to see her, to find out if she was all right, to comfort her, and on every occasion Stefan would talk about Ardennes and his satisfaction at knowing the Allies had been alerted. But the files that passed across her department daily indicated that nothing unexpected was happening. Either the Allies had developed a new way of covering their larger troop movements, or they simply did not appreciate the enormity of what was about to take place.

Finally, Gretl had to voice her worry, and she decided that Farrell was the one to hear it. On a freezing afternoon in a café at the corner of Ackemann Strasse, she told him.

'I can tell when there's a ripple,' she said. 'Requests for more information go out, the Intelligence reports start coming in at double the usual speed, and if anything serious happens the copies we pass along are in code. But nothing's happening. I'd swear the British and the Americans don't know a thing.'

Farrell smiled at her and patted her hand. 'That's the way they want it to look.'

'I find that hard to believe.'

'Look,' Farrell said, and his smile lost a fraction of its brightness, 'you're not in any position to know much, are you? You're guessing.' He had no idea what Gretl did for a living, all he had was her assurance that she had access to official military and security documents. For his money, the kid was a clerk. 'The right people are in the know, just take my word for it.'

Her stubbornness on a point, an endearing thing to Stefan, was something Farrell could quickly find annoying: Gretl could see that, and she ignored it. 'Perhaps your message didn't get through. There could be lots of ways something like that could be lost . . .'

'I told you,' Farrell said grittily, 'they know. It's being taken care of. You just do your bit and keep that cute nose of yours out of trouble.'

Gretl shrugged. 'I'm sure there's something big . . .'

'Honey, let me worry about that, will you?' Farrell smiled again, a visible effort. 'Time you weren't here. You go first, I'll wait around and make sure nobody's got curious about you.'

Gretl stood up, frowning at him. 'I'll see you soon, I suppose.'

'I suppose.'

Farrell watched her leave, and for a while after she had gone he sat fingering the bar of chocolate she had left behind, turning it in his pocket, mauling it as if some sympathetic magic in the act would knock the delivery girl into line, make her walk inside the limits of her job.

A few minutes after he left the café Farrell realized he was getting jumpy, and he knew why. The twanging in his gut every time he thought about what Gretl had said was out of tune with the other thing, the soft, hopeful little surge he got normally. The go-between attracted him, the few times they had met had been enough for Farrell to know she could set off sparks in him. And that could make things good, or very bad indeed.

The same day, just after sunset, Stefan went to Gretl's apartment. As usual he quizzed her about the handover, watched her face carefully when she assured him she was feeling fine.

'You won't be asked to do this much more,' he promised her. 'Soon, very soon, it'll all be over.'

The night outside was like a malevolent shroud, but they could fend it off when they were together, close. When Stefan held Gretl that night he was full of her, and the outside barbs – work, subterfuge, falsehood as a rule of living – could not touch him. For seven precious hours they lay wrapped in each other's warmth. Stefan slept very little but he felt perfectly rested, bathed in a shadowless peace.

In the morning he gave Gretl his reassurances again, and countless times during breakfast he embraced her, letting the food grow cold, preferring to hold her and bestow the mutual therapy of tender contact. When it was time for him to leave, Stefan promised to come again when he could. At the door he mistook a small frown for the natural pain of parting, and kissed Gretl until her brow was smooth again.

When he had gone, Gretl sighed and began to get herself ready for the working day. She had almost said something to Stefan, right at the moment he was leaving, but it would have been wrong, she decided, to burden him with her misgivings.

As she dressed, she concentrated again on what was really worrying her, separating it from the strands of her imagination. The facts were a big enough worry, but there was more. Tentatively, Gretl decided it was Farrell. He was *wrong*. Just how, she had no clear idea yet. The man was repellent, his ways and his thinking were in some way alien.

By the time she was ready to go to the office, Gretl had tightened her assessment of the man she called Janus. It was a negative appraisal, but she felt it was crucial to what nagged at her. Janus, she was sure, added up to something that could never be an ally, hers or Stefan's.

On the morning of the 13th Stefan was called to Secretary Bormann's office, and there he was introduced to a bright-eyed young SS officer, Untersturmführer Ulrich Lang.

'Lang is with Dr Goebbels' front-line propaganda unit,' Bormann explained. 'You have been assigned to accompany him on an important mission, Gaiser. At noon you will draw winter field dress from the Quartermaster's depot at Jagow Strasse. Report back here at two, when the Führer will see you.'

'May I ask the nature of the mission?' Stefan asked.

'You will be informed in due course,' Bormann told him. 'In the meantime, go with Untersturmführer Lang and he will acquaint you with the work he does.'

Lang turned out to be friendly, a boyish recruit to the cause who was more absorbed with doing his job well than he was with protocol or the distinctions of rank. He insisted on calling Stefan by his first name, and when they reached the propaganda unit's headquarters on Dreilinden Strasse he set about explaining his job with the proud, excited air of one schoolboy showing another his collection of stamps.

'This was built to my own specifications,' he said, hoisting a bulky, black-cased 35 millimetre motion-picture camera from its case. 'Lenses by Carl Zeiss, Stefan. Motor by Bolex of Switzerland. Isn't it beautiful?'

Stefan nodded, smiling at the way Lang's eyes danced over the handles and knobs and the way he caressed the film magazine on top, as if it were a mistress. 'You're a cameraman, then?'

Lang nodded vigorously. 'I was second assistant to Leni Riefenstahl at the 1936 Olympic Games. Since then I've worked on more than twenty propaganda feature films. After the war, I want to set up my own unit to make travel films.'

'Have you any idea what this mission is all about, Ulrich?'

'None at all. But it must be something big. I've been told to requisition as much negative as I want, and they've got an armoured vehicle out in the yard with an adapted gun tower, so I can mount my camera on top. No expense spared, as far as I can tell.'

Stefan looked around the big room, seeing piles of film canisters and racks of transit boxes. This was the place the Allies would dearly love to lay hands on. All the suppressed ghetto films were here, all the damning footage from Warsaw, Belsen, Buchenwald. Somewhere in the collection, too, was the famed motion picture of Himmler's slaughter squad killing twenty young Communists at a secret meeting in the Weisensee district. How an outfit like this could concern him, Stefan had no idea.

'I think I'm looking forward to working with you,' Ulrich Lang said as he slid the camera back into its case. 'You don't seem so stuffy as the others.'

'Thank you,' Stefan said. 'I just hope that whatever it is, we'll both enjoy doing it.'

At two o'clock precisely, an adjutant ushered Stefan into Hitler's private quarters. The Führer was sitting at his writing table in full uniform, looking as gaunt and ill as Stefan had ever seen him. The old man's eyes were bright, nevertheless, and he smiled warmly.

'I'm sorry if you have been kept in some suspense, Gaiser, but I wanted to issue your briefing personally. You've become acquainted with Ulrich Lang, I presume?'

'Yes, sir, we've spent a few hours together today.'

Hitler nodded, tightening the grip of one hand around the other. 'He is a valuable servant of the Reich. As you are.' He looked down for a moment, clearing his throat. 'In three days' time, I will launch the most ambitious assault of this war, Gaiser. It will be a momentous occasion, a landmark in our history. I want it to be recorded for our people. I wish every German to see the power and determination of our armies as we turn the tide against the Allies.' Again he cleared the rattling phlegm from his throat. 'Lang is the man to record the scenes with a camera, there is no one better. You, Gaiser, have a task almost as important. I want you to make a record of everything you see, each and every act of valour. I want you to talk to our soldiers and capture their *spirit* – most of all I want you to set down words that will eventually match the glory of Lang's pictures. You have imagination and flair, I know you are up to the task.'

'I am honoured, Führer.'

'There will be danger, of course,' Hitler went on, 'but you will be afforded as much protection as possible. Lang is being briefed to cover the first three days of the offensive, and I want you to stay with him during that time and make your observations. The ordinary military propaganda units will continue to film our campaign, of course, but after three days I wish to have you back in Berlin, working alongside Lang to produce his film's commentary.' Hitler took a deep, careful breath. 'My reason for wishing you to be at the front is double-edged, I confess.' The warmth in his look increased suddenly, and in the tightening of the wrinkles around his eyes Stefan detected something familiar, an echo of the moment after the Rastenburg explosion when the Führer had clasped his hand so firmly. 'I am a believer in talismans, Gaiser. At the front you will be just that, my talisman, and a token of my presence.'

For a few moments Stefan let the silence hang around them, a mingling of emotion and mild embarrassment. Then he asked Hitler when he would be leaving.

'Today. At the front you will have the protection of the Sixth Panzer Army, and from here in Berlin you will have the added shelter of my own good wishes.' Hitler smiled wearily and nodded towards the door. 'Secretary Bormann will give you the details of your itinerary. Good luck, Gaiser.'

Stefan thanked the Führer and left the room, making

his way in a daze towards Bormann's office. *He was going to the Ardennes.*

It had happened too quickly for him to reason carefully. There was no time to get in touch with Gretl, no foreseeable chance to contact Farrell. With the Allies ready and waiting for the offensive there would be ample opportunity to get lost, to get over to the Allied side, but to do that without first making arrangements for Gretl was out of the question. Worries and panics whirled around in Stefan's head.

Steady, Gaiser, he warned himself. One step at a time was the only way, with an eye open for opportunity at each step. He thought of Gretl in the instant his knuckles rapped on Bormann's door, and he had to fight off a sudden wave of anxiety, a stifling premonition of irrevocable loss.

In the early hours of the 16th, everything on the Ghost Front was as quiet as it had been for the previous two months. Along the eighty-five mile stretch of hilly, wooded country the tired men of six American divisions huddled in their tanks and their billets, some sleeping, others watching out for nothing in particular. Three of the units were new, the other three were battle-hammered and weakened: they watched the Germans in the same way the Germans kept an eye on them, warily and discreetly, seeking to cause no trouble.

The previous night, Field Marshal Montgomery had reasserted his belief that the Germans were in no condition to stage major offensives. He had found things on the Ardennes front so boring and predictably inactive that he had asked the Supreme Commander, General Eisenhower, if it would be in order for him to take some leave in England the following week.

By midnight on the 15th, there were two hundred and fifty thousand soldiers – three complete armies – and thousands of war machines lined up at their assault positions. The rumble and clatter of wheels and half-tracks had been covered by low-flying aircraft, and with a precision backed by fanatical determination the generals and field commanders had put every unit of men, every lethal clutch of weaponry, just where their maps and charts said they should go.

The offensive began at 5.30 am, spearheaded through the freezing fog by General Sepp Dietrich's 6th Panzer Army, supported on the right by the 7th Panzer under General Branderburger, and on the left by General Manteuffel's 5th Panzer. The entire Ghost Front seemed, to the startled and confused Americans, to have exploded. Eruptions of smoke and flame accompanied the deafening crash of mortar and shell fire, and as rockets hissed off their launch vehicles hundreds of tanks came lumbering forward. Eerie white-clad figures walked between the tank formations, fifteen abreast, their guns at the ready as they advanced with supernatural steadiness on the panicking American forward positions.

Some of the American soldiers bolted. Others stood their ground, summoning their battle-readiness from the drowsiness of weeks of inactivity. Overhead, to add more confusion and white-knuckled terror, Hitler's new, odd-sounding aircraft swept past in formation, their high-mounted jets screaming like amplified banshees in the mist-shrouded nightmare. A young soldier of the US 28th Infantry, unable in his fear to do anything with his gun but wave it, distinctly heard one German voice above the rattle and the flaming chaos. It could have been a scream from hell, harsh and terrifying: '*Zieg um jeden Preis*!' The soldier did not know what that meant, but it rang with a determination he could never match or even understand. He turned to run with the others, feeling the rain of disrupted earth on his face, and straight ahead of him he saw one of his comrades, a boy of twenty, shove the muzzle of his revolver in his mouth and blow the side off his head.

In places the Americans miraculously held their positions, in others they fell easily before the onslaught.

Standaftenführer Otto Skorzeny and his commando unit had already penetrated the American rear, driving US vehicles and wearing American uniforms, and they had disrupted communications and transport pathways. They changed road signs, turned others around, cut telephone wires and even managed to feign panicking terror so well that they drove would-be American defence units back without having to fire a bullet. To synchronize with the attack at the front, one thousand Germans were parachuted into the open fields near Malmedy. They set themselves up in dozens of gun emplacements to stop Allied reinforcements coming into Ardennes from the north, and before the battle was an hour old a huge bulge was beginning to develop in General Courtney Hodge's 1st Army.

For Stefan, helmeted and strapped into the armoured half-track beside Ulrich Lang, the experience was a nightmare. On either side, since the start of the advance, giant tanks had deafened him with their whining motors and steady cannon-fire. Speech was a kind of communication too feeble now: only the roar of engines and guns, the ear-bursting crack of ripping trees and the crashing of exploding armour made commentary on the ghastliness of what was happening. Lang had the long lens of his camera shoved through the gunslit of the tower, twisting it left and right, his finger jabbing the trigger and capturing slices of the murderous onslaught. Beside him Stefan gripped the support bar and watched, frozen-faced, as one form of life spat fire and lead and extinguished another.

Ahead of them was a King Tiger in its green, buff and brown livery, with the Commander sitting high on the turret and screaming his orders into his mouthpiece. Stefan had never believed that combat could be this savage, that men and machines would ever visit such mindless hell on virtually defenceless enemies. Five fleeing Americans, one of them injured already, cowered against a tree as a tank shell exploded into the snow ten yards beyond them. The King Tiger ahead of Stefan's vehicle swerved gracefully, almost casually, and ploughed into the men, ripping apart both them and the tree with the same easy indifference before returning to its straight-line advance. Stefan glanced down as they passed the spot and saw one man still twitching in the bloody snow, his left arm severed and the brown tissue of his lung flopping from the side of his mouth.

As the half-track lumbered over a fallen tree-trunk something jabbed at Stefan's leg and he turned, startled, to see Lang's assistant in the well of the vehicle, begging for help with yelling, soundless lips. A fragment of shell had glanced off an overhanging branch and embedded itself in his groin. Blood poured out over one hand as he jabbed at Stefan with the other. Before Stefan could move Ulrich Lang turned and climbed down, pushing the screaming young soldier on to his back. Arterial blood began to spout from the wound but Lang made no effort to stop it. Instead, he grasped up the magazine the soldier had been loading and finished threading the acetate himself, then climbed with it back on to the tower. Stefan had taken one step down into the well when the soldier's face stiffened suddenly and his eyes rolled back.

Lang pushed his face down close to Stefan's, shouting at him. 'Nothing we could do,' he mouthed. 'Nothing.' He shrugged and went back to his camera.

Stefan resumed his grip on the bar beneath the gunslit, biting down on his nausea. Lang, he thought, was just the man to be at this slaughter. A solid professional, single-minded, objective.

Another thought, one that had been delayed by the noise, the turbulent movement and the terrible sights, began to descend on Stefan as the half-track accelerated through a gulley in the wake of the King Tiger. *The Allies had clearly not been ready for this.* Nowhere was there a sign of counter-attack, ambush or solid defence. The Americans were scattering like rabbits, open and undefended fodder for the German guns and rockets. In the crescendo of battle it was impossible to reason further; all he could be aware of was the fact, the sickening evidence of piled corpses and running men.

The half-track turned left sharply at the end of the gulley, bypassing a smoking American tank. Ahead, the King Tiger mounted a sloping bank and sank suddenly, its exhausts spitting and hissing as snow closed over them. The Commander was shaking both fists over his head, bawling at the air above them. His tank had crashed through concealed ice and now it was tilting into a pond. The tracks churned furiously, throwing snow, ice and mud straight at the following vehicle. The half-track slid to a halt and Stefan ducked down under the showering, slicing chunks of ice and frozen earth. Beside him, Lang was cursing just audibly.

'Look! Look at my bloody fucking camera!'

A chunk of ice like a golf ball had rammed straight into the lens hood and splintered the front element of the lens.

'My only telephoto! I had to beg to get that! The only fucking one!'

'Nothing you could do,' Stefan shouted, and shrugged.

Lang began unscrewing the lens, muttering his curses into the upturned lapels of his greatcoat.

The King Tiger was almost totally submerged. Its weight was carrying it deep into the muddy bottom of the pond and the crew were frantically scrambling out through the turret. Stefan watched, almost amused, as the Commander struggled to a spot where he could stand up without the danger of submersion, and started a demented war dance. Then, in an instant, everything was gone in a soaking mist of flying snow with bright, crashing light at the centre. Stefan felt himself jolted up and back, and in less than a second he was falling head first into deep soft snow.

For an age he thought he was going to suffocate as he struggled to get himself upright and free of the freezing powder that clogged his nose, lips and ears. Sound came back suddenly and he was standing waist-deep in a drift ten feet from the half track. Stefan brushed the snow from his eyes and looked across at where the explosion had occurred. There was a deep, black hole in the bank where the tank Commander had been standing. Somewhere, the Allies were beginning to hit back.

When he tried to walk, the snow dragged at his legs and twice he toppled face-down and had to flounder himself upright. Tanks were passing on either side, flanked by foot soldiers. Stefan waved to one man, but he kept on walking, taking high, strenuous steps to stabilize himself. Another man looked straight at Stefan and his face showed nothing but disdain. It dawned on Stefan that his expensive SS greatcoat and the white armband with the word FILM stencilled on it were doing nothing towards gaining him sympathy. He began emulating the soldiers, high-stepping through the numbing snow, making for the partly-buried half-track.

The wild scream of another shell came at him, dangerously low, disturbing the air around his head. Stefan ducked, felt the momentary stillness before impact, then had his feet swept from him in an avalanche of snow, tree branches and enveloping noise. This time he was not submerged but marooned on a newly-formed hillock, spitting snow and dirt from his mouth. He sat up, wiped his eyes, and saw the steel-helmeted head and upper torso of a German soldier lying a few feet away. At first he thought the body was half-buried in snow, but when he crept nearer Stefan saw that the man had been cut in two. Dizzy, half-deaf and with no sense of direction, Stefan started to run, ploughing up the snow as his feet chopped a path through the grey and white debris.

The half-track came into view again, on its side now. Someone was scrambling over the side of the cabin.

'Stefan!'

It was Ulrich Lang, still clinging to his camera. His forehead was bleeding and he held one arm awkwardly to his side. He crab-walked towards Stefan and when he was close enough Stefan grabbed him and led the way to the shelter of a huge, torn tree.

'I thought I was finished.' Lang was shaking, putting uncoordinated movements together in an effort to wrap his coat tighter around him. 'When the truck went over that time I was halfway out. It fell on me, but the snow stopped it . . .'

'Just keep still and get your wits about you.'

'This is a mess, Stefan. It wasn't planned like this.'

Stefan remembered the curious assurance in Hitler's voice: *you will have the protection of the Sixth Panzer Army.* That was how the old man saw it, unified strength going forward like a steel wall to mow down the enemy. The 6th Panzer Army was in splinters already. Snow, fog, the rough terrain and now the Allied resistance; that was all it took to break up the advance. Tanks were no longer running in straight lines. They had zig-zagged into each other to avoid the shelling, the foot soldiers had broken formation and the smaller transports were bogging down all over the front.

'What about your film?' Stefan asked, and had to repeat the question: Lang had gone partially deaf.

'Ruined. Most of it's under the half-track. Soaked by now, exposed.' Lang shook his head and fingered the wound on his head. 'Two hours of it. Gone.'

'I'd dump the camera if I were you,' Stefan told him. 'Nobody would want a record of this.'

Lang blinked through the snow on his eyebrows and cheeks. 'I can't understand it. The front was so strong, so massive . . .'

'Inflexible,' Stefan said. 'It's being split into leaderless groups. And we're one of them.'

Three shells landed almost at once, blasting craters into the soft ground and sending up showers of earth and ice.

'We'll have to move,' Stefan shouted. 'We won't be this lucky for much longer. Come on.'

Reluctantly Lang dropped his camera into the snow

and followed Stefan at a crouch, weaving through tree branches and around the dead, twisted remains of trucks and tanks. It had started to snow again and already the craters were being covered over with a white film. It was difficult to see any form to the landscape, and even the line between ground and sky was indistinct. They half walked, half rolled down a slope and fell in beside a group of soldiers walking in a huddle behind a King Tiger.

For ten minutes they plodded along, legs and hands numb, heads filled with the noise of the tank. The soldiers moved like faulty robots, their eyes averted from exhaust fumes and swirling snow as their feet sliced awkwardly to left and right on the smoothed, slippery path cut by the King Tiger.

Suddenly there was a muffled roar somewhere ahead, and a moment later the shock wave came along either side of the tank, making miniature blizzards that swirled inwards and closed on the men. The tank stopped abruptly, its turret swinging. Three soldiers with snow in their eyes walked straight into the back of the tank, another two slid and fell when they tried to stop too quickly. At the rear, watching the small drama, Stefan signalled Lang to stop walking, then gripped his companion's sleeve in a panic when he saw the flurry of chopped snow around the tank's tracks.

'Run! Get out of the way for Christ's sake!'

The tank was reversing. One of the men on the ground went under the left track, his face a soundless mask of alarm and agony as the treads tore into his legs. Another soldier was trying to clamber over two others; for a second they became motionless, balanced among each others' legs and arms, then they slipped backwards, the man on top crashing into the rear armour and the other two falling into the oncoming tracks. The tank accelerated sharply as Stefan and Ulrich Lang side-jumped into the drifts beside the path. Stefan jammed his eyes shut on the image of a soldier's chest being flattened and another being spun by the track edge and thrown clear with one arm missing.

The tank's gun fired and the vibrating roar brought down snow, branches and clods of earth from the banking. Bent double, Stefan pointed himself away from the noise and began loping over the drifts. He was aware of Lang close behind, and when eventually they dropped into a newly-blasted crater Lang's howling, hysterical voice broke through the sounds of machines and gunfire.

'We've got to get out! We'll get killed! Stefan!' He was hanging on to the lapel of Stefan's coat, shaking harder than ever, his face stiff with fear.

'Right! Right!' Stefan slapped Lang's shoulder hard, calming him a little. 'If you want to get out you'll have to get hold of yourself. Settle down, Ulrich. Take deep breaths, sit as still as you can, and *wait*.'

'Wait? *Wait*? I'm not going to wait to get blown to bits . . .'

'We're near the back of the advance,' Stefan said, enunciating his words clearly, trying to force reason past Lang's terror. 'The Allies are resisting but our tanks are still moving forward. It'll get quieter soon. Just hold on. You've no alternative, unless you want to take your chances out there.'

Lang nodded, but his face still showed fear, dark lines along the sides of his eyes and mouth that aged him.

In the following hour neither man moved further than the edge of the crater. The number of tanks and wheeled guns that passed grew less, and the sounds of battle became slowly distanced. Shells still fell nearby but the impact was feeble compared to the blasting before. The fight, as Stefan had said, was moving away from them.

It was two in the afternoon by Stefan's watch when they crawled out of the crater and began heading east. Without maps or even a clear idea of just where they were, it was impossible to adopt any fixed route, but the rumbling to their left was a guide: if they maintained the same relative position to the shellfire, they stood a reasonable chance of finding a German rearguard unit.

Just after three o'clock, with fresh snow flurrying around his head, and with cold pain tearing along both legs and slowing every step, Stefan sighted a cluster of vehicles and two prefabricated machine-gun emplacements, gathered in defence formation on the perimeter of a small wood. He took hold of Lang's arm and began leading him to the spot, but before they reached it somebody by the nearest gun nest began yelling a warning, and a second later there was an explosion and bright orange flame tore apart the tank at the centre of the group.

Men were running in every direction. An American tank with blazing machine-guns was coming down on the outpost from a pitted hillside opposite. The big cannon swung low and fired another shell, hitting a half-track which exploded and blew up the two vehicles next to it. Flat on his face in the snow, Stefan felt his own terror rising to match Lang's. In the savagery of that kind of combat there was no chance for subtlety. No American was going to stop and listen while someone in an SS field uniform explained he was really on the side of the Allies. The only hope was to play dead.

With a suddenness that shocked Stefan, Lang was up on his feet and running towards the American tank, two hundred yards away.

'Non-combatant!' he was yelling, waving his arms wildly. 'Non-combatant!' Twice he fell, and when he stood up the second time he stopped and looked around him, wild-eyed, half mad with fear. Dead bodies like coarse-chopped meat were lying in the snow and hanging from overhead branches. Wounded men were moaning and screaming, clawing at the snow as the machine-guns rattled on remorselessly.

An American soldier in a field cape appeared a few yards from Lang. He was bare-headed, a young man with an expressionless face, his eyes slitted against the snow.

Lang threw up his arms again, holding them high over his head, and began ploughing towards the soldier, who did not move.

'Non-combatant! Non-combatant!' Lang was almost exhausted when he drew near the soldier, panting, covered in snow and the dried blood from his forehead. From where he lay, teeth locked painfully, Stefan watched as the American took one slow step back then threw his stiff arms forward. The glinting point of a bayonet came from under his cape and met Ulrich Lang with fierce, dedicated impact in the chest. Lang screamed and fell backward. The young soldier stood over him and drove the bayonet in three more times, then turned and made his way back to the side of the American tank.

For a shuddering eternity Stefan lay still in the snow, feeling himself grow more and more numb as his brain seethed with futile escape plans and crazy notions of hope. The Americans had stayed where they were, beside the wiped-out German defence emplacement. They were eating their rations and setting up camouflage covers over the tank. Even from Stefan's close position, the ambush arrangement looked sound: the place would soon look like just another burned-out post, littered with useless vehicles and dead personnel.

It was growing dark when Stefan decided to move. By rolling in half turns and pausing before moving again, he was able to ease himself away from the Americans and simultaneously create a deepening furrow in the snow, making him invisible after the first few turns.

Progress was agonizing. Two layers of thermal underwear were enough to keep a man from freezing when he was upright and moving at a good pace. Lying in the snow, Stefan had gradually absorbed several pints of melted snow into the warm cloisters beneath his uniform and greatcoat, and when that had begun to cool his circulation had become dangerously sluggish. Movement was something that needed thought and massive will power to initiate, and the numbness in some parts of his body was as bad as the pain in others. It took half an hour to move less than twenty feet, but by that time there was a natural barrier of drifting snow between Stefan and the American soldiers.

The first time he tried to stand up he failed. His knees simply refused to hold him. On the second attempt he made it, but had to keep his feet spread wide when he walked. He had no idea where he was going: his only initiative was to watch for German units and hide from Americans. The darkness gathered around him like a shroud, and as Stefan wandered on he focussed all his concentration on the mechanics of walking and kept his thoughts rigorously away from the area of self-pity. Even so, it was difficult not to think of Gretl from time to time, and when he did the pain of it put tears in his eyes.

An edge of delirium began to creep over him, a detachment so gradual that it took hold within an hour without Stefan once being suspicious that anything new was wrong. An inner dialogue was taking place between himself and Farrell: it began as deliberate imagination, but soon it built up its own momentum. They were both there in the knee-deep snow, Farrell somewhere to the left, invisible only because Stefan chose not to look at him.

'You read things all wrong,' Farrell said, after minutes of back-and-forth arguing about the battle. The voice was authentic, the words and inflections were Farrell's, right down to the muffled, unechoing tone induced by the surrounding snow drifts.

'Reading things accurately is my business,' Stefan countered. 'They weren't ready. They could have flattened the Germans if they'd been *ready*. Either they were too slow or they just didn't know what was going to happen.'

'They were ready, all right. With bright sunshine and flat territory it would have been a pushover. In this shitty country, who can say what'll happen? Snow everywhere. Low cloud so no fucker can get a plane up, unless he plans on putting on a freaky display. Fog. The best defence plans in the world go down the can with conditions like that.'

'No defences,' Stefan said stubbornly. 'I didn't see any organized defence lines.'

'They were geared for counter-attack. Which is just what they're doing, goddamnit.'

'Not well enough.'

'Too many cooks,' Farrell's disembodied voice growled. 'Eisenhower, Montgomery, Patton . . .'

'Just the same,' Stefan insisted, 'on previous performance they've done a lot better on things less important.'

The expected, subconsciously-concocted response from Farrell did not come. Instead, Stefan was shocked back to stark, bare-nerved reality by the hissing scream of a shell arcing down overhead and exploding in the snow half a mile ahead of him. For a moment he saw buildings, one of them a farmhouse, illuminated by the flash, and then there were more flashes, too many of them to comprehend, with noise so harsh and battering that Stefan dropped to his knees and clamped his hands over his ears.

The shapes of King Tigers made silhouetted interchange with the dark figures of men and smaller vehicles, all of them moving, firing as they ran from their cover. Increased shock brought Stefan back to his feet: *I'm in the middle!* he thought desperately. The American shells were coming from directly behind him, and now German guns were returning the fire right over his head. Stefan tightened the strap of his helmet with frozen, unfeeling fingers and began running to the right. *Out!* a voice screamed in his head. *Get yourself out!*

Abrupt, jarring pain in his spine stopped him dead. He had run headlong into something, it felt like a rock, and there was suddenly no strength left. Stefan felt himself roll over and over, powerless, one more fragment in the millions flying all over the Ardennes. He came to a stop on his back, lying on ground that was harder than the rest, smooth impacted snow. Bright tracer bullets and zooming shells hurtled back and forward above him, and Stefan detected a mysterious pattern in them as he started to pass out. He rallied slightly when the ground beneath him vibrated and lights cut across his vision, swerving sideways with a sound like tearing cloth. It was a vehicle, he realized, it had stopped just a few yards from him. Consciousness was breaking up again, sharding like glass, too complex for him to hold together.

A man, two men, came running from the vehicle. They were Americans, carrying guns and galloping on determined feet. Stefan heard his own breath sighing out of him and had one darkening glimpse of a torchlit face, bending over him and grinning. *Gretl*, he thought feebly: *let me think about Gretl until it's over.*

Light came back in a surge, hurting his eyes and sending a jolt of nausea through his belly. Inside he still felt cold but the air around him was warm. Stefan realized he was sitting up, propped on blanket rolls in the rear of a truck. An American truck.

Three GIs were watching him, their faces a trinity of concern. It made no sense. The truck was moving and a big fan heater was blowing warm draughts over his face and legs. Nobody said anything, they just watched, and smiled a little when Stefan moved a stiff arm and rubbed the side of his head.

The truck jolted to a halt. The soldiers moved away, climbing out through the canvas flaps. A minute or so later a man in US sergeant's uniform climbed in and picked up a wad of papers from the blankets beside Stefan.

'Your papers, Untersturmführer,' he said, and tucked them into Stefan's pocket.

German! Stefan thought. *He's a German!*

The flap opened again and a tall man in American officer's uniform folded himself in through the opening. He smiled across at Stefan and extended his hand. Truth dawned and mystery vanished. Stefan knew the face well.

SS Standartenführer Otto Skorzeny, the Führer's favourite commando.

'You were lucky,' Skorzeny said. 'How do you feel?'

'Content to be alive,' Stefan told him. 'I gather from your disguise you've been making mischief.'

'A little. To tell you the truth, I've found it very exhilarating. But I have to go back to Berlin tonight.'

'Who's winning out there?'

Skorzeny shrugged, and discreetly made no reply. 'You'll be travelling back to Berlin with me, you'll be glad to hear.'

Stefan nodded, taking in the news slowly. He was one of the very few with a choice. Back to Berlin. It hardly seemed possible. 'Yes,' he said, 'I'm very glad to hear that.'

In Berlin there was one soldier, at least, who had taken no pleasure whatever in the initial German success at Ardennes. He was General Heinz Guderian, the man who was appointed, on the day following Stauffenberg's bomb plot, to succeed General Zeitzler as Chief of General Staff. Guderian had exceptional gifts as a military theorist and commander: he had engineered Panzer victories in France during May, 1940, and in Russia in 1941, and he was the author of a widely-acclaimed textbook on tank warfare – *Achtung Panzer.*

But Hitler did not like Guderian. The root causes were complex, a mingling of the Führer's ingrained distrust of clever soldiers, a fear of all people who were too articulate, and an illogical, persistent distaste for Guderian's face. Although Hitler could not easily ignore the general's abilities, he steadfastly ignored his advice.

'It is discouraging, to say the least,' Guderian confided in a fellow officer. 'I present the man with reason and logic, and he resists me with superstition and glass-eyed disdain.'

In Guderian's experience of war, he had learned that a strong army on the offensive always needed an equally strong reserve – and that reserve, he had frequently insisted, had to be put into action before the main force was exhausted. At Ardennes, Hitler had used every available battle-ready soldier he possessed; there was no reserve. Worse still, in Guderian's opinion, was the fact that vital offensives elsewhere were now impossible. In particular, he feared a mass assault by the Russians, now that they were making such headway in Hungary.

By 24th December the tide of battle was turning against the Germans. Manteuffel's 5th Panzer army was getting close to the River Meuse, but the supporting infantry were too far behind, rendering no support at all. The Allies had meanwhile pulled themselves together and were offering a balanced resistance. Hitler refused to take the news seriously. In spite of the fact that Manteuffel's forward Panzer division was being obliterated on the 25th and 26th, the Führer would not give permission for the attack on Bastogne to be abandoned.

'Success is inevitable if there is enough determination!' Hitler screeched at his generals. Despite the danger he had left the Chancellory bunker and travelled to the Berghof. There, he began to display signs of the feverish, wild-eyed dictator who had started it all. With one arm hanging uselessly at his side he waved the other, threatening, accusing, demanding extremes of effort from everyone. When news arrived that a bloodbath was developing near the Meuse, where US General Harmon's Armoured Division was smashing the Panzers in dozens of small engagements, Hitler slammed his fist on the table and called his rumbling subordinates to order.

'We are suffering setbacks, nothing more!' He glared at General Jodl, then at the white-faced Goering. 'If my plan had been followed to the letter none of this would have happened. I can trust no one, it seems.' The yellow pallor of his skin gave him the appearance of a wax effigy, a stooped memorial of the once bright, self-assured master of the Reich. 'All has not been lost, despite the bungling and the disobedience. I have a revised plan.'

Standing behind Jodl, General Guderian sighed quietly and cast his eyes round the gloomy salon. He saw fear on some faces, resignation on others. Germany was on its knees, dying, and the Führer was still revising plans for a last-ditch battle. Offence was what Guderian felt, the unprofessional approach and the idiotic refusal to face facts made him pine, keenly, for the days when military bearing and civilized behaviour counted for something.

'Three new divisions,' Hitler snapped. 'Fresh men, twenty-five thousand of them. Even if we can't obliterate the Allies with one firm blow as I planned, we can do it piecemeal.'

Jodl looked bewildered. He was on the point of telling the Führer that he could never find five hundred fresh men, let alone twenty-five thousand, when Goering spoke up.

'We have lost the war,' he said gravely. Hitler's head snapped round, his eyes narrowed furiously. Goering continued, looking at the floor as he spoke. 'We must seek a truce, Führer. Count Bernadotte will act as our mediator.'

'That is defeatist talk!' Hitler shouted.

'With respect, sir, my words are reasoned – I can't see that we will achieve anything by prolonging this struggle. The weather at Ardennes has improved. The American C-47s are dropping supplies to their armoured divisions, they are growing stronger as we get weaker . . .'

'You are defiling this air with your cowardice!' Hitler's raging whine forced Goering back a pace, and some of the others turned aside, shocked and embarrassed. The Führer was raving, spitting his fury at Goering as if he were blasting him with a gun. 'You would betray me and the entire Reich! Coward! Traitor! How dare you come here with your snivelling treachery and try to force it down my throat!'

'Führer,' Goering replied calmly, 'I would never betray you. Never.'

'I forbid you,' Hitler rasped, 'to have any involvement in this matter. If you disobey me, you will be shot.'

None of them could believe their ears. Goering left in a silence that was almost tangible. When he had gone, Hitler turned to General Jodl again.

'Twenty-five thousand men,' he said grimly. 'Pour them into the Ardennes.'

Two days later, the Führer broadcast to the German people, telling them that Germany would rise like a Phoenix from the ashes of war. Later he attended a gathering at the Berghof, where he talked to his aides and his generals with drug-induced enthusiasm, telling them he would personally create a resurgence of power within the Reich during 1945. At that same gathering General Heinz Guderian took Stefan Gaiser aside, when he was sure that Bormann was not watching.

'I want to speak to you for a minute,' Guderian whispered. 'Where can we go?'

Stefan told the general to go into the adjoining drawing room. A little later, Stefan joined him there.

'I realize I'm putting you in an awkward position,' Guderian said, 'but it really is important. I need your opinion.'

Of all the high-ranking officers who frequented Führer Headquarters, Guderian was the only one Stefan liked without reservation. The general had the fine, sharp-featured head of a born commander, a handsome face with a warmth in the eyes that tempered the otherwise military appearance. At fifty-seven he looked vigorous, the kind of man who sailed rather than limped towards old age.

'I'll be glad to help, if I can,' Stefan assured him.

'It's about the Führer, of course. I've noticed you're close to him, and perhaps you have a chance to observe him when he isn't performing, so to speak. Tell me frankly, Gaiser – does he really know what's happening? Would an appeal for sanity get through to him?'

The question assumed a lot about Stefan's attitude to

Hitler. 'The Führer receives all the facts,' he said carefully, 'nothing ever escapes him. I believe he does know the severity of the situation, but he has such a capacity for hope . . .'

'Or self-delusion,' Guderian said glumly. 'I want to talk to him, alone, but I would like some kind of reassurance that it'll produce something. I'm tired of brick walls, dead-ends. We're in terrible danger, Gaiser. From the Russians. Have you any idea what will happen if they ever gain control of Germany?'

'I can guess,' Stefan said. He knew that Guderian would never go so far as to urge Hitler to make a separate peace with the Allies, but the commonsense of such a move would never be lost on a man like the general. 'You could try to convince the Führer, of course . . .'

'No, that isn't my point,' Guderian said firmly. 'I have to know that I won't be turned away with such finality that I'm operationally neutered. It's not simply a matter of offering a point of view and having it rejected, as you know.'

Stefan knew. No one would forget what had happened to Goering, just because he stated his opinion. 'I would say, sir, that your experience and your undoubted place in military history would save you from anything too extreme. But it *is* only my opinion.'

'Thank you.' Guderian slapped Stefan's shoulder. 'It was kind of you to help me.'

For a long time afterwards Stefan felt curiously touched by those final words. And he felt a little guilty. There was something immeasurably sad about being the technical enemy of a gentleman like Heinz Guderian.

A few days later the general was granted his interview with Hitler. With maps and charts and coolly reasoned argument, he tried to convince the Führer that it would be wise, in fact essential, for East Prussia to be evacuated and a defensive ring of troops placed around Berlin. Hitler looked at the maps, consulted the charts closely, and finally shook his head.

Guderian had been uncomfortable from the start of the meeting. Hitler had insisted that Stefan be present, thereby avoiding the awkwardness of facing Guderian alone: ever since the general had begun to put his case, the Führer had been glancing towards Stefan, who was standing stiffly by the row of filing cabinets, and that little trick had disconcerted Guderian so badly that several times he had faltered. Now, still shaking his head, Hitler looked at Stefan again with an expression that suggested he was mildly amused.

Guderian held his peace as long as he could, then he asked, 'Is there some irregularity? The papers were put together with some care . . .'

'These are the work of a madman,' Hitler rasped. 'He should be put away in an asylum.'

Stefan was painfully embarrassed. Since his return from the Ardennes the Führer had treated him like a pet dog, keeping him nearby on every possible pretext, acting out an unspoken plea for forgiveness. It was as if Hitler were saying he was sorry for risking the life of a trusted aide and was trying clumsily to undo the mistake, but in effect he only made matters worse. Several times a day Stefan was privy to the mean, often brutal treatment handed out to men who deserved compassion, thanks, even praise. Now, meeting the quick glance of General Guderian, Stefan tried to convey sympathy. Guderian inhaled sharply and put his hands on the Führer's desk.

'These are the work of *General Gehlen*,' he said, looking straight into Hitler's eyes and taking no care to moderate his voice. 'He is my chief of Intelligence and one of the ablest men who ever served you. If you want to have him stuck in an asylum, you'd better put me in there with him, for I agree totally with Gehlen. Totally!'

Hitler said nothing for almost a minute. Again, when General Guderian glanced his way, Stefan made an attempt to show there was at least one corner of sympathy and respect in the room. Guderian looked weary, worn down by frustration.

'I was hasty,' Hitler said suddenly. He was looking beyond Guderian, fixing his gaze on a picture of himself taken years before at Nuremberg. 'Of course, Gehlen is a fine man, a trusted servant of the Reich. And as for the Eastern Front, its reserves have never been so strong as they are now. You have been responsible for that and you have my deepest gratitude.'

Stefan watched Guderian's feet shift restlessly on the carpet. There could be little worse, at that point, than being a man in the general's position. A fine wit, a sparkling intellect and an intuitive grasp of warfare: for a man with such gifts to have to stand there and be insulted by the Führer's offhand, patronizing dismissal – it amounted to no more than that – must have been agony.

With ill-contained patience, Guderian said, 'The Eastern Front is not strong.' He glared at Hitler, a proud soldier no longer caring if he was sent to the firing squad for what he said. 'We have only twelve divisions there, far too few men to hold such an extended position. They could be flattened by one decently organized Russian assault force.'

'You exaggerate,' Hitler said quietly.

'Führer, I do not!'

Stefan closed his eyes, almost praying for the general. He was pushing too far, and there was no point. Hitler had no intention of giving in.

'We *must* halt the Russian advance,' Guderian went on. 'Our guns have to be in the east, and there's very little time. If things get any worse at Ardennes there won't be any guns to bring back anyway.'

Stop! Stefan pleaded silently. *For God's sake* . . .

'That is enough.' Hitler pushed back his chair and stood up. 'Gaiser, see General Guderian out.'

Guderian picked up his bundle of papers and tucked them under his arm. Hitler had already turned away by the time he reached the door. Stefan led the way to the guarded exit door, and at the top of the steps he told the general that he was sorry.

'Thank you,' Guderian said hoarsely. 'I am sorry too, for all of us.'

Outside, Stefan watched Guderian climb into his car. He had lost, but he was still a soldier, still in possession of his authority and his rank. Stefan wondered how much value that had now for the general. To most of the others who were still wearing their uniforms and their medals, it meant practically nothing.

BOOK THREE

The information Gretl had brought to the man she knew as Janus was scant, but Stefan had thought it was important enough to be passed on at once. It was a listing of field positions around Bastogne, Houffalize and Echternach where Hitler proposed to set up reinforcements and counter-attack units. In the *Treffpunkt*, one of the last coffee houses still in business along Munich's Arnulfstrasse, she sat by as usual while her contact picked up the bar of chocolate and pocketed it. For the third time in a month, just as Gretl had feared, he did not leave at once, but sat down opposite her and smiled.

'Doesn't your solemn little face ever change?' he asked.

'Sometimes. I'm just nervous.'

'Nervous behaviour's one thing that can land you in trouble. Just relax. You're a girl, I'm an officer, we're talking. That's natural, it attracts no special attention.'

'No, really . . .' Gretl made to stand up, but Farrell put his hand over hers, detaining her.

'Look,' he said softly, 'this could be the last time we meet, right? It's nearly over now, this could be my last chocolate bar. Have a drink with me, a farewell cup.'

'Very well,' she said.

Farrell went to the counter and came back with two glasses of red wine.

'You must have influence,' Gretl said.

'Charm. And enough money to pay three times the usual price.' He sat down and held his glass close to hers. 'To us, and the success of all we do.'

The wine tasted rather sour, Gretl thought, but it was still pleasant. Stefan sometimes brought her wine, and they would sit by her fireside sipping it from the English crystal goblets that had been her mother's. She reflected now that it was probably the warmth and closeness of those occasions that gave Stefan's wine its charm.

'I know a place,' Farrell murmured, 'where you can eat real steak – well, nearly real, and listen to good music while you drink more of this.'

'In Munich?'

'Yes. Less than a mile from here. Why don't you come with me? We could enjoy ourselves. It's a miserable enough life, without passing up the chance of some fun occasionally.'

Gretl shook her head firmly. 'No. I have to get back.'

He grinned. 'Mother waiting up for you?'

'Something like that.' She was growing uncomfortable again, gulping the wine to get rid of it.

'Boyfriend maybe?'

'I just want to get away. These meetings frighten me . . .'

'I'll drive you home, if you like.'

'No, I'll manage it on my own.' Stefan had told her once that she could be too sensitive, but she could not help that. Certain people, certain *men*, just made her feel itchy.

Farrell sat staring at her for a moment, then he suddenly tipped back his glass and drained it. 'Right,' he said, 'time to go, just as you keep saying.'

Flustered, Gretl took another sip from her glass then stood up. Even the business of leaving the drop points together had startled her at the beginning, and she still found it disturbing. Stefan had told her these meetings would be discreet and brief, and to Gretl that made sense. Janus seemed to have his own rules, however. He walked with her to the door and held it open for her.

'Well, then,' Gretl said, standing awkwardly on the pavement. 'This may be goodbye.'

Farrell said nothing. Instead, he took her by the elbow and steered her firmly along the street towards his parked car. Gretl resisted only for a second, then realised how dangerous it would be to make a scene. She stumbled along beside Farrell, feeling the flush rising in her cheeks.

'Hop in,' he said as he unlocked the passenger door, keeping a tight grip on her elbow.

'But I want to go home on my own!'

'Relax, I'm only taking you as far as the station. You'll accept at least *some* of my hospitality.'

Gretl eased into the seat and Farrell closed the door, locking it again. When he got in beside her he was whistling, and when Gretl took one sidelong glance at him he winked.

'Cosy,' he said, and started the engine.

They drove for only a few blocks, then Farrell pulled the car into a side turning with derelict buildings on either side. The sight of the scarred brick and glassless windows made Gretl feel threatened.

'What are you doing?' She watched his hand on the ignition key, turning it. He had a large hand, a fearfully strong hand.

'It seemed to me the only way to have a real good talk with you was to get you away from where you felt vulnerable.' He gave her the smile again. 'You're never in half the danger you seem to think you are. With me, you're safe.'

'I'd still rather get home.'

'And where's that?'

'I – I'm not supposed to say.'

'You were told that? Your contact said that to you?'

Gretl shook her head and drew her coat around her. 'No, but it makes sense. We shouldn't know anything about each other.'

'In case either of us gets caught and tortured and all that business, eh?' He was laughing at her now, and on balance Gretl preferred the smile. 'In this city,' Farrell went on, 'nobody's watching out for spies any more. They're all too busy getting their stories organized for the big day when they have to answer some tricky questions. The ones who haven't deserted, that is.'

Gretl sighed. She was feeling miserable. Could Janus not get it into his head that she just *disliked* him? Did she have to say it? 'I admire your confidence,' she said, 'I really do, but I'm not built that way. Could I please get out of the car now and go home?'

Farrell frowned. 'All that way to the Pienzenauerstrasse on your own?' He shook his head. 'Seems a risk, what with the air raids.'

Shocked, Gretl said, 'How did you know where I live?'

'You never would tell me, so I checked.' He winked slowly. 'I'm a spy, remember.'

'I suppose you know my name, too.'

'Of course. You're Gretl Bauer. I got it from your name plate.'

Gretl began to feel more insecure than she had before. It was bad enough to be in this man's mind, but to be there with a name, an address . . . 'Please, I insist, let me get out.'

Farrell leaned across and put a hand deliberately on her knee. 'Did it ever occur to you, Gretl, that we could all be dead tomorrow?'

It had occurred to her often, and she had heard the line before, too. It was usually delivered in the same heavily dramatic tone Farrell had used, and the hand on the knee was another familiar feature.

'Life's unpredictable,' he persisted, tightening his fingers, making Gretl's stomach contract. 'You and me, just one evening, what does it matter?'

'It would matter to me,' she said.

'Aw, that's just because you're nervous, you don't know me well enough.'

Gretl inhaled deeply, then said, 'I know you well enough to realise you repel me. I'm not the prude you probably imagine, I'm just rather selective.'

'So what's wrong with me?' The expression on his face was supposed to be funny, but his eyes gave away the seriousness behind it.

'To some women, to lots of women probably, nothing

at all. To me – well, we just wouldn't get on, even having a meal and a drink somewhere.' She edged her leg away from his hand and he let her. 'Let me out, now.'

Farrell said no more to her. He got out, unlocked Gretl's door, and stood aside as she stepped on the pavement and began walking towards the main road. Back in the car he sat for minutes drumming his fingers on the wheel, staring ahead, his face blank. It was growing dark when he finally moved off, gunning the engine too hard, tearing through the gears. He reached the Sonnerstrasse in ten minutes and parked the car at the end of the street. Before he got out he straightened his tie, patted his uniform lapels into place and buffed the toes of his boots with the window cloth. On the pavement he stood and watched for a while as couples strolled past, enjoying the few hours before curfew. When he saw two girls walking together, he started to follow them.

They turned out to be attractive, for whores. One was blonde, with tiny doll's features and a thin razor scar down one cheek. Her name was Eve, she told Farrell, and her dark-haired companion, fuller in the figure and older, was Annabel. He took them for a drink in a crowded, sweat-smelling bar that sold the weakest beer Farrell had ever tasted. As he talked to the girls, asking them superficial questions and not troubling to listen to the lies they concocted for answers, he could see they were starting to compete. Eve kept cutting in on what her friend was saying, and Annabel was holding her breath at every opportunity, letting him see the shape and firmness of her breasts. Farrell put them at their ease by saying he wanted both of them.

They went to Annabel's place, a cold-water flat with two rooms, one of them almost entirely filled by the bed. Farrell produced a hip flask with whisky in it, and Annabel brought glasses. They all three sat on the bed and drank every drop, then Eve went off to rinse the glasses, and a moment later Annabel followed her. When they came back they were in their underwear, sadly improvised garments that had obviously been fashioned from dress material.

'Shall I undress you?' Eve asked Farrell in a coy, childish voice.

He shook his head. 'Undress each other,' he said, and stood up from the bed, indicating that the girls should get on to it. He stood in the doorway and watched as they bounded eagerly on the counterpane. Their movements were exaggerated as they toyed with each other's garments, and when they were naked Eve looked knowingly at Farrell. She cupped one of Annabel's large breasts, and Farrell nodded. He folded his arms and leaned against the door frame, watching, his face expressionless.

It was not working, Farrell thought. There were other times when the combined beauty and outrageousness of two women making love could take the rawness from his mind, soothe him and level his anger. Farrell moved away into the other room before they were through.

Eve came out of the bedroom a few minutes later. She looked anxious, as if she might not have pleased him, as if she may not get paid.

'It was good?' she asked in a small voice.

Farrell nodded and handed her some folded notes. 'It was good,' he said. He turned and went to the door, leaving the girl standing on the threadbare carpet, counting the money as she watched him go.

Back in the car he sat for a while and watched the stragglers go by. When he moved his eyes and stared, instead, on the patch of black where the windscreen looked out on the darkened end of the street, he could see Gretl Bauer's face perfectly clearly. The rejection was still a pain in him, but now it had shifted and was shifting still. It was becoming the sharp prod of vindication. Farrell was focusing blame.

The humiliation and disappointment were hard enough, between them, to push a switch. Farrell began to decide, and having decided he felt the pain diffuse. The girl was a threat, *that* was what he had to remember. She was curious, nosey, a snooper who had the credentials, for all he knew, to light a fire under him. It was his duty to act.

A Gestapo car appeared at the far end of the street and began cruising. Farrell started the engine and put his own car into a smooth, unhurried turn. It was time for him to be off the streets, time to take his little plan home and polish it.

On the ninth day of the new year General Guderian again warned Hitler that the Eastern Front was like a house of cards. A few days later, fourteen Russian infantry divisions, plus two independent tank corps advanced across the Upper Vistula. It was the start of an offensive that grew in size and ferocity until Stalin tanks, massive artillery units and over three million Red Army troops stormed a four hundred-mile front from the Baltic Sea to the centre of Poland. Guderian's defence system collapsed. Strong forces now threatened Germany from east and west, and as Hitler withdrew to the concrete safety of his bunker in Berlin, Stefan Gaiser scanned every available communiqué, ready for any chance to short-cut the death throes of the Reich.

It was when a secretary fell ill and Stefan was appointed to put her office in order that he discovered the file on camp closures. The mimeographed orders were unsigned, but the style was undoubtedly Himmler's. Camps at Dora, Ebensee, Kemna, Maidanke and Monowitz were to be destroyed within the month, while continuing destruction of the larger camps such as Auschwitz, Belsen and Ravensbruck had to be stepped-up. In his panic, Himmler was trying to eradicate every trace of his death and torture establishments: to Stefan, who knew already that there were pitifully few units available to carry out the work, it was clear that the task Himmler had set was impossible. However, it was just as clear that the extermination squads would try to follow the Reichsführer's orders, and that meant they would use the most direct means at their disposal. There were still tens of thousands of internees in the camps, and within a couple of weeks half of them could be dead.

Stefan copied out the orders and coded them on tissue sheets as usual. He added a note, explaining that the camp at Ravensbruck should receive priority – it was full of children. The Allies, he suggested, could easily parachute troops in to ensure that the Totenkopf divisions, exhausted and shrunken in numbers, did not achieve their murderous objectives.

That same evening Stefan travelled to Munich with three other officers. Courier duty was being performed at every level by mid-January, since Hitler placed no trust in the few remaining telephone and radio links. Each man carried a packed briefcase and a complex list of assignments, ranging from delivery of papers to SD monitoring points, to the distribution of the names and descriptions of deserting officers. Stefan had the authority to choose his own work load, and he had selected the dockets and sealed packets that would take him closest to Gretl's apartment.

It was after three in the morning when he let himself into her little hallway and tiptoed to her bedroom. In the dark, he could hear her soft, steady breathing. Stefan leaned over by the bed and kissed Gretl's cheek. She woke up instantly, terrified.

'It's only me,' he whispered.

Gretl was shaking. She switched on the lamp and got out of bed. In her thin nightdress she looked more vulnerable than ever.

'I was having a dream,' she said. For the first time she did not come close to Stefan. Instead, she stood awkwardly by the wall.

'A bad dream?'

'Terrible.' She sat down on the bed again and drew a hand across her mouth. She looked ill, Stefan thought. The work she had been doing for him was producing a strain. That, and the fact that the offices where she worked during the day had twice been nearly hit by Allied bombers. Stefan went and sat beside her, wrapping his arm around her waist. The tremor against his palm was violent, the steady rhythm of an overburdened nervous system.

'Are you staying?' Gretl asked.

'No. I can't. I have to get back to Berlin as soon as I can. I'm not on my own, anyway, so I have to be extra careful this time.'

'Then why have you come?' She sounded resentful, like a petulant child being shown a toy, then told she cannot have it.

'I want you to take one more message to Janus . . .'

'No! Don't ask me, Stefan, I won't!'

He stared at her wild eyes, closed his fingers tightly around her trembling arm. 'Gretl, just one, there won't be any more. I'll be finished with this work soon, then we'll both get away, I'll see to that. But just this one message, my love. Please.'

She shook her head.

'It's important,' Stefan insisted. 'It involves the saving of lives.'

'I thought they all did that.'

'Of course. But this time I'm talking about people with no defences at all, prisoners in camps. They're all to be slaughtered, Gretl, Himmler's trying to wipe out every filthy trace of his extermination centres, and he plans to do it by the fastest means. We can stop it, or a lot of it, if word gets through to the Allies.'

Gretl was holding on to herself grimly as she turned and looked at Stefan. The shaking had invaded her face, making her lips tremble. 'Why can't you deliver the last message yourself?'

'How can I? I have to account for my movements hourly. Getting here was quite a feat.'

There was nothing she could tell him, nothing she wanted to impart of her fear, her dislike. It would have sounded petty, even though Gretl knew it was more than that. Laid out plain it would all sound so trite and silly, yet the facts were the basis for an endless disquiet that made her careless at work and sickeningly lonely at home.

'Gretl – please, will you do it?'

'Stefan, it's so much you're asking . . .' And so little, she managed to think. A small message, to be passed from one hand to another. Her squeamish nature should not be accounted as part of the equation. A communication went from Stefan to her, from her to Janus, and after that there was no involvement for Gretl at all. Good would come of the transaction, a great deal of good at a tiny cost, whatever her nerves and her imagination told her to the contrary.

'I know what I'm asking,' Stefan said.

Gretl sighed and reached for his fingers, wrapping her own around them. 'Very well,' she whispered, 'I'll do it. One more time. Then come back to me as soon as you can. Get us both away from all this misery.'

He kissed her and Gretl relaxed suddenly against him. The softening produced an identical reaction in Stefan. In spite of haste, urgency and the thronging pressures that should have driven him out of there, he wanted to stay. He pressed Gretl back on to the bed, and when they were both lying down he made no move to stop her when Gretl began undressing him.

'Crazy,' he whispered. 'I should be going.' By her ear he smelled perfume, light and flowery.

To her own small surprise Gretl rolled on top of him, enclosing him with her thighs, a gentle imprisonment. 'Soon, you can go soon,' she whispered, then buried her face in his shoulder.

A pain touched Stefan then, a sharp stab he had felt before. This body, so fragrant and soft and willing, had been penetrated by someone else. It was irrational to dwell on that, but he did and it scalded him.

'I love you so much,' Gretl moaned, quickening her hips.

'And I love you . . .' He was responding to her, fondling

the moistness between her thighs, tasting the skin of her neck, breathing her. The thought of another lover had never pained or even troubled him with other women. With Gretl it impelled him, a vortex of sweet agony, an awareness of something lost.

She rolled away from him and he followed, eager for her, oblivious now of time. To love her, at that moment, was the most important thing in the world.

The following afternoon Stefan was called to Bormann's office in the bunker. When he arrived he found the small room cluttered with metal boxes and despatch cases. Bormann sat at the centre of the muddle, his hair carefully combed as usual, his uniform tidy and correct. He tapped a folder that lay in front of him as Stefan took a chair.

'Some work for you, Gaiser. Your speciality.'

'Interrogations?'

'Correct. Two Russians, believed to be in radio contact from an unknown address in Berlin to a GRU outpost.'

Stefan had never interrogated Russians, let alone the very special kind who carried ratings with the GRU. 'Russian Military Intelligence might be outside the range of my talent,' he told Bormann. 'They're very hard men. All graduates of the Military Academy of the Red Army. That's tantamount to dealing with gorillas.'

'You should never let yourself believe the rumours put about by the enemy,' Bormann snapped. 'They're men, they feel fear and pain like any other men.'

'And what is it we want to find out, specifically?'

'Their base of operations,' Bormann said, 'and the precise nature of their work. They were caught by the Gestapo, who acted on anonymous information. They probably became careless, in view of the recent reports of Red Army successes. Anyway, I want to find their hideout. There will be records there, records we could still use. Treat these men as important, Gaiser, but don't treat them as superhuman.'

When Stefan arrived in the cellar under the Gestapo

building on the Bellevue Allee, he could see that someone had put in preliminary softening work on the prisoners. Both men were in a tiny room, tied to separate chairs. One had blood oozing from his mouth and his eyes were puffed and discoloured. The other one had a crimson patch on top of his head where a clump of hair had been torn out.

'They won't say anything,' the Gestapo officer in charge told Stefan.

'I'll be the judge of that. Where can we talk?'

The man led the way to a damp, dimly lighted office with mould growing in the corners.

'Why do these places always have to look like dungeons?' Stefan asked. 'And the smell!'

'It's seepage,' the officer said. 'When we tried to heat this room, the walls got even damper. You get used to it, in time.'

'Only if you have to.' Stefan brushed the seat of a chair with his document case and sat down. 'Now, tell me what's happened with these two, right from the start.'

'They were picked up on the Kurfürsten Damm. They tried to make a run for it when they were challenged. We've had them here since early this morning, and they haven't said a word. They make out they can't speak German.'

'We'll be in a mess if that's true,' Stefan murmured. 'I don't speak Russian.' He knew they would be fluent in German, because if they operated inside Berlin they had to be very special, as Bormann had guessed. There was every chance they were co-ordinators for the Red spy network in Western Europe – Heydrich himself had suspected there was an organising cell in the capital. 'What subtleties have you used on them, so far?'

'They've been beaten,' the officer said coldly. 'We did nothing special, though. Orders from the Chancellery. We were to await your arrival.'

'I could have wished you hadn't touched them at all,' Stefan sighed. 'It makes them numb, you know. A pinprick might have hurt a few hours ago. Now, I doubt if either one of them would feel the odd jab from a bayonet.' On the way, Stefan had done some careful thinking. He had determined to abandon as many humanitarian principles as he had to in the pursuit of information. There would be a neat irony in enabling the Nazis to hold off some of the Russian fire until the Americans were closer.

'Separate them,' he told the officer in charge. 'Put one in a cell and leave the other with me.'

When Stefan entered the little room a few minutes later, he found they had left him the prisoner with the painfully inflicted bald patch. The man was fully conscious and rather more alert than before: as Stefan had expected, the prisoner was worried about what might be happening to his partner elsewhere.

'Good afternoon,' Stefan said brightly. He could see the man's glowering hatred for the uniform, a little fire that would eat at his reserves of caution and energy. 'We're going to talk, you and I. First, I'll tell you what I know about you. You are an agent of the Russians – not a difficult thing for me to guess, since the only mumbles you've passed since coming here have been in that ridiculous tongue. No doubt you work for GRU, Division One.' Stefan put his back to the door and leaned on it, smiling almost casually. 'Now you'll answer some of my questions. First, I want to know exactly where you've been working from.'

The man shook his head, simultaneously making it clear that he understood, and that he had no intention of talking.

'You think you are stronger than our torture, do you?'

The big square head nodded.

'Then you have been misinformed about us. Sometimes, we find that the most effective way to punish a man is to let him go free.'

The prisoner frowned for a moment, then resumed his scowl.

'A man like you, for instance,' Stefan went on. 'You were arrested at a place that is probably near your operations centre. That place would be recognized by your masters if they heard its name on the radio. We know they intercept our signals, of course, and we could make sure they pick up one travelling between SD Headquarters and a Reich Security unit at, say, Breslau.' Stefan stood away from the door suddenly, as if he had made a decision. 'Frankly, matters have reached a stage where we don't care too strongly what you're hiding from us. There remains the satisfaction, however, of knowing that the GRU will send some people to look for you – and butcher you, I've no doubt.'

'Explain that!' the man blurted in clear German.

'Ah, I see you care about your skin after all. Or is it your reputation at home that worries you more?'

'I want you to tell me what you mean about a radio signal!'

'You know perfectly well,' Stefan shouted back. 'It's one of your own techniques. Or perhaps you're not aware of that – maybe such things are kept from the labourers in field work.' He lowered his voice and said, 'GRU will learn you've talked. They'll hear you've told us things.'

'They would never believe that!'

'Of course they would. Their high standards wouldn't allow them to doubt it. And we would make sure they didn't take long to find you. We'd colour the message with the news that you'd escaped in such-and-such an area, and were believed to be making a run for the Allied lines. You'd be garbage within hours – and so would your family, no doubt.'

Again, as Stefan had observed so dismally often, the fear of reprisals against kin was enough to pull the joists from under a strong man's will. He had gone into that room prepared to do worse, but a straightforward threat of evil – someone else's this time – had worked. Stefan felt a small surge of relief.

'If I tell you,' the prisoner said, 'what happens?'

Within a buckling system Stefan thought it was safe enough to turn benign, if only once. 'I'll have you released.'

'What?' Suspicion came back and hardened the man's face.

'You'll be set free.'

'That sounds like clemency. What is it, really?'

'Perhaps it's the act of an officer of the Reich who might need a good word afterwards.'

'And there would be no radio signal?'

'None. It'll be up to you to make your way to the Allied lines, and render yourself useful enough to warrant asylum, before the German or Russian authorities know what you're doing.'

The man considered it gravely for some minutes. Then he nodded at Stefan.

'Speak slowly,' Stefan said. 'I want to get everything down.'

'We've been using an attic above a derelict pharmacy. Taunte Kleist Strasse, number sixteen.'

'Who is your senior co-ordinator?'

'I don't know his name.' The Russian caught Stefan's frown and spread his hands. 'It's true. Nobody gets to know names . . .'

'But most operatives know them anyway.' Stefan murmured.

The man sighed. 'The network – our network, that is, there could be more – was organized by a man called Zamyatin. He's something powerful with the Party and he's in the field himself. I've never seen him, but I know he established everything here and in Munich. The one directly controlling us is called Zartoff, David Zartoff. I've no idea where he hides out, there's no way of knowing with any of them.'

Stefan wrote it down. 'Call signs?' he said, and waited.

'Look, there's a limit . . .'

'The limits to my patience are a shade finer,' Stefan warned. 'Call signs, as many as you know.'

During the next hour the Russian began to talk more easily. Stefan covered four sheets with detailed notes. After another hour, when investigators had been to the hideout and came back with documents, radio equipment and some small arms, Stefan again spoke alone with the prisoner.

'You will be released soon – you and your companion. No record of this arrest will be made, and it will probably appear to Moscow that you've been killed, or simply gone into hiding. Your families should be safe, at least until the Allies can make some arrangement for them.'

The man's hopes were slim, he clearly knew that, but he also knew they were a lot better than before. 'I believe I can take your word,' he told Stefan, 'even though you are a Nazi.'

'Appearances can be deceptive,' Stefan said. He left the prisoner then and went upstairs to the controller's office, where he commandeered the radio telephone. He dialled the Chancellery number and spoke directly with Bormann in the bunker. After explaining what he had uncovered, and adding that he believed there was nothing to be gained from further questioning, Stefan listened impassively as Bormann stiffly congratulated him, and ordered Stefan to see to the execution of both prisoners.

To the respectful witnesses in the office, Stefan explained what would now happen. 'Secretary Bormann has ordered that the Russians be taken to the northern outskirts of the city, and then released.' He smiled thinly at their blank faces. 'The GRU will already be aware that their servants have talked. We will let them be dealt with by their own kind.'

The news was easy enough for the others to believe. Authority made fewer openly harsh decisions than before, and as Ralph Farrell had observed at his first meeting with Stefan, no one really knew who had the power to sanction what: nowadays that was truer than ever, with the Gestapo spending half the time looking over their own shoulders instead of other people's, and SD officials conserving energy for cleansing operations on their personal dossiers.

Stefan spent the remainder of the afternoon in a tidying exercise. The report of his interrogation was filed at SD headquarters. Since the time in February, 1944, when SD had finally absorbed the SA, a lot of confusion had entered the mountains of filed documents, and the meticulous double-checking instituted by Heydrich had been abandoned. To be doubly sure there would be no later scrutiny and back-checking with Gestapo, Stefan deliberately filed the docket under the wrong month and year. Back at the bunker, where Bormann still struggled to control his own flood of top-secret documents, Stefan deposited a copy of his report, knowing it would simply be scanned, set aside for filing, and ultimately forgotten. The confirmation of the execution of the Russian prisoners was clipped to the report, counter-signed by a Gestapo officer too new to the job and too confused to know what he was doing.

Bormann, as anticipated, skimmed through the report while Stefan stood by, then threw it on top of his filing tray.

'Where are the captured files?' he asked.

Stefan told him they were piled in the corridor outside.

'Good.' Bormann immediately set to clearing a space on his cluttered office floor, and Stefan helped him. When they had heaped most of the locked boxes, sealed dockets and routine sheaves of multi-coloured paper against two walls, the Russian files were brought in and bundled against the front of the desk.

'That will be all, Gaiser,' Bormann said.

'I'd be quite happy to help you go through them,' Stefan told him.

'No, no, that'll be all, just leave me to it.' The eagerness on Bormann's face was a novelty. It was as if he saw the files as a direct means of harming the Russians, of halting their advance.

Stefan returned to his own quarters. There was still

work to do, most of it dull and predictable, but he was feeling good. Taking a measured risk with the decaying fabric of Reich security had been exhilarating, a refreshing crunch across the eggshells he had been tiptoeing on for so long. He stripped to the waist and began washing at the small basin in the corner, humming to himself as he lathered his arms, smiling at the thought of Bormann on his knees, poring over the captured Russian files. For Stefan it had been a smooth operation with a touch of careful sabotage. There were no movements in the air, no portents to signify that the day's work had in fact been momentous, that Stefan had uncovered something that would change his life as abruptly as it had been changed ten years before.

When Gretl spoke to Janus on the telephone he was as curt and brief as usual.

'We should meet,' she told him.

'Very well. The third place. Does that suit you?'

She said it did.

'Today. Five o'clock.'

Gretl left work at a little after four. She picked her way through the rubble of a bombed building across the way from SD Records and began walking towards the Nussbaumstrasse, a journey that would take her fifty minutes on foot. Since the bombings had started she preferred to walk; there was nothing worse she could think of than to be shut in a bus or train, unable to fight her way out if a raid started. Since childhood, she had applied the advice about thunder storms to other potential emergencies: never shelter and become a standing target, but move into the widest spaces available.

The bar of chocolate weighed like lead in her coat pocket. Since lunchtime the anxiety had grown, the inordinate fear that she had somehow advertised her treason. She could barely look people in the eye when she felt like that, and even though the records office was in chaos, with files and heavy-bound records being destroyed, moved to the Chancellory, altered or re-written, with people working at fever pitch to keep up with the hysterical memos issuing from a dozen directions, Gretl still felt she stood out. It had been a relief to get away from the office, but as she walked on through the busy streets the tension began to grow again. From imagined jeopardy she was heading for the real thing, the concrete act of subversion.

The meeting point was called *Der Trutathn*. It was a small place where a year before people were able to buy tea, coffee, sandwiches and cakes. Now they served only a synthetic coffee but people still went there, because it gave them an excuse to sit together for a while with the thick cups warming their hands. Gretl arrived earlier than she had expected to, but she went inside anyway and sat down at a table near the back. She ordered the coffee and sat forward in her chair, turning up her coat collar and wishing, as she often did on these occasions, that she was a smoker.

At five, as the old battered clock across the road was chiming the hour, Gretl heard the door open. She did not look up. She went on sipping the acrid liquid from her cup and casually laid the bar of chocolate on the edge of the table beside her. There was a murmured exchange at the counter, then the expected tread of footsteps towards her table, making Gretl's heart pound at her throat.

'Fräulein Bauer?'

She looked up, startled, almost dropping her cup. The face was unfamiliar, forbidding.

'You are Fräulein Gretl Bauer?'

There was another man standing by the door, watching, and he was dressed the same, black leather overcoat, black hat. Gretl's heart was lurching now. 'Yes,' she said, and felt her features moving the wrong way as she tried to look innocent.

The man picked up the bar of chocolate and put it in his pocket. 'Come with us, please.'

'But I'm waiting for a friend.'

'Come along.' The man took her by the arm and lifted her roughly from the chair.

'Where are you taking me?' Gretl stared round at the other customers, appealing for help with her eyes, but they were all too engrossed with other things, reading old newspapers, drawing shapes in the wet puddles on the tables.

Outside, the two men led Gretl by the arms to a car and bundled her into the back. She sat rigidly, her hands clamped in her lap as one man got in beside her and the other started up the engine. *Stefan!* her mind screamed, *they're taking me away! Please God, Stefan, help me!*

The driver looked at Gretl in his mirror for a moment and he shook his head, perhaps in pity. Then he drove off.

Moving in the dark and finding several of the reliable landmarks missing, Stefan took an hour to cover a distance that could be walked in half the time during daylight.

The block next to Gretl's had been flattened as a safety measure, after Allied bombing had reduced it to a swaying shell. The bank opposite was almost gone, too. Twice Gretl had been on the point of moving, but then the raids had moved further north and she had decided to stay. Munich looked nothing like itself, light entered rooms at new and disturbing angles and whole streets and skylines had vanished. At the dark of the moon, the city was a puzzle. Climbing the steps to the big black front door, Stefan had to pause twice and convince himself he had located the right place.

There was no reply to his knock on the apartment door. Using the key he always carried inside his necktie, he let himself in and closed the door softly behind him.

Gretl was not there. Her bed was neatly made up, the customary wine bottle and glasses were set on the table near the fireplace, everything sat with the familiar tidiness, but the vacancy was disturbing.

Stefan went into the bedroom again and stood there, lost for a solution. He had no inclination to panic; what he felt rather was a small disruption. The regular meetings following a drop were a strong feature of his life, they had come to mean what religious belief meant to other people, they were a spiritual comfort. Of all the contingencies he had prepared himself for on the trip across the city, this was one Stefan had overlooked, and he stood still for a whole minute, transfixed by a shapeless worry.

Then he remembered Fräu Webel. She was old and lived alone two streets away. Several evenings a week Gretl had taken to visiting the widow and sitting with her, talking, listening to reminiscences of happier times in Munich. Gretl had told Stefan how much she liked the old woman and how she worried about her. She would be there now, Stefan decided. It was a reasonable assumption. He would sit down and wait.

A car door slamming brought him out of the chair just as he was starting to drowse. Stefan put out the light and moved to the window, pulling the blackout curtain aside carefully. Three torches were flashing down on the street, illuminating a Gestapo car and four or five men, two of them in SS uniform. It was a routine search squad, and they were coming up the front steps.

Stefan was out of the apartment before they had the main door open. He ran to the fire escape window at the back of the building, and jerked it open, then swung his leg out over the sill. He had slid down almost his full length, probing with his foot, before he realized the escape had gone. He was hanging twenty feet above tangled ironwork and rubble.

Getting back through the window was difficult, the frail wood crumbled and splintered under his hands, and when Stefan put his knee on the ledge one ragged shard stabbed into him. The sudden pain unbalanced him and he began to fall backwards. A hand saved him, a strong hairy fist bunched around his lapels, dragging Stefan through the window and down on to the carpet.

'Who are you?'

The voice was as harsh as the torch beam, shining into Stefan's eyes past the muzzle of a Luger. For an instant he saw the face, young and tough, breathing through the mouth with the effort of running up the stairs ahead of the others. His collar flashes identified him as an SS Scharführer.

'That was close,' Stefan breathed. He got himself to a crouch, one hand on the wall behind him.

'Identify yourself, please!'

'Of course.' Stefan rose slowly, letting his fingers move towards his tunic pocket. The papers were half removed when he swung his head sideways and down, cracking the man on the bridge of the nose. When the gun hand came up Stefan grabbed the wrist and forced it up faster. The Luger's barrel smashed through the Scharführer's teeth. He was starting to howl when Stefan thumbed the trigger and blew the back of his neck away.

Time and space became a jumble. The others were in the passage, Stefan saw their flailing torch beams and heard their noise. He knew he was moving at them, running too fast to brake, and when he ran into the first man his angle altered. Stefan was falling. His inertia and a nearby wall righted him again and a wild punch hit a chin, clearing the way at the top of the stairs. Something thick and heavy struck the top of his head and he took the stairs without the benefit of balance. Stefan tripped, fell several steps, and was on his feet again, still running. When he reached the main door the handle struck his stomach, winding him and saving him from the brink of unconsciousness. He jerked the door open and leapt out on to the street.

Nobody followed him, probably because there was no trail that anything less than a tracker dog could find. For an hour Stefan kept to the rubble-strewn back streets, losing himself, and when he was too exhausted to go any further he crawled under the wreckage of a railway hut and covered his entrance with stones.

He moved off again just before daylight. The pain in his skull was blinding, and he had jarred his right knee badly. It took another hour of limping progress to locate the hotel where he was registered, and a further twenty minutes to get up the fire-escape and into his room without being seen.

By nine o'clock repairs were complete. Stefan had bathed, field-bandaged his knee and rearranged his hair to cover the grazed swelling on his scalp. Contingency measures had paid off to the extent of making him look good as new in a fresh, well-pressed uniform, shirt, tie and polished boots. Another habitual measure had ensured that he came out of his own room at the right time; Stefan always left a window open.

While he was pretending to eat breakfast, he went over the night again, scanning it with growing objectivity. He was comfortably sure of two things: Gretl was safe, and so was he. Attacks on search squads were nothing new, and the only one who had seen him clearly was the dead Scharführer. As a resident of the block and a Government employee at that, the only harassment Gretl might possibly have suffered would be a routine questioning and an identification check. It had been a mess, but it was over without anything important being damaged.

Stefan was on the way back to Berlin with a bagful of despatches before mid-day. He was tired and aching, and he was deeply sad not to have seen Gretl. Next time, he promised himself, he would go to her earlier, and stay longer. The peace of that decision eased him into a long, dreamless sleep.

Two days after the capture of the Russian documents, Stefan left the bunker on a three-day transfer to administrative duty at his old stamping ground on the Reichenhallerstrasse, the Black House. By that time, the place was only partially occupied, and was used as a munitions store. Bormann had insisted that order be restored: consignments of small arms, components and ammunition were being issued on a prodigal basis, and the flow had to be controlled. Sensing Stefan's slight annoyance at being posted to a job that would have been filled, normally, by a senior bureaucrat, Bormann pointed out that the manpower shortage made it necessary to appoint hundreds of men to posts they were not actually trained for.

'Besides,' Bormann added sarcastically, 'the Führer still appears to think you're too precious to be sent out on really dangerous work.'

The staff operating the arms depot were mostly old or disabled Wehrmacht personnel. They moved slowly and their work was haphazard. Boxes of Luger ammunition were left lying in corridors, and crates of precious replacements and servicing kits sat in open rooms where anyone with enough superficial authority could help himself. Stefan sensed the tightening at his arrival, the speeding up of the slapdash routine. The Wehrmacht could never be conditioned to like the SS, but their obedience was usually instinctive.

Stefan took the officer in charge, a lame Oberleutnant called Arenz, up to the old administrative office and told him to sit down. The man was over fifty, with the permanently weary eyes of a soldier who had spent too many days and months scanning horizons.

'You have come to discipline us,' he said.

Stefan shrugged at him. 'I don't know. It could be that the system here is at fault. I'll rectify what needs rectifying. First of all, I want you to tell me if you have any complaints.'

Arenz looked surprised. 'A few, I suppose.'

'Air them, then. Don't trouble yourself that I'll go running back to SD headquarters and file you as a dissident. You're a soldier, a man who's seen honourable service.' Stefan pointed to the Knight's Cross at Arenz's throat, and lower to the gold Wound Badge on his tunic pocket. 'I always respect mature judgment.'

Haltingly at first, then more fluently as he got used to

the idea of complaining to an ear that was listening, Arenz told Stefan about the obstructions he laboured under daily. First, there was the erratic supply position. Items turned up for which no order could be located, others never appeared at all, although they were listed on the monthly inventories. Sometimes the boxes were wrongly labelled. Then there was the staff problem. Arenz had been landed with the dregs, he said. Men who should have been in military hospitals, men with pain, partial derangement, battle fatigue and crushing grief were herded in and expected to work like fresh young recruits to the Quartermaster's depot. But the root cause of inefficiency, according to Arenz, was the system of requisitions. It was simply too lax. Three different forms of requisition were accepted, and there was no way of telling who had the right to sign those forms.

Stefan listened, and within ten minutes he outlined a plan. First, a supplies clerk would be appointed, someone who was alert enough to check all incoming materials and refuse to accept consignments that were short, and chase up others that did not arrive. There would be staff revisions, too. Fresher men, with a clearer routine to follow. Finally, a new requisition would be drafted, and Arenz would be provided with a check list of the signatures he could accept.

'What do you think?' Stefan asked. 'Will these proposals improve matters for you?'

'If they are ever implemented . . .'

'They will be. Within ten days.'

'I'd no idea things could be organized that quickly any more.' Arenz stood up, beaming his gratitude. 'I'm grateful to you, sir. For listening to me, as much as anything else.'

Stefan accompanied Arenz back downstairs, and asked to see the emergency reserve of guns and ammunition in the annexe. To get there, it was necessary to go out through the front door of the Black House and through a locked gate at the side. As they went down the steps, a man moved to the edge of the opposite pavement. Arenz and Stefan noticed him at the same time, both pairs of trained eyes spotting the irregularity, the singular purpose in the man's stride.

'Watch out!' Arenz yelled and threw himself on the steps, the keys flying out of his hand. The man across the road already had his gun drawn and as the first shot was fired Stefan leapt over the stone balustrade and landed on the stony soil at the side. He rolled once and came up at a crouch, slamming his body against the stonework as a second and third bullet ploughed into the ground beside him. The gunman ran to the middle of the road, sighting on Stefan with a double-handed grip, but by that time Arenz was up and hobbling at him, aiming his own pistol, and the man turned and ran.

Stefan followed him. They ran the length of two streets and when the gunman tried to swing into an alley he slipped and landed on his elbow. Ten yards behind Stefan heard the howl of pain and in seconds he was on top of the man, twisting the injured arm across his back.

'Right! Identify yourself!'

'My arm!' the man screamed. 'For Christ's sake!'

'Your name, if you don't want the arm snapped!'

'Luscher! My name's Luscher!'

Stefan released him suddenly, and as the man tried to flex the arm he found himself being hoisted by the collar of his raincoat and dragged backwards into the alley he had been heading for. There was a fractured slat fence and Stefan yanked his prisoner through the narrow opening, banging his head on either side. One sharp, final tug put the man against a wall at speed, and the impact on his ribs drove the remaining breath out of him.

'When you can talk again,' Stefan said, 'I want a detailed explanation.' He pulled the automatic from the man's jacket and waved it under his nose. 'As mysteries go, this one intrigues me.'

The man was young, with a sharp-eyed, squat-nosed face, the face of someone who was naturally tough but had no instinct for viciousness. His eyes were following the track of the gun muzzle as he gulped desperately, getting together enough air to make speech possible.

'My name is Luscher,' he eventually gasped, then howled as Stefan thumped the gun butt against his breastbone.

'The truth.'

'I told you – aah!' Again the heavy metal struck his chest.

'Luscher isn't an English name,' Stefan hissed.

The man blinked, set his lips. 'What?'

'You have a minute. One minute. Then I'll swallow my curiosity and put a bullet through your neck.'

Fear and pain collided and the man slumped against the wall. 'My name's Aitken,' he said. 'How did you know . . .'

'When a man's in agony he loses control of his skills. Your Munich accent slipped towards Yorkshire when I twisted your arm.' Stefan pulled his victim away from the wall and dragged him closer to the fence. 'I'll have reinforcements in a minute. It would be a good idea if you told me just what you are and why you tried to kill me, before they get here.'

Aitken showed a glimmer of resistance, but it died when Stefan raised the gun again. 'I was ordered,' he said.'

'Who ordered you?'

'London. Whitehall.'

'That makes no sense to me,' Stefan warned.

'It doesn't make much more to me. Honestly. I was sent your name and description, and told where to watch out for you. The order was to shoot you.'

'Why me? Who exactly do you work for?' When Aitken clamped his mouth shut Stefan put the muzzle of the gun on his cheek. 'You'll tell me, Aitken.'

'I'm not required to divulge . . .'

'And I'm not required to keep you alive.'

A long, shuddering sigh escaped Aitken's throat. 'I'm with Special Operations Executive.'

'That's a lie!'

'It's not, I swear.'

Stefan looked at the man hard, and he saw it was true. 'And you don't know why they want me dead?'

'I do what I'm told. All I know is that you're a German officer. I've got no special information about you.'

Stefan released Aitken's lapel and pushed him towards the rubble and half-ruined buildings at the far end of the fence. 'Get moving. Run. And keep running.'

Aitken looked suddenly bewildered. 'You're letting me go?'

'I'm letting you go. Run, I said!' Stefan thrust the gun back in the young man's hand and pushed him again. 'Get yourself out of Berlin, or you won't last a week.' He stood and watched as Aitken began darting through the mounds of brick and stone, then he turned and went back through the gap in the fence. There were three soldiers at the corner with their guns drawn, and they were looking confused.

'Forget it,' Stefan shouted to them. 'We've lost him.'

For two days following the encounter with Aitken Stefan went about his work in a daze. He racked his brain, reviewed every move he had made since joining the Nazis, and still found no clue. He did manage to feel some resentment: he had laboured hard in the interests of the SOE, harder and at more personal risk than duty required, and if he had expected anything from them it was not a bullet. Stefan wondered, vaguely, if this was what they planned to do with all their well-informed agents now that the war was virtually over. Kill them, erase whatever threat they might pose to a post-war show of clean hands.

When he returned to the Chancellery bunker, Hitler was being given the news that the Russians were on the brink of taking Warsaw. On the upper floor, Bormann was surprisingly buoyant. The two Red spies, he told Stefan, had been the gateway to much bigger things.

'They were couriers, it seems. Most of the files contained nothing but old intelligence. But there was one coded address, Gaiser, and that was the bonus. It led us straight to the GRU co-ordinators.'

'You've had them questioned?'

Bormann shook his head. 'They're dead. Shot themselves when our men broke in. They tried to destroy their papers, too. But they failed.' He rubbed his hands. 'We have details of espionage operations in Berlin, Hamburg, Kiel, Munich and Hanover. We now know exactly who organized the bombings at Bremen and Dusseldorf. And we have a complete listing of all GRU spies operating in Western Europe.'

Stefan wondered how much good Bormann thought all that would do the Reich now, but he did not ask. Instead he offered polite congratulations. Then he went on to explain what he had done to straighten out the problems at the Black House.

'Excellent,' Bormann said. 'You have my clearance to go ahead with the proposals. Do it quickly, though. There is other work for you.'

The other work turned out to be security filing. It was a tedious job, but it reflected Bormann's enhanced trust in Stefan, since the papers he was now allowed to handle were normally kept well away from anyone other than Bormann himself and his confidential secretaries. The irony did not amuse Stefan. A week before he would have felt he was in Aladdin's cave, privy to a wealth of information that would be of immense value to the Allies. Now, Stefan felt no compunction at ignoring the material. As soon as he could, he would get himself away from Berlin and take Gretl with him. After that, he would do whatever the prevailing conditions required him to do.

It was late in the evening, as he sorted a sheaf of protective custody orders into alphabetical order, that one name jumped up at Stefan from the paper. He blinked and read it again. Konrad Bauer. On the orders of SS Gruppenführer Elbogen, Gretl's father had been arrested and sent for questioning to Gestapo headquarters in Berlin. Only a summary of findings was attached to the order, and when Stefan turned to the small sheet his fingers were shaking. He read the words and then read them again, willing them to change.

> Bauer's complicity in his daughter's espionage activites was not confirmed. Transportation to Dachau effected this date.

Frantically Stefan began to rummage through the other papers, his mind whirling as urgency and haste made him drop folders and scatter reports on the floor. Then he found it, an arrest order with Gretl's name at the top in terrifying capitals.

At first he could not read the summary. It was as if he had stepped into an area of time that was reversible, if only he could pull himself back. Then he caught himself, took a deep, shaking breath and let the words stab into his brain.

> No formal confession was made. It was determined that the prisoner passed information received at her place of employment, the Records and Statistical Unit of the Sicherheitsdienst, to a second party whose identity she did not know. Transportation to Dachau effected this date.

Minutes passed before he could move. When he did, Stefan began to straighten the papers and push them back into their folders. His mind was paralysed. All he could feel was a tremendous pressure, a crushing weight of guilt that did not break through on him until he was in his own quarters, huddled in a chair with his hand clamped over his mouth. As the pain washed over him he moaned and felt everything begin to break, his courage, his certainty, his hope.

'Gretl,' he whispered when it was safe to uncover his

mouth. The full blast of horror hit Stefan then, the understanding that she had been taken from him, all he wanted in life. And he was the one who had made it happen.

The pattern of loss, when it finally stood out clear in his mind, was obscene. No one knew better than he, a seasoned officer of the SD, just what a risk anyone took when they raised a finger against the administration. Yet he had argued with Gretl, *cajoled . . .*

Shame, an agonizing torrent, poured over him. Self-loathing was a curdled lump in his stomach that erupted with devastating suddenness: Stefan threw himself at the washbasin and vomited.

A little later the urgency established itself. He had to get to her, *save her*. Simultaneously he wanted to know how it had happened, why and where, but those details would be filed at the Gestapo building in Prinz Albrecht-strasse. He knew where she was, that was all he needed.

A plan of procedure began to form as he cleaned himself up. Stefan had power and authority enough to cross the minor official barriers: he also had more cause to do so now than ever before.

Drying his hands, he glanced at himself momentarily in the mirror. His face was gaunt, drawn. The eyes looked sunken. Stefan had never seen himself look so ill. Nor had he ever loathed himself quite so much.

January, 1945

The Dachau complex sprawled behind double wired fences in a valley near Munich. In huts, labour blocks, medical experimentation units, punishment areas and on open ground at the rear of the camp, more than seventy thousand people were held prisoner. The death rate was high, but it was more than equalled by the rate of intake. Since the spring of 1944 it had been impossible to maintain even a semblance of hygiene. There were regular outbreaks of spotted fever, typhoid and dysentery. While every effort was made by the SS to keep prisoners segregated, the sheer vastness of numbers and the desperate staffing problems led to an inevitable mixing of races, age groups and even sexes. Identities were lost, small family units were split and it became hard for the camp administration to tell Jew from Gentile, Russian from Pole or Czech.

'You have to expect chaos,' Sturmbahnführer Pierkowski said wearily. He was sitting behind his plywood desk in one of the few clean rooms in Dachau, the office used by himself and his deputy, Ziel. 'Controlling this place is the same as controlling a town, and not a small town, either.' He looked up at his visitor to see if he was eliciting sympathy. 'We have a munitions factory within the complex, you know. That has to be heavily guarded, which means I don't have the men to spare for ordinary disciplinary work or simple maintenance. And the disease, it creates havoc.'

'I know you labour under difficulties,' Stefan said. 'I'm here merely to assess the extent of your problems.'

'And to report back to the Führer.' Pierkowski shook his head and pointed to a pile of papers almost a foot high, lying on a chair by the door. 'One week's admissions, Captain, and there are maybe thirty names on every sheet of paper. What does Berlin expect of me?'

'I told you, this isn't the start of a disciplinary move against you, Sturmbahnführer. There is genuine concern on your behalf.'

'You'll forgive me if I find that difficult to believe. This place should have been closed down long ago. Instead, it's been allowed to grow and grow until it's reached the point where it's out of hand. And all that time I've had to cope. I've had to see whole weeks and months of hard work go for nothing while the authorities turned this into a human dumping ground. It's rather late in the day for concern, if you ask me. What can anybody do now, anyway?'

'That isn't for me to say,' Stefan replied. 'I have to note what I see and make my report. My involvement ends there.'

Pierkowski looked down glumly at the Access Order on the desk. It was signed by Bormann. 'I suppose I should be grateful that Berlin remembers we're here. You'll need an escort. If you'll wait, I'll get it arranged.' He lumbered to his feet, pulled on his cap, and left the office.

As soon as the door closed Stefan snatched up a pile of the admission records and began scanning the names. He had known in advance that Dachau was overcrowded, he had anticipated the turmoil and equipped himself with a plan of the camp; but when he had arrived and shown his forged permit to the guard at the main gate, the enormity of the task dawned on him, adding more pain to the agony he already suffered. The place was just as the commandant had described it, a town, a rambling, disease-ridden community where a hundred people could vanish without trace, let alone one.

He found Gretl's name near the bottom of a crumpled sheet, and opposite it a scrawled letter L. Her father's name was on the same slip, but there was no mark opposite his name at all. Stefan put the papers back and sat down, feeling the exhaustion catch him for a moment, trying to draw him into rest.

Stefan knew a great deal about Dachau now, and he could not sit there and pretend he had not remembered.

Top secret documents in the bunker were crammed with the reports of visiting health supervisors, SS administrators, statistical officers and the senior camp officials themselves. Pierkowski could whine about being an embattled functionary, but what he amounted to in reality was a butcher, a man who regularly killed prisoners on his own whim, or the whims of the lunatics who worked alongside him. To make space he killed, to punish he killed, and when a new wave of disease broke out he slaughtered wholesale with the official blessing of Reichsführer Himmler.

On the evening before making the trip to Dachau, Stefan had spent three hours in Bormann's restricted file room, filling his head with the atrocities that were commonplace at the camp. Why he did that, he had no clear idea, but it had seemed imperative. Perhaps he had been looking for a glimpse of hope in the last place it was likely to be found.

The facts jolted through his mind as he sat and waited. There were a number of doctors and surgeons at Dachau engaged on experimental work that appeared to have no scientific purpose at all. The effects of prolonged immersion in ice-cold water had been observed in hundreds of prisoners, men and women. The water tests were comprehensive and lacked any concern or respect for humanity: the prisoners were placed in the freezing water and kept there until they went unconscious, then blood was removed from the neck at intervals as body temperature dropped. No prisoner was ever allowed to come out of the water alive, since it was an important part of the test to determine just how long, on average, it took a human being to die in those conditions. Then there were the malaria experiments. Sporozoites taken from mosquitos were injected into prisoners in quantities much greater than anyone would suffer in the tropics, and then the doctors would experiment with possible cures for the resulting illness. The cures were usually bizarre and always ineffective. Patients who did not actually die of the disease, or of the attempted cure, were either left to die or executed to make room for fresh guinea pigs. There were also pressurization tests that ruptured livers and brains, gas tests which scarred and shrank the victims' skins. It was dangerous for any prisoner to have a good skull and sound teeth, for Dachau had regularly supplied the best skulls for medical tuition throughout Germany. In a place where human life was thrown away, practically nothing else was. Hair was processed and used for weaving fabrics, and even human skin was dried and fashioned into boots, saddles and ladies' handbags.

Stefan realized he was shaking again and he stood up, forcing himself to stay calm, refusing to think one inch ahead.

Pierkowski returned with an armed soldier, who waited for Stefan by the door.

'Please remember,' the commandant said, 'that it is easy to form harsh judgments when you take no account of root causes.'

'I'll bear that in mind,' Stefan assured him.

The guard led the way through the passage and out on to the compound. Rows of black huts, eighty and ninety feet long, stretched off in angular streets and alleys towards the centre of the camp. The ground was soggy, and as Stefan walked along behind the soldier he could smell rotting vegetation, or so he thought, until he realized the same stench was coming from broken windows on all of the huts he passed.

'How many people in each block?' he asked the guard.

The soldier looked doubtful. 'A hundred, maybe more.'

'Beds?'

'Forty to a block.'

They stopped at the door of a block that was longer than the others, and the guard asked Stefan if he wanted to go inside.

'I'll just look,' Stefan said.

He was appalled. Men in filthy prison uniforms were huddled along the walls and around a solitary stove, their faces gaunt from starvation, hands like the talons of birds as they hugged themselves and each other, conserving their scant, precious body heat. One man on a pallet by the door looked dead. Another, sitting on the floor in a corner with his chin on his knees, looked insane. The most frightful thing of all, worse even than the stink and the multitude of suffering faces, was the silence. They made no sound at all; there was nothing left in the world to communicate.

Stefan had planned to preserve his act carefully, to go around the camp as any other SS inspector would, but when he turned from the door of the long hut he knew that would be impossible.

'What does the letter L denote?' he asked the guard.

'It's a code notation, sir. It refers to the surgical department.'

Stefan made a show of looking at his watch. 'I've been told to take a look at that place. Time's short, I think we should proceed there at once.'

They trudged on past more huts and taller, windowless buildings, until they came to a block that resembled a field bunker.

'This is the surgical department, sir.'

Stefan nodded, and felt his senses swim. *She was here, within his reach . . .*

The soldier touched Stefan's arm. 'Are you all right, sir?'

'Yes, yes. It's the smells in this place, I think.' He knew he had turned pale, he could feel the wind like ice on his face. He stood and stared at the little building, desperate to go inside, terrified of what he might find.

The guard opened the door and stood aside. Stefan went in, and immediately he was approached by a man in a once-white coat. He was old and thin, with eyes like jet beads behind his glasses.

'Who are you?' Stefan demanded.

'An attendant, sir,' the man stammered.

'Tell me about this place.'

'Surgery is performed here, sir.'

Stefan was taking in the new smell, the scent of ether and carbolic. 'Is that all you can say? What kind of surgery? And where are the surgeons?'

'Experimental surgery,' the man mumbled, and from his trembling and the way his eyes darted from side to side, Stefan guessed he was probably a prisoner, one of the privileged. Privileges were supposed to be extended to German detainees, so perhaps Gretl worked in this place. Perhaps she was safe.

'And the surgeons?' Stefan demanded.

'They are usually in the hospital, sir. There are none here, at present.'

Stefan turned to the guard. 'Wait here. This man will show me round.' When they were at the far end of the corridor, Stefan asked the attendant quietly where the patients were, and the other members of the staff.

'I am the only one working here,' the man told him, and Stefan's heart sank. 'There are four patients, I'll show you them.'

The department's beds, ten in all, were in one small ward. As Stefan walked in, the brightness of the overhead light assaulted his eyes and he blinked, seeing nothing at first but the coarse white counterpanes, the empty beds. Then he turned and saw two faces, unfamiliar, sleeping, their bodies making hardly any movement as they breathed. He turned the other way and saw another two, and his heart wrenched at the sight of Gretl, paler than he had ever known her. He stepped close to the bed, leaned down to her and saw that she was not asleep. Her eyes were half shut but they were on him, and her lips were starting to move.

'Wait outside,' Stefan told the attendant, and as the man shuffled out he turned back to Gretl and put his hand on her forehead. She was cold, unbelievably cold.

'Stefan.' He could not recognize her voice. It was dry, cracked, like an old woman's.

'Oh, my love.' He knelt by the bed and watched her dear face through a welling of tears. Whatever they had done to her, it had encroached on her spirit, her personality. 'Are you in pain?' he whispered.

Her head turned a fraction, the fine hair rustling on the grimy pillow. 'Pain,' she said. 'Terrible. Can't move.'

Stefan raised a corner of the sheet that covered Gretl and saw bandages along her sides, wooden braces strapped over them. He dropped the sheet and put his face close to hers. He began to sob like a child. He had no need to know what had been done to her, there was no room for more anguish. Something precious had been violated to the point where his sanity was retreating, and Stefan moaned his despair against Gretl's cold cheek, and he wet her mouth with his tears.

Awareness of Gretl's pain brought back an icy clarity to his mind. She was still alive, and that could only mean there was some use left in her body, some scope for further brutality.

Stefan fumbled in his pocket and moved back from the bed a little. 'I love you, Gretl. You're all I love.'

'Love you,' Gretl said.

'Forgive me.' With unsteady hands Stefan opened the small box and took out the tablet he had been given ten years before. He brushed his hand across Gretl's forehead, kissed her once and placed the tablet at her lips. 'Take it, my darling. It'll take away all the pain.' He eased the white pellet into her mouth, and watched for a second as it began to dissolve. His angel, the only person in the world he cared for; the madness of grief caught him and threatened to force him to his knees.

Stefan made a supreme effort and stepped back. He mopped his eyes briefly with his handkerchief and told Gretl again that he loved her. He waited only until the peace began to spread on her face and her eyes closed gently, then he turned and strode out of the room. He did not pause to look back.

Activity in the Führerbunker remained feverish as the war outside came closer to Berlin. Desperate measures were now being taken with the regularity of routine work, and Hitler continued to draw optimism from thin air. He had placed Himmler in charge of an emergency army group in the East, in the belief that the Reichsführer's very name would be enough to inspire the troops to maximum effort. Bormann, who had personally come up with the idea of sending Himmler to certain disgrace at the hands of Marshal Zhukov, used his strengthened hold on the Führer to steer the old man clear of the more distressing bulletins that reached the bunker. Hitler did not learn the details of how the Red Army had liberated Auschwitz, nor did he hear that despite Nazi efforts to obliterate the camp, the Red Cross had found mountains of evidence – including seven tons of human hair – and had located the mass graves of several hundred thousand people. He did not hear, either, that by 27th January the Russians were within one hundred miles of Berlin.

On the morning of the 28th Bormann assigned Stefan Gaiser the task of organizing a list of Russian agents known to be operating in and around Munich. Compiling the list was no easy matter, for the captured Soviet documents were put together haphazardly, with the agents' photographs separated from their names. The match was made laboriously by decoding a cross-reference system that had been deliberately scrambled. The files made sense only when a face could be put to a name, and only then was it possible to know a spy's approximate sphere of operation.

It took an hour to get the first two pictures isolated and labelled. Stefan's mind would not stay on the job. Grief cornered him and his awareness fled, leaving him shaking for minutes on end. He should have been out of Berlin by then, he knew that, but the drive was missing. Staying in the bunker was easier because it was automatic, a routine feature of life needing no thought or planning. When he fought his grief he was assailed with guilt, and only in the brief, exhausted moments between one emotion and the other was he able to carry out any work. He knew he was ill, but he saw no point in caring.

He was working on the third name for his list when an alarm flickered at the edge of his reason. It had to do with the big yellow card he had been handling, one of several with identification snapshots pasted on. Stefan snatched it up and peered along the rows of faces, once, twice, and suddenly the flicker was a rush of noise, his own pounding blood. He gaped, astonished. The hard eyes, the scar, the awful familiarity. Farrell. He was gazing at a picture of Farrell.

Alert for the first time in days, Stefan made the necessary match. The name that tied was Zamyatin, but the face was Farrell's. He was listed as a senior co-ordinator and field operator for the GRU, working under OSS cover.

Hate began to dance between his own sense of criminal neglect and the person of Farrell. He went to the washbasin, splashed cold water on his face, dashing it against his eyes again and again, and then he stood with the towel at his forehead, waiting for something logical to emerge. The dawning was mercifully gradual; he could not have taken it all at once.

By early afternoon he was in a controlled rage. He completed the list and passed it on to Bormann, then made an excuse to leave the bunker. For an hour or more Stefan walked the streets, seeing and hearing nothing, preoccupied with his anger. He had wasted years, risked his own life and others, destroyed what should have been cherished. He had been feeding information to the Russians with the dedication of the best Communist spy.

No wonder London had ordered his execution. *That bastard Farrell!*

Returning to the bunker, feeling no less agitated than when he had left, Stefan was brought to a halt by a new realization, a terrible suspicion that had finally managed to break into certainty. He turned back the way he had come, walking faster than before, heading for the Gestapo building on Prinz Albrechtstrasse.

At the Office of Interrogations they knew him and promptly supplied the records Stefan demanded. Alone with the closely-typed papers he felt a stab at his heart when he found Gretl's name, and reading the detailed account of her interrogation was like tearing off his own skin.

It was in the final pages of notes that he found what he was looking for. Gretl had been arrested on the basis of information received by telephone. The Gestapo had been provided with name, time of rendezvous, and even the method of transferring the information. It was noted that no other person had turned up for the rendezvous. Only Gretl.

Later, using one of the precious telephone lines that still operated between the Chancellery and the outside world, Stefan called Farrell's Munich number. There was no reply the first time he rang, but the second time the receiver at the other end was lifted at once.

'I think we should meet,' Stefan said.

Farrell was silent for a moment, then he said, 'Risky.'

'Nevertheless, I think we should.' The unsteadiness in his voice was hard to control and Stefan paused before going on. 'It's very urgent.'

'Whatever you say. Tonight?'

'Tomorrow. Keep your schedule open. I'll call you an hour beforehand and tell you the place.'

'Why not tell me now?'

'I can't.' Stefan dropped the receiver and stood looking at it. He was wondering how much of his new knowledge, if any, had coloured his speech. Spies' ears were tuned very finely. When he killed Farrell, Stefan wanted to be sure he was killing a man with as little forewarning as possible.

By his own telephone, Farrell was motionless too. He had picked up the strain in Stefan's voice, the effort to sound controlled. Farrell did not operate where there were doubts, and something told him there was a big one here. Maybe it could be something simple, like Stefan getting upset over the loss of the go-between – and that would make it logical for him to make contact in person. There was an outside chance that he had found out just how the girl had been fingered to the Gestapo: Farrell considered that, but not for long. Doubt equalled unplanned risk, so he would skip the meeting. The Nazis were finished now, the role of field Intelligence was practically over. It was time to move on: there were big plans brewing at GRU, and they involved Ralph Farrell.

He spent a few more minutes by his telephone, considering the matter of finesse. There was one move he had always been ready to make if he had to, and the notion of making it now was appealing. The idea had not originated with Farrell, it had been devised by a Russian Intelligence sleeper in London with contacts that ran deep and wide, and he had supplied the means of making it work. Farrell drummed his fingers, looked out at the grey sky, and nodded slowly. There was no need to let the contact between him and the dashing Nazi officer just evaporate. Farrell would end it sharply, the way he always liked to end things.

By the airshaft grille, holding a bundle of reports and stapled memos under his arm, Hauptsturmführer Hugo Gresch stood and watched Stefan Gaiser as he emerged from the communications room. Passing the room a minute before, Gresch had noted that Gaiser was holding the telephone close to his face, partly shielding the mouthpiece, the way a man did when he did not want to be overheard.

In the young breast of Hugo Gresch, suspicion had grown and flourished the way comradeship did in other people. Suspicion was his business, a natural trait had been turned to professional profit when Hugo had accepted Reichsführer Himmler's invitation to join a very special security squad, two months after the assassination attempt at Rastenburg. Secretary Bormann admired the young officer's efficiency as much as Himmler did, and was glad to have Gresch on his personal staff. Superficially, Gresch was another SS clerk: covertly, he was both a bodyguard for the Führer and a security ferret. He knew that in the five weeks he had been working in the bunker, Gaiser had paid no attention to him, for Gresch was adept, among other things, at making himself insignificant. He also knew that Gaiser, for all his upstanding features and spotless record, was not the kind of man he pretended to be.

'Ah, Hauptsturmführer Gaiser, if you have a moment . . .'

Stefan stopped, spun on his heel with the too-quick reaction of a man trying to pretend he was behaving normally.

'I'm sorry if I startled you,' Gresch said amiably. His face was maturely cherubic, shining with health and confidence. He had already been nicknamed Pretty Boy by a few of the typists. 'There are one or two matters I'd like to discuss with you, if you have the time.'

Stefan frowned, preoccupied, even faintly annoyed. 'Can't it wait?'

'I suppose so.' Gresch stepped forward, hefting the bundle under his arm and smiling. 'I'd much rather you spared me the time now, though.' The smile remained, but the dark eyes hardened.

Perhaps sensing that there was more to the request than routine business, Stefan shrugged and pointed in the direction of his quarters. 'As long as it doesn't take too long.'

'I'd rather we went somewhere else,' Gresch said.

'Might I suggest the Chancellery library? I'm sure we won't be disturbed there.' It was easy for the trained eye to spot the small confusion on Gaiser's stiffening face, the worry. 'I have permission to use the library,' Gresch added. 'Only for special purposes, of course.'

Ten minutes later they were alone in the cold, echoing chamber, empty of books and most of the furniture now, a place that resembled nothing so much as a gilt and marble tomb, with yawning shelves waiting to receive the dead.

'Forbidding,' Gresch observed as he closed the door, 'but private.' There was one long table in the middle of the room, and two chairs. 'Do sit down, Hauptsturmführer.'

Stefan strode smartly across the floor, his footfalls resounding like drums, and sat himself stiffly by the table. Gresch followed at a slower pace, emphasizing a special authority that was evident in nothing other than his manner. When he sat down opposite Stefan he was smiling again, like a friendly personnel officer.

'Cigarette?'

Stefan shook his head. 'What's this all about?'

Gresch lit his cigarette slowly, almost leisurely, reading more confusion, an accumulation of surfacing guilts. He blew smoke in the direction of Stefan's hands and picked a tiny flake of tobacco from his lip. 'You probably have some idea already.'

'None at all,' Stefan snapped.

'Oh, come now. You're a smart man, your record is eloquent testimony to that. Are you honestly telling me you haven't even a suspicion of why we're here?'

'That's what I'm telling you. I don't even know why an officer with your rank thinks he can get away with addressing me as if I was a subordinate.'

'But you have let me, haven't you?' The swirl of smoke around Gresch was as lazy as the movement of his hand, waving his words forward at Stefan. 'You are smart, you know there are people – people like yourself – who can operate outside the barriers of rank. When there's sound cause.'

'So you're in security of some kind. I don't need to be smart to know that.' Stefan ran impatient fingers through his hair. 'I still can't imagine what you want with me.'

Gresch turned his eyes to the barricaded window, fixing them on the one slit where feeble daylight entered. 'After the bomb plot last year, the Reichsführer realized quickly that our internal security, complex as it was, still left much to be desired. Refinement was necessary. An élite with standards twice as high as the existing élite had to be formed.' Gresch looked at Stefan again, his eyes arrogantly bright and wide. 'There are less than fifty of us, Gaiser, but we've weeded out hundreds.'

'Admirable,' Stefan said.

'I'm especially good at my job,' Gresch went on. 'That's why I work here, right at the Führer's side. I admit I am proud, and selfish. I never share glory. My father was an honoured Oberdienstleiter of the NSDAP, and he gave me that advice – what you achieve, you keep for yourself, all of it. And I've been keeping you to myself, Gaiser.' In the brief silence Gresch leaned forward, enveloping Stefan with his gaze.

'You're talking rubbish,' Stefan told him.

'You know I'm not.' Gresch folded his arms, comfortable in his certainty. 'I've been waiting to pull you in. I almost did it yesterday, but today I have more time.'

'What's your evidence? What am I supposed to have done?'

Gresch said nothing for a moment. He was trying to decipher the change in Stefan's attitude. It was complex, he had gone almost chalk white, but it did not look like fear: it even suggested that the previous nervousness had been some kind of act. 'Don't rush me, Gaiser. Don't you want to know how I spotted you? It was quite easy, with my capabilities. You see, when a man has something to hide, he can normally conceal it when he's in a crowd. But my kind of scrutiny takes no account of the crowd.

They become invisible and I concentrate on my quarry. And the flaws show.'

'Describe the flaws.'

There was no doubting it now, Gaiser was not being properly intimidated. That irritated Gresch, but he reminded himself it hardly mattered. He still had his man. 'Gaps in your timetable, for one thing. Secretiveness, too. The more I've watched, the more obvious it's become. Your eye is always looking just a little beyond – that might sound fanciful to some people, but it's just that kind of observation that's given me my success rate. You've been under a lot of strain lately, too, and there's nothing here that's changed so much it could affect you that way.' Casually, Gresch unbuttoned his holster and took out his Walther, pointing it at Stefan. 'Lay your gun on the table, Gaiser. Carefully.'

Stefan did as he was told. 'You're making a very bad mistake,' he said.

'Never. Where my work is concerned I have a faultless record.' Gresch took Stefan's gun and slipped it into his tunic pocket. 'My suspicions are all I need. The evidence will come later. I'll admit I don't know just what it is you're up to, but I've seen traitors with your pattern. The interrogation will bring out the details.'

'Your bad mistake,' Stefan said levelly, 'was in letting your selfishness and your sense of the dramatic get in the way of simple caution. Nobody knows we're here.'

Gersch waved the gun gently. 'So?'

'You should have challenged me in the bunker, in front of witnesses.' Stefan was motionless, his face taut and white, his hands clasped before him on the table.

'I don't need witnesses, Gaiser. I can act on my suspicions alone, I told you that. You're not thinking clearly.'

'Your suspicions haven't spread. You haven't shared. A terrible, terrible error.'

Gresch pushed back his chair and stood up. 'On your feet,' he snapped. 'The safety catch is off and my gun has a sensitive trigger. You know what will happen if you try to implement your veiled threat. Get moving!'

They began walking towards the tall door, Stefan in front, Gresch close behind with the Walther extended.

'There was a man,' Stefan murmured, 'called Albert Murray. He taught me a lot, more than I could remember, probably, but he always emphasized one thing I've never forgotten.'

'And what was that?'

'Nothing you'd understand.'

Gresch blinked at the back of Stefan's head. 'Then why mention it at all?'

The small sequence of events took its start from Gresch's moment of annoyed distraction. Stefan stopped walking. The barrel of the Walther touched his back and as it did he grasped it, spinning his body and yanking the gun out of Gresch's hand. There was one fraction of a second when Gresch was motionless in a limbo of surprise, and in that moment Stefan's stiffened fingers jabbed savagely at the left side of his neck. The breath gurgled in Gresch's throat and his face darkened as he dropped to his knees, then on to his back. Stefan watched and waited until the twitching in the hands had stopped, then stooped to retrieve his own gun and to put Gresch's back in its holster.

Albert Murray had expressed great pride in the technique and Stefan had never doubted it would be effective, but even so he was impressed. The vagus nerve, surfacing only at one point – and only when there was excitement, agitation, tension – was tragically vulnerable. A blow on the narrow fibres put a shock wave through the entire body, disrupting the lungs, heart, even the kidneys, and invariably the result was instant death. There was need for skill in applying the fatal blow, and when he taught Stefan how to do it Albert Murray had laboured the key to success. 'It's like throwing a dart at a dartboard. Never mind the dart, just look where you want to hit, and throw.'

It took less than five minutes to get Gresch back in the chair and arranged in a slump with his arms across the table. For added dressing Stefan took some papers from the dead officer's pocket and put them on the table, then wound the cooling fingers around a fountain pen. Any doctor who was not a reasonably gifted pathologist would know, after the briefest examination, that Gresch had died of a heart attack. Even an autopsy would confirm that.

Stefan got back to the bunker by the stairs leading from the Chancellery hallway, after waiting for the two guards to go off to the illicit warmth of the security booth, which they did every half hour. It had been luck, nothing else, that had put him on the guards' blind side as he had gone into the library with Gresch. Noting the fact had given Stefan the first inkling of an emergency plan, and there again he had been acting on the advice of Albert Murray. Careful observation of trivia, Albert insisted, could often be the groundwork for salvation.

In the aftermath Stefan began to feel uneasy. Even when the word had gone round that the guards had found Hauptsturmführer Gresch dead in the library, and that Hitler's personal physician had pronounced the cause of death as being a heart seizure, the queasy, anxious feeling persisted. Nobody was getting particularly upset over the death, people were being killed in their hundreds and thousands every day, and death from overwork and plain stress had been commonplace in Government departments for a long time. So why, Stefan asked himself, did he feel so exposed, so open to disaster?

Throughout the afternoon the strange sensation lasted, and Stefan decided it had nothing to do with the murder he had committed. Not directly. That event had simply made him properly aware of the black miasma he moved in, the reeking shadow of the Reich, where his personal safety relied on flimsy, minute-to-minute stratagems and where his ache for vengeance was the only thing resembling consolation. He was sick to the heart, and all around him the air was thick with foreboding.

In the evening the Führer had dinner in the conference room, and as before Stefan was invited to attend. Hitler did not have much to say, for a change, and it was left to Bormann to supply the topics for conversation. The typists, weary from long periods of work without daylight or proper exercise, sat glumly and listened. The secretaries tried to be brighter, and an aide on Stefan's left managed to laugh occasionally, but the overall atmosphere was one of strain: people were afraid, they needed to be occupied or left alone with their thoughts.

Dr Morrell was present that evening, and when the small gathering was at an end he spent a few minutes privately with Hitler, then made his way up to Stefan's quarters, as he had done a couple of times before. Stefan was in no mood for talk, but he sat and listened as Morrell went on about Hitler's health.

'Do you know something, Gaiser? One month's holiday would do more for the Führer than all the medicines he's had over the past year. The man is exhausted, he has a dozen ailments that will never even start on the way to cure unless he rests.'

'A difficult time,' Stefan murmured.

'Maybe so, but it is the difficult times that put the most pressure on him. If he would only delegate some of the work, that alone would make a difference.'

Stefan could read the concern behind Morrell's words. The Führer had become increasingly dependent on stimulant drugs, and the chemical balance of his body was so disturbed that he needed other drugs to make him sleep. The doctor's constant fear, which could be detected by anyone who watched him, was that Hitler would overdose on either the stimulants or the depressants, and then the blame would fall on Morrell. One soldier had already killed himself with tablets prescribed by the Führer's physician, and the suicide had focussed unwelcome attention on the leader's treatment. Morrell valued his alliance with Bormann, but it would be the same Bormann who would bring down the axe if anything happened to Hitler.

After rambling for a few more minutes about the curative properties of rest and the need for proper exercise, Morrell came abruptly to the point of his visit.

'I would be grateful to you, Gaiser, if you would advise the Führer to rest. He would listen to you.'

That surprised Stefan. 'I would have thought that it would come better from yourself, Doctor, or from Secretary Bormann.'

Morrell shook his head. 'He thinks we conspire to make him ease his grip on the reins. He is not a man to relinquish power easily. If you spoke to him, it would be different, he would know that you spoke from concern and no other motive.'

'You believe he regards my opinion that highly?'

'But of course. He has much affection for you.'

'If I have an opportunity,' Stefan said, 'I'll raise the matter.'

At ten o'clock that evening Bormann received a sealed packet from Gestapo headquarters in Munich, brought by an SS courier officer. He put the envelope on his desk and ignored it for a while. There were other things to do, a tide of priorities that threatened to swamp him. At 10.30 he stopped work to have his customary cup of black coffee, and almost offhandedly he opened the Gestapo communiqué. There was a letter from Obersturmbahnführer Hilger, explaining that the enclosed document had been sent anonymously to his office, and that he felt it raised a matter best handled by Bormann himself.

Bormann sighed and drank some more of his coffee. The passing-on of responsibility was reaching ludicrous proportions. The Gestapo were the prime offenders lately. Since Himmler had gone off to the front they had assailed the Chancellery with matters they were perfectly well equipped to handle themselves. The document was a photographic copy of a letter, Bormann observed, and it was in English. Attached to the picture there was a translation in German. Bormann read two lines and slammed down his cup, spilling coffee across the desk.

'Guards! Guards!' He went roaring into the passage and grabbed the nearest soldier by the arm. 'Bring Gaiser here! Bring him at gunpoint!' The soldier ran off and Bormann went back to his office, panting, his face almost purple. He snatched up the letter again and stared at it as if it might explode. It was on the headed notepaper of the British Minister of Economic Warfare. Briefly, the letter confirmed the Parliamentary responsibility for the appointment of Stefan Gaiser, domiciled at Dorfen, Bavaria, as an Intelligence agent of the British Government. Bormann glared at the date on the letter. January, 1935. *Ten years.*

Stefan was brought to the office with the guard's pistol against his back. He had been asleep in his chair when the guard burst in and he was pale, shaken.

'Stand there,' Bormann snapped, pointing to the vacant area on his carpet, surrounded by piles of boxes. 'And if you move, this man will shoot you.'

'What's all this about?' Stefan asked quietly.

'It's about this!' Bormann stuck the letter under his nose, then drew it back so that Stefan could read it. 'Well? Have you any nice, glib explanation?'

The colour had surged back into Stefan's face. 'I've nothing to say.'

'Oh, but you will have!' Bormann turned to the guard and told him to wait outside the open door, then he turned back to Stefan.

That was when Stefan moved. In that instant of events moving from one phase to another there was a chance and Stefan was swift to take it. His elbow slammed into Bormann's face and a second after he was pushing the guard ahead of him with stiffened arms, ramming the man against the corridor wall with enough force to stun him. There was another guard by the spiral stairs, a man too daunted by Stefan's rank to do anything before it was too late. Stefan ran straight at him, swerved, and kicked the guard in the groin. As he went down Stefan grabbed his gun and rushed up the staircase.

The door to his quarters was lying open and he ducked inside just long enough to grab his cap and his own pistol, then he made for the nearest exit, a stairway that led to the Chancellery building. Someone was behind him, how far behind he could not tell, and he could hear Bormann screeching for reinforcements. Stefan leapt up the concrete steps three at a time, then braked by the tall door to the Chancellery hallway. He put on his cap, strapped his gun in position and pocketed the other gun. His hand was on the door handle when pain sliced across his arm. He brought it up, staring at the blood, a free-running stream pouring through his gaping sleeve.

'Get back down. Move!'

Stefan saw the young guard and barely believed he was there. The approach had been soundless, but he was real enough, his jaw clenched, ready for anything with the service dagger clenched in his hand.

'Certainly,' Stefan said, and brought up his knee with such force that the thigh muscles wrenched on contact with the guard's stomach. The man fell back, slashing wildly with the knife, putting another wound beside the first. Stefan's good arm, his left, crossed to his holster and fumbled out the gun. The guard hit the bottom of the stairs as the first and second bullets pounded into his chest. The third bullet struck the following guard on the arm, spinning him, and when he collided with the man behind him the fourth bullet ploughed through his back and into the belly of the man he was tangled with.

'Back!' Stefan yelled, and the force of the command made one more guard stop, gaping. In the two seconds it took him to react, Stefan had the door open and was rolling across the floor beyond. A startled SS Sturmann, running towards the sounds of gunfire, was bowled over and fell sideways on the marble floor. His steel helmet clanged once as he landed and twice more as Stefan rolled upright and kicked him on the back of the neck. One more bullet put a dark caution on the two guards by the main door and Stefan ran out past them.

It was pitch dark. Stefan galloped to where he knew there was a sandbag store and rammed the fragile door with his back as he closed on it. There was no pain in his injured arm, even when he clambered over the front pile of bags and dropped behind it. When he pushed himself into a corner with sand in his mouth and eyes, he realized he had used up most of his strength. There was no pain because a nerve had been severed, but the loss of blood was serious, pain or no pain. Stefan touched the sleeve where it was cut and felt the warm, sticky fluid fill his palm and spill between his fingers. The effort of running and climbing had set his heart pumping furiously, and it was sending his life blood out into the open at terrifying speed.

He began to feel clammy cold on his face and legs. His hand dropped and hit something colder, a metal plate. As footsteps began to scuffle on the Chancellery steps twenty yards away, Stefan discovered he was touching a sewer cover. Kneeling up, feeling the dizziness clawing along the back of his skull, he wrenched at the cover with his left hand and lifted it. The sandbag stores, he knew, had been thrown up randomly all over the city. He took a moment to bless the careless squad that had built this one over a manhole, before he dropped down on to the narrow ladder and pulled the cover shut behind him.

It took twenty minutes of knee-deep trudging through the accumulated filth before he found a service lay-by and pushed himself into it. By then he was breathless and dangerously off-balance. By kicking and groping around in the dark Stefan found the service unit, a crate filled with emergency materials, and he opened it. There was a battery lantern, which he lit, and in its beams he started pulling out the other equipment.

A length of rope made a tourniquet, and he bound it hard around his arm, using a spanner for leverage. When he was satisfied the bleeding had stopped he ran the lantern beam over himself. His tunic and breeches were covered in dark blood, and around his boots he was coated with a stiff layer of sewage. One sight of him on the street would be enough to have him picked up. He looked like a scarecrow.

Stefan decided that rest was essential. In the box, among other things, were three packs of the glucose tablets issued to all municipal workers since the time rations had diminished to the bare nutritional level. He ate all three, gagging on the final handful, and gulped down a litre of sterile water from an aluminium canister. The dizziness turned to nausea for a small eternity but Stefan held on, and finally, with pain buzzing in his head and ears, he sank into a rest that was half shock, half exhaustion.

Bormann was so excited that twice he almost took to the streets himself. As it was, he had managed to appoint three full squads of mobile police and over fifty Gestapo personnel to a combing search, less than twenty minutes after Stefan had made his escape.

'I want him,' he told the senior bunker guard, Fresch, as they stood over a spread map of the city. 'Alive or dead, although I'd prefer him breathing.'

'Everything possible is being done, sir.'

'And when I have him,' Bormann grated, 'I'll drag him before the Führer.' The prospect lit up his face. He had the look of a man embarking on a delicious act of gluttony.

Fresch cleared his throat. 'Shall I alert the SS posts on the city boundaries? I suppose there's just a chance Gaiser could make it that far . . .'

'There'd better be no such chance!' For a second Bormann looked outraged, then he sighed and nodded. 'Alert them, anyway. And see that I'm called immediately any news comes in. I'll be in my office.'

The air around the lower level of the bunker felt thick.

Bormann kicked absently at the ventilator shaft behind his desk, turned, saw the letter again and closed his eyes. He was desperately tired. All the high-energy diets and stimulant pills in the world were useless when a man simply went too long without sleep or even rest. There was so much to do, so much to control and direct. Even now, with nothing but Gaiser dominating his mind, Bormann felt the other priorities crowding in on every side, clamouring for attention. He sat down, glaring at his telephone, willing it to ring. The need to lay hands on Gaiser was making him shake, the way Hitler did when his frustration had no outlet.

When the telephone did ring it startled Bormann and he nearly dropped the receiver before he got it jammed to his ear.

'Yes?'

'They've had to call off the search for the moment, sir.' It was Fresch, sounding huskily apologetic.

'Had to? *Had* to?'

'A raid, sir. There's an air raid . . .'

'To hell with the air raid! I want that man found, I want him located and brought here within the hour!'

'Very good, sir.'

Bormann threw the receiver back in the cradle and banged the side of his fist on the desk, sending pencils and pens scattering. He could have stood up then and marched straight to the Führer's quarters. Hitler would be angry at being disturbed, but it would be worth the risk, just to see the incredulity spreading over him. His beloved Gaiser, a spy! He would want to disbelieve but he would be forced to accept, he would be compelled to realize that there was only one man, *one*, that he could ever trust.

The impulse passed. It would be better to wait, to confront Hitler with the culprit, manacled, head bowed, exposed. Bormann clasped his trembling hands and glared at the telephone.

A fall of rubble in the main tunnel brought Stefan awake. For minutes he sat still, trying to remember. He was cold and weak, and there was no feeling in his right hand. The memory flooded back suddenly and he leaned forward, reaching for the switch on the lantern.

During his sleep the tourniquet had loosened a little, and for that he was grateful. A minimal blood supply had reached the forearm and hand, but the surge had not been strong enough to upset the clotting on the wounds. By painful stages Stefan took off the pressure entirely and gasped at the burning when the full pulse restored itself. The larger wound began to ooze again, and there were no proper field dressings in the box – only rat-bite salve, some thick disinfectant and a packet of cotton wool. Stefan tore open the pack with his teeth and bundled the cotton wool against the wound, then strapped the dressing in place with the black tape supplied for binding the handles of shovels.

More rubble fell nearby. He stood up and felt the giddiness again. By leaning on the wall and spreading his feet he could make himself feel more stable, and in that position it was possible to shine the lamp out into the tunnel and see both ways. The fallen brick had not obstructed the walkways, but it was diverting the slow-moving sewage out over the slippery cobbles. A far-off rumble confirmed what Stefan had thought. There was an air raid, and he stood a good chance of being walled in if he stayed in the sewer much longer.

Walking was nearly impossible. With the torch beam wavering ahead of him, Stefan moved with his left shoulder to the wall, testing each step before transferring his weight, slipping sometimes and once landing painfully on his knees. He had no idea of time or distance travelled, his shallow pool of consciousness was directed solely on the mechanics of movement.

At an intersection of the tunnel he found a signpost, bolted to the wall. At first it was hard to understand, but it became clearer as he traced the zig-zagging black lines with his finger. He was standing under the Hohenzollern Damm, at the crossroads with Berkaer Strasse. Stefan flicked the lamp beam up for an instant and saw the manhole cover, twenty feet above him. The ladder was spindly and frail looking, but there was no alternative.

He waited a few minutes to muster his strength, then he switched off the lantern, laid it at the foot of the ladder, and started to climb.

His body weight seemed tremendous, and it got greater with each successive rung. Because he could use only one hand, he had to put his chin over the iron spars to hold himself in position before each step was taken. When he estimated he was halfway up there was a crash somewhere above, and the ladder creaked against the brick.

Stefan stayed in the same position for a count of twenty, then began climbing again. He was convinced the manhole would be piled high with rubble, or that he would come up under an armoured SS wagon. The hopelessness was draining the resolve from him. Then he had a thought, so clear it might have come from outside. Stefan put his chin on the second rung from the top and touched the cover lightly, checking his thought, racking his memory to be sure.

The cover opened to the combined pressure of his hand and shoulder. Through the two-inch gap Stefan saw nothing but the dark road surface and the edge of a pavement six feet away. The air carried the smell of smoke and cordite, but its coolness revived him a little. With an effort that almost felled him he pushed himself out on to the road and lay there for over a minute, unable to move any further, the manhole cover still resting on his ankle. Stefan could see the sky and the criss-crossing searchlights, and he heard the drone and whine of Allied aircraft making their return run over the south of the city.

He got himself into the cover of the shell of a building and waited there to check his bearings. Berkaer Strasse ran for another hundred yards beyond the crossing, and then there was a short street running off at a tangent, the

Reichenhallerstrasse, where all his hope lay. It was not the best of times to rely on instincts, but Stefan believed he had made a friend down there.

He reached the Black House with less trouble than he had anticipated. A bomb had torn up the road a few yards from where he surfaced, and everybody appeared to have fled. Feeling weirdly alone on the echoing street, Stefan hobbled up the steps and pushed the bell by the door post.

When the door opened, the first thing to appear was a gun, clamped in a steady, experienced hand.

'Arenz,' Stefan hissed. His relief, when he saw the familiar face of the old officer, was monumental.

'Good God, let me help you.' Arenz put both hands under Stefan's arms and drew him into the building. There was a chair to the side of the door and he lowered Stefan into it carefully and stood back. 'You look terrible, sir. I'll call the ambulance team at once.'

'No.' Stefan shook his head wearily. 'Don't do that. Just listen to me for a minute.' He swallowed, trying to make his voice less of a croak. 'I'm out of favour, Arenz. Totally. I believe the Gestapo will be looking for me.'

Arenz took the news calmly. He holstered his gun and folded his arms, listening.

'I can't tell you much more than that. I'm in need of medical attention, rest, fresh clothes, and somewhere to hide until it's safer for me to move. Can I rely on your help?'

Arenz nodded.

'You'll be placing yourself in great danger, and in the meantime you might learn things about me that would make you change your mind . . .'

'We're all in danger, sir. I want the war over and I'm sure you do. I don't care what I hear. I formed my opinion a while ago and it won't change. If there are enemies around me, I'm sure you're not one of them.' Arenz smiled, then took another step back. 'I never saw such a mess. But we'll get you fixed. This place is stacked with just about everything you need . . .'

'Except doctors.' Stefan pointed to his injured arm. 'I think this is pretty bad, and I've lost plenty of blood.'

'You'll have to make do with a medical orderly.' Arenz held up his hands and spread the fingers. 'The Great War. These managed to save a life or two. Now let's get you somewhere more private.'

Stefan leaned on the old man's shoulder as they went down the winding steps to the cellars. Part of him could hardly see the point in it: most of the people who were obliged to stay in the city had less than a fifty-fifty chance as it was, and somebody with Bormann on his tail probably had no chance at all. But the other part of Stefan wanted to try, just the same. There was still a point, after all; there was still a reason.

Two days later, when posters bearing Stefan's photograph were pinned up in police stations, SS security posts and Gestapo offices, a revitalized Hauptsturmführer Gaiser emerged from the rear door of the Black House and climbed into a purloined SS staff car. By the window Oberleutnant Arenz stood, smiling and waving. He had conducted the entire operation with the kind of flair he had shown in the old days, before they had decided a lame man was of no use in the field.

Stefan checked the gauges before he started the engine. Both tanks were full. He flexed his right arm, feeling the throb of healing, and as the engine fired he glanced down at his new uniform, grinning at Arenz's ingenuity. On reflection, it was obvious the old man had been right. It was still best to travel as an officer of the SS, and beyond the city limits very few people would find his identification curious: even the hawk-eyed border men would have trouble identifying the fake, and anyway, Stefan's route was designed to take him well wide of them.

He waved one last time to Arenz and drove out on to the side street, turning right at the end and heading south.

Stefan's eyes were steady on the road, and his brain was as clear as ice.

All missions, allegiances and intrigues were gone. Vengeance was the only mission that mattered any more. Stefan sat behind the wheel and felt the peace of simple determination. For the suffering and death of those kept in the dark, for his own wasted years, for Gretl – that was the cause. Ralph Farrell would be the sacrifice.

February, 1945

When the Russians crossed the Oder River on the last day of January, there remained no real barriers between them and Berlin. On 3rd February, nine hundred American bombers flattened vast areas in the centre of the city. Water supplies became polluted and essential services were cut off, and even the Führer's headquarters were affected. Water had to be carried from a water cart parked outside the Chancellery, and emergency power generators were moved into the bunker, making the place even more cramped and uncomfortable.

Stolidly, Hitler went on finding reasons for hope. He even spent long hours with his architect, Paul Giesler, going over the plans for the new city of Linz, and when he was given the finished model of the city he shuffled around it with clasped hands, like a child on Christmas morning. He only ever became angry when General Guderian arrived at the bunker, as he did increasingly, and demanded that the inept Himmler be replaced by his own deputy, General Wenck, if there was to be any hope of counterattacking at the Oder. Hitler finally gave in and appointed Wenck chief of staff at Army Group Vistula, but not before he had raged at Guderian for his presumption and for his lack of respect for Reichsführer Himmler.

'It was not disrespect I offered,' Guderian said. 'It was reasoned opinion. The Reichsführer is no military tactician.'

'And who knows what anybody is nowadays?' Hitler barked.

Bormann and a few others at the meeting knew what lay behind that. The Führer had gone silent for an entire day when he heard the news about Stefan Gaiser. Later, he ordered that Gaiser's name never be mentioned in the bunker again.

In Munich, the air raids had been less selective than those on Berlin. Great chunks of the city centre had been destroyed but just as much remained standing, and in the suburbs undamaged rows of houses stood by the craters of others that had disappeared.

The bombs had not touched the lower end of the Jagerstrasse, but when Stefan went to the safe house there on the 4th, there was no trace of the big American. Farrell had taken off.

Stefan decided to stay in the house for the night. There was canned food and a stove, and after he had made himself a meal and eaten it, he went and sat by the rear window. The sun blazing westward on the horizon had turned the crippled city into a gilded canvas. He had loved that city for a long time, and never more than when *she* had been there, at its heart. His grief soared, and for a time he let it.

In the morning he felt refreshed. Down on the streets he saw people wandering about, confused, most of them, dispossessed. The war had finally detached them from their realities. Alone in that building, Stefan felt he was the only person in Munich with any purpose in him.

It was safe enough to drive through the city in daylight; no one was looking for him there. Stefan took the car through remembered back streets, knowing precisely where he was going. He would take his time, for haste would decoy him away from Farrell's trail. Stefan knew that in his blood.

When he reached the place he stopped the engine and stared out at the wreckage. Another dead end. It was as if he was being taunted. But he would not go under, he knew of still one more address, and as Stefan drove off again he carefully prodded his hatred, like an anchorite fingering his beads to keep him close to his God.

Although the offensive at Ardennes had ended, on a major scale, by 25th January, a secondary conflict had broken out to the south, in the territory of Alsace-Lorraine.

The 6th Army Group of US General Devers had been covering an area known as the Laverne Gap, left by the 3rd Army troops who had gone north to the Ardennes. General Obstfelder had driven an attack towards the gap with the German 1st Army, and at first the assault was successful. But the Allies quickly co-ordinated their forces and began driving the Germans back into the guns of the 1st French Army, under the leadership of General Lattre de Tassigny.

Towards the end of that battle, it became clear that a unit of the SS Einsatzgruppen had been involved. French and American soldiers came across some dead Germans wearing the unmistakable battle regalia of the Nazi murder squads, and later the mutilated bodies of eight tortured American soldiers were found in a shallow grave outside the town of Briand.

On the 4th of February Ralph Farrell already knew about the presence of the Einsatz unit in that area. GRU had made it their business to keep tracks on all elements of the SS branch that had slaughtered half a million Russians. In the brief operational hiatus that existed while the Soviet troops moved on Berlin, Farrell was advised that the time had come for him to get behind the advancing Soviet line and join up with a newly-established Russian Intelligence unit, where he would be needed. To his OSS contacts, Farrell would simply be out of touch for a while, and that would hardly be surprising.

The GRU had estimated that there were about one hundred men in the Einsatzgruppe. Their work, usually, was to clean up after the German Army, slaughtering partisans, arresting enemy soldiers and torturing information from them. In places like Minsk and Kharkov they had interpreted the word 'partisan' freely, and had exterminated men, women and infants with no regard for fine distinctions. Farrell carried a headful of the atrocities, together with a knowledge of the Einsatz unit's whereabouts. GRU tactical officers believed that the centre of operations for the Laverne Gap struggle would be one of two places – the town of Dizier, or the nearby village of Challerange. Despite clear orders to avoid the areas, Farrell arrived in the region of Challerange on the 5th of February.

It was only a small detour, Farrell reasoned. He knew the Einsatzgruppe had to be hiding somewhere, because the Germans were being squeezed out from north and south and there was no room in the meantime for a butcher squad to operate. He would just take a look, Farrell told himself, and if there was any chance to do some harm, he would do it.

It was easy for a man with genuine purpose in his head to make progress in that area. En route Farrell had killed two people, the first a Wehrmacht despatch rider, the second an SS Unterscharführer, detached from his tank unit and trying to beg a lift on the stolen motorcycle. Farrell could have wiped out ten times as many people and still have made no ripples. There were small engagements all over the place, men running singly and in groups and colliding with their enemies when all they wanted to do, by then, was get to somewhere safe. Buttoned into his field greatcoat, goggled and helmeted, Farrell had taken a clear line to his destination.

At Challerange there was only silence and death. Bodies of German soldiers were lying on the narrow streets and others were huddled in disabled tanks. The only sounds were distant, the rumble of gunfire fifteen miles to the east.

Dizier was quiet too, but the marks of living presence were there: the main roads in and out of the town had been kept clear, and around the perimeter dozens of tree branches had been lopped off recently. On foot and under cover, Farrell found the missing branches. They were piled like huge beehives around half-tracks, staff cars and motorcycles.

Farrell decided to set up some kind of temporary base

before he made any other exploratory forays. There was a house, a detached residence on a small rise at the north of the village, with windows that looked out on all sides. A couple of shells had torn off the roof and removed the staircase and part of the ground floor, but there was still plenty of room for a man to set up base, and ample opportunity to escape in an emergency. Farrell detached the two panniers from the motorcycle and dragged them to the house, and in the kitchen he unpacked his tinned food, weapons and spare clothing. Depending on circumstances he could pass himself off as Wehrmacht, SS, or a US infantry sergeant. Some minor details of uniform were inaccurate or missing, but that would make no difference on a battlefield where a lot of men had no boots or jackets.

Late at night, in almost total darkness, Farrell walked soundlessly through the twisting streets, keeping himself close to the walls, and within half an hour he found the Nazis. The dim lights of their storm lanterns were like beacons beyond the small windows of the church where they were sheltering. Farrell detoured to the rear of the building and climbed on an overturned water butt. From there he eased himself on to the edge of the roof and crawled on his belly to the nearest crater in the tiles. Voices drifted up to him as he lay with his ear above the opening. They were hushed voices, most of them young, the hissing conversation of murderers bickering with murderers.

In ten minutes Farrell had the picture, or most of it. The Einsatzgruppe leader, Oberführer Naumann, was still alive and still very much in command, even though he had been wounded. Naumann was insisting that the group remain under cover and inactive until the battle was further away from them. He proposed to make a run for it to the north, through the flattened French villages and farm land as far as Nancy, then veer north east towards the German border. Farrell could have departed as soon as he learned that much. There was less than one chance in a hundred that the unit would survive the proposed retreat. He could simply leave them to the American guns. But Farrell would not consider the easy solution: he was there, he decided, to destroy, to punish, to bludgeon the life out of those animals.

The bickering, it seemed, was over the way Naumann had rationed the food. In the cleaner's quarters at the back of the church the men's supplies were kept under lock and key, and Naumann permitted one meal per day, measured out by himself and an Untersturmführer. Already the men were feeling the effects of the kind of hunger they had imposed on others, a permanent gnawing in the gut, an inability to stay warm even when they were close to the stove. On his way down off the roof, Farrell decided that his campaign could start there and then. The only lookout being maintained was at the front of the church, and it was a straightforward matter to get in at the back. Farrell hoisted himself through a broken window and padded along the short corridor until he found the old oak door with its new, improvised bolt and padlock.

He was inside in less than two minutes, unscrewing the entire bolt and lock and setting it noiselessly on the floor. A quick scan with his torch showed him two boxes piled with food – tinned beef, biscuits, dried fruit and some tough-skinned local cheese. He pocketed as much of the stuff as he could carry, then cast about for a means of destroying the rest. There was a can of kerosene in the corner, the fuel for the lamps, and Farrell poured half of it over the cheese and fruit. He then punctured all of the cans, leaving wide tears along their ends where the kerosene could seep in easily, and set them in a puddle of the liquid on the floor. The packs of biscuits were crumbled and left otherwise unharmed, for it pleased Farrell to think of the Nazis spending their last few hours on earth eating handfuls of crumbs.

Before leaving he replaced the lock and bolt, then made his way back to the house. A few yards from the place where the road merged into the overgrown lawn he sensed something move, and he dropped to the damp ground, cursing the small rattle of the cans in his pockets. There was a scuttling to his left, then the pounding of feet, running in a panic straight towards him. In one move Farrell drew the knife from his boot and grabbed a leg as it ploughed past, inches from his head. The running man stumbled and fell headlong, landing with a thump as Farrell straddled his back and put the point of the knife to his throat.

'One move and you die,' Farrell whispered harshly, then took a grip on his torch and twisted the man's head round into the beam. He was young, with pleasant features and a stubbly beard. Sitting back a little Farrell took in the torn uniform jacket and the sleeve chevrons.

'Please,' the young man whined. The mercy he sought lined his face, narrowing his eyes.

'American?' Farrell whispered.

'Yes.'

Farrell stood up, keeping the knife in contact with the soldier's neck. 'Move.'

The soldier got to his knees and Farrell lifted him the rest of the way, pushing him towards the house before he was properly standing. In the kitchen, Farrell pushed the youth into a chair and flipped the switch on his battery lantern, which he had set on the floor under the sink. The light was a dim yellow, throwing high, unnatural shadows on both their faces.

'What outfit are you with?' Farrell demanded.

'I'm only obliged to . . .'

'Cut the crap! I'm not a fuckin' Nazi – but I don't know *you* aren't. What's your outfit, and what the hell are you doing here?'

The soldier blinked, clearly having trouble reconciling Farrell's accent with his German uniform.

'I'll twist your balls off if you don't talk, sonny.'

'I'm with US Seventh Army – or I was.'

'Under whose command?'

'General Patch.'

Farrell shook his head. 'It doesn't gel. Patch is at the Moder River. You're here. Are you telling me you deserted and made it all this way on foot?' Farrell waved the knife, making long shadows on the walls.

'I was in a medic transport,' the soldier said. He pulled up his trouser leg and showed a filthy bandage, black at the middle with congealed blood. 'I got shot and I was being taken back with nineteen other guys—'

'Back to where?'

'Mortagne. There's a field medical station there. But we didn't make it. The ambulance got ambushed about seven, eight miles north of here. That was a week ago, near enough.'

Farrell sighed. 'You're making it hard to believe, kid. You're telling me you've survived in the open for a week – wounded, at that.'

The soldier nodded. 'I did. I've been moving at night most of the time, trying to catch up with an American unit, any unit at all. Five French resistance guys helped me for a couple of days, but the same squad got them that got the ambulance. I was lucky, I was still in the barn where they'd hidden me.'

'Well,' Farrell sighed, 'you've jumped out of the skillet into the charcoal. When I grabbed you just now you were heading in the direction of some holed-up SS boys down the road a way. Here, let's see that leg.'

The wound was cratered, with puffy yellow flesh around the edge. 'It hurts like hell,' the boy said.

'I'm not surprised. It'll have to hurt some more before it gets better.'

Farrell brought his emergency field medical kit and used it on the soldier the way he had been taught to use it on himself, ruthlessly, ignoring pain in the greater interest of arresting infection. With a sterile blade he released the pus and scraped away the granular floor of the developing ulcer, then he washed the wound with a sachet of antibacterial solution, dusted it with Sulfoxone powder and put on a padded dressing.

'That should hold it for a few days,' Farrell announced when he had finished.

The soldier was sweating and pale. 'I thought I'd faint,' he said weakly. 'But thanks.'

'It wasn't charity, kid. I need help, and you just got yourself enlisted. I like my hired hands to be in good shape.'

'Who are you, anyway?'

'You don't need to know,' Farrell said. 'Just as I don't need to know who you are. Just accept that I'm working under cover, and right now I'm working against those shits down the road.'

The soldier flexed his leg, patted the bandage gingerly. 'How many of them?' he asked.

'More than fifty,' Farrell said casually.

'Jesus Christ! How are you going to cope with that many?'

Farrell dug around in one of the panniers and hauled out a bottle of Schnapps. He poured two measures in metal cups and handed the soldier one. 'Swallow it all at once, then I'll give you one to sip.' He gulped his own drink and sucked in a breath as it burned his throat and spread warmth to his stomach. He waited until the soldier stopped coughing before he explained. 'The enemy is all in one place. They're armed, they've got transport, but they're hiding in one neat little lump – and they don't know we're here, which gives us quite an advantage.'

'So?' the soldier croaked, holding out his cup for a refill. 'What do you plan on doing?'

Farrell smiled. 'They're in a church. It would be poetic justice, I suppose, if we locked them in and burned the place. But I don't want to do it that way. These men are special, you see. They're a murder team, clean-up artists. They deserve some imagination. Besides, I want to *see* the bastards die.'

The soldier was looking at Farrell as if he might be a different species. 'But how can two of us—'

'You'll find out. Could pick up a medal for yourself in

the process. Before it's daylight, we'll go down the road to where they keep their transport and their heavy ammunition. We'll find us a good car, and then we'll use the rest of the stuff to bring them out in the open.'

At six o'clock the following morning, Oberführer Naumann lifted himself painfully from the pile of rugs where he had been sleeping and draped his blanket around his shoulders. He crossed from the shattered altar to the bottom of the nave and kicked the wadded coat and rug that rested against the foot of a pew. Untersturmführer Gratz came rolling out of the covers and flung himself to his feet, buttoning his tunic before his eyes had focussed. His hair stood up in grey spikes and his nail-bitten fingers tried to press it flat as Naumann waved his arm over the other huddled shapes around the little building.

'Get them up,' Naumann snapped, 'then come with me to the food store.' It was customary to start setting out the portions in the morning; then each man was issued his ration mid-morning. It was up to individuals to spread their nourishment over the day as best they could.

Gratz started yelling at the others and his shouts brought in the night guard from the front of the building. He had been sleeping as soundly as the others, because his boredom and hunger had been a match for the cold that could normally keep a man awake. He was stiff and limping, carrying his submachine-gun as if it weighed a ton.

'I'm starving,' he announced to the first man he bumped into.

'Who isn't?' The two men moved off to where the buckets were lined, filled the day before with precious water that had to be used for washing three times before it was discarded. Shaving was out of the question.

The first freezing splash brought the guard to a painful alertness. 'We could move out now,' he moaned, burying his face in the towel that was almost as wet as his skin.

'The fighting's moved on, I could hardly hear the guns at all last night.'

His companion stared down at the greasy water, reluctant to put himself any nearer it. 'Tell Naumann,' he murmured. 'He might let you off with a broken leg.'

The Oberführer was unlocking the door of the food store when Gratz joined him. They went inside together, and for a minute they just stood and stared at the mess inside. Then Naumann turned and examined the lock, turned back and glared at the ruined meat and fruit and biscuits.

'How did this happen?' Gratz said stupidly.

'Somebody has decided to force the issue,' Naumann replied. His voice was calm, which meant he was on the border edges of rage. 'Get the men lined up. Now.'

Gratz hurried away, and Naumann remained for a few more minutes with the vandalized provisions. He was not an old man, but the past year had aged him to a point where he often heard his mouth whisper the sounds of weary despair. Everything seemed draped in tragedy, all the way down from the grand tragedy that was enveloping Naumann's beloved Fatherland to the daily indignities that mocked his idealism. Not long before, he had stood at a round table with other senior men of the SS, dressed in his fine uniform, listening to Reichsführer Himmler's words of inspiration. Blood and Soil, Herrenmensch-Untermensch – the litany of the only faith that meant anything to Naumann. It had been easy, then, to see himself as a knight, an instrument of divine wrath cleansing the way towards the glorious day of the Master Race. He ran his gaze over the ruptured cans, the kerosene-drenched cheese and the sodden, stinking wads of fruit and had to muster his anger from the growing despair. The wound on his hip began to burn as he turned and went back to the church.

The men, standing in five rows in the cleared central area of the stone floor, looked comprehensively miserable. Unshaven, bleary, half-starved, they reminded Naumann of the miserable half-humans he had lined up outside villages in Poland, Czechoslovakia and Russia.

'Without food,' Naumann said, 'we cannot remain entrenched. Among us there is a man who seeks to use that fact to put an end to our waiting.' He paused, running his eyes along the rows of faces, looking for one more fearful than the others, less mystified. 'We have no food. It has been destroyed. But the saboteur in our ranks has not succeeded. We will remain in this place until he confesses, or until his comrades find him out. That is all.' He turned away, hearing the rumble behind his back, the sounds of disbelief, astonishment. He was two paces from the altar when the rear of the church exploded, belching fire and smoke at him, shaking the roof and bringing down plaster and bricks.

The men ran from the building by every exit they could find, kicking down doors and bursting windows as they charged in disorder on to the sloping lawn and ran for the road. As the first twenty reached the cobbles, the concealed vehicle pool, twenty yards away, exploded with a roar fifty times louder than the first one, and the air became filled with flying metal, burning rubber and acrid, billowing smoke. By then there were nearly seventy men on the lawn and on the road, kneeling, lying down, rolling in the hope of finding cover. A few guns were being waved but there was no target, only the wall of fire and smoke vomiting up from the vehicles. Lying a few yards from the church door, Untersturmführer Gratz looked up and saw Naumann come staggering out, yelling something that was inaudible above the roaring flames and crackling branches and the terrified shouts of the scattered soldiers.

The church was blazing and the heat, channelled forward by the old stone passageways, fanned down across the lawn, driving the men into the road where the smoke gathered to choke them and send them running for the sparse wooded ground to the west. They came to the trees at a gallop with their heads lowered against the rain of debris, as fuel tanks continued to blow and burning wood fell in red-hot chunks. Farrell waited until he could see them in a mass, disordered, scared and leaderless in the semi-dark, then he pushed the nozzle of the flame-thrower ahead of him and seared the eyes out of thirty men with the first blast.

As the first wave went down screaming and burning the ones behind veered off the only way they could, up the steep rise that led to the fields behind the church, and more than half of them were hit by the hail of bullets from two machine-guns, fired in unison and swung feverishly from side to side by Farrell's assistant. One man, miraculously escaping injury, turned and made back for the road, which was shrouded in smoke. Somewhere in that suffocating black fog, as he screamed his wife's name, he saw the dawning of an orange light and took one long stride towards it before it spread, grew, and enveloped him in a heat that fused his brain before he ever comprehended it.

The machine-gun fire stopped and the young American soldier began spraying death in another direction with another gun as Farrell ploughed back towards the blazing church with the flame-thrower. Some pistol shots were fired and one German even managed to get his submachine-gun going, but there was no target in the fierce contrast of smoke and flame. In their gas masks it was easy for Farrell and his companion to work methodically through the carnage with pistols and finish what they had started. In less than ten minutes they had killed the entire Einsatzgruppe, with the exception of one man who had forced himself to remain close to the church in spite of the fire and the scorching heat, a solitary man who had sensed a trap in all the confusion. As Farrell and the young soldier stood in the road opposite the church and surveyed the piles of burnt corpses, the irregular lines of bullet-torn dead, that one man still clung behind the clump of bushes on the lawn, his hair and the backs of his hands scorched, his will intact.

The smoke was lifting, letting through the weak morning sun, and Farrell pulled off his gas mask, drop-kicking it at a folded corpse ten feet away. It landed with a thud that seemed to please Farrell enormously. He grinned and slapped his companion's shoulder, and when the rear of the old church building collapsed suddenly, quenching the remains of the fire inside, he actually began laughing.

When the soldier took off his mask he looked as pale and distant from life as some of the ones who lay around. He turned his face towards Farrell, staring at the beaming confidence of the man. 'Jesus God,' he said weakly, 'that was terrible. I never saw—'

'It was a successful operation, kid. Don't let it overwhelm you. We planned, we executed, we succeeded.'

'But so many of them, so fast.'

The German flame-thrower was lying in the road and Farrell jerked his thumb at it. 'Those babies are worth a platoon, in the right hands. Close range is what you need, close range and a clear head.' He slapped the soldier's shoulder again. 'You did pretty good yourself. Close range again, you see?'

'Yeah.' The soldier turned aside, then began walking to the debris-littered grass in front of the church. He stopped suddenly and dropped to his knees, then vomited. The nausea took him in three great waves, and when he had finished he remained on his knees, shaking and too weak to stand. Farrell was going to him when Oberführer Naumann stood up from behind the clump of bush five yards away and levelled his pistol. The first bullet slammed into the young soldier's chest, the second whined inches past Farrell's ear. There was no time for Naumann to steady his hands for another shot. Farrell was running at him and even as the burned hands struggled to hold the unbelievable weight of the Luger, it was wrenched aside and Naumann felt blazing pain as a solid fist knocked him into temporary darkness.

Farrell examined the soldier, convinced himself the boy was dead, then went back to Naumann. He tied the officer's hands behind his back and rolled the still-unconscious body up to the blackened doorway of the church. The stone was giving off a powerful heat and Farrell stood close to it for a few minutes, relishing the sensation, like sun after a long spell of winter. He gazed around at the dead again, letting his eyes rest with puckering regret on the young American. He had no doubt the boy would have died anyway, he had been the type who generated only enough luck for short-term survival. It was just a pity he had gone down like that.

Farrell spent fifteen minutes making ready for his move out. He had put a staff car in the grounds beside his base of operations, with spare cans of fuel in the back and a box of guns and ammunition he had found in one of the half-tracks. He piled food and clothing into the boot and put ten grenades on a folded blanket on the front passenger seat where they would be handy in an emergency, then he drove the car to the edge of the town and parked it.

Back at the church he dug a grave with a trench shovel and buried the American soldier, in full view of Naumann who lay on his side, conscious again and in pain, in the dry heat of the arched doorway. When the grave was filled again and the rectangles of turf had been patted into place with the shovel, Farrell pushed a stick into the mound and tied the soldier's dog tags to it. He had been called Harvey O'Neill. That was a sound Irish name, Farrell thought, as he walked slowly to the place where Naumann was lying. He squatted by the man and spoke to him in German.

'You're special, aren't you?' He turned for a moment and waved his hand towards the dead. 'You led this garbage, right?'

Naumann said nothing. The pain of the belt on his burned wrists was only slightly less than that in his face, where Farrell's punch had dislocated the nasal bone. He set his teeth, diverting himself with his hatred.

'I'm going to treat you as something special,' Farrell said. He reached out and patted the tense cheek, then let his fingers grip on the side of Naumann's neck, forcing a groan from him. 'Really special, Herr Oberführer. One last taste of glory.'

Division One of GRU, known lengthily in Moscow as the Chief Intelligence Administration of the General Staff of the Red Army, had almost doubled the numbers of its agents in Western Europe during 1943 and 1944. Operating on the thesis that more spies produced more information, the GRU lost over two hundred men to the Germans in a period of eighteen months, but the hard core of their spy network survived the Gestapo raids and continued to operate early in 1945. With the imminence of Germany's defeat, the hierarchy of Russian Intelligence began to reorganize the field operators, and the nature of their work was changed, too. Before there could be too much obstruction from Americans and British with charity in their hearts, GRU headquarters at Arbatskaya Ploshehad, in Moscow, issued a clear directive to all espionage co-ordinators: retributive punishment would be carried out against the Nazis, and no method of achieving that end should be considered too extreme. Dozens of agents, who had made vengeance a part of their work all along, became full-time instruments of Moscow's wrath. Other men, such as David Zartoff, remained co-ordinators, but now they co-ordinated campaigns of mutilation and slaughter.

Zartoff was forty, a soldier's son from Aleksandrov who had trained first to be a teacher and had attracted the attention of the authorities when, at a youth rally in Moscow, he had denounced Western imperialism and bourgeois decadence with such fire and virulence that his audience had been moved to cheering. He worked for a time as an indoctrination officer for the KGB, and in 1935 he was transferred for training with the GRU. By 1943 he was working as a field co-ordinator in Munich.

Co-ordinators stayed out of sight most of the time, spending their days like moles in their cover addresses, maintaining the structure of their networks like sightless creatures who worked by touch and instinct. It was work for introverts and fanatics, men who did not need the company of others and who drew their warmth from their cause. The co-ordinator did not have to be so brave as the field operatives he controlled, for he was exposed to less danger: if he was ever caught, he would be ready to kill himself without hesitation, because as a good Communist he knew in his bones that the cause was more important than its servants. Zartoff was the ideal co-ordinator, and on the evening of 5th February, when a tall, stern-faced SS officer kicked in the door of his hideout, he picked up his Stechkin automatic and turned it on himself.

The gun failed to fire, because the safety catch was still on. In two quick strides Stefan was across the room and one kick sent the pistol flying out of Zartoff's hand. He jumped up and tried to hurl himself at the window, but he was held by then, gasping with pain as his arm was twisted against his spine.

'Let's have you sitting down, Comrade.' Stefan threw the thin little man into an armchair and stood over him with his hands hanging loose, ready to counter any sudden movement. 'I know who you are, and it didn't take very long to find you. It's been reasonably simple all along, so it would be nice to keep it like that. Tell me where I can find Ralph Farrell.'

'I don't understand.'

Stefan booted one scrawny shin, then the other, making Zartoff howl. 'I'll break them. Then the arms. Then the fingers. Talk!'

Pain terrified Zartoff; a toothache could put him in a state of depression and collapse. But there was the cause to think of, and martyrdom was easier to take than simple punishment. 'I told you,' he gasped, 'I do not understand what you mean.'

The words had the familiarity of an old song. Stefan walked to the door, far enough for Zartoff to take in the entirety of the physical threat. 'I'll explain, then. I got your name from a list – a list of Soviet agents and supervisory operators working in Western Europe. The list was taken by the SS when two of your colleagues were uncovered on the north side of Reinickendorf. They're dead, Comrade, but their files live on.'

The lines of worry deepened on Zartoff's face. If he persisted in saying he did not understand he would be hurt again. If he said anything other than that, he would be a traitor. When Stefan's foot began tapping its warning, Zartoff said, 'You must believe me when I say I can't tell you anything.'

'You can be made to,' Stefan replied. 'I can exercise the kind of power that will draw full submission from you.' He believed he had read this man accurately. Zartoff had great moral courage, but no physical valour at all. '*You* must believe *that*,' he added.

Zartoff shook his head with a trembling sigh.

Stefan lifted the unresisting body from the chair by the shirtfront and walked it to the centre of the floor. With his free hand he caught three or four of the sparse hairs on Zartoff's scalp and pulled them out. Zartoff yelled and closed his eyes tightly. In Moscow he had been taught to fight, he had been shown myriad ways to cause pain and disablement, but he had known all along that he would never be able to defend himself against a real assailant. David Zartoff's anger and strength resided in his spirit; nowhere else.

'That's the tiniest pain you'll feel,' Stefan said. 'It'll get worse and worse, and eventually you'll tell me what I want to know, anyway. Why not save yourself the agony?'

'You'll kill me anyway,' Zartoff said hoarsely.

'If you tell me where I can locate Ralph Farrell, I'll let you go free.'

'I don't believe you.'

'It's true. And it's very little I'm asking, anyway. I simply want to reach Farrell. I know he's left Munich. Where has he gone?'

To be free, Zartoff was thinking, was everything he wanted right then. He could run, he knew plenty of places to go. But why was he tempted to believe the Nazi? All his experience and his loathing dictated the opposite reaction. 'Why only him?' he asked Stefan.

'It's a personal matter.'

Zartoff was staring at him. 'What is your name?'

'Gaiser.' As he spoke, Stefan relaxed his grip on the man, seeing the dawn of something on his troubled face.

'You were a contact.' Zartoff was still staring. 'You broke the line of communication . . .'

'Farrell broke it.'

'I will tell you as much as I know,' Zartoff said finally. 'It may be of no help to you at all.'

That same evening Stefan drove to Kaiserslauten. There he stormed into the Gestapo headquarters and found everything as he had expected. Confusion and desertion were whittling away at order, there was no communication possible with Berlin or Munich, and the presence of an officer with a pocketful of passes and permits signed by Bormann put a bolt of fear through the administration. Stefan commandeered the only good vehicle left at the place, a semi-armoured car with twin fuel tanks, and left the sweating Obersturmführer with the assurance that his co-operation would be noted at SD headquarters.

The following morning, after taking two hours' sleep in the back of the vehicle, Stefan drove to the nearest main road and waited for a convoy. The first one to come along was only five vehicles long, a detachment of boy soldiers being hurried to the Oder, where attempts were still being made to hold back the Russians. Stefan drove with them for twenty miles, then turned west, heading for the French border.

Avoiding the main line of the fighting was difficult, but the tactical geometry of both sides became clearer as the journey into France progressed. Moving steadily south west, Stefan saw only three skirmishes, and they were all at a safe distance. Closer, however, were the signs of earlier fighting, the dead men and their dead tanks, the sundered flesh of countless soldiers surrounding and mingled with the smashed and upturned remains of vehicles and weapons. At one point, in order to keep to his route, Stefan had to take his car over a mound of bodies, ambushed Germans caught in a steep pass. The blackened corpses slithered across each other as the wheels passed over them, and the car filled with the putrid stink of death as it ploughed on to the road ahead.

At nightfall the petrol ran out. Stefan had been expecting it much earlier, and took the last five miles of the drive as a bonus. He ditched the car outside a deserted farm house, then he buttoned his greatcoat to the neck, put on two pairs of gloves, and moved off on foot.

Exhaustion caught up with him before daylight. In a half-burned cluster of trees overlooking a main road he sat down and drew the heavy coat up over his face. In the woollen darkness Stefan heard the rasping of his breath like an engine, a labouring device that dragged him towards sleep. For one moment he had a flash of awareness, a revelation of hopelessness. But it passed. There was no chance of despair clinging where there was only room for slow burning determination. Stefan slept.

It was bright daylight when he awoke with the sound of clanking metal and motors in his ears. He stood up and rubbed the stiffness from his legs, wriggling his toes to bring back the circulation. There was a convoy on the road, and stiff-backed men were visible in flack wagons and light armoured vehicles. Stefan moved to the trees on the edge of his shelter and peered across the fifty-yard distance. It was an SS formation, and that encouraged him before he was quite sure what he planned to do.

By crossing the field that sloped down behind him, he was in the hedges by the roadside before the convoy came around the wide bend. Stefan waited until every one of the vehicles had passed, then he moved out of cover and stood at the side of the road with his coat unbuttoned, his rank visible. For a minute he wondered if he had miscalculated, then he heard the rumble of the officers' transport. Since ambushes of convoys had become common, senior personnel always travelled a clear half mile behind the main body of troops. Stefan moved into the centre of the road as the squat armoured car rounded the bend. He waved with one hand and kept the other in his coat pocket, wrapped around his Luger.

The car stopped and a Hauptsturmführer promptly stuck his head out of the window. On top of the car, the gunner stood bracing himself on the sides of his little steel tower. Stefan approached them, smiling apologetically.

'What are you doing here?' The officer's face was as taut as his voice, but Stefan detected no suspicion. The man was simply annoyed at having to stop.

'You'll never believe it, sir.' Stefan grinned and quickly took a count of the occupants. Only four officers, two of them asleep.

'Well?'

Stefan took one step back, removing the gun as he did. His arm was out and straight in an instant, and as it swung rapidly upwards he pulled the trigger twice, hitting the gunner with both bullets. The startled face of the Hauptsturmführer took the third shot, and as he slumped against the windscreen Stefan moved close and pumped the remainder of the clip into the others. One of the sleeping officers remained as he was, but the other woke up for a second, his eyes wide and desperate as blood spilled out of his mouth.

Stefan moved quickly. He opened the side and rear doors and rolled the bodies on to the road. The officer who had been driving was wearing a belt with two Walther P38 pistols in stout leather holsters. Unfortunately for him, both holsters were firmly buttoned. Stefan strapped the belt on to himself, then climbed up to the gun tower and pushed the dead gunner over the side. There were two racks of ammunition for the Erma MP40, and a spare gun slotted into the side of the tower. Stefan took the spare and half the ammunition into the cab with him. He drove off across the field where he had slept and down on to the road on the other side. He had the map in his head, he knew just where he was and how long it would be before he reached his destination. Russian Intelligence was combining the efforts of five infiltration squads, and they were operating from a village called Chabrier. To get there, Stefan had decided to go through the town of Dizier, saving himself probably two hours. With luck, and his armoury, he could allow himself a fair amount of hope that he would locate Farrell before the day was out.

A unit of the disrupted US 424th infantry regiment arrested the driver of an SS staff vehicle twenty-four hours after he had left Dizier. A dozen men closed on the car as it was easing through the narrow arch of an old road bridge. When Farrell saw the muzzles of five rifles all pointing at his windshield, he simply switched off the engine and sat back.

At first the soldiers were hostile, and the big sergeant who pulled Farrell out of the car was careful to punch him towards the wall, rather than pushing him. Farrell remained silent while he was searched and the car was stripped. He saw the confusion spread when the uniforms turned up, and watched the sergeant decide, huffily, that this was one for the colonel.

The unit had made its headquarters in a school two miles from the place Farrell was picked up, on the outskirts of Septforges, near the southern Belgian border. Farrell was tied and energetically frog-marched the entire distance to the school, and when they arrived he was hustled into an empty classroom and left there.

Colonel Sutton entered the room twenty minutes later and introduced himself in halting German. He was a friendly-looking man with close-cropped white hair and a leathery face; his bright, searching eyes reminded Farrell of his own father's. In the same mis-accented German he ordered Farrell to identify himself.

My name's Ralph Farrell,' Farrell said. 'I'm an American.'

The colonel frowned. 'An American? Then what in hell were you doing in a German staff vehicle, armed to the teeth with German weaponry, and wearing that uniform?'

'I believe your men found my other uniforms, Colonel. My work requires me to adopt various identities, as circumstances dictate.'

'I see.' Colonel Sutton sat on the edge of a table opposite Farrell, scratching his chin. 'How come you didn't say anything to my men? They might have shot you.'

'I only say something when it's absolutely necessary, and to as small an audience as possible. My work is delicate, you understand.'

Sutton nodded. 'With army Intelligence, are you?'

'I'm not supposed to say who I'm with,' Farrell said, 'but at a time like this, I can't see it'll hurt. I'm with OSS.'

'Holy shit!' The colonel was impressed. He stood up and went to the door, then shouted at the woodwork. 'Daniels! In here at the double!'

The sergeant came in and Colonel Sutton ordered him to untie the prisoner. Sergeant Daniels seemed reluctant.

'Do it, man! This isn't a German, he's as American as you and me.'

Daniels narrowed his eyes, giving Farrell the same look of menacing dislike he had when they first met. 'I heard of a lot of Germans passing themselves off as Americans,' he said slowly. 'Whole platoons of them.'

The colonel groaned. 'Skorzeny's boys aren't around any more, Daniels. And if they were, they wouldn't be going about in kraut uniforms, would they?'

'I should've put on my infantry sergeant's outfit before I hit this region,' Farrell said amiably. 'If I might make a suggestion, Colonel – why not let the sergeant here put me to the test? Let's face it, you do only have my word for it that I'm American.'

'And your bearing and your accent,' the colonel said. 'I have the right nose for these things. But sure, let's put Daniels' mind at rest. Fire away, Sergeant. Let's see how you uncover spies.'

The sergeant was looking embarrassed, just as Farrell had intended he should. He shuffled his feet for a second then cleared his throat. 'What's the date of George Washington's birthday?'

'Aw, shit, Daniels.' The colonel thumped the table. 'Anybody can memorize stuff like that. Some interrogator you'd make.'

Red-faced, the sergeant tried again. 'Who's Helen Keller?'

'That does it, Daniels. Untie this man, right now.'

'Ask me about something more personal,' Farrell said. He was enjoying the sergeant's discomfort. 'The sort of things guys jawing in a bar would talk about.'

Daniels looked blank for a second, then he narrowed his eyes again, an action he obviously believed made him look cunning. 'What's your favourite Barbara Stanwyck movie?'

Farrell hammed confusion. 'There's so many . . .'

'So maybe you'd like to name a few,' Daniels insisted, glancing at the colonel.

'Let me see, now.' Farrell looked up at the ceiling and stayed like that until the instant he knew Daniels was going to wade in with the accusations. Then he said, 'My real favourite, I suppose, was *Ten Cents a Dance*, although that's a real old picture. *His Brother's Wife*, that was good, and I enjoyed *Stella Dallas*. I didn't get a chance to see *Meet John Doe*, but I've heard it's worth a visit.'

'Daniels,' the colonel murmured, and the sergeant began untying the rope around Farrell's arms and hands.

'I'm a Frederic March fan, myself,' Farrell said, smiling up at the sergeant. '*Jekyll and Hyde* is what I call a movie – and *Anthony Adverse*. Did you ever catch either of those?'

Daniels mumbled something and stepped back, taking the rope with him.

'Find our guest something to eat,' the colonel said, and when Daniels had gone he turned to Farrell and winked. 'Some of these boys learned all their soldiering at the movies. You should have asked him about those.'

When Farrell had eaten, and when the colonel had ordered that the German staff car be brought to the school and reloaded, the matter of procedure was raised. Colonel Sutton explained that he had to keep a daily journal, even in his present position as leader of an amputated unit.

'Maybe you know more about it than I do,' he said. 'Do I put it on paper that you turned up here?'

'It would be better if you forgot me, Colonel. I was on my way to carry out a specific mission when your men waylaid me. If I still arrive on time, events along the road can be omitted from my own record, so why not yours?'

'Happy to comply,' Sutton said. 'That's all that really worried me. If you'd mentioned this, and we hadn't – well.'

'Colonel, in Washington they like to play it like I don't exist, so let's neither of us upset things.'

The colonel was on the point of explaining how he hoped to be joined by two other scattered units within a couple of days when there was an explosion outside that shook the building and threw clods of earth against the windows.

'Stay here!' Farrell yelled. He ran to the back of the school and jumped through an open window, then pushed himself against the wall and sidled to the end of the building. In a field opposite, grinding through the ruins of houses, he saw two King Tigers. They were moving towards the road, and the one shell they had fired had made a direct hit on the unit's solitary Sherman M4, which was now blazing and spewing burning fuel across the yard in front of the school. As Farrell watched, the big 88 millimetre gun on the leading King Tiger began to swivel and dip, ready for another shot.

'Out!' Farrell shouted, running back to the window. 'Out, everybody! Out!'

Bodies began falling through doors and windows and as they landed Farrell waved them to the wooded land at the rear. The colonel tumbled through the smallest window carrying piles of folders and a submachine-gun, and Farrell helped him into the trees. They had just hit the ground when the second shell landed, ripping through the front of the building and ploughing its way to the rear. For a second the structure swayed, and then it collapsed, sending billows of brick dust and shattered wood into the trees where the soldiers were lying. When the cloud of debris began to settle, the King Tigers could be seen clearly, almost at the road now, their commanders leaning out of the turrets.

'Where in hell did they come from?' The colonel was lying with his documents piled under his chest, staring through dust-rimmed eyes as the rattling monsters came down the slope.

'There're busted Panzer units all over the place,' Farrell told him. 'They go marauding in twos and threes until they meet up with other groups, then they find themselves a battle somewhere. Where's your ammo?'

'Over there.' The colonel pointed to a hut by a large tree which, until a couple of minutes before, had sheltered one side of the school building.

'Can I take your sergeant?'

'What are you going to do?'

'Stop those bastards,' Farrell hissed.

'That's crazy! Those are the biggest tanks in this war!'

'They're machines, Colonel, and machines can always be stopped. Now can I take your sergeant, before they get up here and grind us into the dirt?'

'Sure.'

'I suggest you move the rest of the men as far back as you can.' Farrell stood up and beckoned to Daniels. The sergeant frowned at him for a second, then the colonel gave him an impatient thumbs-up and he scuttled over to where Farrell was standing.

'The guns on top of the tanks are MG34s,' Farrell said. 'We have to watch out for them, they're designed to knock out aircraft, and they fire nearly three thousand rounds non-stop. As soon as you see anybody start swinging one of them, hit the floor.'

'What are we going to do?' Daniels demanded.

'Get some ammunition first.' Before Daniels had any time to consider that, Farrell dragged him by the arm and they began running towards the hut. The door was locked but one kick opened it. Farrell began rummaging furiously among the cartons and boxes, then found what he was looking for. He passed three grenades to Daniels and put another five in his own pockets.

'We have to get around behind them, Sergeant. Which means we take off out of here and run away from the place. They'll see us, but they won't do too much about it. Now let's go, before they get a bead on this hut.'

They had sprinted almost one hundred yards when the hut blew up. The resulting fire and smoke covered them as they put another hundred yards on their distance from the school yard. Then Farrell turned sharp right, with Daniels panting and grunting behind him. There was a bend in the road at the point where Farrell had veered off, and when they crossed it they were out of sight of the tanks. The ground on the opposite side was dotted with half-ruined buildings with wide, irregular spaces between. It took five minutes for both men to put themselves in a position directly opposite the ruins of the school. They crouched behind a low wall for a further three minutes to catch their breath. Then Farrell explained the next step of the operation.

'There are weak spots on the King Tiger,' he said, 'and nearly all of them are at the back. Once we're beside them, we have fifteen seconds, that's all. One grenade goes on top of each radiator grille, and one goes into the turret.'

'And you think that'll stop them?' Daniels was scowling, resentful at being commandeered and dragged off on such a lunatic mission. 'The armour is six inches thick – I know a thing or two about those mothers myself. The only grenades that are going to do any good are the ones we lob inside, and I don't see any chance of us doing that.'

Farrell was silent for a moment, watching the tanks. They had stopped in the middle of the road and both commanders were scanning the territory ahead with their field glasses. 'The front armour is six inches thick,' he said eventually, 'but the rear is thinner, a lot thinner. But that isn't the point. The blast on the upper radiator grilles will hit the fuel tanks – there are seven of them. The grenade through the turret will carry the damage deeper, into the motor. Knockouts on King Tigers have to be thorough, Sergeant.'

'And what about the guys up top? They're bound to see us.'

'You're just looking for difficulties. Come on.'

They went down the slope at a crouch and moved out on to the road. The tank commanders were still scanning the horizon, and as Farrell moved in under the rear plating of one tank he winked at Daniels and mouthed, 'I told you so.'

When they were both ready, grenades set on the road beside them, Farrell gave Daniels the beat, and in unison they pulled the pins and set one grenade up on each tank, squarely on the grille mesh. More rapidly they de-pinned their second grenades and planted them; then they moved back, arming the final ones and getting ready to throw. At that moment the commander of Farrell's tank turned round. He reacted with the speed of an athlete, throwing himself out of the turret and down over the forward plating as the grenade sailed into the cavity he had just vacated. Daniels' grenade struck the second commander on the shoulder and fell down into the turret. The man had time to turn and see the saboteurs running away across the field, then his tank and the one beside it exploded almost in unison. The first loud bangs were drowned by a sudden roaring from within the vehicles as the fuel tanks blew and buckled the side and top armour.

Flattened on the ground, Farrell watched as the secondary explosions ruptured the forward bulkheads and sent engine-blowers and steel-cased fans hurtling through the radiators and on to the road. A second later the ammunition racks started to explode and within a minute both tanks were engulfed in flame. Farrell stood up and grinned at Sergeant Daniels, the second man in two days to help Farrell discharge his hate at the Germans.

Farrell's smile faded suddenly when he recalled the strongest similarity between that day's assault and the one the day before.

'Where did that guy go?'

Daniels blinked at him. 'What guy? They're all fruit salad.'

Farrell ran down on to the road, shielding his face from the heat. There was no sign of a body on the road. He ran up the rise towards the rubble of the school and saw Colonel Sutton coming towards him, waving happily like a man whose team had just won.

'Amazing!' the colonel yelled. 'Just amazing!'

As he drew closer, Farrell saw some of the other men coming out of the trees. They had a black-uniformed soldier with them, they were dragging him by the arms. Farrell felt a little jolt of pleasure.

'I see you caught the sprightly one,' he said.

Colonel Sutton took Farrell's hand and shook it vigorously. 'For an impromptu massacre, that was really something.' He turned and looked at the prisoner. 'He ran right into us. I think he's dazed, he was only halfway to the school when the tanks started to go up.'

'I'd like a word with him later,' Farrell said. 'If you've no objections, that is.' The sensation of pleasure grew stronger as he took in the German's uniform. He was a

Panzergrenadier of the SS, one of the élite, a flashy young Hauptsturmführer with the build and looks the Nazis stuck on their propaganda posters.

'Be my guest,' Sutton told him. 'There's nothing I want him to tell me, anyway.'

In the early evening the unit retrenched on a hillside a few miles from the ruined school. Without spare ammunition they were vulnerable, but in Colonel Sutton's estimation they were better off than before; up on the windy hill they could see the enemy coming. Sergeant Daniels, a hero now with the other men, organized the erection of small tents and moved two labourers' huts on to the site. One hut became the colonel's office and the other was used to lock up the prisoner. The only transport remaining was a truck and two jeeps, and Sutton generously donated one jeep to Farrell, whose German staff car had been blown up along with the school.

'It's the least I can do,' the colonel said, 'and since you don't appear to be too fussy what uniform you wear, I can let you have one of mine. It'll be a little rumpled, but it'll look better than that Nazi number you've got on.'

Over a supper of K rations the colonel apologized for having obstructed Farrell, but admitted he was glad it had happened. 'That Panzer outfit would have had us for sure. I'm inclined to view your arrival on the scene as an act of providence. To you it's probably been one big pain in the ass.'

'Not at all,' Farrell said.

'When do you plan on leaving us, Ralph?'

'As soon as it's dark. Which is right now, by the look of things.' He stood up and peered out of the grimy window. 'I'll just check out that prisoner before I go, though. He might know something I could use.'

Alone in his hut, the young German sat huddled in a corner with a blanket around his shoulders. He did not look up as Farrell came in and hung his lantern on a coat hook on the wall. He closed the door carefully and approached the prisoner.

'What's your name?' Farrell asked softly in German.

There was defiance on the face as he glanced up. 'Heckel, Karl, SS-Panzergrenadier. I hold the rank of Haupsturmführer.' His eyes were hard and in the faint yellow light Farrell could see that quality of resentment he knew so well, the arrogant certainty of a man who knew he should not be the prisoner of his inferiors.

'Onto your feet, Heckel.'

The prisoner complied, and stood brushing the dust and grass from his black uniform. He jumped back against the wall when Farrell slapped the side of his head.

'This is outrageous!' He fingered the stinging weal and for a moment it looked as if he might retaliate.

'I was establishing your position here,' Farrell said, as softly as before. 'It's nice to get off on the right footing. Now I want you to tell me something . . .'

'I am required to tell you nothing!'

Farrell hit him again, in the stomach, and Heckel doubled over, groaning.

'While you get your breath back, I'll tell you what I want to know.' Farrell stepped closer so that there would be no need to raise his voice. 'Tell me the approximate location of the nearest Russian division.'

Heckel breathed deeply, trying to drive the pain from his abdomen. 'I know nothing of such matters,' he grunted.

'Don't you? Well, I know a few things that might change your song. I know about places like Treblinka, Belsen, Buchenwald, Wolzec – and I know what goes on in those places. I know the people who run those slaughterhouses are people like you, and I'm prepared right now to work a medley of SS torture techniques on your arrogant carcass until you'll be glad to talk. Am I making myself understood?'

'I am a prisoner of war! I demand . . .'

'Fuck your demands.' Farrell rammed his fist into Heckel's mouth, splitting the lip. The German started to howl and another punch in the stomach silenced him. He crouched, gasping, blood dribbling from his mouth. Farrell stood watching, and was taken off guard when the German suddenly sprang at him, butting him in the groin.

'You shit bastard!' Farrell rode on the slicing pain, leaping behind the prisoner and taking him by the hair. He ran Heckel at the wall, clamped his injured face there, then dragged him the entire length of the hut, smearing the rough wood with blood. Heckel was barely conscious when Farrell dropped him in the corner again.

For five minutes there was no activity in the hut and nothing said. Farrell remained standing over Heckel, listening to his moans, waiting for the pain to recall him to the present. When he was sure the German would hear him, Farrell bent low over him, staring at the pulped mouth and torn, bleeding nose. 'We've only just begun, Karl. Do you want some more, or do you want to talk?'

Heckel talked. It was difficult to make out what he said and he had to repeat it several times. He gave Farrell the location of a rearguard Russian division, forty miles to the east.

Before he left the hut, Farrell made the prisoner stand up. Heckel was in shock and had to lean hard against the wall to support himself. Without a word, Farrell put one hand on Heckel's chest, steadying him, and with his other hand he drew out the knife from his pocket. Heckel's eyes widened suddenly as the knife-point moved like fire into his groin, but he could not scream, he could only remain where he was, staring at the calm determined face of his tormentor as the agony devoured him.

When Farrell came out of the prisoner's hut he closed the door and replaced the padlock. Colonel Sutton came out of his own hut and held out his hand. In the faint light he did not see that there was blood on Farrell.

'It's farewell time, then,' the colonel said. 'Was our prisoner any help?'

'Some,' Farrell replied. 'Let's just say that none of this has been a waste, Colonel.' He turned to the jeep, parked by the hut door, and hauled out the US Army greatcoat he had been given. 'Thanks for everything.' He shook Sutton's hand again and got into the driving seat.

'I hope my sergeant picked up a few tips,' Sutton said over the rumble of the jeep's engine. 'You never can say who's going to drop by.'

'I'm sure it'll be quieter from here on,' Farrell assured him. 'Say goodbye to everybody for me, and tell Daniels thanks.' He waved and jerked the vehicle into gear, then drove off down the hillside towards the road. Colonel Sutton watched until he was out of sight then returned to the hut, smiling to himself.

At ten o'clock, before the watch was changed, Sergeant Daniels went to check on the prisoner. Given his own way, he would have put the kraut against a wall and shot him. The unit was in bad enough shape without having to carry a prisoner around the countryside with them. But the colonel was hot on the Geneva Convention, so that was that.

The first thing Daniels saw when he looked through the small window was the lantern, still hanging on the wall hook. He had to crane his neck to see the prisoner, and when he saw him Daniels could not understand. He moved further along, to another window, and looked through that one. The German was kneeling, and he was rocking back and forth. Daniels watched for a minute, then decided to go inside.

The man continued to kneel and rock even when the lock was clanked open and Daniels strode in.

'What's the matter, fella?' Daniels approached slowly, his gun levelled. 'You sick, or something?' The prisoner was moaning, and when Daniels came round in front of him he saw the man's face was covered with blood. 'Christ Almighty, what did that lunatic do?' Daniels put down the gun and tried to raise the German, but when he put his hands in the man's armpits and heaved, the prisoner opened his broken mouth and howled. Daniels looked down, saw the cupped, trembling hands and then realized what had happened. He let the man slump down again and turned, feeling his mouth drying as he charged to the door and started yelling for the medic.

Later, when they had done as much as they could for the prisoner, Daniels took himself off along the hillside and sat down on a rock, wishing the whole day had never happened, wishing he could stop the twitching in his shoulders and the terrible feeling that he was trapped, even out there with space all around him.

'That crazy bastard,' Daniels murmured, and saw the German's broken face and heard his moans again. Maybe if there had been a frenzy of pain and screaming it would have been more bearable. As things stood, the image was set hard into Daniels' brain: a man, kneeling, moaning, with two handfuls of his own bowels. As he sat there and shivered against the wind, Daniels' dearest wish was that time would reverse and that Nazi staff car would take another turning, another route all together. Daniels would have been content with that, he would have been glad to take his chances with the King Tigers, without the help of a raving psycho.

Half a mile from Dizier, Stefan knew something very bad had happened. The day-old stench of burning was in the air and on the high approach road he could see the disruption, the burned trees and the blackened walls. The silence of the place was dispiriting.

On the main street he saw the bodies, scattered like grisly toy soldiers from a carelessly shaken packet. They were all over the place, frozen in their last convulsions. Stefan got out of the armoured car and walked among the dead, some burned black, others torn by bullets. In front of the ruined church he saw the new grave and fingered the dog tags on it. As he straightened his breath caught. On the church doors, charred but still standing, a man in the uniform of an SS Oberführer had been crucified, his hands nailed to the ancient wood. Like the others he was dead, but there was wide-eyed agony on his face, as if the pain had followed him into his silence.

A truck was coming down the main road. Stefan turned at its sound, reacting too late. A man with a rifle had already leapt out and was running in his direction, warning him to get his hands up. Stefan did as he was told.

They were Americans, advance spotters for the artillery. The leader of the five-man squad, the one with the gun, was a captain. He was younger than Stefan, with short black hair and a stubble like fine ash on his chin and upper lip. As soon as Stefan raised his hands the captain stopped running and slowed to a saunter, keeping the gun firmly levelled. When he was close, and in a voice that was nowhere as rough as his appearance, he told Stefan to identify himself.

'My name's Gaiser. I work for the British.'

'That so?' The gun did not move. 'And what's been going on here?'

'A small massacre, I'd say. I only just got here myself.'

A corporal came up alongside the officer. 'Trouble?' he asked.

'Probably. The guy in the SS uniform tells me he works for the British.'

The corporal grinned. He had a mean, ferrety face. 'What'll we do with him?'

'I'm not sure yet.' The captain's gun had dipped, but only a couple of inches. 'Tell me, ah . . .'

'Gaiser.'

'Gaiser. What is it you do for the British? Are you telling us you're an undercover man, something like that?'

'Something like that,' Stefan said.

The captain looked at his corporal, then back at Stefan. 'Your accent's not bad. In fact it sounds perfect. But I hear that more than one Nazi officer went to public school in England.'

Stefan shrugged wearily. 'I've no proof of who I am.'

The corporal spat on the ground and made mud with his toe. 'I say put a hole in him. I never saw anybody looked more like a Nazi in my life.'

The captain's jaw stiffened. 'What you say, Corporal, isn't worth a jug of warm piss to me after yesterday's performance on signal reading. Get your ass back in the truck.' When the soldier had gone, the captain told Stefan to unbuckle his guns and drop them. Then he searched the tunic and trousers, keeping the gun on Stefan's ribs. Satisfied there was nothing else to find apart from some fancy-looking documents, he stood back. 'What are you doing out here, Gaiser?'

'I was passing through, heading for a village near here. I've urgent business, Captain.'

The captain was staring at the man nailed to the door. 'Not a run-of-the-mill massacre, by the look of it. Any theories?'

'None.' But already there was the suspicion; Stefan could trust some instincts completely. A dead American, carefully buried. Dead Nazis, left to moulder and stink on the streets. If Farrell had not been there, then someone with his talent for hatred had. Americans, the ordinary soldiers, would never have left one of their own in that churchyard, just as they would never leave their victims scattered in that bizarre, chaotic memorial of multiple slaughter.

'Nasty. Very nasty.' The captain stared at Stefan for nearly a minute, chewing his lip, considering. Finally he twitched the gun towards his truck. 'I'm taking you back with me. Somebody else can figure out what to do with you.'

In the back of the truck Stefan was put in cuffs and laid on his side on the floor.

'One tricky move,' the corporal warned him, 'and you get ventilated.'

Stefan nodded and put his cheek against the scuffed metal tread. Any move he made, he decided, would be chance, accident. For the time being he was void of useful intention, and by the time they had covered a mile of the bumpy road north of Dizier, he was sound asleep.

A bored, dejected Hauptscharführer called Koerner had been left to man the solitary gun on the rim of the crater where his tank, a King Tiger with a ruptured fuel system, had lain tilted for two days. Koerner had been an electrician in civilian life, not a plumber, and he had taken it hard when the tank commander, Vocke, had screeched and punched at him when he had failed to understand the tank's fuel feed, let alone repair it. Vocke had called Koerner inept, stupid, an imbecile. Koerner knew otherwise, he had certificates and letters of recommendation to prove he was probably the only man in the tank crew who knew much about anything besides butchery and Aryan supremacy. His mistake, he realized far too late, had been in joining the SS. He should have gone into the Luftwaffe, or even the army. In outfits like that they still remembered what being human was all about.

Everything was cold, damp, miserable. Even the landscape gave the impression it had succumbed; the green on the fields and hills around Dieuze was nearer grey than emerald, and the trees and shrubbery had the clenched, brooding character of growths impatient to become fossils. Sometimes the wind blew on Koerner's back in long chilling gusts, and strangely those were the times he felt best: that wind came from Germany, a land he would go back to on his hands and knees if just once somebody would give him the chance.

The purpose of Koerner's nine-hour stint on lookout was to spot any German transports that might stray that way. So far, all they had seen had been one American tank and a straggling detachment of Wehrmacht, looking for someone to surrender to. It was Koerner's opinion that they were doomed to stay where they were until they rotted. The gun was for defence, since the angle and deployment of the King Tiger was such that any attempt to use its artillery would result, in Vocke's view, in nothing less than annihilation for the entire four-man crew. Towards sunset, Vocke warned Koerner that he had better spot *something*. Koerner sank deeper into his gloom, staring at the austere landscape and trying to remember his girlfriend's face. When something did appear down on the road, he let out a yelp that brought Vocke running.

'What is it? Let me see, you clown! Give me the glasses!' Vocke wedged his long nose into the gap between the eyepieces and twirled the focussing ring frantically. He inhaled once, deeply, and held his breath while he steadied the glasses. He looked hard for a second, then breathed out. 'Americans.' He went on looking, then dropped the glasses suddenly into Koerner's lap. 'I think we have a chance here. Get out of the way.'

Koerner stepped back from the gun, more depressed than ever. A fight was the last thing he wanted.

Vocke swung the gun round and took aim on the truck that was bumping along five hundred yards away. Through the open top he had counted three men sitting in the back and there were two in the cabin. They only had rifles and side arms. Obersturmführer Vocke saw it as his duty to attack an enemy whenever possible, and in this case it was a clear possibility. As his men looked on from the rim of the crater he squeezed the trigger and began strafing the ground around the truck. When the driver braked, Vocke corrected his aim and began spattering the sitting target.

The corporal was the first to be hit. The bullets caught him halfway out of the truck and the velocity threw him back inside, right on top of Stefan. Another man had his shoulder and one hand blown away when he tried to get out on the blind side. Standing up, screaming, he was hit by three more bullets and fell out on to the road. The captain and the driver were mowed down before they were clear of the cabin, and the last ringing volley tore through the back and head of the remaining soldier, who had been huddling under the rear of the truck.

Koerner and a Sturmann were sent down to collect anything worth rescuing from the wreck. It was Koerner, heaving the dead American corporal out of the back, who saw Stefan first. He let go of the body and jumped back, dumbfounded.

'Don't stand there gawping!' Stefan snapped at him. 'Help me up!'

Koerner blinked, then collected himself and pushed the Sturmann. 'Come on, you hear the officer. Help me get him out.'

Between them they got Stefan on to the road. The key for the cuffs was found on the corporal's body and they were unlocked.

Vocke came running down on to the road while Koerner was distractedly dusting at Stefan's tunic.

'Are you the officer in charge?' Stefan demanded.

Voke nodded. 'That's correct, sir.' He was looking edgily at Stefan's flashes. The difference in rank was only one grade, but the SD triangle on Stefan's sleeve made an ominous distinction. 'I'm terribly sorry, we had no way of knowing you were in the transport . . .'

'I was a prisoner,' Stefan said quietly, 'and now I am not. There's no need to apologize, Obersturmführer.'

'May I ask what happened, sir?'

'I was on liaison duty with an Einsatzgruppe in a place called Dizier,' Stefan told him, 'and we were attacked by an American division.'

'You were the only prisoner?'

Stefan nodded. 'My special standing, shall we say, made me a valuable prize.'

Increased respect crept across Vocke's birdlike features. 'Special standing?'

'I am with the Führer's bodyguard.' Stefan pointed at the dead captain, hanging halfway out of the cab. 'That man is carrying my papers. Get them for me, will you? And then, perhaps, you could get me to wherever it is you're hiding. This road is rather exposed, as your bullets have just demonstrated.'

Later, in the gathering gloom, Stefan was given an outsize portion of the tank crew's rations and Koerner surrendered his only blanket to keep the distinguished guest warm. They sat round a tiny fire lit in a fuel can, eating and shivering, while Vocke tried his best to look efficient. He yelped senseless orders at the men and sat stiffly on his makeshift seat, watching Stefan, nodding reassuringly to him every time their eyes met.

'And what do you intend to do?' Stefan asked finally, setting his metal plate aside.

'Do?'

'Yes, do, Obersturmführer. You can't sit up here forever. I doubt it there's a German unit of any size for miles. The Americans and French have the upper hand in this territory.' Stefan watched the other men turn their attention to Vocke. On his orders, they had been waiting for a German transport. Two days out in the cold had made them despondent, and now their leader was squirming on the plain accusation that he had been wasting time.

'It is difficult to know how to proceed,' Vocke said lamely.

'Then let me make a suggestion.' Stefan put enough hard-edged authority into his tone to make it clear the suggestion was nothing short of an order. 'You have a duty to return to action by the quickest means. To do that, you must gather what armaments you have and leave this spot, preferably under cover of darkness. As the fighting goes at the moment, your best bet is to make directly for the German border, moving north most of the time. That way, you would avoid the major skirmishes and keep ahead of the Russian advance.'

Vocke looked out towards the darkened hills. 'You're sure we would have a chance that way, sir?'

'More than you have sitting here.'

Vocke sighed and stood up, rubbing his hands. 'Very well. As you appear to have more up-to-date information than I do, sir, perhaps you would assist me to work out a route.'

'Of course.'

With maps and tactical charts of the region Stefan began to paint a battle picture for Vocke, while the men unloaded the portable equipment from the tank and packed the supplies into mess tins and canisters. The detailed fiction that took shape in front of Vocke was, for Stefan, one of the best pieces of work he had done. He shaded in areas of probable danger and outlined others where, he told Vocke, engagements were already taking place. By inventing two American tank divisions he was able to show a pincer action fifty miles north west, making progress at an estimated fifteen miles a day. With something like that to avoid, Vocke's angle of escape had to be arranged uncomfortably close to the advancing Russian front – and Vocke knew it. Nevertheless, with so many American troops and tanks to his left, sharp right was the only way to go.

'I have given a great deal of thought to the route,' Stefan assured the tank commander. 'I will demonstrate my faith in it by accompanying you.'

In the surge of his pleasure at having such exalted company for the journey, Vocke took no time to consider that he was doing Stefan a favour by providing cover for him. And there was no way at all that he could know the route was designed to take them right through the village of Chabrier, eight miles away, where Russian Intelligence had recently welcomed their own visitor.

So much of the carnage at Ardennes and Alsace-Lorraine had been caused by the weather: Colonel Tom Delaney of the US 2nd Armoured Division had known it for a long time, but there was no way round the problem. In wooded country with deep snow covering the ground, the heavy armoured units had to keep to the roads or sink. Men and machines on both sides were ambushed regularly, out in the open, and Colonel Delaney had seen a roadbound line of Nazi tanks outside Bastogne, full of dead personnel who had been caught by the guns and grenades of one small unit of foot soldiers.

At Cezoine, twelve miles north east of Dizier, the problem had cropped up again. Delaney had four tanks and eighteen soldiers to man them. Looted fuel from German tanks had kept them moving for nearly a week, and progress had been reasonable. But Cezoine had the look of a custom-built trap and Delay gazed at it through his field glasses for a long time before he voiced his feelings.

'If we got caught down there,' he told his sergeant, 'they could blast us to shit.'

Sergeant Moore accepted the glasses and had a look for himself. The road ahead of them dipped to a long gradient and the ground on either side got gradually higher. At the bottom was a crossroads.

'Somebody could be sitting right around the corner,' Moore said.

'Or up on the hill, or behind some trees,' Delaney grunted. 'Anywhere. There's a dozen places.' He looked around at the wet, muddy terrain. The men in the turrets of the three tanks behind him were doing the same, as if just for once they would spot a dry, hard route across the battered, soggy landscape.

'So what do we do, sir?' Sergeant Moore had lost a fingertip a week before, and now the chilly morning air was making the wound throb inside its bandage. The pain did a lot to deepen Moore's misery, and it whittled away the remains of his patience. If it had been up to him, he would have gone roaring down that road with guns blazing. If enough of the surrounding area was shelled, there would be no worry about ambushes.

'We go very carefully,' Delaney said. He was not like his sergeant. Tom Delaney fancied himself as a man of tactics, a fox. 'With machine-gun cover on both sides we'll have a fighting chance.' He caught the frown on Moore's beefy face and read the dissent accurately. 'If we tried shelling we'd most likely bring down a landslide.'

'Right, sir,' Moore said throatily. 'Will I pass on the order?'

'Sure.' Delaney eased himself back down inside the tank as Moore started bellowing the command. Through the forward slit he could see only the road, and he felt it was better that way. Blinkered, he had the clear certainty of the route ahead; if he had been able to see those gradients and clumps of trees it would have made him jumpy.

As the tanks started moving again, the turrets of two King Tigers swung round and their guns were levelled at the road, half a mile ahead of Delaney's tank. The German armour, one of the several remaining splinters of the 10th SS Panzerdivision 'Frundsberg', had been in position above the roadway for three days. They had approached the position from the west, travelling on a spur road that had ended abruptly and left them floundering in mud and slime. Retreat was pointless, since they would simply be delivering themselves to the Allies, so it had been hastily decided to take the tanks ahead as far as possible, until there was at least some cover. The cover was good, when eventually they found it: a group of trees at the top of a crumbling hillside, overlooking a road. In time, when the clogged mechanisms of the tanks were cleared, the King Tigers would attempt a descent of the hillside and make use of the road. Until then, they would diligently observe the conditions of their commanders' oaths as loyal SS officers. They would wage savage war on any enemy in sight.

If the appearance of the American tanks sent a surge of glee through the waiting Nazis, it was nothing compared with Obersturmführer Vocke's joy at the sight of the King Tigers. Stefan Gaiser had spotted the tanks first but he had said nothing. They were off from his intended route; they represented the cancellation of his plans.

'Quickly!' Vocke hissed, breaking into a run. Koerner and the others behind him were exhausted already from lugging the equipment, but they tried to keep up with their commander. The SS tanks were less than a hundred yards away, their rear bulk exposed through the trees. Stefan remained motionless for a second, calculating the chances of running off on his own, but they had been seen. Two SS men with rifles had come out of the trees and were waving frantically, indicating that everybody should keep low. Stefan moved forward, glumly treading mud, and joined the others behind one of the tanks.

A Hauptscharführer explained what was going on, and exhorted the newcomers to keep under cover. There would be time for introductions later. As Vocke, Koerner and the others laid themselves out on the ground, Stefan moved to the far side of the tanks, out of their sight. He lay down at the bottom of a tree and watched the American tanks moving over the crossroads, two hundred yards away. In a flash, Stefan realized he *had* to run, his only chance of getting to Chabrier was to take off there and then, while the Germans were fully occupied with their ambush. On his knees, Stefan shuffled away from the tanks, moving sideways, making for another cluster of trees.

It was Sergeant Moore who spotted the solitary figure up on the hillside. On his roaring command the machine-gunner opened fire and in the first sweep his bullets ricocheted off the concealed plating of one of the King Tigers. All four American tanks stopped, churning the road surface as their tracks swerved.

'Up there!' Colonel Delaney was shouting, waving his arm at the gap in the trees where the two massive cannons were re-aiming, tearing down branches as they moved.

Orders were transmitted at speed and Delaney's tank opened fire first. The shell landed wide and ploughed a chunk out of the hillside. The second shell was closer to the target and blew down four trees. Obersturmführer Vocke was under one of the trees and its trunk landed diagonally across him, shattering his spine. Koerner, gaping across at the twisted corpse of his commander, was decapitated when the third American shell sent a King Tiger's rear plating spinning through the trees in a hundred lethal fragments.

Stefan was on the road. The second shell had lifted him, literally, with its ground impact, and thrown him on to the slope, where he rolled until he struck the edge of the ditch. When he stood up, dazed, spitting mud and wondering if he had broken a rib, the King Tigers opened fire simultaneously. The third American tank was hit by both shells and the explosion, a roaring, blazing hell of fire and metal, enveloped the fourth tank in the line. Stefan saw bodies flying, bodies running in flames, bodies motionless in the smoke and debris. His legs felt wooden; he tried to move them and they refused to obey.

Another American shell struck the hillside, and as Stefan began to move again, bewildered and directionless, stunned by the noise, the King Tigers started to slide forward. The Americans fired again. The entire hillside for a length of fifty yards was sliding down to the road, bringing the German tanks with it. The impact of trees, tons of earth and clattering armoury shook the ground so viciously that Stefan was knocked over and had to scramble halfway up the opposite hillside to avoid being buried. With his head against the shuddering foot of a tall tree, he took a deep, agonizing breath and cried out, soundless in the tumult and roar around him. Something in his chest *was* broken, too late he realized it and tried to ride the pain. He was unconscious before he could try to take another breath.

After a long dark passage, a time when he laboured in a half dream to drag air into his burning chest, there was abrupt daylight. The chest pain was like a ball of knives, with edges shifting and stabbing as the lung struggled to move. There was another pain, a wrenching at his shoulder, and when Stefan tried to ease it he found he was held.

'Just hold it there, bastard!'

The voice was behind him, hot on his ear, and it was American. Stefan blinked, trying to gather understanding from the fragments of awareness. He was standing, someone was holding him upright. The jagged pain made it hard to comprehend. He saw the crossroads, only a few yards away. Turning a fraction, he saw men in SS uniforms, four or five of them, being herded towards the crossroads by Americans with guns.

'My chest,' Stefan said in English. 'I've got a broken rib . . .'

'Shut it!' The restraining hands jerked his arm up an inch, making the pain worse.

Two American soldiers, one with a bloodied bandage on his head, came up the slope and stopped in front of Stefan. The one without a bandage, the younger of the pair, worked his mouth from side to side, collecting saliva, then spat into Stefan's face.

'The colonel's coming,' the one with the bandage told the invisible captor. 'Hang on to him.'

Stefan looked over to his left and saw the small mountain obstructing the road. One King Tiger was sticking up out of the top. The other one was under it, its cannon pointing impotently down at the trees and rubble around the bottom. The two American tanks that had been hit were just smoking now, there was no trace of fire, and it dawned on Stefan that he must have been lying unconscious for a long time.

'Please,' he groaned, 'if you could just let me sit down . . .'

The man behind him responded by bringing up his knee and slamming it against the base of Stefan's spine. Consciousness began to swirl away, and then his vision cleared and he was looking into the eyes of Colonel Delaney.

'It speaks English,' the voice at the back said.

Delaney nodded. 'Name?'

'Gaiser,' Stefan croaked. 'I work for British Intelligence.'

The colonel nodded again, his face blank, passionless. 'I suppose the rest of your brethren are with the British as well.'

'They're SS. I'm no part of that unit.' Stefan wanted to tell the colonel what he was doing there, he wanted to sit down and have a reasoned talk, but the pain and the exhaustion made too big a barrier.

Sergeant Moore, with an arm wound to add to his throbbing, truncated finger, came forward and thrust his gun belligerently at Stefan. 'They're all down on the road,' he said, addressing the colonel but keeping his eyes on Stefan. 'We shoot them, or what?'

'This one's SD,' Delaney said. 'Maybe we should keep him.'

Moore was having trouble minding his place. 'Where do you suggest, sir? We got two tanks, ten men. Where's the sense keeping him? The creep would knife you first chance he got, anyway.'

Stefan was blacking out again. The man at his back jabbed him twice with an elbow and the pain sliced through Stefan's chest, making him whine.

'He's injured,' Moore pointed out. 'He'd be a barrel of trouble if we took him along.'

The colonel shrugged. 'What has Templeton got on the radio? Anything?'

'Same as before, sir. There's a big US unit ten miles north west. It's our best chance.'

'Right.' Delaney turned away, staring down at the rumpled, despondent Nazis on the road. He turned back and looked at Stefan. 'Let him sit down. He can travel in the second tank. The others, rope them together. We'll walk them to base.'

'Jesus Christ Almighty.'

'What was that again, Sergeant?' The colonel had a glint of sudden anger in his eyes.

'Nothing, sir.'

'Just keep your face buttoned, Sergeant, and do what I ordered you to do.' Delaney went clumping down the hillside and started yelling at his other men, giving them the orders to turn the tanks around.

Moore remained where he was. 'You heard the colonel, soldier. Let the poor wounded Kraut sit down.' The sergeant's eyes were bulging with malice. 'We can't go doing nothing *un*humane here, can we? Just let Fritz have a rest.' The man behind Stefan was releasing him when Sergeant Moore stepped close. 'Stinkin' fuckin' Nazi shit!' His knee drove into Stefan's groin twice, hard. 'Let him lay down, soldier.'

In a chasm of agony Stefan sank and found himself adrift, nowhere near the ground he had felt beneath his feet. He was swathed in pain, merciless, tearing, and every shred of inward resource began to buckle and twist. Later, still in a crazy darkness, he felt his body being directed; people were carrying him, making the pain worse.

Later still, there was a wave of coolness that numbed him. Stefan was blessedly apart from his pain. It was still there, he knew that in the oddest way, but now it did not seem to matter. A voice, sounding just like his own, came filtering down out of the darkness then, and it told Stefan that he might be dying.

'Costal cartilage got detached,' the white-haired man was saying, 'and the edge of the rib scratched the lung. Nasty, but you're mending nicely.'

Stefan was lying in a bed, covered with crisp white sheets. His awareness of the bed, the sunlit room and the well-dressed man had come to him gradually, and although he was sure he had said something to the man, he had no idea what.

'You still look a shade peaky, but that's only to be expected.' The accent was Cambridge-fed English, and the face and bearing matched. Even the silvery moustache looked as if it had been precisely schooled. It moved, which probably meant the man was smiling. 'Still woozy, are you?'

'Yes, a bit.' Stefan inhaled carefully. The pain was still there, but it was bearable now. His chest had been strapped and his back was supported at a comfortable slope. 'Could you explain . . .'

'What?'

'Everything. I've no idea where I am or how I got here.'

'I thought you were rambling a bit when I spoke to you first.' The man drew up a chair to the side of the bed and sat down, taking care first to draw back the knees of his pin-striped trousers. 'Have you any recollection of what happened to you?'

Stefan nodded. 'I was caught in a tank battle. I remember all of that. After that it's a jumble.'

'Yes, I suppose it would be. Well, it was four days ago you were picked up by the Americans. They took you to one of their field medical stations, and while you were there an Intelligence bod went over your papers. SOE liaison realized who you were, and they had you brought here.'

'And where is here?'

'Paris. You're in a requisitioned hotel. It's being used as HQ for three American Army divisional heads and their entourage. By the way, my name's Webb. British Foreign Office.'

'I see.' Stefan closed his eyes for a moment, clearing his thoughts. Paris. He was further away from Chabrier than ever. And he had lost *four days*. 'What's my status, Mr Webb?'

'You're a prisoner,' Webb said pleasantly.

'That's what I thought. What happens to me now?'

The door opened and Webb held up a hand to Stefan, indicating they should pause. A young American soldier brought in a tray with coffee and set it on the bedside table. When he had gone, Webb poured two cups and handed one carefully to Stefan. As he sat down again, Stefan noticed Webb's expression had altered. Now he had the studied look that long-term authority gives some men. 'First of all, I have to talk to you. At length.' He sighed. 'Quite a headache you've been, y'know.'

'I've had my own headaches, Mr Webb. Most of them for nothing, it seems.'

'By rights,' Webb said slowly, 'you should be dead. Did you know that?'

'Yes, I found out about it. I came across one would-be assassin in Berlin. A man by the name of Aitken.'

Webb sipped his coffee, then looked at the cup as if it had bitten him. 'I suppose you got to Aitken first, eh?'

'I let him go,' Stefan said. 'If anybody got to him, it wasn't me.' He closed his fingers around the warm coffee cup. 'Let's see if I can work it out for myself. The SOE got the idea from somewhere that I'd gone bad on them, so they decided I should be put down before I did any more harm. Is that close?'

'Near enough. Are you saying you didn't go bad?'

Stefan gazed wearily at the man from Whitehall. 'For years, *years*, Mr Webb, I weeviled and battered my way to the heart of Nazi administration, and for too many of those years I was waiting for England to come up with a sign that they still remembered me. Then, when I finally went operational, they gave me a double-agent for a contact. Every scrap of work went for nothing. Risk, hellish risk sometimes, was undertaken to no good end, just because you lot couldn't even set up a reliable line out.'

Webb was studying the figured ceiling. 'You're alive and breathing today, Gaiser, simply because too many people got to know about you at once. Turning up the way you did, you were under what I might describe as collective scrutiny. You're an embarrassment. Frankly, if it could have been arranged to let that jagged bit of rib go on scraping away at your lung, then I've no doubt someone would have arranged it. The American doctor who looked after you was fastidious, so you were patched up and now – well, decisions have to be taken by civilized routes, if you follow me.' He looked across at Stefan again. 'You say your contact was a two-way man. Who else was he working for, besides the Americans?'

'The Russians.'

'Have you proof?'

'I've got no doubts at all.'

Stefan proceeded to tell Mr Webb the whole story, how

he had even passed on advance information about Ardennes, how Farrell had diverted it all and how eventually he discovered that Farrell was with the Russians. 'For Christ's sake, don't you see?' Stefan said. 'The Russians *wanted* Ardennes to happen. Guderian knew. Once Hitler took his reserves off the Hungarian front, it was only a matter of time before Farrell's friends reached Berlin.'

Webb was looking faintly troubled. 'As an untruth your tale has ingenuity – not that I'm saying you're a liar, mind you. But there's a certain roundness that would suit a fiction. Yes.' He scratched his chin. 'The Reds *have* made some pretty astute moves lately. Puzzling, to say the least. And they were quick to press their advantage when the Ardennes business started up.'

'Mr Webb,' Stefan sighed, 'where do I stand?'

'Difficult to say. I'm briefed to assess the situation and report back. First thing we can do, I fancy, is check up on your former contact.' Webb stood up and buttoned his jacket. 'You won't be uncomfortable here, Gaiser. Concentrate on getting fit.'

'I want to get fit and get out of here and kill Farrell,' Stefan said flatly.

'Mm. After that?'

Stefan shook his head. 'One day I'd like to go back to England. Perhaps. I don't really know, Mr Webb. With Farrell out of the way I'd be able to see farther ahead. But he isn't, so I can't.'

'Yes, well. It's all in the future, isn't it?' Webb was moving to the door, his expression troubled again.

'There's just one thing,' Stefan said. 'My mother. I'd like you to send her a message, whenever it's possible. We've been out of touch for a long time.'

Delicately, Webb cleared his throat. 'Your mother believes you're dead. Killed in action, that sort of thing.'

Stefan's precarious composure slipped. All he could do was glare at the man.

'I might as well tell you,' Webb added, his voice heavy

with embarrassment, 'it could end that way yet. As things stand, there's a lot of evidence against you that could be damning.'

'Then get somebody to look into Farrell.'

Webb raised his eyebrows. 'My dear chap, that's precisely what I intend to do. What I'm saying is, you shouldn't build up too many hopes at this stage.'

'No, I won't do that, Mr Webb.' Stefan turned his head away and heard the door close softly.

April, 1945

In March General Sokolovsky's 1st White Russian Army Group had made a thirty-mile bridgehead across the Oder River. The German forces in the region were inadequate: Hitler had despatched five Panzer Divisions to Prague, where, according to his instincts, the main Russian onslaught would take place. The Russians massed their troops, artillery, tanks and aircraft for the final push on Berlin, and on 16th April the barrage commenced. Escorted by six thousand fighters and bombers, and headed by the Russian 8th Guards, the Soviet tanks left the bridgehead and made for the capital of the Reich. The Germans retreated to their second line of defence, and the Russians rumbled on.

In her quarters at the Führerbunker, Eva Braun had sat for two hours on the evening of the 17th, listening to Hitler raving in the conference room outside. He had told Bormann, several times, that he was surrounded by liars and traitors, and although Bormann himself was never directly attacked, the possibility lurked as the Führer's tone became more and more hostile. Reports were piling up, each worse than the one before, and as Bormann and the others tried to placate Hitler his voice grew louder.

Returning to the bunker had been easier for Eva than she had thought it might. Outside the world was being torn apart, people ran back and forth in terror and barely acknowledged each other's existence. The bunker might be a prison, but there were faces there she knew, and a few people she trusted. When Hitler had seen her he had wept, and the sight of his tears clarified what Eva had known, in a confused way, all along. She would stay with him whatever happened, and she would subject herself completely to his will. It was not penance, nor was it really love. She simply did not care what happened, and it would be no hardship to give the Führer the loyalty, in the end, that he had demanded all along.

Hitler's voice stopped suddenly in mid-sentence and Eva stiffened, then rose and put her ear to the door. Feet were shuffling urgently, someone was whispering and a chair was squeaking across the floor. Although it was forbidden her, Eva opened the door and walked into the conference room. Two worried-looking generals were leaning across the map table, and Eva had to walk completely around it before she could see what had happened. Hitler was slumped, half-out of his chair, supported by Bormann and an aide. His face was white and his eyes were closed. His entire body was trembling, as if he were being electrocuted.

'Get him into his bedroom!' Eva shouted.

Bormann glared at her. 'You have no business in here.'

'And you have no business taking it on yourself to do that!'

Bormann looked both puzzled and angry. He had hoisted the Führer back into the chair, but the old man was still shaking and his eyes were still closed. 'What are you implying?' Bormann said.

'I'm telling you that you're mishandling a sick man. He must lie down at once, you'll only make him worse doing that.'

Hitler's eyes opened suddenly and through shuddering teeth he grunted, 'Bed, get me on my bed.'

Wordlessly Bormann and the aide carried him into the chamber, then Bormann went off to call the doctor. The aide assisted Eva to put a blanket over the Führer; then he left, too.

'Lie still,' Eva whispered. She smoothed back Hitler's hair and felt the clamminess of his skin. She had seen only one attack like this one, and it had been much less severe. The fear was in her that he would die and leave her exposed to Bormann and the others, but Eva fought it back and felt the panic recede as the trembling left him and Hitler turned his eyes to her.

'I lost my temper,' he told her huskily. 'I should not do that.' He took a long, sighing breath. 'But who can blame me? Liars, traitors . . .'

'Please,' Eva insisted, 'you must put all that from your mind. You must rest.'

With some difficulty the old man took her hand and squeezed it. 'You are a wonderful girl,' he told her. 'You came back here to share my fate . . .'

The first Russian shells to hit Berlin landed to the north of the city on 21st April. General Zhukov and General Koniev began shelling from the east and the south shortly after, and infantry troops pushed their way in, setting up dozens of street battles. On the night of the 21st Ralph Farrell identified himself to a Russian colonel commanding a tank unit on the outskirts of Treptow, in the south west of the city, and he was immediately granted the protection of the unit.

Farrell bedded down in a truck, snug in his Russian winter uniform and greatcoat. Although he had not rested for an entire day, he found he was too agitated to sleep.

The idea of returning to Berlin had come to him suddenly, and grew steadily during the five days he had spent with the Russian forces south of the Oder River. The notion was part expedient, part ambition. There were sound political reasons for a man of Farrell's initiative to go back into the battered capital of the Reich, and as they were outlined to him by a Czech network co-ordinator the lusting ideologist in Farrell reared, ready, eager.

The co-ordinator, Wolker, had been sinking into disillusionment since the loss of half his network to the SS. He was well-informed, a man with Party roots going back to 1925, and a series of cover identities that had taken him into more battle zones than the average general. Sharing a flask of vodka with Farrell on the freezing Red Army flank by the Oder, Wolker passed on his information in a weary, hollow voice.

'I'm sick of it. Make no secret of the fact. Sick. The

army can wave a few victory banners, but the GRU might as well disband and start again.'

At first Farrell had thought the man was rambling. 'We've been invaluable to the war effort,' he pointed out stiffly. 'I can't see any cause for despondency. You lost a few men, it's true, but . . .'

'That's not what I mean.' Wolker swirled his vodka in the metal cup, watching the dim reflected light turn blue and green in the slick of fusel-oil on the top. 'The clerks are our undoing, my friend. They're everybody's undoing.'

Farrell pressed him to explain.

'Papers,' Wolker said, and shook his large, grey head. 'Records. For what they call cohesive purposes, GRU made a full listing of all their operatives working in Western Europe. A *complete list*, mind you. Photographs, status of operatives, everything. It was supposed to be safe.'

'What happened?'

'The field copy, housed in Berlin, was discovered by the Nazis.'

Farrell could hardly believe it. 'Weren't the papers in code? And what were they doing inside Germany in the first place?'

'I told you, for cohesive purposes. Whatever that means. And what if they were in code? Germans crack codes the way you and I crack walnuts.'

'But they're no use to the Germans . . .' It was faint but stubborn hope which made that thought surface first in Farrell's head. The obvious reason for Wolker's gloom came at him a second later. 'Christ, the Americans.'

'Precisely. If the Americans get to the papers first, much of GRU's future planning evaporates.'

The news was a severe blow. There were plans for Farrell to go on working inside American Intelligence after the war, but that would be impossible if the papers were found. 'You're sure about this, Wolker?'

'Positive. I even know where the sacred list is, although it doesn't take much guessing.'

Farrell drank his vodka without tasting it. 'The bunker?'

'With everything else. We could be lucky, of course. Somebody with his wits about him could make it his business to attend to the destruction of that little dossier before the grander ceremonies take place. It's a shallow hope, though.' Wolker emptied his cup. 'Clerks. They've done more damage to mankind than all the soldiers we've ever reared.'

From then on Farrell had stopped listening. Men like Wolker courted failure, they sat around waiting for an excuse to throw in their hand. If Lenin had preached one message louder than any other, it was that action in the face of terrible odds produced the most spectacular results, if the man taking the action found failure unthinkable. Farrell already had the bit between his teeth when he handed Wolker back the metal cup and bade him good night.

Later that night, Farrell contacted an army field Intelligence officer and received the information he had expected. The bunker was now almost impregnable. Since the Oder bridgehead had been formed, Hitler had put an armoured unit around the Chancellery, and it was known that guards with mortars and machine-guns were posted in the garden. Internal security had tightened, too. To a man who needed terrible odds, the news was invigorating.

After five days at the Oder Farrell could wait no longer. He had been having dreams, orgiastic, fevered scenarios of violence and victory. He wanted blood as much as he wanted that list, and in his imagination the two goals became fused: to lay murderous hands on a few top Nazis and to carry off the precious papers, or destroy them so that his secret would remain intact. On the evening of the fifth day Farrell left the Oder. His intention was clear, uncluttered by doubt. Lenin would have been proud of a man like him. He had to be there when the security was breached, and get himself into the records section.

The hugeness of the task was dizzying, but as Farrell pieced together his strategy, prospects even more dizzying arose, exciting him, shoring up his determination. He would be careful not to lose sight of the prime objective: his whole future as an agent depended on that. But the bonuses made Farrell's head sing. Hitler was in the bunker, and Bormann, and probably a dozen others with names and faces that had kept his hate simmering for years. Daytime fantasies of gutting Bormann interchanged with flashing dreams of throwing the Führer's corpse across a Russian tank. And there was Hitler's whore to think about – would she be there too? The more he thought about it, the more Farrell believed that this was much, much more than a dangerous mission he had assigned himself. He was being granted access to glory, and all it took was his own determination.

In the following weeks he contacted OSS field workers three times, passing on snippets, planting the story that he was on to a major Intelligence unit in Berlin.

'Hush-hush,' he told each one, 'and tricky as all hell. But I'll keep you posted. Rely on your Uncle Ralph.'

His contacts were glad enough he had survived the Munich bombings, and they passed back the news that Farrell was still on the job, still making progress. Farrell already knew the location of a medium-size Intelligence outfit in Berlin and in time he intended to reveal it to the Americans, since it was of no particular importance any more: in the meantime, it provided a perfect alibi for a short spell of absence from the OSS contact chain.

The rest was timing. Farrell now carried an identification tag that was recognized by every Russian unit commander. By moving from one unit to another, he could take himself to the front line with safety and speed, until the time came when he would be right there beside the Chancellery, ready to show those cornered Nazis what wrath was really all about.

The Tempelhof airfield was taken by the Russians on 26th April, and they began pushing rapidly towards the centre of the city. Within hours they had reached Unter Den Linden and the Tiergarten. Whole streets were blasted to rubble as German soldiers, many of them no more than children, made feeble attempts to stem the most ferocious tide any city had ever seen. Berlin was bleeding to death and at its heart the creator of the Third Reich made sombre preparations for his own end.

Secretary Bormann had been living for some time with a bottled-up hysteria that threatened daily to surface and boil over. The funereal activity around him was horrific; he watched and listened and increasingly wondered if he were really there. The Führer had refused earnest advice to leave for Berchtesgaden and negotiate a surrender. Instead, he bellowed that he would never leave Berlin, he would defend it to his last breath. Goering, in an attempt to save something from the disaster still being enacted around them, had sent a message from Obersalzberg, asking Hitler to appoint him as successor, so that he might start negotiations with the Americans at once. Hitler's reply was to have Goering arrested on a charge of treason. Guderian had been sacked, Keitel and his deputy Jodl were panicking hourly, and Goebbels had taken up residence in the bunker with his family, obviously to await some grim finale.

Bormann observed it all, and he wondered how much of a chance he would have when the time came to run. His wife and children were at Berchtesgaden, ready to flee to the Tyrol. So far Bormann had no firm plan for himself: running was all he could think of, but where, and into what? Strategies for a breakout, like all other survival strategies, were being rejected by the Führer, and he had ordered the immediate shooting of anyone attempting to leave the bunker without permission.

Bormann moved, watched, and listened, and his terror mounted.

On the morning of 27th April, after weeks of dreary confinement in his hotel room, Stefan was called to the third meeting with Mr Webb.

The days in his room had wrought changes in Stefan. For one thing, the inactivity had imposed a new level of calm. Daily contemplation of his whole life had produced the conclusion, painfully accepted, that it had been a total waste. Stefan also concluded that vengeance did have a place in a life that had been useless: he still wanted Farrell, it was probably his only spiritual desire. As for love, it was a continual mourning. The memory of Gretl was cherished with as much remorse as grief.

Webb was waiting in an elegant suite along the corridor from Stefan's room. He looked gruff and starchy that morning. At the second meeting, three weeks earlier, he had pressed Stefan for more details about Farrell, more evidence of his subversion, but Stefan had no more to give. Webb had left that meeting with misgivings, and he did not appear any brighter now.

'Sit down, Gaiser. How have you been?'

'Idle,' Stefan said. 'There's no other way to be, in the circumstances.' He sat down, and noticed that Webb chose to remain on his feet.

'We had our final discussions on your case yesterday. The United States authorities have been very co-operative, everyone has. We've done all we can to be fair to you.'

'Instead of shooting me out of hand, as was originally intended.'

Webb frowned. 'I think you know I bear some sympathy for you. I've tried to convey to the others the impression of sincerity you give, but . . .' He waved a futile hand. 'So much is against you. The agent Janus, on the other hand, has come out of the investigation looking cleaner than he went in. The Americans insist that he's one hundred percent loyal - he was selected by General Donovan himself.'

'The Americans are wrong,' Stefan said flatly.

'They have no proof of that, and neither have we.' Webb decided to sit down after all. 'To be frank, Gaiser, I'm more sympathetic towards you than I properly should be, although on the evidence I must be off my chump. On paper you're one of the most rabid Nazis extant. But then if other people at Whitehall would place less faith in paperwork, the whole world might be a different place by now. I'm sorry for you, Gaiser. That's putting it plainly. You've lost your property at Dorfen, you can't return to England a free man, and if the Germans are on to you as you've said, then they'd reduce you to a pile of bones without hesitating.' Webb sighed and patted his knee, as if it might be Stefan's shoulder. 'Frankly, if I had the power, I'd let you go to Berlin and settle your vendetta. But I have no such power, and it's probably just as well.'

'Berlin?' Stefan said. 'What do you mean?'

'That's where this Janus fellow is. Don't ask me why, old chap. The Americans simply say they're satisfied he's on active duty there. He's made recent contact with other OSS people.'

'But Berlin must be falling apart by now.'

Webb smiled. 'I must say, I gave the matter some thought on the way here. Assuming Janus *is* a good servant of the Soviets, I'd say he's probably in Berlin to flush out the kind of personnel they'd rather take prisoner than kill outright. Administrative johnnies and the like.' He cleared his throat discreetly. 'I know that's what our own people will be doing.'

And then Stefan knew. There was only one place Ralph Farrell could be. 'I'd find him, Mr Webb. I'd find him.'

'No doubt.' Webb stood up again. 'But there will be no opportunity, I'm afraid.' His face was serious again.

'All right,' Stefan said, 'tell me what's been decided.'

'You're to be returned to England where you'll be imprisoned and, eventually, tried for treason.'

Stefan said nothing.

'You'll leave first thing tomorrow morning.' Webb came

forward and extended his hand. 'I'm sorry, Gaiser, truly I am.'

Stefan rose and shook hands, forcing a tight smile. 'Thanks for trying, Mr Webb.'

A few minutes later Stefan was escorted back to his room and locked in, as usual. For a long time he just stood by the door, testing his reactions. With all roads closed, submission was the natural course. One open path, however small, would have made a world of difference. He turned, surveying his tidy prison, and decided on the instant that if there was no avenue, he would make a fierce effort to create one.

In place of his SS uniform he had been given civilian clothing - black trousers, white shirt, sports jacket and shoes. Dressed like that, he looked like any citizen of just about any country. Anonymity was a sudden blessing. Stefan went to the bedside and pressed the button to summon the guard, then went back and stood by the door.

The key clanked in the lock after a second, then the door was pushed open. The young soldier stepped straight into the room, his face friendly, his gun pointed down slightly.

'I'd appreciate it if you made your check on me now,' Stefan said. 'I've had some bad news, I think I want to rest for a while.'

The guard looked round the room, keeping himself between Stefan and the door. 'You know the rule,' he said, almost apologetically. 'Every ten, fifteen minutes I've gotta look in on you.' Long weeks of passive behaviour had endeared Stefan to his guards. This one, the youngest, was the most sympathetic. He shrugged. 'This time maybe I'll make it twenty minutes. And I'll be quiet as I can. That way maybe you'll sleep longer.' He smiled and stepped outside again, then closed the door and locked it.

Stefan checked his watch. Twenty minutes. He could have used twice as long, but a bonus was a bonus.

The window was barred, but the bars were anchored to a square frame that was screwed into the wall on either side of the casement. Effectively, only four screws kept the bars in place. Stefan knelt beside the small electric radiator by the window and hooked his fingers through the grille. One sharp tug, according to his long-standing theory, should be enough to dislodge one steel spar. He set his shoulders and yanked back on the grille. It came away so easily he almost fell over.

Sliding one spar free from its groove he laid the others aside quietly, then got to work on the first screw. By chipping away at the plaster and brick around the screw he gradually made a hole an inch in diameter and half an inch deep. The spar began to heat up at the digging end as the fragments of brick were dislodged. Stefan withdrew it, blew on the end, and started on the second screw. There was no saying how long the anchor screws were, but the framework had the look of hasty construction about it. By his watch he had taken three minutes to make the first hole. Half an inch would *have* to be enough.

By the time the second hole was made, eight minutes had passed. The spar was slippery with Stefan's sweat and both ends were blunted. There was a sound at the door and Stefan spun, staring at the handle. For five loud beats of his heart he crouched motionless. Nothing happened. He looked at his watch. Nine minutes.

Two holes would have to do, there was no more time. Stefan stood up and put on his jacket. He grasped the bottom of the steel frame, breathing deeply. Two holes at the bottom, two firmly fixed screws at the top. He inhaled sharply and tugged. Plaster showered down from the top of the frame as it moved forward a fraction. But the lower screws were still holding. Stefan breathed out through his mouth and set his foot on the skirting board. Ten minutes. He wrenched savagely at the frame and felt a sharp warning pain in his back. The plaster crumbled some more but the frame resisted. Groaning with the tension,

Stefan leaned back with both feet braced on the skirting and wrenched again, torturing his arms and back. The frame gave way suddenly and plaster and brick dust showered down on him.

He had his gap, and beyond it clear, vulnerable glass. Hastily he brushed the dust from his clothes, then slid up through the gap. The window lock was standard, a simple swivel and clasp. He pushed it forward and eased the bottom of the framework upwards. It squeaked alarmingly, and before it was open a foot it jammed. Stefan twisted himself sideways and forced his head and shoulders through the gap. There was a stone balcony ten feet below. His watch said twelve minutes. Stefan rolled out on to the ledge, hung there for a second, then let himself drop.

The shock jarred through his legs a moment before he let them collapse under him. As he rolled he struck his shoulder on sharp stone and the pain tautened him again. He crouched in one corner of the balcony, riding a wave of pain that touched every part of him. Facing him were two tall glass doors that led on to a room that looked empty.

Stefan stood up and stamped his feet, checking he was intact. He turned the handle of one door. Locked. He turned the other and it opened.

The room was plush and orderly, a conference chamber by the look of it, and Stefan's feet made no sound on the deep carpet as he sprinted across to the main door. He stood with his ear against the panelling for a moment. He could hear nothing but his blood pulsing in his ears. He opened the door a fraction and peered out.

There was a short passage straight ahead. As Stefan watched, a guard appeared in profile, patrolling the narrow space between ornate elevator gates and the door of a suite like the one where Webb had delivered his news. Stefan counted under his breath as the soldier disappeared from sight. After eight seconds he was back again and turning, his hand resting on the revolver at his hip.

Stefan was counting again as he ran down the passage. On the count of five he was at the corner, but the guard had turned already and his face began to register alarm as Stefan ran straight at him. They collided by the elevator gates and fell sideways against the heavy bronze bars. Stefan had one hand on the guard's throat, smothering his attempt to raise the alarm, and the guard had both arms round Stefan's waist, trying to force him down. The gates rattled harshly as both men struggled; then the guard's boot slipped on the carpet and his head struck the brass gate handle. Stefan seized the opportunity and banged the soldier's temple against the handle again twice, viciously, then released his throat and stood back.

The guard was not unconscious but he was dazed enough to be off-balance. When he tried to get up Stefan punched him low in the stomach, then on the jaw. He went over on his back, eyes glazing, and Stefan jerked open the elevator gate and jumped inside.

The descent to the ground floor was endless. The ancient mechanism laboured and squeaked, and once when it lurched Stefan was sure they had caught him.

Sweating and struggling to maintain something like composure, he looked at his watch again. Time was up. If the guard outside his door was charitable, he might make it. But that was nothing to depend on. The elevator was suddenly a prison. It lurched again and Stefan felt his fingernails stabbing into his palms. They must be on to him by now. The squeaking cables and shuddering cabin were issuing fair warning.

But at the bottom, when he stepped out into the busy foyer, nobody paid any attention to him. Even so, he wanted to run. There were civilians and military walking around with file boxes and papers, carrying out the business of rationalizing the chaos that was still raging to the northeast. Before Stefan got to the door, an American officer stopped him. The hand on his arm was insistent.

'Are you one of the observers?' the man asked.

Observers. Stefan's mind raced. The war was nearly over, civilian observers would be gathering in Berlin; journalists, sociologists, political commentators.

'Yes,' Stefan replied. 'Why do you ask?'

'Your transport's been switched,' the officer said. He had a clipboard and he was scanning a list on it. 'Which one are you?'

Stefan had read two names upside down. 'Mitchell,' he grunted. There was no tick opposite that name.

'Hmm. Let's see.'

Stefan had to struggle to control his breathing. The officer was plodding through his list and time was passing. Every face around began to look dangerous. They would have found that guard by now. One more second, Stefan thought, one single second, then he was going to make a run for the doors.

'Ah. Mitchell.' The tick was made and the officer looked up at Stefan again. 'I wish you guys would all stay in one place, it'd make my job easier. You take the bus with the yellow flash on the side. It's right outside. All your stuff's been transferred from the other vehicle already.'

'Thanks,' Stefan said. Turning away, he felt the pressure behind him, as if something wrathful was galloping after him. He made it to the doors and stepped outside, inhaling the crisp, cold air. The bus was there, right in front of him. A clear choice existed: make it to Berlin under his own steam, or accept providence and hope it did not turn into a disaster halfway through. The bus was tempting, and Stefan was mounting the step before the decision had properly formed.

There were twelve other men inside, and they did not give the impression they knew each other. Most were bundled up in overcoats and scarves, and a couple of them looked curiously at Stefan's light, summery attire. He ignored them and sat down near the door, in case it became necessary to get off again in a hurry.

Three minutes ticked past. By that time Stefan was ready to leap through the door at the first sign of unusual activity in the hotel. A small detachment of military police arrived and parked their jeep behind the bus. Stefan eased forward, one foot ready to grip the floor tread and the other curled in to push him forward.

'We'll have to leave now,' the driver announced, loudly enough to make Stefan jump. 'Some of the observers are still missing so they'll have to wait until tomorrow. When we've off-loaded their bags, we'll get going.'

Now the seconds were like hammer blows, timed to thud with Stefan's pulse as two elderly Frenchmen heaved the holdalls and rucksacks out of the luggage compartment. He fought to ignore the possibility of the real Mitchell turning up and confounding the officer's typed list.

By the hotel door, something was happening that made three of the other observers get up and peer out of the windows. A barrier gate was being erected, people were being asked to keep outside and others, stuck inside, were shouting to be let out. Stefan rose and heaved himself at the door, then suddenly the bus revved and he was thrown back towards his seat as the old vehicle swerved away from the roadside. Stefan stared through the window, watching the hotel receding, watching for anything or anybody that might be following. He sat like that until the building was out of sight, then eased down on the seat and let out the breath he had been holding for nearly a minute.

On the journey out across the battered suburbs he pretended to sleep, and listened to the conversations going on around him. Somebody with a deep, rumbling American drawl told the others he was a correspondent for a paper and, by God, he was going to tell the story of the battle of Berlin like it really was. He sounded as if he would favour the Germans over the Russians any day, no matter who prevailed. In the dark behind his eyelids,

Stefan wondered just how far he would get with no gun and no credentials.

After forty minutes' driving they arrived outside a temporary military airfield. Stefan saw two howitzer motor carriages by the barbed wire gates, and beyond them a Locust tank that looked as if it had been there for a long time. The tracks and turret were flaked with rust, and as he began to scan the area beyond the front gate, Stefan saw similar signs of decay on aircraft and metal outbuildings. The place was obviously one of the less important units, and Stefan clung to a sudden hope that the security was as rundown as everything else.

The driver addressed his passengers in a monotone that suggested he had made the speech many times before.

'When you get outside, take your bags and other gear out of the luggage compartment and go to the checkpoint. Show your passes to the people there, then assemble behind the checkpoint until you're assigned to a flight. Good luck.'

Stefan waited behind the others while they located their property, then straggled behind as they began to walk towards the gate. He had no plan beyond keeping himself ready for whatever might turn up. By the gates, as a soldier was telling them they would have to wait a few minutes before he could open up and let them in, the gravel-voiced American suddenly cut in and demanded to know were the toilets were.

'I've been bustin' for a piss for half an hour.'

The soldier pointed to a square cement building standing beyond the rusty Locust. 'It ain't the Ritz in there,' he warned smilingly, 'but it does the job.'

The journalist turned and walked off, and after a couple of seconds Stefan followed him. The American was big and wide, a shambling man in his fifties. For that much Stefan was thankful.

Inside the latrine the air was redolent of stale urine and cigarette smoke. Stefan waited until the other man was straddled by the stall, then he moved up close behind him.

'I don't want you to make any sound.'

The man made to turn and Stefan jabbed a knuckle into his back.

'What in hell is this?'

'I said no sound.' Stefan glanced at the door, and as he did the man inhaled sharply, preparing to let out a yell. The hard knuckle rapped his skull suddenly and he sagged. 'I want your pass,' Stefan hissed. 'Hand it to me. *Now*!'

The man fumbled in his jacket and handed a grey oblong card over his shoulder. Stefan flipped it open with one hand. The document carried a warning that the Allied Authorities would take no responsibility for the safety of the bearer while he was in Berlin.The only personal data on the card were the man's name, John Cully, his occupation, journalist, and his home address in Wisconsin. There was no photograph.

'Give me your wallet, too.'

'Now hold on, Mister . . .'

'I'm prepared to shoot you, Mr Cully.'

The fat, scuffed wallet was passed across. Stefan thumbed out the money and gave it back to Cully. 'I don't need this.' There was a press card in the wallet, some news clippings with Cully's by-line and various press agency addresses on small file cards. That would be enough additional identification, Stefan hoped, if he was ever asked for any.

'What are you going to do now?' Cully was trembling, his face still inches from the grey wall.

'My friend here will be positioned under the tank outside. If you make any attempt to leave the building before one hour is up, he'll shoot you.' Stefan eased the knuckle higher across Cully's head. 'I'll be across the way, just in case you try to take any other way out.'

'Why? Why are you doing it?'

'We simply don't want you to take this trip to Berlin.'

Taking short steps, Stefan began to back away. 'Go into the cubicle and close the door. If anyone comes looking for you before the time's up, tell them you're ill.'

'Suppression, is that it?' Without looking round, Cully edged himself into the rickety cubicle and sat down on the pedestal. 'You don't want the truth coming out of Berlin, huh?' The voice was shaky but the thread of defiance was strong enough.

'Form whatever conclusion you like, Mr Cully.' Stefan was at the door now. 'I'd advise you to dwell on certainties, though. Wait in here for an hour, and you'll go on living.' Cully's canvas satchel was by the doorway and Stefan picked it up. 'The timing starts now.'

Stefan returned to the gate. There was confusion, some of the observers had gone the wrong way when the gates were opened and they were being herded back. Stefan mingled and jostled and gaped as witlessly as the others. Eventually he was passed through the checkpoint by the impatient soldier there, and ten minutes later he boarded a seatless USAF freighter, where he settled himself on a bale of Red Cross blankets. In the discomfort, the noise and the edgy fear, only one man seemed to notice that the American journalist was missing.

'I think he took ill,' Stefan said.

'There's always one,' the man said wryly. 'All gab and gas until it's post time, then the chicken feathers start sprouting.'

The engines roared louder as the plane accelerated for take-off, and nobody tried to talk after that. Stefan leaned back on the blankets and felt his legs shaking in the sudden slackening of tension. The weeks of inactivity had softened him a little, but now his determination was as strong as ever.

He closed his eyes and tried to sleep. It might be his last chance for a while. As the droning engines began to ease him into a light slumber, Stefan was still hoping, for all he was worth, that in spite of the odds his luck would hold and he would keep a grip on his purpose. It was all he had.

He woke up with a start as the plane's engines changed pitch. Around him several men were kneeling by the windows, and Stefan sat up, stretching, questioning the nearest man with his eyes.

'Berlin,' the man shouted above the roar.

Stefan got up and scrambled to the nearest window. They were flying at less than a thousand feet, taking a wide approach to the airfield. The last time Stefan had seen the city, the bombs had made huge inroads on the major buildings and industrial developments, but what he saw now was harrowing. Hardly anything appeared to be standing. Vast piles of rubble surrounded craters and pits like some bizarre disease, pock-marking the landscape and obliterating the former orderliness of streets and highways. There were fires everywhere, some of them very large, spewing smoke towards the aircraft in swirling black billows.

'How are the mighty fallen,' somebody said.

'You should have seen Dresden.'

Stefan tried hard, but he could identify nothing. He had seen Berlin from the air many times and from many approaches, and always the shapes had registered with him and directed his eye along known territories. Now, the disjointing was total; places that had once been mere adjuncts now stood out as sole surviving structures: small squares, crescents and alleys stood in pathetic isolation, like dying fingers and limbs poking through suffocating rubble.

When they landed the processing was perfunctory and totally lacking in diplomacy. Russian soldiers stared blankly at papers, stamped them and pushed the bearers towards the transports waiting by the main gates. Stefan was bundled into a seatless bus with thirty or more other men, and a soldier with the word *Interpreter* embroidered on his greatcoat bawled at them in broken English.

'You will be taken as far as the Reinickendorf observers' post. After that you must make arrangements of your own. The Russian Army takes no responsibility for any of you after you leave the custody of the transport. Is this understood?'

Without waiting for a reply the man jumped down from the step and the pneumatic doors closed. The bus shuddered and crunched into gear, then started out through the gates.

They travelled for an hour, over roads cracked and sundered and occasionally missing for long stretches. Hanging on to a bar by the front windows, Stefan watched for something he recognized, but there was nothing. All he saw were the rough, abstract remains of houses and shops, the random piles of wood and brick and the faceless Russian foot patrols, picking their way towards the centre of the city. Stefan knew he was in Berlin, but it was hard to make himself believe it. Centuries of character had been eradicated, leaving only a duplicate of the torn cities in Poland, Czechoslovakia and Russia.

The observers' post at Reinickendorf turned out to be a tiny school building, modified only to the extent of having the assembly room cleared of chairs. Correspondents, photographers, political observers and Red Cross officials wandered aimlessly about the place, drinking cups of weak coffee and asking each other what they should do next. The Russian soldiers in charge were no help: they manned the doors, courtyard and coffee urns in stolid silence, making it clear they would put up with the visitors, but that was all.

Stefan remained at the post for less than an hour. In that time he managed to steal an overcoat, and crammed the pockets with the more useful contents of John Cully's satchel – chocolate, cigarettes, a torch, brandy and an ornate silver propelling pencil. He walked to the front gate, and when it was clear no one would take the trouble to stop him, he started walking in the approximate direction of the Tiergarten district.

It was getting dark when he stepped into the doorway of a ruined bomb shelter and started to eat one of the bars of chocolate. Rain was falling and the wind was swirling the dirt on the ground into muddy whorls that clogged the welts of Stefan's shoes and made his feet slip on the broken paving. He would have to find somewhere to rest eventually, and with no street lighting it would be sensible to find a spot before it was really dark. Pocketing the remaining half of the chocolate bar, Stefan took out the torch and shone it into the cavernous remains of the shelter. He almost dropped the torch when the beam hit the white, staring face of a man huddled in the farthest corner.

'Please,' the man said simply.

Stefan moved closer. He was old and thin, wrapped in a moth-eaten black overcoat. His sparse hair stood up in clumps and the torch picked out glinting particles of stone and glass on his cheeks.

'It's all right,' Stefan said, 'I won't harm you. Where did you come from?'

'Olgenstrasse. My house, it was bombed.' Although he was clearly frightened, the man spoke with the vague, distant tone of someone in a trance.

'Here.' Stefan handed him the chocolate. 'How long have you been in here?'

'I don't know. It was yesterday, I think.' The man began chewing at the bar, tearing shreds of foil with his teeth. 'The noise outside . . . it was bad. I came in here and lay down.'

'You'll freeze to death if you stay here another night. Eat up your chocolate and I'll get you to a medical station.'

'No!' The old man was shaking his head violently. 'The Russians are out there.'

'They won't hurt you.'

'They hate us! The boys next door, they killed them. Right in front of us! Two children.'

Stefan nodded, moving closer still and patting the old

man's shoulder. 'But the Red Cross are the ones out there now. The fighting's moved away, miles away to the centre of the city.'

The old man said nothing. He munched the chocolate and stared at the patch of light by the door with scared, wary eyes.

It was after seven and pitch dark when Stefan eventually led the old man out on to the street. Distant shelling lit up the sky, silhouetting the ruins, and the thunder of the guns echoed from corner to corner until it was impossible to tell which direction they came from. Keeping close to whatever walls they could find, the two men made their way to the south of the sector. Just before nine o'clock, Stefan sighted the dim blue light of a medical unit, set up in the ruins of a church.

The unit was manned by a Swiss doctor and five French nurses. They were working in appalling conditions, and their ten beds were full. Outside the main tent, several people were lying on pallets under mounds of blankets.

Stefan explained to the doctor that the old man had been sleeping in a damp shelter, and was probably suffering from exposure.

'Like half the population,' the doctor sighed. He was young, with the eyes of an older, cynical man. 'We can feed him, keep him reasonably warm, and hope he isn't blown up by a shell in the meantime.'

Stefan thanked the doctor, then spent five minutes convincing the old man that he would be safe and cared for.

At midnight, with a warm meal inside him, Stefan said goodbye to the doctor and stepped outside the remaining arch of the church. The rain had stopped and a cool breeze was blowing from the north east. Shading the torch with his hand, he picked his way back to the edge of the road, then froze as a voice no more than five yards away yelled, 'You! Over here!'

Stefan turned his head, seeing only the dim glow of a cigarette. 'Who's that?'

'I said over here!'

He moved towards the tiny light, and gradually the shapes of three men appeared, gathered by a buckled lamp standard. When he was a yard from the one with the cigarette, Stefan felt a hand grab his coat lapel and drag him forward. Warm sour breath assailed his face.

'What's in there?' The voice was hoarse and the grip was nervous.

Stefan decided to play it passively. 'It's a medical unit. They're looking after the homeless and injured people.'

'And you? Who are you?'

'I'm a civilian, homeless like the ones in there.'

A torch went on and Stefan averted his eyes. For an instant he saw a sleeve flash protruding from a greatcoat cuff. They were Wehrmacht.

'What's your name?'

'Gaiser. Why are you detaining me? I only want to get back to where I come from . . .' A certain truth, Stefan realized, was underlying his fiction.

The torch went out. 'Are there any men with guns in the medical unit?' the same voice asked.

'No. Just a doctor and his nurses, and their patients.'

'Right. We'll be needing your coat, friend Gaiser.'

As the coat was being pulled off him Stefan saw the two other men move into the ruined church. A moment later somebody screamed, a woman, then there was the sound of breaking glass. They were plundering the unit. Stefan suddenly crossed his arms, preventing the man from pulling the coat clear.

'Give it to me! Bastard!' A knee jerked up and made searing contact with Stefan's groin. His legs buckled, but he kept his arms crossed. In the medical unit, more people were crying out. A fist struck Stefan's ear, making his head sing and taking away his balance. He threw his arms up and struck a gun, halfway out of its holster. With a supreme effort he grabbed with both hands and spun on one knee, unbalancing his shadowy assailant and wresting the gun away from him. As the man hit the ground Stefan rose to a squatting position and took a hold on the pistol with two hands. The shadow of the head came up, panting and cursing, and Stefan squeezed the trigger. The shot echoed round the broken buildings and the flash illuminated an angry face with a jagged hole between the eyes. The man fell back and was silent.

Stefan leapt over the body, the pain from his groin still making him breathless. As he reached the archway of the church the two other men were coming out, one of them waving a pistol. The first man was too close and Stefan wheeled aside, clipping him over the ear with the gun butt. As he went down his companion slithered to a halt and took aim. Stefan brought up the pistol, pumping the trigger as he did, and put three bullets into the man before he could fire. At a sound behind him he turned and put the remaining two bullets in the man he had knocked over.

The doctor met him at the front of the main tent.

'I think we owe you our lives,' he said.

It was several minutes before Stefan felt able to speak. Some reserve had gone, something vital to his alertness. He was shaking, and when the doctor gave him a half-filled cup of brandy, he had to hold it with both hands.

'Is everyone all right?' he asked eventually.

'Shaken up, but alive.'

In the morning Stefan left the medical unit, and on the way he paused to look at the three dead soldiers, lying where he had shot them. Not one of them looked any different from the ordinary people in the unit.

Stefan walked until mid-day, keeping his head down in the lapels of his overcoat, stopping at intervals to marvel at the weird, alien landscape that Berlin had become. Even the major streets where the old buildings had seemed so dauntingly permanent were blasted, shapeless memorials to the thousand-year ideal. A few civilians picked their way across the rubble, most of them looking bewildered, a few carrying belongings in bundles on their backs. At a wide intersection Stefan crossed the road to avoid looking at a dead child, curled under his small winter coat as if he were only asleep.

Outside the hollow-windowed front of a café in the Tiergarten he sat down on the pavement and opened his remaining bar of chocolate. He was chewing and staring at a mangled sculpture across the square – a statue of Wagner bisected by the armour plate of an infantry vehicle – when a scuffed, dented Mercedes saloon drew up beside him.

'Hey,' somebody shouted. 'Going our way?'

It was one of the men from the plane, a Swedish war correspondent. He was packed into the back of the car with three others.

'I want to get a look at the Chancellery,' Stefan shouted back.

'I think we all do. Jump in.'

By the late evening of 28th April, the fighting was less than a mile from the bunker. German divisions, beaten down to the size of battalions and scattered without lines of communication, bunched defensively in streets and on top of buildings, saving ammunition and suffering a hundred blows for every one they landed.

The Russians, free at last to visit their wrath on the enemy, were moving about the fringes of the battle in units of ten and twenty, slaughtering and plundering in the name of revenge, while the larger groups concentrated on hemming the Germans in. Street after street was piled with German dead. From lamp posts in the Chausee Strasse, less than half a mile from the Chancellery, the mutilated corpses of SS and Gestapo officers dangled, sometimes in groups of three, some by the necks and others by the ankles. Boy soldiers, children who had never before seen fighting or bloodshed, had to face the naked savagery of Russians with more hate inside them than they could discharge in ten Berlins. The Reich was dead, only the death-throes remained.

On Hagenstrasse one Russian ran into ten Germans,

all armed. The Russian opened fire, certain he was about to die fighting, and he killed all of the Germans. They had not one live round between them.

In the bunker, Hitler dictated his last political will. It was a harsh, biting catalogue of accusation and spite, and the Führer ended it by saying that he had never wanted war. It had been brought about by statesmen of many nations, men who were either of Jewish origin, or who worked in the interests of the Jews.

The Führer then dictated his personal will, in which he revealed that he would marry Eva Braun, 'at the close of my career on earth'. He further revealed that Eva had agreed to go to her death with him, as she had, that same morning. Hitler bequeathed his possessions to the Party, and appointed Bormann his executor. The will ended on a dramatic note: 'My wife and I have chosen death as an alternative to humiliation in defeat. We wish our bodies to be burned in this place where I have carried out the major part of my work during the twelve years I have served the German people.'

Towards midnight, in the presence of Bormann, Josef Goebbels and his wife Magda, the head of the Hitler Youth and four other guests, Hitler and Eva were married. Eva wore a long black taffeta gown and the Führer donned his best uniform for the occasion. The couple behaved calmly, and at the celebration feast later they even displayed a little gaiety. There was music from a gramophone and some bottles of wine; the cook, Fraulein Manzialy, had prepared pastries and a modest wedding cake, in spite of the desperate situation with supplies. As word travelled through the bunker smaller parties erupted. People appeared almost to be enjoying themselves, while outside the guns rumbled and roared.

At 5 am, when Hitler had signed the transcript of his political testament and passed it into Bormann's keeping, he retired to his chamber with Eva. His bride helped him undress and get into bed; then she undressed herself and for the last time cradled his face against her breasts.

'Loyalty to the grave and beyond,' the Führer murmured.

Eva nodded and made herself smile. Holding him, feeling the permanent tremor, she experienced a brief surge of pity. 'Sleep, Adolf,' she whispered, and kissed his brow.

By early morning on the 30th Stefan was inside the broken structure of the Chancellery. For twenty-four hours he had lived through a maelstrom. The happy band of observers had been broken up the morning before when a trio of Russian soldiers fired on the car. No one was injured, and the Russians offered gruff apologies for their mistake, but without transport the group spirit diminished on the spot. Only Stefan and one other observer, a Canadian, had decided to press forward on foot.

For hours the Canadian went on about the Russians' unwillingness to compromise on anything, and he cited yards of memorized history on the topic. Later, he switched to the way they treated observers and news correspondents, in fact Allied non-combatants in general.

'They'd kill every one of us, if they could get away with it,' he said.

Stefan managed to lose his companion when they walked right into a shelling raid on Bendler Strasse, but he kept the advice in mind. One bad-tempered Russian soldier could easily make an act of murder look like an accident of war.

The short distance from Bendler Strasse to Wilhelm Strasse had become the equal, in terms of difficulty of crossing, to the Sahara. The remaining German units were gathered around the Chancellery and on all of the approach roads, raining shells and bullets on the Russians, who returned the fire tenfold. The entire region was cut off with scissoring gun- and mortar-fire. Stefan had found himself a cellar with three possible exits, and he had remained there during most of the previous day and all through the night. It was only when the fighting moved nearer the Chancellery that he decided it would be relatively safe to move.

Now, in the dark and awesome seclusion of the big, empty building, Stefan suddenly began to shake again. He had climbed through the remains of the side wall and into the reception clerk's office, and the respite from so much noise, violent ground tremors, flaring guns and stark carnage was so sudden it had thrown his nervous system into chaos. He decided to rest, even though a part of him did not want to.

He came awake, suddenly, hearing his own cry of alarm. There was a tremendous crashing above him and Stefan threw himself sideways, landing on all fours. There was another crash, louder this time, and he stood up and ran. As he did, the main ceiling of the Chancellory reception hall collapsed. Stefan dived for cover under a big oak table and as he tucked himself between its legs a roaring downpour of plaster, steel and concrete rained on the table and all around. He put his hands against the table, feeling it strain under the impact; then there was a pain in his foot that made him yell, his voice drowning in the noise.

He lay still, waiting for the pain to slacken, watching brick dust seep under the table. Parts of the building were still collapsing but the direction of shell fire had changed. The Russians were right outside, Stefan guessed, and they would be turning their guns on the bunker.

He was reluctant to inspect his injury. If there was a broken bone, then he was finished, and if that was to be the case he felt he would rather delay knowing about it. If the damage was not serious, a few more minutes could hardly hurt. Stefan listened to the muffled *pop-pop* of anti-tank guns and the myriad noises of splintering, splitting, collapsing and exploding. He was in the middle of a kind of savage symphony, he thought fancifully. For a few minutes while his system moved from light shock to prickly awareness, Stefan did not care about anything beyond the abstract melodies of battle.

When he did try to sit up he realized he had been lying

on a fragment of brick. Rubbing the grazed skin of his back gingerly, he decided to examine his foot and saw it was buried by a lump of concrete the size of a dinner plate. It weighed considerably more, and with the greatest of care Stefan shifted the thing and drew up his foot carefully. He was bleeding and it hurt when he moved his ankle, but he was sure nothing was broken. As soon as it appeared safe to do so, he crawled out over the mound of rubble by the table and took a few hesitant steps. He could walk, but it was extremely painful. Hobbling to the Chancellery's main doors Stefan decided to consider himself fortunate. The law of averages being what it was, some kind of wound had been inevitable. Better a damaged foot than a cratered skull.

There was a small sentry post on top of an iron stairway beside the doors. Stefan limped up to the top and found that the slit window gave him a clear view into the garden, where the main bunker exit was sited. One rumour of many circulating among the Russians maintained that Hitler and his staff had left the bunker days before the fighting entered the city. Stefan could not believe that. He had watched Hitler draw himself together in his concrete domain, entrenching. He would never leave the place until he was forced, and that kind of force could not be applied by his staff or advisors. Down in the garden there were a few machine-gunners and SS guards; they were still defending their Messiah.

It became hard, after an hour of watching, to believe in the purpose of his mission, and Stefan began to wonder if it was all that had brought him to that place. His whole fascination, for a time, had been in seeing his former centre of activity under siege. Stefan was keen to watch the end of the story after being part of it for so long. Only once or twice did he think about Farrell and wonder if he would ever come for the GRU files. With the passing of an hour, Stefan began to think it was the longest of long shots. One glimmering hope persisted in the growing doubt: if Farrell truly was in Berlin, and if he was alive, he would have no dearer wish than to lay his maniacal hands on the architects of the Reich.

By mid-morning the shelling was in the street beside the bunker, and Stefan could hear tanks. Windows high on the remaining frontage of the Chancellery began to crack and shatter with the vibration, and brickwork started dropping past Stefan's vantage point. A few soldiers were scattering on the street and a light armoured car chugged past with its engine exposed and damaged. The high garden wall had withstood some battering already and a shell, plummeting in a neat, dying arc, hit the weakened stonework and blasted a wide gap in it. Stefan moved away from the window and eased himself painfully down the stairs. It was time for something momentous to happen, and he wanted to be near when it did.

In the afternoon three Russian tanks and supporting artillery cleared the open area around the Chancellory. Buildings had been destroyed and the few remaining guard units were obliterated. On a couch in their bunker suite, the Hitlers sat and listened to the fearful noise penetrating the earth above them.

'The sole regret I have,' the Führer said wearily, 'is that there was no standard bearer, no son with my blood and ideals.' He turned his head and looked at Eva. She was pale, with the serenity of a sleepwalker. 'You should know, my love, that there was once a child. A son.' He sighed and stared at the closed door. The deep wrinkles on his cheeks had given his eyes the look of death already. 'I think it is time,' he said, and turned to Eva again.

She said goodbye to him in a small voice, and kissed him on the cheek. The small metal phial had been in her hand since she entered the room minutes before, and when Eva uncapped it and raised it to her lips she did not tremble, and she hesitated only a moment before pouring the liquid into her mouth.

The cyanide acted instantly. A sharp pain seized Eva's throat and chest, and she heard her heart change and felt the beat become faster. She set her lips against the pain and forced her mind on a picture, a room full of laughing people where there was music and dancing and she was at the centre, twirling, twirling. She could not breathe, everything in the real world was turning black. Grimly Eva held the picture, saw it move and heard the music.

Hitler watched with tears in his eyes until her body became still. He touched her arm, fingered her hair, then drew back. His Walther pistol was beside him and he handled it for a moment, held as he had often been by its dimensions and its weight. He looked one more time at Eva, started to speak to her dead face, then abruptly put the gun to his temple and pulled the trigger.

From the centre of a mound of stones and brick that had formed an accidental shelter only yards from the bunker exit, Stefan saw the valet, Heinz Linge, help another man to carry a blanket-covered body into the middle of the garden. A few seconds later two men carried out Eva's body, uncovered. Goebbels and Bormann stood inside the bunker doorway, watching.

Stefan felt giddy. It was over, they were dead. He could see Eva's pale hair blowing in the wind. Minutes later there was a soft popping, then a dull roar as the bodies began to burn.

In the lower level of the bunker Bormann's terror was finally surfacing. For a lifetime he had lived at the side of an eminence that was now gone. He had worshipped Hitler, clung to his presence like a jealous dog, and now that the master was departed the dog was ownerless, abandoned. In his records office he stood still for a long time, knowing what was going on outside, imagining he could hear the flames consuming the bodies. The others in the bunker were making their plans for escape, organizing themselves into groups: only Bormann remained separate from the planning, he belonged to no natural group, he wished to accompany nobody out of there. After long minutes he sat down at his desk, hands trembling on the stained blotter, and tried to make preparations for leaving. But something had to break, he could not withstand the pressure in his head, and suddenly it happened. Despair, fear and grief gathered and broke from him in a long whine and he clung to the sides of the desk, wracked by emotions he had kept buried for years.

The upper level was deserted. Telephonists, orderlies and a dozen clerical staff had made their way out by the Chancellery exit: half of them were already dead on the street outside. A young driver, climbing the steps and seeing the bodies scattered beyond the door, had gone back to the bunker and shot himself. His body lay in the passageway. Books, office chairs and file boxes were littered everywhere, and a bundle of useless money had been dumped in a waste basket. No one on the lower level realized that the upper chambers had been so completely abandoned, and nobody was in a position to care. There would have been concern, however, if it had been known that the driver, in the seconds before he killed himself, had come down the stairs in such a state of anguish that he had forgotten to bolt the door.

Stefan had left the garden and crawled back to the cover of the Chancellery walls. A small, fanatical unit of SS guards had appeared from a cellar under the ruins of an office building, and they were dug into the rubble around the garden on three sides. They had two mortars, machine-guns and a supply of grenades. Nothing could live in the three hundred yards between them and the opposing groups of Russian foot soldiers. They had knocked out a tank, and its wreckage was blocking the progress of another. Stefan lay half hidden among the stones in the Chancellery doorway, dazed by the noise, but certain now of the two-pronged compulsion that had brought him here. He *had* to see it die, the need was as strong as his drive for vengeance. There was a grim, sensual thrill in seeing the recoil of violence on the murderous heart of the regime that had started it all. Oblivious suddenly to the danger, deaf to the screaming of the ferocious soldiers manning the German guns, Stefan heaved himself down the slope of rubble and rolled to the nearest opening in the garden wall. Pain sang through his foot and leg, but it was not enough to stop him. He stood up and began limping towards the bunker door.

Ten yards away, a man in Russian uniform lowered his field glasses and knelt up among the bushes where he had been lying for nearly half an hour. At first he had not believed it, the dirty overcoat and tousled hair had made him doubt his eyes. But now he was sure. The man he could see shuffling through the garden and into the shade of the bunker door was Stefan Gaiser.

A Russian shell hit the armoured stanchion by the door and Stefan jumped with the blast, throwing himself through the door and landing a yard behind it on his good foot. He clung to the wall and began hopping down the stairs, smelling the familiar odour of machine-fanned air and cold, damp concrete.

At the foot of the stairs he stopped and leaned on the wall. There were sounds on the lower level, a confusion of footsteps on the hard floor, low and high voices, doors slamming. The rats were cornered and scurrying, Stefan thought. He could imagine them, their disorder and fear. It soothed his pain, and a precarious calm descended on him. It could be fate, ending his life there, staying until the place caved in. Gretl had been a believer in fate.

Stefan moved to the top of the spiral staircase that led to the lower level. He passed the body of the dead driver and saw the look of frightened despair on his stiff features. It was a look Stefan had seen all over the ruined capital, the expression of total defeat.

He rested his hands on the rail, listening. This was a time he had often imagined, a time he had sometimes believed would never come. In his absorption, Stefan did not notice the tiny sound behind him.

He turned too late as Farrell closed on him and grabbed his collar, swinging him and shoving him into the small room adjacent to the staircase. It was the room where

Stefan had lived and done most of his work. He fell into the chair by the desk, wracked with pain.

'Fancy meeting you here,' Farrell grunted. He stood with arms folded and feet spread, smiling at Stefan. 'I thought you were long gone.'

The melancholy mood had been shattered; Stefan was alert and tingling. 'I left,' Stefan said. 'Then I decided to come back.'

'Came to gloat, did you?'

Stefan shook his head. 'Not entirely. I came to get you.'

'Really?' Farrell was breathing easily, and his grin was widening. 'Smart figuring, hotshot. I never thought you'd have the balls to survive this long.'

'You're filth, Farrell.'

'And what are you going to do about that, huh?'

Stefan watched as Farrell took the gun from his holster, felt cold, sickening loss as the muzzle levelled with his chest.

'You wore that SS uniform too long, Stefan. It gave you delusions.' Farrell slipped the safety-catch and tightened his grip.

'No delusions about you. You're filth, the same kind that's scuttling about downstairs. No distinction, Farrell. You're vermin.'

Farrell leaned forward and struck Stefan across the cheek with the back of his hand. 'The number of times I wanted to do that,' he grated, showing his teeth. 'That smug pretty face of yours, superior bastard . . .' He hit Stefan again, snapping his head back.

'Butchering,' Stefan grunted. 'That's what you need. Kosher killing.' Stefan was not afraid, but he could feel the edging of despair. He had never been less equipped for vengeance.

'It's one thing to want, baby, another thing to get.' Farrell waved the gun. 'Men like me always win, didn't you learn that? Didn't you take in the signs?'

Perhaps he had. Stefan was in no position to consider

the point. 'You're not a man, Farrell. You're a mindless *animal*, and somebody's hate will get you. Somebody's.'

For an instant it looked as if Farrell would hit him again, but instead he stepped back, glanced through the door, then came close again. 'I'm going to do it slow, Stefan. I'll get you screaming for mercy, you'll beg me to kill you. And you know what? The more you beg me the slower I'll make it.'

Stefan closed his eyes. *It shouldn't end like this.* He opened them again, glaring at Farrell.

'Take a nice long look at me, motherfucker. Take my face with you down the long black hole.'

The trigger moved a fraction and every nerve in Stefan reacted. The injured foot shot up and kicked the gun aside. As the bullet tore into the wall Stefan's head slammed under Farrell's chin. Farrell dropped to his knees, cursing, and Stefan's fist slammed down on the gun, knocking it across the floor. Then the damaged foot gave out suddenly and Stefan toppled over on his back, roaring in protest.

'I'll show you, motherfucker! I'll show you!' Farrell was on top of Stefan, shouting in his ear. Stefan bent his knee, the wrong one, trying to lever himself up. The pain almost made him black out. The cold fear of loss shuddered through him as he felt Farrell's breath, struggling under the crushing weight. There was an animal smell, a stifling closeness, then searing pain as Farrell's teeth closed on the side of his neck.

Channels of panic stiffened Stefan's arms. His hand grazed something hard, his fingers closed around it. It was a knife, Farrell's knife, dangling from his belt. The crazed jaws worked ferociously on his neck and Stefan heard himself yell, and only half of the cry was for himself. He could not move, he could only suffer, and even as he tried to make his arms work he began to sink into unconsciousness. Farrell was growling like a mad dog and Stefan's hand jerked out, holding the knife. Sinking deeper into darkness he jabbed and jabbed, not sure if he was even touching Farrell. Then the savage teeth were gone suddenly, and Farrell was whining, sitting up and trying to scramble away.

Stefan struggled to a sitting position and saw his arm outstretched and the knife clamped in his fingers. The blade was covered in blood, and more blood oozed through a tear in Farrell's tunic.

Time shifted. Faster than he thought he was able, Stefan knelt up, holding the knife in front of Farrell's whitening face. There was shock there, fear, as Farrell clutched his side and tried to stop the terrifying flow. Stefan took in every detail of the fright and confusion and strengthened himself with it. At the instant Farrell looked into his eyes, Stefan swung the blade in a swift sideways arc and slit through the skin and cartilage of his throat. Blood surged through the gurgling mouth and spilled in a torrent over Farrell's chest, then he fell slowly back, the gash on his neck wide and flowing.

Stefan stood up, steadying himself by the wall, watching the life shudder out of Farrell. He stayed like that for a long time, until the spasms in the arms and legs had stopped and the chest caught on the last rasping breath.

It was over. Triumph had surged through Stefan for a while, but the sense of loss had overtaken it. He was empty, bereft of the gnawing hate, the drive that had carried him for so long. He took a last look at Farrell's bloody corpse, then turned and limped into the passage. The pain in his neck had grown severe, but even so it did not quite touch him.

He knew the foot would not carry him far. That would have mattered more if he had possessed some idea of where he was going. By the body of the driver he stooped and picked up the man's pistol, then made his way slowly back up the stairs.

The fighting in the streets was closer now, the remaining SS men were gathered in one cluster a few yards from the bunker. Stefan walked out on to the crumbling road and limped his way to the cover of a wrecked truck. He leaned there for a few minutes, wondering how much medical attention he needed. When he felt for the piece of card that had been his passport across the city, he could not find it. There was nothing to do, he decided, but wait.

A grenade exploded in the Chancellery garden and Stefan moved around the front of the truck, seeing three huddled, uniformed bodies where there had been fighting men a moment before. Russian voices were shouting excitedly, another grenade went off and the showering earth and brick landed all around Stefan.

'Move,' he told his legs. There was another truck a few yards away, and it looked like a better shelter. Stefan hobbled towards it and to his left he saw someone running, making for the same cover as himself. It was a man in civilian clothes, carrying a small suitcase. He had a machine-pistol in his other hand, and the sight of it made Stefan tighten his grip on his own gun.

The urge to take cover dropped away, abruptly, as Stefan recognized the man's face. It was Bormann, his eyes wide with terror as he galloped for the big wounded truck. At a distance of less than five yards he swerved, seeing Stefan motionless there in the road, and his own face lit with recognition.

Stefan knew his reactions were too slow. Bormann had the machine-pistol up and aimed before the Luger was even pointing at him. An explosion nearby made Bormann waver for a second, but he fired before Stefan did. Just as the Luger's recoil pounded on Stefan's wrist he felt the blow on his skull, saw the street tilt sideways and heard his face strike the ground.

Everything dimmed quickly and painlessly. Stefan saw his hand on the gun. Beyond, there was Bormann, sprawled on his back, part of his face gone. Then, in a soothing silence, there was nothing.

EPILOGUE

August, 1981
The Kossmann Veterans' Hospital stands in two acres of pleasant countryside to the north of Braunschweig. The main building, an elegantly restored mansion built at the turn of the century, is designed on the lines of a sanatorium. Eighty patients are accommodated on three floors, each with its sun lounge, sitting room and verandahs. From any window it is possible to look out over carefully tended lawns and gardens, and the view beyond is of hills and forests. The late Dr Kossmann bequeathed the hospital in 1946, and in accordance with the terms of his will only long-term patients are cared for, the surviving victims of war. There is always a long waiting list for places at the hospital, and these are only granted when patients die. No one is ever discharged.

The records at the hospital offer sad testimony to the chaos and destruction left behind by the war. There are men with no memories, others without limbs or sight. Some are so badly mutilated that new nurses have to be warned in advance, in case they might react with shock and so distress the patients. Even after thirty-five years, there are men who have nightmares about what happened to them; one man who was buried alive for five days still cannot sleep in a room with closed windows.

But the Kossmann Veterans' Hospital is not a place of sadness or grief, it is a retreat where peace and kindness are applied to counteract sorrow. Patients are pampered as a matter of policy, and the majority of them are genuinely happy, for most of the time.

On the top floor, spending his days in a neat room with a splendid view of rolling fields and wooded horizons, the old man called Karl is one of the few cases who have not responded visibly to the hospital's lavish care. He was the fifth patient to be admitted in 1946, and he has occupied the same room since then.

Karl's record shows that he was one of many pulled out of the rubble in Berlin on the last day of the war. Of two hundred and forty-seven people taken to an emergency hospital set up by the Allies, Karl was one of the twenty-three survivors. On 30th April, 1945, he had a bullet removed from the cortex of the left frontal lobe of his brain. He was also treated for severe lacerations on the right side of his neck. Tendon damage to his right foot was discovered later, and treatment there was less than expert, with the result that Karl now walks with a limp.

For a year, until he was admitted to the Kossmann Veterans' Hospital, Karl lay in one temporary care centre after another. Together with the crippled and blinded of three cities, he was nursed in wards and huts that sometimes housed as many as three hundred patients at a time. Once, Karl contracted pneumonia and almost died, and shortly after he recovered he was savagely beaten by another patient, a man whose mind had been split apart by the terror of Dresden. Throughout all that time Karl remained passive. He ate his meals, bathed himself with the assistance of nurses, and lay on his bed, never speaking or displaying the least sign of emotion. The name Karl was given to him by the first matron of the Kossman Veterans' Hospital, because it was a name she liked, and the man's real identity was unknown.

Physical health has been no problem with Karl for over thirty years. He is somewhere in his late sixties, with a vigorous head of grey hair, and although he stoops from the years of inactivity, his heart, lungs and general physique are admirably sound.

Occasionally, Karl's normally placid face will become troubled. At such times he fingers the only possession he brought with him to the hospital, a silver watch fob on a chain around his neck, and if there is anyone else in the room he will talk to them. The flow is jumbled and agitated. Karl's eyes fill with tears, his shoulders twitch and his voice becomes assertive and mumbling by turns. There is something approaching a rhythm in the things he says, a repeated pattern of words that are disjointed in themselves. He talks about Dorfen, Deanfield, someone called Eric. At his most distracted he calls out other names – Sara, and over and over again Gretl, Gretl. The staff have heard it all many times, but they smile and pat Karl's shoulder as if they understand, and someone will always stay with him until he is calm again.

When there are visitors to the hospital, Government officials or members of the Board of Management, Matron Ender always assures them that Karl is a happy man.

'He doesn't show very much on the outside,' she will say, 'but we're certain he has found a great deal of peace here.'

The visitors smile and nod, and sometimes the silent old man will nod back, but usually he makes no response at all. He sits in his chair and looks at the wall, or at the fields and hills beyond his window.